Harry Cole was born [...] south London. He left school when he was fourteen, during the war, and became a cricket-bat maker, soldier, stone-mason and, in 1952, a policeman. For thirty years, until his retirement in 1983, he served at the same police station in London.

He is a former FA Coach, referee and cricketer but his main sporting interests now are swimming, bowls and watching his grandson play cricket and football. The author of the popular *Policeman* books about life on the beat ('Harry Cole is the police's James Herriot' *Sunday Express*), he has also written two volumes of autobiography and two London Sagas, QUEENIE and BILLIE'S BUNCH, also available from Headline.

In 1978 Harry Cole was awarded the British Empire Medal for voluntary work. Since leaving the force, in addition to writing, he has taken up after-dinner speaking.

Praise for QUEENIE and BILLIE'S BUNCH:

'*Billie's Bunch* is a heartwarming, lively and compelling story' *Lancashire Evening Telegraph*

'[A] warmhearted saga with perhaps a little more wit than most' *Reading Chronicle*

'Another knockout saga of London life in the 1920s' *Bolton Evening News*

Also by Harry Cole from Headline

QUEENIE
BILLIE'S BUNCH

Julia's War

Harry Cole

To George
With all best wishes
Harry Cole
September 1998

HEADLINE

First published in 1997 by
HEADLINE BOOK PUBLISHING

First published in paperback in 1998
by HEADLINE BOOK PUBLISHING

10 9 8 7 6 5 4 3 2

ISBN 0 7472 5573 3

Typeset by Avon Dataset Ltd, Bidford-on-Avon, Warks

Printed and bound in Great Britain by
Clays Ltd, St Ives plc

HEADLINE BOOK PUBLISHING
A division of Hodder Headline PLC
338 Euston Road
London NW1 3BH

To Dave and Mary Brooks for their support
during a bad year

ACKNOWLEDGEMENTS

With special thanks to:

Headmistress Carol Thomkin, and the staff and children
of Charles Dickens School.
Ex-Warrant Officer Sid Greenaway (Royal Artillery).
Ex-staff Nurse Jean Smith.
Reminiscence Centre Blackheath Village.
Barbara Garrett.
Dave Brooks, ex-Underwater Search Unit.

1

The huge cross that rose high above the dome of St Paul's
Cathedral caught the full glare of the low October sun and
reflected it like a golden mist. There, beyond the vast riverside
warehouses, 365 feet below, the Thames eased itself lazily
eastward towards Tower Bridge and the sea. The almost eerily
still Sunday morning was deceptively serene considering it
was at the heart of a capital city that had been at war for six
weeks. At first glance there was not a soul to be seen. Even
the scavenging gulls had tired of raking the mud-flats in search
of tubifex worms and water-fleas and seemed content to perch
on the ropes of the tethered barges and quietly enjoy the view.
From across the river the clocks of the city churches could be
heard chiming the ninth hour and, though not all in perfect
unison, the fading of their brief harmony seemed to emphasise
the general tranquillity of the scene.

'I love Sundays at this spot,' said Julia Giles quietly. 'I feel
I've leased the river to the city merchants for the rest of the
week, but Sunday mornings it's all mine again. D'you know
when I was a little girl I always thought God lived up there.'
She folded her arms and leaned on the riverside wall, staring
over the Thames at the spire of the great cathedral.

'Doesn't he, then?' asked her companion as he slipped his
arm around her waist and nuzzled his nose into the side of her
neck. 'I am surprised.'

'Why?' she asked with mild interest. 'I thought you were

1

an atheist. Where God lives – any god, for that matter – surely shouldn't concern you one way or the other.'

'It doesn't. It's just that looking up at it now, it seems that if a god has to live somewhere, then that's as good a place as any. Though I must say at this particular moment if I was compelled to choose a religion, *any* religion, that is, I think sun-worshipping would have the edge on all the others.' He nodded towards the cathedral. 'The sun on that spire is like a fairy wand in *Cinderella*. It transforms this lot' – he removed his arm from her waist and swept it in a grand gesture towards the row of grimy warehouses – 'from pumpkins to palaces.'

She reached quickly for his hand and, recovering it, returned it sharply to her waist. 'If you must pontificate would you kindly do it with the other arm? We have little enough time for touching as it is without you semaphoring when you should be cuddling.'

'What do you mean "little enough time"?' he protested. 'I've got a thirty-six-hour pass, haven't I? I don't have to be back at my unit until eight o'clock tomorrow morning. In any case, I'm disappointed to have to remind you, my pretty Miss, that to the best of my recollections, you and I indulged in a fair bit of touching last night.'

Tugging his arm from her waist she spun to face him. 'Duncan Forbes! I'd like to remind you that far from being your "pretty Miss", as you so crassly put it, I should have been a married woman by now.'

'I couldn't help that now, could I?' he protested. 'It wasn't my fault. I mean to say, I didn't start the bloody war, did I? It wasn't my idea to get a telegram calling me back to my unit on the morning of the wedding, was it? Don't forget, if I hadn't received that telegram I would have been on that course and well on my way to being an officer by now instead of a corporal. It's the krauts you have to blame. If them and that bloody lunatic Hitler hadn't started their performance, you'd probably have been a fortnight into starting a family.'

She placed her hands firmly on her hips and tilted her head forward, her dark eyes glowering at him. 'Oh yes? And who, pray, would be its father? Not you, I trust, Corporal bloody Forbes. You have led me up the garden path so many times in the last few years that I could have spent the time better in the Hampton Court maze. The idea of you fathering my child then sodding off for the duration of the war has no appeal for me at all.' She began to prod his chest to emphasise every word. 'None whatever – understand?'

He grinned at her for a moment then moved his gaze upward towards the gleaming cross. 'If he *does* live up there,' he whispered, 'he's going to have the right hump with you, I can tell you. All this swearing and carrying on; disgraceful, I call it. And on the sabbath too? Tut-tut-tut, shame on you, gel. Still, I'll tell you what I'll do. I'll accept your apologies and forgive you. How's that grab you?'

'*You'll forgive me?*' she exploded. Fists clenched, she launched herself at him and was about to pound his chest when he seized her wrists and, tugging them down to his sides, threw his arms around her in the tightest of embraces. Leaning her backward against the river wall, he then kissed her so passionately she reeled. As he finally released her she stood silently with her eyes closed for some moments. Gradually she opened them and shook her head slowly in reproach. 'One day, you bastard,' she murmured, '*one* day . . . that little ploy is not going to work.' Closing her eyes again she gave a tiny sigh and dropped her head onto his chest. 'But for the time being . . .' she repeated the sigh, '. . . it'll have to do.'

Although Duncan would never have admitted it, her complaint was not without justification. Their ten-year, on-off romance had been punctuated with many difficulties but she had thought it was all behind them as she had prepared for the register office wedding that black Monday two weeks

earlier. At first glance everything had seemed to have worked
out well. She had contrived a few days' leave from her nursing
duties and he was between army courses. Then had come the
bombshell of that cursed telegram. Julia had never been able
to understand how the fate of the entire war was going to
hinge on whether her man reported back to his unit on Monday
morning instead of Tuesday afternoon. Yet the fact remained
that she still loved him and had done so throughout every trial
and tribulation since she had first clapped eyes on him those
many years before. However, as she knew only too well, time
was now racing by. In spite of her outburst moments earlier,
she knew she had always wanted this man's children, but now,
at twenty-nine years of age, who was to know how long this
damn war was going to last?

Many had said 'All over by Christmas', but Duncan had
told her that the only chance of that happening was if the
Martians, the devil and bubonic plague all came in on our
side. So where, she wondered, did that now leave her? Though
she loved this man deeply she was no fool and was painfully
aware of his faults. If he was capable of loving anyone at all –
and there were times when she had her doubts about that little
surmise – then he certainly loved *her*. But Duncan, being
Duncan, took very little in life seriously and that indifference
particularly included women. However, at least he was
constant, he had been like that since they first met and she
saw no prospect of change. Still, she knew their relationship
could never be dull and she would never deny she loved him.
At the end of the day he was her man and for Julia, that was
the top and bottom of it.

Pulling her to him again, this time in more gentle mood, he
kissed the top of her regulation-length hair and smoothed down
the back of her blouse with his hands, before finally resting
them lightly upon her buttocks.

'Will you please take your hands off my bum,' she whispered

into his chest. 'You never know who's looking.'

'But as you've just said,' he whispered into her ear, 'it's a Sunday morning down by the unstaffed warehouses and there's only you, me and the gulls in the whole wide world . . . or at least this part of it.' He eased her even closer and began to run his hands up and down her body.

At first she responded but as his fingers undid the first two buttons of her blouse, discretion finally won. 'Duncan, not here,' she pleaded. 'We've still got the rest of the day and also my room in Queenie and Jim's house. They said they'd be out until lunchtime and it won't take us long to get back to Streatham in their car, will it? Let's go back there, eh?'

'But we only left there an hour ago,' he protested. 'You told me you wanted to spend the early morning here. That, my love, was the only reason I got out of bed.'

'I know, I know,' she repeated, 'but only because I loved this spot so much and, what with the war and everything, well, I wasn't sure how many times we'd be able to come here again.'

He nuzzled into her hair for a second or two. 'For you, sweetie,' he whispered as he re-buttoned her blouse, 'anything.'

'Anyway,' she said, smiling up at him, 'even you wouldn't have made love to me here, especially in uniform, surely. After all, a concrete river wall is not what you'd call romantic, is it? Even if it is only us and the gulls in the whole wide world.' As if suddenly reminding herself of their solitude she glanced about her. 'D'you know it really is strange, Duncan. It's as if the Pied Piper has been through town and led the children away. Although it's not even just children, is it? Apparently some fifty thousand civil servants have gone from London alone.'

'I know, even the BBC has buggered off to Bristol. Still, you may have spoken too soon,' he replied, nodding east along the foreshore. 'There's at least three kids there the piper seems to have missed.' His eyes focused intently on them for a moment. 'On the other hand, the way they are clambering all over that barge, they look like three little hooligans out on the prowl. Perhaps he didn't want them in the first place?'

'Where?' she said, raising herself on her toes. 'I can't see them.'

Lifting her as if she were a child, he perched her on the river wall and turned her towards the foot of Southwark Bridge. 'On the furthest of those three barges, see them? Three right little brats, I'd say.'

She peered for a moment. 'Duncan Forbes!' she exclaimed. 'Little brats indeed! The tallest one is Benji Diamond. You know him, surely? He's Grace and Dave Diamond's son. Bloody hell, I'm almost his aunt! The other two look like his friends, Fat Freddie Foskett and that little girl . . . oh, what's her name, it's on the tip of my tongue. You know, the one without a mum. Her knickers always hang a couple of inches below the hem of her dress. The poor cow died of TB a year or two ago. Her dad's a Billingsgate fish porter. He keeps his boots outside on the windowsill because they smell a lot. You *must* remember that, surely? They live in the same block as Grace Diamond . . . oh what *is* that child's name?'

'How the hell do I know?' he protested. 'Anyway, I thought all orphans were called Annie.'

'That's it!' she cried.

'What, Annie?'

'No *Rosie*, Rosie Blackwell. In any case, you idiot, how can she be an orphan if she's got a dad?'

'If the poor kid has no mother and a father whose feet smell so bad he has to keep his boots on the windowsill – and that's to say nothing of the fact that her drawers hang down below her frock – then in my book she's about as orphaned as anyone's likely to get.'

'It's not his feet that smell, you fool, it's his boots. Apparently they are special boots, it's all to do with his work.'

'Hm,' murmured the unconvinced Duncan. 'This TB her mum was alleged to have died from, didn't stand for "Two Boots" did it?'

'Duncan Forbes, you're a wicked sod! Anyway, enough of this, go and get those kids off that barge, it's dangerous. Knowing Grace, if she finds out where they've been playing she'll tan the hide off Benji, and most likely the other two as well.'

'Well, tell me this,' replied Duncan disapprovingly, 'why weren't they evacuated with the other local kids? London will be no place for a child when the war really hots up.'

'I think if it was down to Grace Diamond, Benji would have certainly gone, but David was reluctant to part with him and at the end of the day all three kids said they didn't want to go away. It's as simple as that.'

'Good God, woman, they shouldn't have had any say in the matter! Bloody kids, they should do as they are told. If it was down to me I'd say, "Oi you lot, off to the countryside, double-quick," and that'd be the end of it.'

'Oh, you are so masterful at times,' she mocked as she placed her hands reverently between her knees and fluttered her eyelids up at him.

'Yeah I know,' he agreed, as he moved away towards the barges, 'because when I come back here I intend to put you over my knee and spank your bum substantially. Oh, by the way,' he added, 'that'll be after I drown the three little buggers.'

'Promises! Promises!' she laughed as she threw her head back and rocked to and fro on the wall in merriment.

On reaching the riverside steps Duncan glanced ruefully back at her and decided he had never seen her look so beautiful. 'Little buggers!' he repeated to himself, wagging a large warning finger to no one in particular. 'If I had those Billingsgate boots here at this moment I'd brain all three of 'em!'

The approach of the irritable Guards corporal had not been noticed by the trio of playing children who were particularly preoccupied with fighting a naval battle with invisible German pirates. The three barges were moored alongside each other and the battling trio were heavily engaged in repelling imaginary boarders from the furthest barge. The first question that Duncan asked himself was exactly how the children had reached the barge to begin with. High water had been thirty minutes earlier and, whilst the tide was just ebbing, the water was probably some twenty feet deep and the undertow deceptively strong. They had obviously crossed from barge to barge but all three vessels were moored to buoys at least twenty yards out into the river. He looked around for a boat of some description that the children could have possibly used but there was none to be seen. It took some little time before he finally realised that the only way they could possibly have reached the barges was to swing hand-over-hand across the mooring-rope to the first barge. They would then have to have jumped to the second and then the third. Cupping his hands he was about to call when he realised all three children had suddenly disappeared from view. An instant fear arose. The fast-flowing tide was bad enough but the danger of falling beneath the flat-bottomed barge was the most perilous risk of all. Each year a dozen or so youngsters would perish this way. Even the strongest of swimmers would panic when trying to break surface beneath a flat-bottomed, hundred-ton coal-barge.

'Blast!' he exclaimed. 'Now what the hell did she say their names were?' He quickly racked his brain but the only one that came readily to mind was 'Annie'. Yes, of course, that was it! Taking a deep breath he bellowed, 'ANNIE . . . WHERE ARE YOU?'

It was not that the three brave heroes – now in conference deep in the hold – did not hear the call, they heard it only too clearly. But Annie – any Annie – was completely unknown to them so they dismissed it from their considerations as an irrelevance.

When no response was made to his call Duncan felt that time was running out fast. To dash for help would take much too long in such a treacherously-running tide. On the other hand, if he just blindly dived in the river his chance of finding three children in the almost impenetrable waters of the ebbing Thames was remote, to say the least. There was only one thing for it and that was to reach the barges the same way the children must have done, hand-over-hand on the rope. However, unbeknown to him, there was a certain difficulty with this solution. The fair Rosie had decided to cut the evil German pirates adrift into the swirling current. Her compatriots had agreed with her plan and though the rope appeared taut enough, it was now only wrapped loosely around the bollard and was beginning to slip. 'I'm going across on the rope,' he called to Julia, 'because I can't see the kids anywhere. Shan't be long.'

Her merriment faded instantly and she put her hands to her face as, Guardsman-trained, he jumped confidently out into space to reach for the rope. 'Be careful darl—' she began but before the sentence was complete Duncan hit the water like a small bomb. Hordes of squawking gulls suddenly rose in protest. The chill of the autumn Thames was as nothing to the debris that floated in it. It takes seven tides for any item of debris to finally find its way out of the estuary. Up and down it goes, day in and day out. Cats by the dozen, driftwood, bloated dogs, cartons, tins, bottles, boxes and a seemingly endless stream of contraceptives. They floated by the hundreds just inches below the surface like transparent, tapering jellyfish.

The shock of hitting the water had caused Duncan to gasp for breath at the very moment of impact. As a result, a generous amount of vintage Thames flooded his throat. After an explosion of chokes and splutters he composed himself quickly but not before Julia's screams and the cacophony of gulls had caused the children to return to the deck to investigate the commotion. The trio, however, were not the only ones to be drawn by the cries.

Rita Roberts was cycling home from a twelve-hour stint on the Auxiliary Fire Service switchboard. Rita was a particularly vivacious young woman, yet there was something hard that seemed to show through even her most routine of gestures. She was smart, dark and petite with a short fringe and flick-up sides that rarely showed a hair out of place. She spoke quickly and her movements were always made as if she were responding to an emergency, which in wartime was no little asset. 'What is it?' she snapped, leaping from her cycle.

'I think three kids are adrift and my fiancé has fallen in the river trying to save them. Oh God, please help, I can't swim!'

'I don't think that should bother you, dear,' reassured the newcomer, pointing to the water. 'He seems to have recovered himself well enough. Look.'

Duncan had returned to the surface and, even though still in uniform, was gliding round to the front of the barges with the ease of an accomplished swimmer.

However, a soldier swimming in the Thames in full uniform understandably caught the instant interest of the three children. 'Oi mister! Wot you doin' in the water?' called down a scruffy girl with sagging knickers and a candle running from her nose. ''S all dirty dahn there.'

With great restraint Duncan ignored the question and was about to order the castaways to try to re-loop the rope to the bollard but before he could do so, the rope slipped smoothly from the barge and plopped softly into the river.

'WHAT THE HELL ARE YOU DOING THERE, SOLDIER?' boomed a sudden metallic voice.

Glancing up he saw a small motor launch fighting its way

upstream and emerging from the south arch of Southwark Bridge.

'It's the cops,' said Rita curtly, 'come to claim all the glory, no doubt.'

'Thank God they've come!' cried Julia with a swift but thankful glance up at the golden cross.

'Shouldn't think God had much to do with this one, love. You probably woke the lazy bastards up from a kip. Come on, I'll give you a hand to pull your man back on land.'

Duncan, seeing the police were about to rope in the barges, decided he could achieve little else and so struck out for the shore. As he did so the loudspeaker again cut through the morning silence. 'SOLDIER! MAKE FOR THE STEPS AND WAIT FOR US THERE. THE MUD AT EITHER SIDE IS TREACHEROUS.'

Duncan waved an acknowledgement and ploughed through what seemed to be half of London's sewage before reaching the sanctuary of the greasy granite staircase in front of the Bankside Power Station.

As both women struggled to assist him up the steps to the safety of the river wall, Julia could not help but notice Duncan's immediate interest in her companion. His eyes swept the newcomer from top to bottom as he seemed to absorb every detail of her. In spite of herself Julia felt an instant jealousy.

'You do look a poor soldier-boy,' smiled Rita. 'You'd have been safer fighting the Germans than saving that bunch. Especially that little bastard Benji Diamond. Him and that bloody girl are right out of hell. Shame the coppers arrived, with any luck the three of 'em might have been swept out to sea and dro—'

Before Julia could begin a tirade of protest Duncan cut in sharply. 'Thank you for your help, Miss . . . er, sorry didn't get your name. My fiancée here is Benji Diamond's . . . well, sort of aunt, I suppose you'd call her. So you see, er – perhaps

11

it might be a good idea and less embarrassing if we changed the subject?' His voice faded but he gave a friendly enough smile.

Far from being embarrassed the newcomer gave a harsh little laugh. 'I'll remember that when I'm trying to sleep and the three of them are crashing their bloody skates up and down the staircase. I live two floors below them. Rita Roberts is the name. Anyway, I must go because the law will soon be here and I can't stand coppers. But if I was you I'd get out of those wet clothes before you putrefy.' She fanned her hand rapidly across the front of her face 'Phew! You seem a nice enough lad but you don't half stink. See you.'

With that she leaped to her cycle and rode briskly away towards Southwark Bridge. 'Well of all the damn cheek!' exploded Julia. 'Fancy saying that about the kids! That's evil, that's what it is. They could have so easily all been drowned.'

'Oh come on,' chided Duncan. 'I mean to say, be fair, they're hardly a trio of bloody angels, are they?' He pointed out to where the police were just about to board the barge. 'Look at them now, they've cut three barges adrift. Another ten minutes and they'd have probably sunk half the merchant shipping in the Pool of London.'

'Don't make excuses for her, Duncan Forbes,' she replied primly. 'I saw the way you stared at her, you lecher. It was only too obvious what you were thinking.'

'For your information, young lady,' began Duncan wearily, 'I'll tell you, yes, she is a very attractive girl. And yes, I could understand any man fancying her. And yes, I would like to know more about her. But there is a hardness about that lass that even for the short time she was here, made me feel uncomfortable. I'd say that woman has been through a great deal. That was why I was staring.'

'Well, she was certainly right about one thing,' responded Julia huffily. 'You do stink!'

Further debate was interrupted by a shout from one of the river police who had just been landed on the Bankside steps. 'My two mates are securing the barges,' said the policeman, pointing to the launch. 'Can I just get a quick statement from you before you go to hospital?'

'Hospital?' echoed the puzzled Duncan. 'I don't need a hospital. I'm not hurt. A bit bloody cold, perhaps, and I don't imagine my quartermaster's going to be too thrilled about the state of this uniform, but other than that I'm fine.'

'You won't be,' prophesied the policeman, 'not unless you get your stomach pumped out double-quick.' He jerked his thumb back towards the river. 'If you swallowed as much as a mouthful of that stuff you'll shit for a month. Sorry mate, but it's Guy's Hospital for you. Cheer up, it won't take long, the nurses are quite used to it there. We've got a body-cover on the launch, it'll keep the chill off until you're out of those wet things. Now, just tell me what happened and how those kids got on the barge and we'll call an ambulance, then you can be on your way. Okay?'

Duncan groaned in self-pity. 'Look, Constable,' he began, 'nothing personal, I assure you, but I'm supposed to be enjoying a thirty-six-hour pass. So far I've upset my girlfriend, ruined my uniform, bloody nigh drowned, poisoned myself with sewage and now you're telling me to "cheer up" because you're going to wrap me in a body-cover and some bloody butcher of a nurse is going to pump out my stomach.'

'Well,' said the constable, without looking up from his notebook, 'there *is* a war on.'

'And don't we damn well know it!' interjected the furious Julia. 'If it hadn't been for the war, as you call it, I'd probably be on a relaxing honeymoon in the Isle of Wight by now. Instead I'm taking this goof to Guy's to pump out his intestines.' She turned sharply to Duncan. 'And what was it you just called us nurses – butchers, did I hear you say? Right mate, you just get in that car and I'll take you to the out-patients' department at Guy's and I'll show you just what a "butcher" is. If I have anything to do with it, sweetie, you won't even know you're having your stomach pumped. Oh no,' she assured him, 'you'll probably think your appendix is being removed . . . *without* an anaesthetic!'

'Here,' said the policeman, as a thought suddenly struck him. 'She said if it wasn't for the war she'd be on a honeymoon. It wouldn't have been with you, by any chance, would it?'

'Uh huh.' Duncan nodded.

The officer made no reply but raised his eyes slowly to the heavens.

'How about the kids?' said Duncan. 'We can't just leave them here now, can we?'

'No I suppose you're right,' said Julia reluctantly. 'Though, heaven knows, they deserve it.'

'They with you, then?' asked the policeman suspiciously.

'Not strictly,' replied Julia. 'We just know the family of one of them quite well, practically related. Coincidentally, his dad's a copper.'

'What's his name and where's he stationed?'

'Diamond, Dave Diamond. He works out of Stones End police station, I think. Why, do you know him?'

'A little,' nodded the officer. 'Enough to realise he'll wallop the daylights out of that boy when he finds out.'

'Oh, I should think you can certainly count on that,' agreed Julia.

'Here they are now,' said the policeman, nodding towards the river steps. 'Blimey, what a trio!'

The other policemen on the launch had managed to tether the barges to the buoy and were depositing the children on the foot of the steps. 'Gissa hand, George,' called out a fat sergeant. 'We don't want 'em falling in the river after all this.'

'Can't think why,' muttered Duncan.

'One of 'em's Davy Diamond's boy,' said George by way of explanation. 'You know him, tall geezer with the great-looking missus with the legs and the knockers. What's the state of the poll with the barges?'

'Well, fortunately they hadn't drifted far,' said the sergeant, 'but if they'd swung out much further they would have separated, then we would have had a problem.' He pointed at Duncan. 'What's the situation with him? Have you called an ambulance?'

George shook his head. 'No, he reckons he don't want one. His fiancée here is a nurse and she's going to run him down to Guy's and either pump out his guts or disembowel him. She's not quite sure which at the moment.'

'Well if we're going to square this job up she's going to have to make up her mind pretty damn quick.'

'What does this "squaring up" actually involve?' asked Duncan dubiously.

The sergeant gave a pronounced sniff and stared thoughtfully at him before replying. ' "Squaring up" in this case means that officially the children hopped onto the barge because they *public spiritedly* saw a loose rope and wanted to secure it. Then you, being a passing brave soldier, *public spiritedly* called out for them to be careful. Unfortunately you leaned out too far and fell into the water.'

'Couldn't he have dived in to save them?' asked Julia naively. 'After all, that's virtually what happened.'

'If he "dived in to save them" as you put it, Miss, then he'd be a bloody hero. Then if he's a bloody hero, I'd have to write a report in triplicate and cop a statement from every bugger present, including the kids. Our inspector would then put two-and-two together and make a dozen and we'd all be in the shit . . . if you'll pardon the expression. So why don't you take this trio and drop them off at home on your way to Guy's Hospital? *They* will have got away lightly, *we* can go in for our breakfast and *you*, Miss, can, if you wish, pump this lad's belly with blacksmith's bellows. Meanwhile, the rest of the country can get on with winning the war. That's a pretty fair offer I'd say, wouldn't you?'

Julia's protest was strangled at birth as Duncan clapped his hands over her mouth and said stoutly, 'The fairest offer I've heard in a long time, Sergeant. Come on, gang, home time.'

2

The meeting had been hastily convened on the fourth floor of the old tenement block of Queen's Buildings. Duncan and Julia had needed little encouragement to avoid this gathering. The interrogators consisted of Benji's parents, Grace and David Diamond; Jack Blackwell, Rosie's father; and Polly and Ted Foskett, Freddie's grandparents. Grace, in her mid-thirties, tall and still lithely beautiful, ducked beneath the cluttered washing line as she handed round the tea to the other adults whilst wearing a suitably pained expression. David, who had only just returned from a twelve-hour stint of duty and was still in his uniform, minus tunic, looked particularly tired and badly in need of a shave. The years had certainly been kinder to Grace than to her husband and his once smooth, clear-cut features now showed visible signs of wear.

The slipper-clad, sturdy, bald and bearded Jack Blackwell, the block's air raid warden, was clad in his customary off-duty attire which consisted of trousers, a buttoned-up waistcoat and an open-necked shirt, plus of course his arm-band that denoted his official position as warden. Since the day the war had begun, on or off duty, Jack had yet to be seen without this arm-band. His boots may have been kept on the windowsill but his arm-band never left his body. In addition he also carried a small notebook that listed every man, woman, child and animal (some even claimed cockroach) who was likely to be residing either long- or short-term in the buildings. At first his

17

zeal for his job had caused great amusement amongst the tenants. It was claimed he could spot a chink in an otherwise blacked-out room from two streets distant. His booming cry of 'Put that bloody light out!' would regularly echo round the buildings like the voice of doom and was frequently imitated by the few remaining children. For the residents, however, the novelty of this persistent zeal had long waned. 'Bloody little Hitler' was one of the more repeatable descriptions of him. Yet in spite of his rather intimidating appearance, Jack was an emotional man whose heart was clearly in the right place and who obviously dearly loved his daughter. He would never have admitted it but he had been dreading the impending confrontation with her.

Polly and Ted Foskett, on the other hand, could have never been mistaken for anything else than placid grandparents. Polly, who was in her early sixties, had been born to be the eternal grandmother. Her silver hair, cuddly figure and rounded, gentle and surprisingly unlined face, denoted 'Grandma' even in the largest of gatherings. Summer and winter she was rarely seen without the flat cap that was neatly pinned over her tight bun. Another feature of her attire was a navy-blue shawl that was thrown with surprising elegance around her plump torso and hung halfway down her back. Apprehensively quiet, she instinctively shrugged her left shoulder as she adjusted the shawl with one hand and raised a trembling tea-cup with the other. She and husband Ted had raised Freddie since their youngest daughter had abandoned him by running away from home just weeks after his illegitimate birth.

Ted was a slightly-built man and some ten years senior to his wife and was seldom seen without his white clay pipe which he would remove from his mouth to point at anyone with whom he conversed. He had been a road navvy working the London tramlines for most of his seventy-two years and he walked with the slow but determined gait that most navvies acquire.

During his time he had worked on most of the main roads of the metropolis and though he remembered few of their names, Polly swore he remembered every one of the public houses en route. This assumption came from his habit of always mentioning pubs when giving directions. Since retiring from the roads he had discarded his corduroys, clogs and large-checked shirt and could usually be found in his second best suit, highly polished boots and a soft felt cap. His peak of elegance was reached with his white silk scarf. Even at weddings and funerals he would never wear a collar or a tie, feeling, no doubt, that with such a splendid silk scarf such items were dispensable. He made just a token gesture to formality by his use of a brass collar stud. This he sported like a jewel in the turban of some eastern potentate. Polly and Ted were reasonably compatible but if there was one single thing that bound them together it was their love for their grandson, Freddie.

The five adults almost ritually finished their tea before finally facing the children. Obviously deciding silence was the safest policy, each of the three youngsters sat upright and uncharacteristically quiet on the edge of Benjamin's bed. This bed stood in a curtained recess of the kitchen-cum-living-room of the two-roomed flat. Though the curtains were parted, young Freddie Foskett had tried slowly to ease himself behind them, presumably following a theory that if he could not be seen he might be forgotten. The five grown-ups had been so concerned about working out a solution to the children's now all-too-regular escapades, that his ploy had almost worked. Rosie, though, was having none of it. She was determined Freddie would share the come-uppance whatever it was to be. As he eased the curtain gently one way, she suddenly tugged it violently the other. The result was that five yards of heavy linen curtain promptly dislodged itself from its rail and fell swiftly to the bed, enveloping the whole trio.

'My God will you just look at them!' cried Grace Diamond

19

despairingly. 'It's this damn war, it's only been on six weeks and our kids have already turned into monsters. The sooner someone opens a school the better.'

'But it's Sunday, Mum,' protested Benjamin. 'We never went ter school on a Sunday even before the war.'

'You can go to bloody Borstal on a Sunday, though,' she responded. 'Either there or a reform school. Because I'm quite sure that's where you're going to wind up.'

'We've certainly got to do something about them,' agreed David emphatically. 'They're running wild. How does it look for me being a local copper and trying to maintain law and order, when my kid is cutting loose half the Thames barges!'

'They're not totally to blame though, are they?' said Polly Foskett defensively. 'What with the summer holidays, then all the schools shutting because of the war and now each of you working twelve hours a day in the emergency services,' she waved her arm in the general direction of the four adults, 'well, you can hardly wonder if they go off the rails sometimes. Me and Ted have got seven other grandchildren and Freddie is not the worst by any means, but the other six were all evacuated.'

'Why wasn't Freddie evacuated?' asked David.

'Because all the others lived with their parents and, as he's lived with us since his mum disappeared, we felt responsible for him. We're all he has, you can't just toss a ten-year-old boy around like a second-hand coat, now can you?' she admonished. 'So me and his grandad have kept him with us. Though I must say,' she gave a great sigh, 'it can certainly be wearing at times.'

'The cleaner at Charles Dickens School told me they're thinking of openin' some of the schools part-time,' cut in Jackie Blackwell. 'I turn round and said ter 'er, I said, "It's that or send the buggers ter Australia." I reckon that'd solve the problem soon enough,' he added optimistically.

'Would we all be famous if we went ter Australia, Dad?' asked Rosie hopefully.

'Don't be so bleedin' cheeky an' wipe yer nose,' retorted her father.

David was beginning to think the debate was losing its point, and decided it was time to inject a bit of order. 'Look,' he said, smacking his right fist into the palm of his left hand. 'Let's get this sorted out for once and for all. We agree that the big problem is that we are all away from home for long hours – yes?' There were nods all round. 'I'm in the police, Grace is working in the factory, Jack here is an air raid warden and Polly, you and Ted are manning the mobile canteen for the rescue services, right?' Again he was met by a series of nods. 'Well, I've heard on the grapevine that all these twelve-hour stints are being abolished. After all, you don't want a mobile canteen if there's no one to rescue and you don't want an air raid warden if you haven't had any air raids, so all the emergency hours are being cut very soon. So what with that and the schools thinking of opening part-time, things should soon improve considerably.'

A murmur of optimism ran around the room but noticeably not from the children. David was also disappointed to see that Grace did not seem to enthuse quite as much as the rest. 'Grace,' he said frowning, 'you look as if you have reservations. Don't you want them to go to school?'

'Oh, of course I do,' she replied, 'but listening to Polly there, I'm now beginning to wonder if we're treating this incident too seriously. Yes, I know it was particularly mischievous of the children to do what they did but it is a relatively little thing when there are so many other matters that are much more important.'

'Such as?' queried David irritably.

'Such as what is going to happen to us all in the near future? This war has been on for six weeks now and yet' – she shrugged her shoulders and looked bewilderedly about her – 'I feel that it really hasn't been *on* at all. Don't you see, virtually nothing has happened. Well, it's not going to be like this forever, is it? Sooner or later something is going to happen – but *what*? What horror is coming our way? People don't declare war for nothing, you know. The Germans aren't asleep over there. We know what they did to Poland and Warsaw in particular, now we're next in line and yet we're judging these kids as if they were master criminals instead of poor little sods who've been caught up in something that is completely beyond them and could easily be the death of us all before Christmas.'

'Does that mean they're goin' ter let us off?' whispered Freddie Foskett, still under the fallen curtain.

'Nah,' hissed Rosie, cuffing her nose. 'I think she said we're all goin' ter die afore Christmas.'

Because Freddie was never sure of the validity of any of Rosie's replies he decided to play safe and remain under the curtain.

'But don't you see, dear,' explained Polly Foskett as she reached out for Grace's trembling hand, 'it may be a "little thing", as you call it, but then we're little people. We're *little* people in a *big* war, so to us this little thing is really a big thing. It affects our children, it also worries and alarms us. There is absolutely nothing that us five adults can do if our city is going to be destroyed, but that still doesn't mean there is nothing we can do about our children.'

'Then let us send them away,' demanded Grace. 'I think it was a mistake to have kept them here in the first place. We can still rectify it. I'll go down to the town hall first thing in the morning.'

Realising she was in a minority of one, she stared at David for support but none was forthcoming, although she did sense a hint of guilt. 'Look,' he said, opening his palms to her, 'more and more kids are returning from evacuation every day. We'd be sending our kids away just as everyone else's are coming home. You wouldn't want that, would you?' She made no reply, so feeling suitably encouraged he continued, 'Christmas is only a few weeks away. Why don't we wait until then and see how the situation is developing? Who knows, the war may even be over by then, then you will have upset yourself for nothing at all.'

'Great idea,' she said acidly. 'Hitler probably loves Christmas and would never dream of doing a thing until Santa's been down his chimney and shoved an orange in his stocking.'

'Okay! Okay!' snapped David angrily. 'There he is.' He pointed sharply at Benjamin. 'Ask him yourself. If the boy wants to go away – so be it. Go on, woman, ask him!'

Benjamin, who up until that moment had shown his customary lack of concern in matters that had no interest for him, had been inclined to let the whole proceedings wash over him. He had missed half of the conversation anyway, but even he gathered that his mother now seemed duty-bound to ask him a question of some importance. The trouble was he had no idea what they had been talking about.

She bent over him and took his hands in hers. 'Benji,' she said softly, 'I don't think London is going to be a safe place for much longer. You'd be far better off somewhere in the country. It wouldn't be forever and me and Daddy will write to you every day and come to see you as often as we can. Perhaps even Freddie and Rosie will go with you. What d'you say? Do you want to go?'

Although the boy was looking straight at his mother he could hardly fail to notice Rosie slightly to the rear of Grace, shaking her head frantically. He hadn't heard enough of the case to have made up his own mind but Rosie obviously had. If she wanted to stay in London then that was probably the right thing to do. Not only that but if his mother was going to write to him every day she might even expect a reply just as regularly. That possibility alone condemned it. 'No, Mum,' he replied, 'I think I want to stay here.'

'You only *think*?' queried Grace optimistically, sensing a chink in the armour.

Rosie raised her eyes to the ceiling before again shaking her head, this time quite violently.

'Er – no Mum, I'm sure. I definitely don't want to go.'

Rosie smiled quietly and almost imperceptibly nodded an approval.

'Okay then, that settles it,' began David. 'When I'm on patrol tomorrow I'll pop into the school and make some inquiries. Then hopefully—' His words were cut short by a distant but short scream. Before they could work out the direction of it, it was followed by another, this time more prolonged and far more chilling.

'It's a woman and it's close!' exclaimed Grace. 'It's in this block somewhere, David. It has to be.'

David ran to the door and, on opening it, could already hear voices and an assortment of snatched conversations from both up and down the staircase.

'Who was it?'

'Where did it come from?'

'Is someone being murdered?'

'I'm sure it came from downstairs,' he called over his shoulder as he jumped down most of the first flight. He had reached the second floor when he saw old Ellie Wilkinson bent over her walking stick and standing in her doorway. Her husband Ike stood inquisitively behind her.

'Did you hear a woman scream, Ellie?' snapped David. Before she could respond he added, 'Where'd it come from?'

Ellie opened her mouth but before a word left it she was nudged in the ribs by Ike. Though making no reply she nodded almost imperceptibly towards number 87 and the elderly pair shuffled back into their flat and quickly closed the door. David turned to the door in question and gave an official-sounding rat-tat on the knocker. He was obliged to repeat it twice more before a muffled and weak female voice replied, 'Yes?'

'It's Dave Diamond from up at number ninety-one,' he called through the letter box. 'Are you okay? Did you scream?'

'Sod orf,' came an unexpected, gruff snarl from a thick male voice, 'and mind yer own bloody business.'

This response came as something of a blow to David's professional pride. 'It *is* my bloody business,' he hissed indignantly through the letter box 'I'm also a police officer, so open this door.'

'I don't give a toss who yer are. It's nuffin' ter do with you, I tell yer. It's between me and me missus, so sod orf an' leave us alone.'

'Listen,' said David with deceptive calm, 'I've already worked twelve hours today and I certainly can do without this. Especially in my own time, but if you still refuse to open this door, so I can speak to the woman who screamed, then I'm coming straight through it. Understand?'

'Oh yeh! An' if I say yer not, wot then? *I* pays the rent 'ere an' I thought an Englishman's 'ome's supposed ter be 'is castle. Can't be much of a castle if any nosy bleeder who fancies 'imself can come chargin' in, can it?'

'For the last time,' said David with temper rising, 'open this damn door so I can speak to the lady. If she says she's okay, then that's the end of it. Now open it this very minute or I'll get a couple more coppers and take the whole bloody door apart.'

Several oaths greeted this statement but the policeman was more than relieved when he heard the bolt slide back. This was followed by a click of the lock and a squeak from the hinges as the sturdy old door finally eased open.

To David's surprise the man was not the ogre he expected. He was little more than average height and as far as David could see through the over-sized boiler suit the man was wearing, he was slightly, almost skinnily built. He had an angular face with hollow cheeks and a large nose that was out of all proportion to the rest of his features. His hair was thinning and mousy and a cigarette stub was wedged so tightly behind his right ear that it looked like a permanent feature. To all intents and purposes he should have been an insignificant individual yet there was an air about him that David found sinister. He thought it could perhaps have been his eyes, they were hard blue and piercing and somehow did not seem to belong to the rest of him. The same could be said of his voice. David found a silly question entering his mind. How could a light-weight man have a heavy-weight voice? Also, just who was he? David had lived in the block for almost eighteen years and he must have passed the door a thousand times. He had certainly seen an attractive woman on odd occasions but never a man. He knew that if he had ever seen this creature he would most certainly have remembered him.

'Okay, so yer've got the door open, what nah?' challenged the man.

What now indeed, thought David. The whole thing could have been nothing more than a verbal battle between husband and wife. God knows, they were almost a cottage industry in Queen's Buildings. Legally he was on very slippery ground and he knew it. He had clearly threatened violence both to the man and his property but with what law? It was a good time to fetch into operation the experienced copper's secret weapon – bluff. 'I've had several complaints about screams originating from this flat,' announced David in his most official voice, 'and the Domestic Protection Justice Act, section three, empowers me to use sufficient force as may be necessary to ascertain the causes.'

He could see that, if nothing else, his fictitious Act and section had at least temporarily confused the man and that was good enough. What he needed to do now was to press home his point whilst he still held the advantage. 'I need to assure myself of the lady's welfare, so where is she?'

There was a flickering of doubt in the man's face but he turned and called over his shoulder, 'Come an' speak ter this rozzer, will yer, then perhaps 'e'll sod orf an' leave us in peace. If I'd known there were bloody coppers livin' in the block I'd never've moved 'ere in the first place.'

The man stood aside to reveal a petite, vivacious but bloodstained woman with dark hair, a fringe, and flick-up sides. She was shoeless and clad in only a wet and torn petticoat. Rita Roberts looked a most pathetic creature. 'Yes?' she asked.

'Well I was going to ask you if you're all right, Miss,' said David, 'but I can see that you're anything but.' His eyes narrowed as he looked at her bare shoulders more closely. 'Is that a scald mark?'

'Yes, it's all right though, mate,' she assured him as she eased the door to, 'I've had a little accident with a kettle. Nothing for you to worry about. Good day.'

'Whoa!' cut in David. 'What "little accident" covers you in blood, scalds you, cuts your lip and tears your petticoat?'

She looked round wearily at her partner as much as to say, 'Well you tell him.' The man stepped forward and thrust her roughly aside. 'Look!' he snapped. 'I'm not sure I'm buyin' all this Domestic Protection Justice Act bollocks. I'm warnin' yer that I've done my stint in the pokey and as such yer can't come down 'ere threatening, even if yer do live in the bloody place. She's told yer she's all right, so what more d'yer want?'

'I want to know how she got those injuries,' replied David quietly.

'Okay,' said the man, ' 'ere goes. She was goin' ter wash 'er 'air in the sink so she boiled a kettle on the gas stove. She took off 'er dress an' as she was liftin' the kettle to wet 'er 'ead she realised she 'adn't put in any cold water, so it'd be too 'ot. She reached fer the tap but wiv' the kettle in one 'and an' the tap in the other she lost 'er balance and fell against the sink, cutting 'er lip an' spillin' the 'ot water all over 'er shoulder. That then caused 'er ter fall ter the floor where she banged her brainbox against that old chair. Ain't that right, gel?' he demanded.

'Dead right,' agreed Rita, nodding her head. 'Now if you'll just leave us we can get on with clearing up the kitchen, it's in quite a state.'

David had been to enough violent domestic disputes to know when he had been fed a subtle lie, and this explanation was anything but subtle. On the other hand, he also knew when he had reached the end of a lawful inquiry. There was, however, still the identity of the man. What was it he had just said; 'I've done my stint in the pokey'? It was worth a final chance, thought David. 'So who are you then, guv?' he asked casually.

'What d'yer want ter know fer?' said the man, his aggression now returning.

'Well, I'll need to make a report because she should really go to hospital to get that scald seen to. It's just routine,' he assured him.

'I can't see why yer need ter make out a report. She's all right, she don't need no 'ospital or anyfin'.' He turned to her. 'Ain't that so, gel?'

She nodded in compliance. 'There y'are then,' said the man. 'No report needed. She don't want no treatment. Satisfied?'

'Well, I can't make you go for treatment if you don't want to, ma'am,' agreed David, 'but watch out for that scald. Use plenty of cold water to take the heat out of it and do it as soon as poss—' He jumped back quickly as the door was finally slammed in his face. 'Bloody women,' he muttered to himself. 'Why *do* they stand for it?' He gave a little shrug and made his way back up the damp stone staircase.

'Where was it and what happened?' asked the anxious Grace. 'Was it in this block?'

'It was in the block, right enough,' agreed David. 'Two floors down at number eighty-seven to be precise. The daft cow's in a hell of a state, she's cut, bruised and scalded but she insists she's not going to hospital so there's nowt else to be done.'

'Number eighty-seven?' persisted Grace. 'Not that dark-haired, attractive girl, surely? I always thought she looked particularly self-assured. How on earth did she do it?'

'*She* didn't – *he* did,' replied David. 'What puzzles me is why I've never seen him before. I mean, he's not a bloke you'd forget easily.'

Ted Foskett removed his pipe thoughtfully from his mouth and pointed it at David. 'I know who you're talking about,' he said. 'Skinny geezer. Big hooter. Usually wears a boiler suit. As nasty a piece of work as you're likely to see outside of Madame Tussaud's.' He scratched his head with the stem of his pipe. 'Oh, what's his bloody name now . . .'

'I don't understand how you know him though, Ted,' said David. 'Particularly when you don't even live in the block.'

'Yes, but I helped Jack here to make a register of everyone who lived in the flats during the first few days of the war. It was in case the buildings received a direct hit and we would know how many people we would need to search for.'

'Thas right!' exclaimed Jack Blackwell. 'I remember it nah. I recollect us knockin' on the door and a bloke with a big 'ooter in a boiler suit givin' us a right 'ard time. Said we wuz nosy buggers an' it wuz nothin' ter do with us. At one stage I thought 'e was goin' to duff us up. If I remember right, it wuz 'is missus who gave us the information in the end. I've got it in me register 'ere somewhere.' He reached into his hip pocket and pulled out a well-thumbed and curly-cornered notebook. He ran his fingers quickly over several pages. 'Yeh! 'Ere we are: "Rita and Ewan Roberts and a cat called Tibs." She said 'e'd been workin' abroad fer some years in one o' them colonies but 'e wuz nah back 'ome fer good an' he'd be livin' there permanently. I remember turnin' round ter Ted an' sayin' that if – heaven forbid – a bleedin' bomb did 'appen ter fall on the buildin's, then Mr Ewan bleedin' Roberts would be a bloke I wouldn't try too 'ard ter bleedin' find.'

'So what's this all leading to?' asked Grace, looking up at David with some impatience. 'Are you saying we've got a wife-beater in the block? So what's new? Throughout these buildings we must have scores of them. Right now we should have other priorities. The welfare of our children, for starters.'

He made no reply at first but looked thoughtful for a few moments. 'When I was down at number eighty-seven a few minutes ago, Ewan Roberts said to me, "I've done my stint in the pokey," and Jack, you told us Rita Roberts claimed he'd been working away in the colonies ... Hmm,' he murmured thoughtfully, rubbing his chin, 'I have a vague feeling at the back of my mind about this.'

'About what?' asked Grace.

'A week or two ago I remember reading in one of our police publications about a right nutter who'd been released after doing his time on Dartmoor. I didn't take much notice because it did not give an address but I think I'll take another look at that article.' He glanced up at the mantelpiece clock. 'How long until we eat?' he asked Grace.

'At least an hour,' she replied. 'But why, where are you going?'

'To the station, it's only at the end of the street. I'm going to scan all the recent publications. I'm sure it's there. I won't be long.'

'But you've only just finished a twelve-hour stint and you'll be back there again in a few more hours. Your mates will think you're crackers. Won't it keep?'

'It might, but I won't. I'll be back afore you know it.'

'Can us three come with you, Dad?' asked Benjamin hopefully.

It was a request that caused Freddie Foskett to optimistically slip the curtain from over his head, but the curt reply, 'Not on

30

your life!' caused him to slip it right back again. David hastened down the staircase glancing only briefly at number 87.

Stones End police station was barely two hundred yards away and within five minutes he was sitting in a basement room thumbing through a book of local police information.

'What's the matter, Diamond, can't you stay away from the place?' The well-known voice of old Station Sergeant Andrews came from the doorway. 'I thought twelve hours a day would be sufficent for anyone. Perhaps we don't work you hard enough when you're here.'

'Oh, hello Sarge,' said David without even looking up. 'Perhaps you could help me.' He had barely begun his account of his confrontation with his neighbour when the old sergeant cut him short. 'There's not a bit of good anyone going to the trouble to publish all that information when you buggers don't even read it *before* you go out on the street,' he snapped. 'The whole idea of these circulars is that you know exactly who it is you're dealing with when you *arrive* at the scene, not half an hour later back at the nick! Seeing as you're off duty I'll save you time. You're obviously talking about Ewan Roberts. The man's a bloody psychopath. He's just done a sixteen-year stretch on the Moor. Apparently he fell out with a few of his old gang and done two of them in. The jury cleared him of both murders but Judge Goddard boxed him up with a sixteen-year stretch for GBH on a third. A rose by any other name, as you might say. As he's out now he must have done about twelve years. He was nicked at his wedding party above the Father Red Cap pub in Camberwell, must have been around 1928 to 1929. The bride didn't take too kindly to it as I remember. Hard little cow, nice-looking kid at the time, though.'

'How come you know so much about it, Sarge?'

'I was the one who nicked him. It was the same day I'd been made sergeant so I remember it well. You said he lives in your block? How close?'

'Two floors below. I'm at ninety-one, he's at eighty-seven.'

'Then you'll need to be careful because when he went down for his stretch he vowed he would either do a copper or a copper's family. Of course I know a lot of them say that at the time but this bloke . . .' The sergeant shook his head. 'I'm not so sure. He could just be the bloke to try it. Still, he doesn't know you're in the job, does he?'

'Er, I'm afraid he does, Sarge. I told him.'

The station sergeant sucked on his teeth thoughtfully 'Hmm, shame, that. Perhaps you'd better get home, son, and have a word with your missus. Don't frighten her, mind, but you'll need to be on guard. I'd say you're dealing with a dangerous man . . . a very dangerous man.'

3

Corporal Duncan Forbes was not a happy man. In fact it would
be fair to say he had not been happy since he had returned late
to his unit near Amiens from that eventful thirty-six-hour pass
two months earlier. He had explained to his commanding
officer that it had not been his fault he had been delayed. Of
course he could hardly tell him that Julia's vigorous use of the
stomach pump had not been taken from the best nursing
manuals. On the other hand, he had managed to impart the
disadvantages of falling in the Thames in full uniform. However, it wasn't that which had upset him. After all, his
relationship with the girl had not just survived but practically
prospered on far worse disasters than that. No, what permanently infuriated him and had ever since war was declared,
was the fact that there was no *real* war at all and, as far as the
army was concerned, there seemed very little preparation for
it. Every week he seemed to be sent on a useless course to try
out a variety of useless weapons, most of which a platoon of
very apprehensive men would be expected to use to stem, or
at least delay, a well-equipped enemy. Never one to hide his
feelings, he had made his views known at every opportunity.
The latest week's course had been the last straw. When asked
for a report on the effect of a particularly useless shoulder-
carried anti-tank gun, he had written in the comments section,
'At nine yards, with wind support, this gun could inflict a
worrying dent in a paper hat.'

The colonel had not been amused. 'D'you think you're the only damn soldier in this war who is appalled with what he sees around him, Corporal?' he had asked.

'Not the only *soldier*, sir,' Duncan replied. 'But it's not soldiers who are fighting at the moment. It's politicians, Whitehall Warriors and the bloody bureaucrats. With respect, sir, the only cause they are fighting is the one that allows them to keep their heads up their arses.'

'Why d'you say that?' asked the colonel, who deep down shared a fair proportion of Duncan's frustrations.

'Because I led my squad in a patrol behind enemy lines last week and managed to capture a German sniper. When we returned he sung his head off and I believed him, even though I seem to be in a minority of one.'

'Yes, I remember hearing something about that, I was on leave at the time. The interrogators made their report but GHQ apparently didn't believe he was telling us the truth. They thought he was too obvious and possibly a Walter Mitty character. What was it he said, now?'

'Well, he could speak good English, apparently he had gone to school for some years in Preston where his dad ran a baker's shop. He was certainly mouthy but I believe it's because he expects to be a free man by Easter. He reckons the German army have been building up like mad and the tanks he described sounded alarming. When he saw ours he burst out laughing. He reckons he saw better at the Dodgems in Blackpool in 1937.'

'He's probably right,' muttered the colonel. 'You're not a conscript, Forbes, you've been with the army for some years now and you're a professional soldier. As such you are required to get on with whatever matter is in hand and quite frankly you have fallen short of what I would have expected.' He glanced down at the papers on his desk. 'You were not always so. Some of these earlier reports on you are very encouraging, very encouraging indeed. I see you were due an officer's course in September. Who knows, perhaps another course is only a question of time. With the huge recent intake of men, the army is going to need every good soldier it can lay its hands on and your record indicates you are exactly that – a good soldier. But you know that, surely?'

'I fully realise I'm a *professional* soldier, sir,' Duncan countered. 'Whether I'm any good or not is for others to decide but it's because I am professional that I get so angry at what I see going on around me. Whitehall is so apathetic that I suspect it's doing nothing more than acting this war out. I have the feeling I'm about to take part in an enormous fixed fight and everyone's betting I get stuffed in the first round.'

The colonel leaned back in his chair and, staring across the table at Duncan, he sat tapping his fingers together for a moment. 'Well,' he said finally, 'I'll tell you what I'm prepared to do. According to this circular from GHQ, I am invited to recommend one man from this unit for the officer's course at Sandhurst starting Monday 1st January. You were singularly unlucky last time because someone declared a war, so providing this time no one actually *starts* one, how d'you feel about going to Sandhurst again?'

'Great, sir!' exclaimed Duncan. 'And I'm very much obliged, even though my opinion of the way this war is being tackled has not changed one bit.'

'Well, you never know,' said the colonel with a hint of acidity, 'perhaps if you pass with enough distinction at Sandhurst they'll let you run it yourself. Anyway, report immediately to admin for your pass and travel warrant. There is a train to Dieppe about a quarter to midnight; be on it and with any luck you could find yourself at London Bridge this time tomorrow – Christmas Eve! That would give you a whole week before you report to Sandhurst. Make the most of it because I have an uncomfortable feeling that a whole week's leave is going to be a particularly rare occurrence in this army very soon. Good luck, Corporal.'

'And to you, sir.'

Duncan saluted and, with a brisk right turn and contrasting feelings, strode smartly out towards the admin office. He had certainly been bitterly disappointed when his original course had been cancelled way back in September, but at least, being a corporal, he could moan and groan his head off without too much trouble. However, this discontentment would certainly not be acceptable with a lieutenant's pip resting on his shoulder. Still, first things first; with any luck there was now Christmas with Julia to celebrate. It was ironic that it was times like this, two hundred miles distant, that he appreciated her most. He suddenly realised that at that moment he actually ached for her and the thought of seeing her again was the one overriding thought in his mind. His brisk stride broke into a trot and then a run as he bounded up the admin staircase three at a time.

Grace Diamond stood precariously on an old kitchen chair and endeavoured to pin up the end of a paper-chain to the ceiling. After much grunting she managed to insert the final drawing pin and stepped gingerly down to admire her handiwork. Well, it was hardly the main window at Selfridge's but it would have to do. Christmas Day, falling as it did on Monday, had compelled her to fetch her customary washing day forward to Saturday. This in turn meant a three-hour Sunday stint with the two heavy flat irons. After finishing the last sheet she placed both irons to cool on the stone floor of the outside balcony. She was then able to take down the washing line that criss-crossed the width of the kitchen and replace it with four lines of paper-chains. It was true that Jackie Blackwell had advised against these decorations on the grounds that, in the event of an air raid, they could be fire risks but after more than three months of war, air raids were unheard of. In fact if it hadn't been for the food shortages, queues and the blackout, nothing much would be different. Even most of the kids in the buildings seemed to have returned from evacuation. Her earlier fears seemed to have been needlessly pessimistic. She glanced across as the mantelpiece clock struck four. David was due home at six and several friends and family were all expected to meet in the nearby Winchester public house during the evening. It would be nice to see them all again. That had been one of the biggest drawbacks of the past three months, with everyone working on some national task or other it had been almost impossible to arrange a social evening. Well, judging by the amount of uniforms she had seen around the streets in the last few days, it looked like a truce had been declared throughout all services, both civil and military. Everyone seemed to be on leave and making plans to see everyone else this Christmas. Perhaps her sarcastic remarks about Hitler had been right after all, perhaps he did believe in Santa.

Because of the impending party, the usual Sunday roast had been forsaken as all the gas rings and the hob of the kitchen range would be needed to boil saucepans for the family bath. She would need to fetch in the old galvanised tub from its hook on the wall on the balcony and place it in front of the fireplace. She frequently envied folks with a bathroom, but on a cold day – and the weather had been bitter for some weeks now – a bath in front of a glowing fire had a great deal going for it.

Glancing out of the window she looked down through the December dusk to ensure that Benjamin was still playing in the yard of the flats. There were so many children there now that at first she could not see him. A far cry indeed from those first days of the war when Freddie, Rosie and Benji seemed to be the only kids left in the world. Finally she saw the dreaded threesome. They had obviously each cadged a skate and were heavily engaged in a one-skate race. Grace found this activity particularly reassuring when she remembered that tonight Santa was due to give each of the trio a pair of roller-skates purchased earlier for ten shillings each from a second-hand stall in the market. Rosie, who missed very little, caught sight of her staring down and responded with the briefest of waves. Grace smiled to herself. There was no doubt who was the brains of that little group. The sight of the children reminded her that she had yet to wrap the skates. She guessed that neither Benji nor Rosie still actually believed in Santa Claus, though she suspected that Freddie still clung on.

An hour or so later the presents were wrapped, her clothes were laid out and, as the water boiled, condensation streamed in twisting rivulets down every smooth surface in the flat.

Checking the clock, she thought she would just have time for a quiet bath before Benji and David returned. The usual pecking order was Grace first, Benjamin second, then, after a top-up from another hot saucepan, David last. One by one she lifted the utensils from the stove and poured the swirling water into the tub. Great clouds of steam billowed across the room. After two generous handfuls of soda, she added a cup of soap-flakes and a few splashes of disinfectant. Finally, for hair-washing duties, she placed a pot of Green's soft soap on a stool at the side of tub. With any luck she would even have time for an extended soak before her son arrived. As this was to be the first get-together since war had been declared, Grace guessed that similar preparations were doubtless being made amongst her friends all over town. These would range from the palatial bathroom in the Hampstead mansion of David's grandmother, Billie Bardell, to Jackie Blackwell's strip-wash at the sink on the top floor of the next block. She smiled to herself as she imagined Jack bent over the porcelain, probably still wearing his warden arm-band – even if he was wearing precious little else.

Having drawn the curtains and stoked the fire, she had

turned out the electric light. A bath by the fire-glow seemed somehow more cosy, perhaps it was because she could pretend she was somewhere more exotic than in a tenement kitchen. Discarding her clothes on the back of an armchair, she lowered herself into the comforting heat of the tub. After adjusting to the temperature of the water she briefly ducked her head and was soon massaging a handful of soft soap into her scalp. She began to realise just how much she was looking forward to the evening when she found herself singing; she couldn't recollect doing that for a *very* long time. With eyes shut and a head full of foam, she reached to the stool for the rinsing water, singing, '*There's a land that I heard of once in a lul—*'

Suddenly a firm hand seized her wrist. Her impression of Judy Garland faded quickly as she rubbed most of the soap from her eyes and found herself staring anxiously into the smiling though tired face of her husband. '*David!*' she exclaimed. 'Christ, you frightened the bloody life out of me! How did you get in?'

'Like I always do, with my key, of course. I was going to knock but as I did I listened and thought, "Hello, what's Judy Garland doing in my kitchen?"'

'Well, I never heard you. Anyway, what're you doing in so early? You shouldn't be here for another hour at least.'

'Funny you should say that, because' – David picked up the soap – 'I said to the commissioner, "Now look here, guv," I said, "I'm married to the most beautiful woman in London . . . England . . ." no, I lie, I'm sure I said Europe, "and tonight is her bath-night. Now I realise my police work here is vital and of great national importance but if I don't get home in time to wash her back—" no, I lie again, I believe I actually said her front, "she will consider her Christmas ruined and sue for divorce." Know what the commissioner said to me then? No? Well, I'll tell you. "Got a nice pair of bristols, then, has she?" he said. Commissioners are a bit like that you know – randy buggers. "Well, I wouldn't know that sir," I said. "After all, I've led a very sheltered life and I've never seen another woman's bristols. Although, I must say, her nipples are as big as strawberries – and just as sweet." Then he said to me, "Diamond," he said—'

'I *know* what he said!' cut in Grace, flicking a large handful of foam into his face. 'He said you were the biggest bloody liar in his entire force!'

'But Grace,' protested David indignantly, 'tell me straight, would I lie to you?'

'Not bloody much you wouldn't!' she exclaimed. 'Still, now you're here you can rinse my hair and wash my back.' She looked down at her nipples. 'Strawberries indeed!'

'I didn't just say "big", though, did I?' he protested. 'I also said "sweet". That must count for something, surely?' He bent forward and lightly kissed each of her nipples. 'Bloody hell!' he cried, clapping his hand to his mouth. 'I take that back! Sweet they're definitely not – ugh!'

'Seeing as they are currently covered by a solution of soap flakes, antiseptic, soda and Green's Soft Soap, I don't suppose they are. So unless you'd care to rinse them, then that's the price you'll pay for cleanliness.'

'Actually,' he said, as he picked up the saucepan and began a slow but steady trickle all over her head and shoulders, 'my rinses were once acclaimed by all across the length and breadth of London and I've been told by the very best that I've lost none of my old magic.'

'Uh huh,' she murmured as he kissed her fully on the lips. 'And just who is this "very best" you're on about?'

'Why you, of course, sweetie,' he whispered as he ran his hands down over her wet belly to her thighs. 'Who else?'

'Davy Diamond, you must be the world's most transparent man and I don't know what you're searching for down there but you'll not find it, well, not this week anyway.'

David gave a great sigh, then drew away and reached for the towel. 'Curses!' he groaned. 'Sometimes I wish men had periods, then life wouldn't be so damn frustrating.'

'Heaven protect us from that,' laughed Grace. 'They moan enough as it is, that would just about push them over the top.'

Further debate was interrupted by a pounding on the door. 'Mum, can Rosie and Freddie come in for tea?'

Grace looked up at him and gave a great smile. 'There,' she said soothingly. 'Aren't you pleased with mother nature now? If it hadn't been for her you might have just been at the point of no sexual return. Instead of that you can cook saveloys and chips for the children. That should dampen your ardour.' She turned her head to the closed door. 'Yes, okay, son,' she called with a chuckle in her voice. 'Dad's having a saveloy problem at the moment, he'll call you when he's sorted it out. Don't go away from downstairs, though, because you're next in the tub.'

Sid Pavey, the landlord of the Winchester public house, was busy ensuring the blackout curtains were securely in place in the saloon bar. What with local industry and shops only working a half-day, the pub had been busy enough at lunchtime, but if past experience was anything to go by, Christmas Eve evening would be far busier. For the first time since war was declared it seemed everyone was really determined to enjoy themselves. This determination would in turn present Sid with an ever-recurring problem, namely kids at the door. It did not matter how neatly the heavy curtains were draped, there would always be a dozen or so children waiting at the pub entrance. Adults would attend to their needs from time to time with glasses of lemonade or large arrowroot biscuits – price one penny – that Sid kept in an enormous jar on his counter. Try as he might, kids at the door meant one thing: irregular flashes of light seeping out in all directions. On a busy night, Jackie Blackwell and his team had been known to have apoplexy.

Then there was the pianist, Fat Lill Fanshaw, a lady of some twenty stone of well-corseted female flesh. The parts of her that were not corseted seemed to wobble in every direction as she pounded the ivories and sprayed her fag-ash everywhere, even over her fox fur stole which she would wear around her neck irrespective of the temperature. She hadn't turned up at lunchtime because she had been worse for wear from the night before. Christ, but she could put some booze away, could Lill. On the other hand she was a damn good pub pianist, she could sense the mood of a pub like no piano-player he had ever known but not for nothing was she known as 'Old Mother-gin-guts' or 'Fox-Fag Lill'. Well, anyway, with a final look around he knew he had done the best he could. The worst that could happen was that the curtains would collapse, or Lill might fall off the piano stool and set light to her frock. But what the hell, there was a war on, wasn't there?

Sid need not have worried. That evening, as regulars and occasionals began to pour in, there was an air of bonhomie that he hadn't felt in the pub since August Bank Holiday. Tonight, Sid felt, was going to be just fine. That was providing of course that Fat Lill actually arrived.

Fat Lill, in fact, did not just *arrive* but she was the first in the door. Not only that but she spent half an hour clearing beer stains off the keys. 'It's gonna be a great night tonight, Sid,' she boomed as she adjusted her stole. 'So keep 'em coming, me luvvie.'

Although, of their friends, David and Grace lived the nearest to the Winchester, they were by no means the first to arrive. That honour went to Billie Bardell and her shy maid and companion, Elsie. Billie, a former queen of the music halls, was now well into her sixties but was as smart and healthy as ever. The pair had arrived by taxi from Hampstead after a frustrating journey through the London blackout. 'Sid! You old rogue!' yelled Billie in greeting. 'I s'pose you're still watering the beer?' Then without waiting for a reply she jerked her thumb towards the piano and added, 'In that case two gins. One for Lill, and one for her fox.'

'Gawd bless you, Miss Bardell,' smiled the grateful pianist. 'Just a small couple to be sociable. And will you be giving us a song or two later?'

'Not too much later, Lill. You play better when you're sitting on the stool, not lying on the floor like last time.'

The pianist's raucous laughter coincided with the entrance of Billie's daughter, Queenie Forsythe, and her husband Jim. Mother and daughter greeted each other in a genuinely fond embrace and, on releasing her daughter, Billie promptly seized her son-in-law in a gigantic bear-hug. 'Jim Forsythe!' she cried. 'You have no business to look so good. If I wasn't such a dignified old dear I'd seduce you.' If Jim looked good it was as nothing to Queenie's appearance. She had obviously not only inherited her mother's good looks but also managed to incorporate much of her own. In a neat, tailored two-piece suit with matching hat and gloves she looked quite regal. 'Well, where's my grandson and his family?' asked Billie. 'As they live the nearest I thought they'd be here by now?'

'Jim and I just popped up to see them on the way here,' explained Queenie. 'They were almost ready and said they would follow on in a few minutes.'

'I understand David is working a permanent twelve-hour day,' said Billie.

'That's why we arranged for us all to meet here,' explained Queenie. 'What with the long shifts and Benji, I thought it would be easier for them.'

Billie nodded understandingly. 'And who else is coming?'

'I think it will be mainly David and Grace's friends plus your ex-maid, Julia. She has a room in our house but as she's working up the road at Evalina Hospital she usually stays in the nurses' quarters. She's hoping to get here a little later.'

'How about that fellow of hers, whatshisname? You know, the one who used to be my gardener?'

'You mean Duncan? He's in France somewhere.'

'They are such a suited couple,' said Billie, shaking her head. 'I'm only amazed they haven't married by now.'

'Whatever you do, Mother, when Julia arrives, don't start her off on that subject. Just about *everyone* thought they'd be married by now. Everyone except Duncan, that is.'

'He's such a good-looking brute,' sighed Billie. 'If I was only forty years younger . . .' she gave a little chuckle. 'D'you know, I find I'm saying that more and more lately. I think I'm finally getting old.'

'Not you, Grandma,' said a voice from behind. 'Never you.'

She wheeled and screeched with delight to see her grandson David standing before her with a huge smile and arms wide open. 'Davy! Davy! Davy!' she said as she fell into his arms. 'And where is my great-grandson and his beautiful mother?'

'His beautiful mother is just coming through the door and his nibs himself is currently outside the same door with a few of his mates.'

'You're not leaving the child in the street, surely?'

'Of course, where else?' asked David. 'There's enough of them out there. Anyway, Grace will leave us a little early and take him home. After all, it is Christmas Eve. What kid do you know who ever went to sleep early on that date?'

'I must see him!' she cried, as she fought her way towards the door before disappearing through the ever-growing crowd.

By this time a heavy haze of grey-blue cigarette smoke hung in the air and blurred the outline of everything more than a few yards distant. The pub was now packed and, with the heavy drapes cutting out the draughts as well as the lights, the air became truly oppressive. Not that anyone noticed, though; what with big Lill pounding the piano and a hundred different conversations, the Winchester was at last looking like something it hadn't been for ages – a real, proper south London pub.

It must have been an hour or so later that Julia, hastening the short distance from Evalina Hospital, saw the collection of children outside the saloon bar. As she neared, the first child she noticed had a pair of knickers an inch or two lower than her dress. Benjamin and Freddie took a little longer to identify. She gave them each a sixpenny piece and, by the way the coin jingled as each dropped it into their pockets, it sounded like all three had done rather well for themselves. Probably a guilt complex in most of the grown-ups, she thought.

The difference between the inside and the outside of the pub could have hardly been greater. She had gone from a chilly, dark street into something akin to Dante's inferno but with unquestionably greater smells. She headed towards the piano where Lill was bashing out some ragtime. This was not out of any musical appreciation on Julia's part but simply because on previous visits to the pub she had noticed that its raised plinth had been the best place for making an observation across a packed bar. After a struggle she finally managed to place one foot on its edge and hoisted herself up to see across the room.

'What d'you want to sing, luv?' asked Lill Fanshaw, squinting through the smoke from her own cigarette.

'Oh er – er –' stammered Julia, 'I don't want to sing. I'm just looking for my friends. You see—'

'Only singers allowed on stage. Rule of the house,' snapped Fat Lill curtly as, with a great puff of air, she blew her fag-ash over the piano and resumed pounding the keys.

'Julia! Julia!' called a familiar voice. 'What the hell are you doing up there?'

'Oh, Miss Bardell,' laughed the girl, 'I'm so pleased to see someone I know. That stupid woman thought I wanted to sing! Just as if anyone *would*. I mean, you'd need to be drunk or a lunatic to sing in this place . . .' She stared at Billie for a moment, then placed her hand upon her own mouth. 'I shouldn't have said that, should I, Miss Bardell?' Julia shook her head as if she could not believe her own words. '*You're going to sing aren't you, Miss Bardell?*'

'Yes, I am going to sing,' agreed Billie, 'but as you so rightly say, love, not until I'm pissed or barmy. Depends what comes first.' With that Billie exploded into a fit of laughter and fell upon the girl.

Meantime a very frustrated Guardsman had dashed from his train and called firstly at the nurses' quarters, then at the hospital – all to no avail. Racing around London in a blackout late on Christmas Eve had not been conducive to good temper and Duncan began to think it could well be incorporated into the Sandhurst course as a character test. If it was ever the case then he felt he would fail miserably. Having drawn a blank at the hospital, he was heading towards David Diamond's flat, purely as an act of despair, when he heard the children chattering in the dark outside the Winchester. Rosie Blackwell had a distinctive giggle and, on hearing it, Duncan thought it worth a chance.

'Annie,' he called. There was a momentary silence in the chatter before it resumed at an equal volume. 'Annie!' he repeated this time much more loudly. '*You there?*'

''Ere, Rosie,' a young voice said, 'ain't that the geezer wot jumped in the river wiv 'is clothes on? Yer know, 'im that got the right needle when 'e got wet?'

Rosie! Yes, of course, that was it! Why did he always want to call her Annie? 'Rosie! Freddie! Benji! Is that you?'

A stranger emerging from the dark who knew each of their names caused a twitch in Rosie's suspicious nature but it was soon settled as Duncan explained the real reason for his inquiries. Depositing a sixpence into the hands of the dozen or so kids, he pushed open the door of the bar. Before he could enter, a couple who were leaving pushed by. The man, much the worse for drink, was clad in a dark blue boiler suit but the woman looked vaguely familiar. Duncan looked around quizzically for a moment but as the woman stopped and began to speak to the children he decided her identity was of no importance and dismissed it from his mind.

The one big advantage he had over Julia when searching a smoky, packed bar was his height. He could see just about as far across the room as it was possible in such an atmosphere and soon spotted the heads of both David and Jim. Billie Bardell was still engaged in conversation with Julia when she saw Duncan elbowing his way through the throng.

Immediately changing the tack of their conversation she suddenly cut in with, 'And how's your soldier boy these days?'

'Don't you talk to me about that bugger,' muttered Julia disapprovingly. 'I'm having nothing more to do with—' She jumped as a pair of hands were slid around her waist from behind.

'Still love me?' whispered an all too familiar voice.

'Duncan Forbes!' she exclaimed, wheeling around. 'What the hell are you doing here? I thought you were in Amiens!'

'So I was, sweetheart, so I was. But as I told Hitler, my girl comes first.'

She threw her arms around his neck and after kissing him frantically for a couple of minutes, hissed, 'You bastard! You're the world's greatest bad penny.'

Billie Bardell wet her forefinger and dragged it facetiously across her own brow. 'Oh, I can't stand all this romantic tosh,' she said, turning towards Jim Forsythe. 'Take me away, James, I feel the vapours coming on.'

After finally coming up for air, Duncan dutifully made the rounds of all those he was expected to meet before finally conversing with David. Within a few minutes the subject of the debacle in the river was raised. 'How did it all finish up?'

asked Duncan with mild interest. 'Didn't that girl on a bike know all the kids or some such? I returned to my unit so quick I never heard the end of it. That river boat sergeant was not a happy soul though, was he? Being such a quiet Sunday morning we'd probably kept him from a kip.'

As much as was possible in such a noisy atmosphere, David explained about his subsequent meeting with Rita Roberts and her husband Ewan and even more importantly, his conversation with Station Sergeant Andrews. 'So what happened?' persisted Duncan. 'You can't possibly live in such close proximity with a bloke who's made a threat like that, surely? Can't they move you out to a police flat somewhere?'

'Apparently there are none available. All the empty ones have been requisitioned by the government and even if there was one, no one is allowed to move into them in case they're needed for people who have been bombed.'

'Yes but surely—' began Duncan.

Further conversation was interrupted by Jackie Blackwell. 'Where're all the kids, Davy?'

'Outside the door,' said David. 'Why?'

'No they're not,' replied the worried-looking warden.

'They were certainly there half an hour ago,' said Duncan. 'I spoke to young Annie – I mean Rosie. There was a whole group of them there.'

'I tell yer, there's none there nah!'

Duncan snapped his fingers. 'I remember now – that girl, the one from the river! The one on a bike . . . it was her. She was with a bloke, bit pissed he was. They were talking to the kids as I came in.'

'Rita Roberts!' muttered David, the colour draining from his face. 'This bloke who was with her, what did he look like?'

'Strange-looking geezer in a boiler suit. Big nose, he had. Bit weird really. It's not him, is it? Not the bloke you were talking about, surely?'

All three men suddenly forced their way through the crush of singing people towards the door. Jack Blackwell was the first to arrive and sure enough the spot where the children had been was dark and vacated.

'Hark,' said David, 'that's my Benji's voice. He's calling for help!'

'Look there!' snapped Duncan, pointing to where two small figures were emerging from the dark. As they moved into the light that now shone unabated from the saloon bar door, there were indeed two small figures. What is more, the two small figures were carrying a white-faced and bloodstained third small figure.

4

Freddie Foskett was crying pitifully whilst Benjamin Diamond just stared white-faced. Between them they were half-carrying, half-dragging the barely conscious Rosie. Duncan almost snatched the child up and even in that poor light noticed a glazed stare in her eyes. There were numerous small abrasions on her face and cuts on two of her knuckles as if she had been fighting someone off. Most alarming of all, though, was the blood that trickled from the corner of her mouth.

Within seconds most of the friends had gathered and all gave way to Julia's professional expertise. 'Did she lose consciousness, Benji?' she asked sharply.

Benji looked puzzled for a moment before David clarified the question. 'Was she knocked out, son?'

'Yeh,' replied Benjamin. 'When we picked 'er up she was a bit dozy and didn't know us for a while. Freddie said she was dyin' because when we all got told off about that bloke fallin' in the river, Rosie said then that we were all goin' ter die.'

'Rosie isn't going to die,' soothed Julia, 'but we do need to get her to hospital as soon as possible for an X-ray and an examination. We'd better call an ambulance.'

'I've got my car. That's if I can find it in the blackout,' said Jim Forsythe.

'The Evalina Hospital is only up the road,' pointed out Duncan. 'I can carry her there in a few minutes.'

'If you can do it carefully then I think it would probably be

51

the best policy,' said Julia, 'but I don't like that blood from her mouth. It's not a good sign.'

'I'm going to kill that cowardly bastard!' hissed David. 'Fancy taking it out on a little kid, the man must be demented.'

'Oh no yer not,' murmured Jackie Blackwell quietly, ' 'e's done my Rosie an' now I'm gonna do 'im. Fair's fair.' He reached forward and smoothed back a few strands of blood-stained hair that had matted across the child's forehead. 'But there'll be time enough fer Roberts, 'e can wait. Let's git my little gel to 'ospital first.'

Billie Bardell slipped quickly out of her heavy astrakhan coat. 'Here, put this around the poor mite.'

Duncan wrapped the child gingerly in the coat before cradling her in his arms for the short but swift walk along Southwark Bridge Road to the hospital.

'Look, we can't all go to the Evalina,' said Polly Foskett as she wiped the tearful eyes of her grandson. 'But I don't suppose any of us feel like going back in the Winchester. Let Duncan, Julia and Jack go with Rosie and the rest of you come back to my place and I'll put the kettle on. We can all wait there until we hear how the child is.' The suggestion found general approval as the coatless Billie shivered in the unexpected cold.

'What actually happened to Rosie, son?' asked Grace.

Benji exchanged a quick glance with the still-snivelling Freddie before replying, 'Er – well, Mum, we don't rightly know . . . It was dark y'see . . . an' . . . it sorta happened in no time . . . and well—'

'Let's not worry about it now,' cut in Polly Foskett. 'We can see both of them are distraught, it'll keep and we'll get it from them in the morning.'

'Yes but—' began Grace.

'Now don't worry,' soothed Polly. 'Look, we're almost home now.'

The Fosketts lived in the first of a row of two-storey terraced houses that faced Queen's Buildings in Collinson Street. They rented the ground floor whilst two other families rented the first and second floors. The Fosketts' flat consisted of a bedroom and parlour, scullery and outside lavatory. The parlour was spotlessly clean but horrendously cluttered. It seemed full of useless presents from half the seaside resorts in the south of England. There were tiny houses where a diminutive man came in or out of a different door when the weather changed, there were thimbles by the dozen, paper-weights, ashtrays, glass bells, stuffed birds, pipe-racks and knick-knacks and pictures galore, mainly with the words 'A present from Frinton/ Southend/Margate/Ramsgate/Pevensey Bay' suitably inscribed.

Even at such a time of great stress, the first thought that struck Billie Bardell as she walked into the room was just how long it must have taken to dust the place. Yet in spite of the clutter there was not a speck to be seen. As the company settled, Polly crossed to the glowing fireplace and topped up a huge old kettle that perched on an iron trivet and swung it to the fiercest part of the flames. 'Won't be a few minutes,' she announced, before rubbing her hands briskly together then fanning them wide in front of the fire. The chair to the left of the fireplace was so creased and shaped that it just had to be the customary berth of Ted Foskett. Tea-making and general hospitality was obviously woman's work because Ted made for and dropped into his chair as instinctively as he breathed. 'What are we going to do about the two boys?' asked Polly as she kneeled to gather her best china tea service from the sideboard. 'Seeing as it's so late and they've had such a distressing time, why don't you let Benji sleep here with Freddie?'

Grace was about to say that being Christmas Eve, Santa might find it less confusing if both lads slept in their own beds. But she suddenly realised that if Father Christmas was bright enough to know where the world's children slept, know-ing that Benji was sleeping with Freddie should not be beyond his capabilities at all. Freddie's bed was situated behind a curtain in the only bedroom in the flat and was a minimum-sized single bed. Grace suggested they might have more room if they top-and-tailed. In spite of this somewhat bizarre sleeping arrangement, both boys were so tired that they were asleep almost before their heads had hit their respective pillows.

Ewan Roberts had stood on the kerbside outside the saloon bar of the Winchester for some three minutes waiting for Rita to finish speaking to the children. To Ewan's mind, three minutes was two minutes too long to wait for anyone, especially a wife. Scowling, he stepped back across the pavement and caught hold of Rita's arm and dragged her away. 'I ain't left a warm pub ter stand on a freezin' pavement ter listen ter you talkin' ter a bunch of snotty-nosed kids,' he snarled. 'If we're goin' ter Clinkside, then let's go, afore I lose me enthusiasm.' Truth was, it had taken Rita the best part of the evening to talk him into leaving the Winchester. 'After all it is Christmas,' she had pleaded. 'We can come here any night but shouldn't we be somewhere more grand on Christmas Eve?'

At first she had had a blank refusal but the drink had taken its toll of his intransigence and Rita was never one to give up easily.

'So where's this place yer wanna go then?' he finally conceded.

'Clinkside would be nice. I haven't been for at least two years. It's so smart and at least they have a band and not some fat cow puffing fag-ash over everyone.'

'So yer went there two years ago, did yer?' he said, eyes narrowing. 'Who wiv?'

'Young Wanda Williams, I think. Didn't I write and tell you? I'm sure I did.'

'Nah, as a matter of fact yer didn't. Nah ain't that a surprise?' With his right hand he tugged her arm and pulled her towards him. Then with his left fist he gave her a fierce blow to the ribs.

She gave an involuntary grunt as she closed her eyes and leaned sideways in pain. 'Ewan no!' she cried, obviously expecting another blow.

'Strikes me yer were seeing a lot of that little slut Williams while I wuz away. Up ter yer old tricks agin, were yer?'

She winced with pain before replying, 'I don't know what you're talking about.'

'Oh no? I think yer do. I clocked yer years ago if yer remember. Let's see, who was it then? Margo, I believe the first of 'em wuz called. Then there was that tall tart, nah what was 'er name, Janet somethin' or other wasn't it? Nah it's a Wanda. Well ain't that a posh name? Still, I s'pose that's a posh game yer playin', wouldn't yer say?'

'What game?' she pleaded. 'I'm not playing any game, Ewan. You must believe me.'

'The game, me ol' darlin', is the filthy one yer plays with these women friends of yours. Oh, I well knows that blokes don't concern yer, I knew that almost from the start. Even in our early days it was all yer could do ter let me touch yer. Surely yer didn't think that I didn't notice.' He suddenly pulled her into a doorway. 'Remember this, if I catch yer anywhere near that whore Wanda-whatever-her-name-is, I'll carve yer both up so much yer'll look like yer've spent a weekend on a bacon-slicer. Geddit?'

With the pain in her ribs now relenting, Rita's composure had virtually returned. 'Look Ewan,' she said, 'it's our first Christmas together for almost thirteen years. Let's not fight, let's celebrate. Let's go home and change into some decent clothes and go down to the Clinkside. We can have a nice dance and I might even be able to talk you out of all these nasty suspicions you've built up. After all, what with the war and everything, we don't know if we'll all be alive to enjoy next Christmas. What d'you say?'

The idea slowly began to take root in Ewan's fuddled mind. Suddenly a bit of fancy socialising had begun to appeal to him. Bigot, and half-drunk that he was, even he realised that the chances of entering the Clinkside in his boiler suit were remote. 'All right, we'll go an' change. But if I as much as catch yer even lookin' in the same direction as another tart, I'll slice yer, Rita. I swear it.'

'I know you will, Ewan, I know,' she said, sliding her arm into his, 'but you needn't worry. Now you're back home again that's all that matters.'

A few minutes later she slid the key into the door of number 87 and seconds later she was rummaging through a small wardrobe in the bedroom. With just three dresses to her name choice was not much of a problem. She soon laid a dark green dress – her most recent acquisition – on the bed and began to search the bottom of the wardrobe for a suitable handbag. Finding one, she kicked off her shoes and slipped quickly out of her frock. Before she could make another move her arm was seized in a torturous grip and she found herself thrown face down on the bed. Her husband had tugged down her knickers and was on her back almost before her face had struck the smooth chill of the eiderdown. 'Ewan, no, please,' she begged. 'Not now, darling, later. Let's go out first, eh? It'll be so much nicer when we come back. We can spend all Christmas Day in bed if that's what you want. You can have me any way you like then and I'll do just whatever you wish. That's a promise.'

Though not instantly convinced, he eased himself up a fraction whilst he stopped to consider the offer. 'Yer'll do anything I want without screamin' the place dahn like last time?'

'That's what I promised, didn't I? Have I ever broken a promise to you before?'

'Nah yer ain't, but then I've been away for almost thirteen fuckin' years so it's 'ardly a true test.' He lay immobile for a moment, though she could still feel him hard against her buttocks. 'Okay,' he finally murmured as he pushed himself up to his feet. 'Yer on.'

It was as well she was still face down and he could not see the twin looks of relief and hatred that showed in her face. She was reaching down to pull up her panties when a sudden sharp pain seared through the back of her left thigh as he bit deep into her. 'Just a little sample to whet me appetite, darlin',' he leered.

She gave a weak smile and limped to her feet. Rubbing her wound apprehensively, she began to dress. She had planned this evening long and hard but she knew there were bound to be times when she would need to think on her feet if things did not go strictly to plan. His sudden inclination to bugger her could have almost ruined everything. She glanced quickly at the bedside alarm-clock; her timetable was vital and so far she was on schedule but she could ill afford another such unexpected interlude. Deciding to play the attentive little wife, she brushed him down and straightened his collar. 'You should wear a suit more often, darling,' she said. 'It looks nice on you.'

'I 'ate suits, yer know I do,' he snapped. 'Reminds me of all them petty rules and jumped up little barsteds in the pokey. Do this, do that! Wear this, wear that! Go 'ere, go there! I'm me own man nah an' I can do as I please.' He pulled her roughly towards him. 'As yer just said yerself, I can have yer any way I please, can't I?'

'Yes of course, darling, but that shouldn't deprive me of seeing you look so nice.' She pouted. 'I fully realise why you always wear the boiler suit but it's good for a woman to see that her husband is really a smart-looking brute. We girls do like to show off our menfolk from time to time, y'know.'

'Look, let's get this straight fer once an' fer all. I'm putting this clobber on fer no other reason than I fancy takin' in this

Clinkside place tonight. So don't get carried away an' think yer've talked me into somethin' I don't much fancy – you ain't.'

She took his arm for the second time that night and steered him as firmly as she dared towards the door. 'I wouldn't dream of talking you into anything, Ewan. I'm just so happy that we're going out posh together for the first time for years.'

'Going out posh' hardly filled the description as they faltered their way through the blackout down to the riverside. Rita had a small torch in her handbag but though torches were not too difficult to come by, their batteries were like gold dust. The overriding desire of the user, therefore, was for economy. It was general practice to shine the beam as far as it would reach, then switch off quickly to save power and try to remember the layout of the pavement until that distance had been covered. Well, that was the theory; the practice was usually different. A quick flash would do little to illuminate an uneven drain-cover, ridge, indentation, shallow kerb, or worst of all, dog-excrement. However in spite of these tribulations the couple finally reached their destination. The Clinkside, situated in an alley that ran down to the river, was grandly called a club. In effect it was little more than a small basement drinking dive that, by virtue of its rather secluded situation, tended to ignore the more irritating liquor laws. It was true that it was a cut above the average grog-shop but only on the grounds that it sported an elderly carpet and an equally elderly jazz-band. This group, though bearable to listen to, were impossible to dance to and after a cursory try most couples would settle for just tapping their feet. Even before the war the standard of catering at the Clinkside had peaked at mediocrity; now, with the unarguable excuse of war shortages, the management's total culinary effort amounted to water-biscuits and processed cheese. This inertia, however, did not prevent a half-crown cover-charge. Rita certainly had had qualms about this charge; to such an extent that she had taken the precaution of carrying enough silver to pay for it herself in the event of Ewan baulking at the price. However, it seemed the promise of good things tomorrow had put him in the best mood that she had known since his return from Dartmoor. It was in fact Dartmoor that was to provide her with her second unwelcome interlude. They had been sitting at a table for a little over an hour when a grey-haired barrel of a man approached. He did not say a word but simply reached out and shook her husband's hand almost ritualistically.

'Monkey!' Ewan greeted him. 'Long time no see. Where've yer been 'iding?'

'I don't have to hide nowadays, me old son. I'm almost legit.'

Turning towards Rita, Ewan jerked his thumb back over his shoulder at the newcomer. 'One of the best kite-flyers in the game, was Monkey,' he said reverently. 'Somehow I can't believe yer've gone legit though, not unless yer makin' a right packet.'

'I don't understand,' said Rita, hoping her concern at this interruption was not going to be too obvious. 'What's a kite-flyer?'

Both men laughed at the question. 'Well let's just say,' whispered Ewan, 'that if you were stupid enough to take a cheque from this cunnin' barsted, I'd strangle yer afore the ink 'ad dried.'

'Oh I see,' said Rita, her mind now racing.

'Why don't yer come and share our table?' suggested Monkey. 'There's a dozen or so of us and we're going to make a real night of it. Fingers Wilkinson over there has just come out from doing a five-stretch at the 'Ville. Should be a right good piss up.'

Rita was appalled and now found herself in a real dilemma. If she was to raise an objection, no matter how slight, Ewan would almost certainly slap her down and go to the table if only out of sheer cussedness. Yet she knew if her plan was to succeed she needed to be out of the club by midnight at the latest. 'Oh, I don't think so,' said Ewan, surprisingly. 'I ain't too flushed for loot at the moment and besides—' he gave a quick wink to Monkey. 'It's our first Christmas for thirteen years and I've got some catchin' up ter do . . . know what I mean, Monkey boy?'

Monkey ran his eyes slowly over Rita's body whilst making no attempt to hide his thoughts. He bent forward and quickly whispered a few words into Ewan's left ear.

Giving a humourless little laugh, Ewan replied, 'Well if that's what yer fancy, I'll loan 'er ter yer fer Boxing Day, 'ardly soiled . . . fer a decent price though!' he added.

'Never paid for it in me life,' responded Monkey proudly. 'Anyway, I must be gettin' back to me party, take care me old mate and—' He bent forward again but this time made little attempt to soften his voice. 'Give her one for me, will you?'

The forced smile on Rita's face only just covered a simmering hate which was not helped by her husband's raucous laughter. 'Oh, 'e's a lad is that Monkey,' he chortled. 'Used ter keep us amused fer hours on the Moor.'

'I can imagine,' replied Rita through clenched teeth and tight lips.

A long non-stop selection from the band had finished with a surprisingly good rendition of 'South Rampart Street Parade' when Rita noticed that the time was approaching 11.45 p.m. She was also pleased to see that her husband was now showing visible signs of wear. 'It's near the witching hour, Ewan. Fifteen more minutes and it's Christmas.'

'Oh yeh,' he replied, his eyes almost closed. 'I think I'm suffering from the smoke in that bloody pub.'

'Well, let's make tracks, shall we?' she suggested. 'It's been an exhausting day one way and another and, after all, we mustn't forget I've promised you an even more exhausting day tomorrow.' She leaned across the table and, giving him a prolonged wink, placed her hand reassuringly on his arm.

'Good idea,' he said, sliding back his chair and almost losing his balance. 'Bloody floor, slippery as a choirboy's arse. Let's get out of 'ere afore I breaks me neck.'

With only a cursory wave to his former cell-mate, Ewan placed a balancing arm around his wife's shoulders and stumbled towards the door. 'We're gonna need . . . cab,' he grunted the instant they reached the street. ''S not only fuckin' cold but . . . feel sick an' can't see . . . thing,' he slurred.

'I know, luv,' she assured him, 'but we won't get a taxi down here by the riverside. We'll need to climb the steps up to the bridge. Come on, lean on me but mind the cobblestones.'

They part-walked, part-staggered up the centre of the narrow roadway towards Southwark Bridge. There a granite staircase led up from the riverside to the south side of the bridge. 'Beats me 'ow yer can see anyfin',' he panted. 'Think it's . . . bloody dangerous. 'S like walkin' in a bloody coal-mine.'

'Don't forget I pass this way twice each day on my way to work,' she pointed out. 'I know every step here, you'll be all right.'

If he had looked up and stared intently, he might have just made out the shape of the bridge crossing above them. But Ewan Roberts did not look up, instead he looked down as he explored each stride with his feet.

'Now watch these steps, darling, they're very steep.'

'I just can't unnerstand 'ow yer can see any bloody steps.'

'Can't you see anything at all, then?'

'Not a bloody thing.'

'Never mind, dear, lean forward . . . nearly there,' she encouraged him. 'You should feel the hand-rail soon.'

Ewan never did feel the rail and the only hand he felt was the one that pushed him off the steps that led down to the river. On the all-time list of famous last requests, '*'elp!*' must feature pretty frequently. In most cases it is usually ineffective. For a heavily dressed non-swimmer, in an ink-black river on a coal-black winter night, it was worse than useless. Ewan might just as well have saved his breath. As the distant city clocks began their midnight chimes, Rita congratulated herself on her timing. 'High tide at London Bridge 11.59 p.m.' the newspaper had stated. With Southwark Bridge being just 400 yards upstream from that point, she had just cause to feel smug. The now-deep, icy Thames that had just closed over the head of Ewan Archibald Roberts seemed to chuckle in approval.

Billie Bardell had always been brilliant at assessing an audience but as St George's church clock had struck midnight, she'd needed no experience to tell her that the drama with Rosie had taken the joy out of the family evening. She did her best to keep up her impetuous bubbling, but conversation was painfully stilted until finally, some three hours after their return from the Winchester, there was a knock on the front door. Polly opened it but not without trepidation. She was confronted by the tall figure of Duncan.

'Is everyone still here?' he asked.

'Yes. How is the child?'

'She's going to be fine,' he smiled. 'Julia and Jack are staying for the time being, I've returned to put you all in the picture. I could murder a cup of tea though, Poll.'

'Of course,' said Polly.

Minutes later Duncan began to hold court as they all gathered around him. 'Well first things first,' he said, after taking his first sip of the hot, strong tea. 'The kid is okay and we'd better forget Ewan Roberts for the time being because he's in the clear on this one.'

'But if Roberts didn't do it, who did?' asked David.

'The boys may be able to help on that,' he answered. 'By the way, where are they?'

'They were tired and upset,' said Polly, 'and they've gone to bed.'

'Poor little sods, I don't wonder they're upset,' he replied ruefully. 'They've every reason to be.'

'They didn't do it, surely?' cried Polly, aghast at the idea.

'Oh no, they're also in the clear. In fact Rosie did it herself. It was a fall – not a push or a wallop. She did it in the Gaol Park Playground.'

'The *where*?' exclaimed Billie Bardell.

'The Gaol Park Playground,' he repeated, with a half smile.

'What the hell were they doing at a park at that time of night? And where the hell is Gaol Park anyway?'

'Gaol Park is only a few minutes away,' explained Duncan. 'It's the site of Horsemonger Lane Gaol. Appropriately, it's where the last public execution took place in London. As to what they were doing, according to Rosie they were doing – would you believe – a "Chinese Wot Wot".'

'*What?*' cried Billie.

'I was hoping you wouldn't say that.' Duncan laughed. ' "*What?*" is what everyone at the hospital said when they heard it.' He drained his cup and shook a puzzled head before continuing. 'Apparently all the kids had been arguing about the best way to do this bloody Chinese Wot Wot and Rosie claimed she could do one easily. A couple of larger kids called her bluff and the upshot of it was she was challenged to prove she could do it in the park playground.'

'But it's shut!' gasped Grace.

'Of course it's shut,' replied Duncan with mild irritation. 'We all know that; they simply climbed the fence. In a Christmas Eve blackout who's going to see them? Anyway, as far as I've now been able to ascertain, the best way to do a Chinese Wot Wot is to hook both feet in two looped rope ends hanging from a playground maypole. Apparently it's a kids' playground game. You then hook both arms in another two. You then twist over, and spread out your arms and legs as if you're flying. After this the directions become a bit hazy. They were particularly hazy in Rosie's case because she fell like a stone and landed on the gravel. All the other kids except Freddie and Benji done a runner. Mainly because they thought she was dead. To be fair, Freddie hadn't helped when he told them some tale about how they were all going to die at Christmas anyway.'

'Well at least they carried her back, that was something to be grateful for, I suppose,' sighed Grace.

'That's as maybe,' said old Ted, brandishing his pipe. 'But how about that blood coming from her mouth? I didn't like the look of that. I remember once when I worked on the Kingsway tram tunnel, I saw a fellow crushed and he was bleeding from the mouth because of internal injuries. Died, he did; 'orrible, it was.'

'Well, I'm afraid young Freddie was responsible for that,' laughed Duncan. 'You see, when she fell, she sustained a couple of nasty deep cuts to her hand on the gravel. Freddie told her people died if they lost a lot of blood so she should suck it back in. Who knows, perhaps he remembered your tale from the tunnel? Anyway, Freddie said the best thing to do was put her fingers in her mouth. In fact, other than a few abrasions, she had nothing much wrong with her face. Her knees, knuckles and wrists are certainly in a state and she was badly shaken and probably knocked a bit silly. They are keeping her in for the night – as much for observation as anything else – but she should be home for Christmas dinner.'

'Bloody good job none of us saw the bastard you thought responsible for her injuries though, wasn't it, Davy?' said Billie Bardell thoughtfully. 'Otherwise *someone* might well have died at Christmas.'

'I was always led to believe *someone* did die, Miss Bardell,' murmured Billie's hitherto silent maid Elsie. 'I thought that was what Christmas was all about.'

'No darling,' smiled Billie ruefully. 'That was Easter . . . but I take your point.'

5

The coroner's court was situated in the rear of a small church-
yard in an area steeped in history that seemed positively
Dickensian. Copperfield, Nickleby and Pickwick would have
all frequented the same pavements, with the George Inn and
the riverside steps where Sykes killed Nancy barely five
minutes up the road. Little had changed in the intervening
years. Heavily clad witnessess packed the tiny, windowless
waiting room and condensation tumbled down every wall. The
smell of damp clothing, unwashed bodies and stale tobacco
smoke filled the foul air. Yet, if the protests were any guide,
even the oppressive stench was preferable to the icy blast that
swept through the room when the exterior door was opened. It
was a location that spawned a scene in which Fagin and the
Dodger would have been more than comfortable.

After the Christmas holiday the coroner's list for that
morning was particularly heavy. Though the Germans had yet
to kill, or even injure, a single Londoner, buses, trams, staircases, roadworks, canals and – in Ewan's case – rivers had
taken a formidable toll of them in the blacked-out metropolis.
There were at least six fatalities awaiting a verdict that very
morning.

Station Sergeant Ted Andrews gave a disapproving glance
over the packed throng and was not too surprised to see the
only composed figure in the whole room was sitting by the
door in a sheer white blouse and an elegant, black two-piece

suit with a black fox-fur coat folded neatly over her lap. Her short, almost severe, shiny black fringe was in perfect keeping with the rest of her attire and, even in that poor light, still managed to reflect the glow of the dreary 40-watt bulb. Her whole demeanour placed her above the average tearful female occupant of the room. In spite of his professional disapproval, the old sergeant could not resist a twinge of admiration as he took in her composure. Finally, he tore his eyes away from her legs and glanced down at the list of witnesses on his clipboard. Running his pencil down the page he ticked off each identified name.

'Good! Looks like we're all here, Davy boy. With any luck we may be on early,' he said optimistically. 'Don't much fancy spending too long in this place, it stinks to high heaven.'

David Diamond, who had been deputed for the day to assist the station sergeant to assemble witnesses and present his case, glanced idly over the sergeant's shoulder at the list. 'What d'you reckon, Sarge . . . about the verdict I mean?'

'D'you want my official guess of the verdict or what I suspect *really* happened?'

'Either'll do. You took all the witness statements so you must have a pretty good idea what happened.'

'Oh, I've got an idea what happened, right enough. My idea is that Roberts did *not* come out of that club and get separated from his wife in the blackout. My idea is that being the worse for drink, he did *not* climb the wrong steps and step off into twenty feet of freezing, pitch-black, river water. My idea is that Mrs Rita Roberts did *not* scream the place down when she couldn't find her husband in the dark. My idea is she waited until she heard a reassuring splash, followed by an even more reassuring silence, before she dawdled back to the club for assistance. My idea is that there are – or were – at least half a dozen people within a close proximity on Christmas Eve, whose festive season was improved greatly when they heard Ewan Roberts had spent a week wedged neatly between the bottom of a coal-barge and best Thames silt. That's my idea, lad, or certainly most of it.'

'So if it's a suspicious death, why isn't the CID dealing?' asked David.

The sergeant raised a handful of statements and quickly ran a thumb across the edges, creating a brief whir before he replied. 'There're fourteen statements here and every one of them goes to great pains to say how sorry they were that such a lovable chap as Ewan Roberts had such an unfortunate accident. Thirteen of them say how caring, loving and distraught his poor wife was at his sudden demise. The easiest thing in the world will be to prove that this was a classic case of accidental death. Just look at the information the coroner has in these statements – blackout; too much to drink; high tide; non-swimmer; icy water and close proximity to three flat-bottomed barges. Well, bless me if the man wasn't doomed from the start. The old coroner's eyes will light up when he gets this case. Everyone will be in agreement, there are no arguments, in fact a real tidy little job. He'll then compliment me for all my hard work and there'll be a verdict of "Death by misadventure". Then that'll be the end of it. Now I ask you, what's suspicious about that?'

'Well, you *said* it was,' David reminded him.

'Oh, it's bloody suspicious, all right! Do you know that almost everyone in that club was either a friend of – or a distant relative of – Swinger Baxter? You remember Swinger, don't you? The old running mate and bosom pal of Ewan Roberts? He was the dear pal that Ewan carved up and copped a sixteen-year stretch for. Remember him now? Well, Swinger was in the club that night. It so happens that Roberts never saw him, too drunk, I suppose. Swinger claims that he never saw Roberts either, which is probably true because he lost most of his sight when Roberts carved his face. However,

Swinger still has a powerful presence and I can't believe that no one mentioned to him that Roberts was in the place. I've got statements from at least six villains who were present that night and who I'm pretty sure would have cheerfully dropped Ewan in the Thames for his butter ration. His distressing drowning would have presented no problem at all. It's sad to say but Roberts was a hateful bastard without a friend in the world. Though to give him credit, it didn't seem to bother him none.'

'But how about Rita? It would have bothered her, surely? I'm sure she could never have been a party to her husband's death.'

'Couldn't she?' The old sergeant gave a mirthless laugh. 'If I really had to lay money on it, she'd not only be a party to it, she'd be my bloody number one suspect! I think it's possible all those in the club guessed she'd pulled a stroke somewhere along the line and they are simply backing her up. There's something about that young woman that is totally unnerving. I find her far more intimidating than her husband ever was, but I cannot honestly say why.'

'Now you mention it,' said David thoughtfully, 'when I first met Roberts he had given her a terrible hiding. She was battered, bruised, cut and scalded. She looked a real pathetic creature. Yet at no time did she look scared. She has always struck me as one of the most self-assured people I've ever met in my life.'

'Okay, so look at it this way.' The sergeant glanced quickly around before continuing in a quiet, confidential tone. 'Even though Roberts' death is a great result for the rest of the world, let's pretend I was convinced enough to say I'm not at all happy about the circumstances of his death. What then? I'll tell you – the guv'nor would then be obliged to set up a murder squad and, after a few fruitless and expensive months, when they'd be much better employed on any one of a dozen other tasks, it would be finally stood down with not a thing to show for it. Okay, so someone somewhere along the line gets away with murder but on the credit side we've lost one of the most objectionable pigs I've ever known and the world is a safer place. Your own family are proof of that . . . true?'

'True,' agreed David philosophically, 'but I still can't accept that an explosive bastard like Roberts could get done in by a slip of a girl like her. I just can't see how she managed it.'

'Well, Delilah was allegedly a slip of a girl but she managed it. And remember, Ewan Roberts was no bloody Samson.'

'I still find it hard to believe, though. What did she say happened?'

The sergeant thumbed through the papers for a moment. 'Here it is,' he finally said as he ran a stubby, nicotine-stained finger down a page and read aloud. 'We left the club because he had too much to drink and was becoming rowdy and embarrassing. I tried to humour him but he kept pushing me away. Suddenly he pushed me over and ran off in the dark. I went sprawling so I was not too sure which way he actually went but I did hear him say he was going up the steps to the bridge to try for a taxi. When my husband was in that sort of mood it was best to let him just get on with it. I was certainly worried but it was only when I heard the splash that I realised he must have run up the wrong set of steps. He missed the steps that led up to the bridge and instead must have climbed the ones that led to the top of the river wall. I ran in the direction of the splash and kept calling him but I never heard another sound. I then ran back to the Clinkside and several people came out to assist me to search but it was pointless. It was just too dark. That's when we called the police.'

'So how did we find him?' asked David.

'Well, at first we didn't,' said Andrews. 'The river police searched the surrounding area all that night and most of the following day. They even worked out where the tide could have carried someone of Roberts' build and size. But it was New Year's Eve before the barges were towed downstream and, after the tide receded, some old fisherman scavenging for tubifex worms on the foreshore found the body pressed down flat into the silt. The barge must have risen and fallen a dozen times during that period and just about the only thing about him that wasn't totally flattened was his bloody nose, which must have been buried in a soft section of mud. They reckoned you could have slid the rest of him under the door . . . Are you listening to me, Diamond, or am I just here to talk to myself while you stare up that woman's legs?'

'Sorry, Sarge. I couldn't help but look at her. She actually lives in my block and I must have seen her countless times but I've never seen her look as good as she does today. If we're not careful half the women in the buildings will be shoving their blokes in the Thames if they think they can look like her as a widow.'

Further conversation was interrupted by the elderly usher who whispered briefly in the sergeant's ear. 'Thanks, Sid,' murmured Andrews in reply. He then turned to David. 'We've got a result here, son. They're taking a suicide case first that will be remanded to next week for witnesses, then it's our turn. Go and get our mob ready and tell Rita that after I've addressed the coroner she'll be first witness on. You'll also find it good practice to casually mention to that set of cut-throats from the Clinkside that, if they are not too long-winded in the witness-box, this case could be finished by the time the pubs open. That usually concentrates their minds wonderfully. Oh, and by the way,' he tugged at the constable's sleeve as he was about to depart, 'no lingering over Rita.'

David Diamond had long admired most everything about Station Sergeant Andrews. He particularly admired his confidence, competence and assurance. That icy January morning was no exception. The Crown public house in Borough High

Street was the nearest hostelry to the court and its doors had been open just three minutes as Arnold Westow, known as 'Monkey' to his friends, acquaintances and most of the warders on Dartmoor, led the charge from the court to the saloon bar. Death by misadventure had been the station sergeant's forecast and death by misadventure had been the coroner's verdict. He even complimented the sergeant on his sheer hard work.

The gathering at the Crown public house bore more resemblance to a wedding than a wake but after all, there was no one to grieve over Ewan. As Monkey said in his eulogy to the assembled company, 'Far be it from us to speak ill of the dead but thank Gawd the bastard's gone.' He had barely stepped down from the chair when he saw the street door open and an attractive woman quietly enter. She made no attempt to join the throng but made her way to the end of the bar and stood waiting patiently to be served. He left his own drink on a table and sidled his way through the group towards her. 'Rita!' he greeted her. 'I'm sorry I haven't had a chance to tell you how sorry I am about your loss. But I haven't seen you since Christmas Eve and it was all we could do to breathe in that court waiting room. Will you have a drink with me?'

'I'll have a brandy, please,' she agreed.

'Make that two brandies, Cedric old mate,' he called cheerily to the barman whom he had never seen before. On receiving the drinks he lifted them high over several heads and nodded towards a small empty corner table. 'Sit there, shall we?' he asked. 'It's a bit more private.'

She followed him to the table and had actually raised her drink to her mouth before asking, 'Why this desire to be private?'

Her composure caused him to falter slightly. 'Er . . . no particular reason. Er – I suppose I was thinking you might still be a little distressed. I mean, losing Ewan and all that. It goes without saying that you have my sympathy.'

'Mr . . . ? Look, I'm sorry, I can't possibly call you "Monkey". What *is* your name?'

'Arnold, Arnold Westow.'

'Well, Mr Westow, thank you but I don't need your sympathy and I am not now, nor ever have I been, distressed. Ewan Roberts was a man I married when I was a starry-eyed kid and obsessed about the whole idea of marriage. I was barely eighteen at the time and, looking back, I think I would have married anyone. Fortunately my mother was desperate to get rid of me and so I married Ewan. But he was a wicked bastard and now he is no more. *I* know it, *you* know it – and by the sound of it, everyone in this pub knows it. So please, no false sympathy or crocodile tears. It doesn't suit you and what's more it doesn't work.'

'You say your marriage to Ewan was fortunate. Yet you appear to have hated him. Why is that?'

'It was fortunate because, even though he was a truly vicious, uncaring bastard, he also got banged up for more than twelve years within a few weeks of our marriage. There are not many young brides who are that lucky, Mr Westow.'

'I take it you didn't enjoy marriage, then?'

'I enjoyed the wedding itself because my mum treated me to a new outfit, but that's about the sum total of it.'

'Why do you think that Ewan wanted to marry you in the first place?'

'Well, I wasn't a bad-looking girl, but I think his main reason was he knew he was due an appointment at the Old Bailey and he thought he might get a shorter stretch if he was newly married.' She gave just a hint of a smile. 'Didn't work, though, did it?'

Monkey stared at her in silence for a few moments before replying. 'Did you push him in the Thames, Mrs Roberts?'

'Mr Westow! How could you possibly say such a thing? Especially when – after hearing all the evidence – the coroner has just said that my poor Ewan's death was caused by mis-adventure.'

'That old station sergeant didn't seem to share that opinion, though, did he?'

She gave him a dazzling smile and leaned across the table and, with her face almost touching his, whispered, 'When coroners have said "Misadventure", Mr Westow, station sergeants don't matter a toss. M-i-s-a-d-v-e-n-t-u-r-e,' she repeated, rolling her tongue slowly around the word. 'What a lovely-sounding old English word that is. Doesn't it conjure up a hero carrying out some majestic deed of derring-do yet gallantly coming unstuck in the process? You know, like Scott of the Antarctic . . . or perhaps Nelson?' She gave a great sigh. 'There you are, you see, I was particularly fortunate. How many girls are lucky enough to marry a man who dies of misadventure? Very few, I'd say, Mr Westow, wouldn't you?'

'You know, girl,' he said curtly, 'I don't think you have any idea at all what the situation was with your husband. Perhaps if I told you, you might not feel quite so bloody clever.' He moved his chair around to her side and sat so close he was almost touching her. In spite of this proximity she instinctively realised it was a move for confidentiality rather than companionship. 'When you entered that club on Christmas Eve, I was under strict instructions to get your husband over to our table. If I'd managed that, you can take it from me he would have had a far less peaceful finish than the one you gave him. I'm not normally a violent man, Mrs Roberts, that was never my way, as Ewan well knew. That's obviously why I was sent as a messenger. That's also why I didn't make too much of an issue of it when Ewan declined my offer. It was lucky for me you left when you did, because if you'd left an hour later I would have been up to my neck in it. If nothing else I owe you for that.'

'In that case, Mr Westow,' she murmured, 'perhaps you'll

now be good enough to tell me exactly where this leaves me?'

'I thought you might ask that.' He grinned. 'It leaves you, my pretty lass, in the best of positions. You're now an honest widow, you have a clearance from the law and you have the undying gratitude of a certain Swinger Baxter. Short of receiving the freedom of Paris, you're about as tops as you're ever likely to be. You see, if that mob had got their hands on Ewan – bearing in mind they were all best-part pissed – subtlety would not have been their strong point. They would have probably each carved a slice off him. One thing would have been sure, whatever they did would never have resulted in a verdict of misadventure. "Butchery" would have been the least they could have hoped for. But whatever it was, it would have caused the bogies to be clumping about all over the place for bloody weeks. So for the moment, lass, as far as Swinger's mob's concerned, you can walk on water. If you take my advice you'll make the most of it.'

Rita drummed her fingers thoughtfully against her bottom lip for some time. 'I see, Mr Westow . . . that's very interesting . . . very interesting indeed.' She gave a little smile. 'Though I don't think walking on water is a trick my family have yet perfected. I'd say one misadventure is more than enough, wouldn't you?'

'Listen,' he said, his tone changing to a softer hue as he reached for her wrist. 'Why don't you come and meet the rest of the mob? I'm sure they'd like to meet a cool-headed girl like you and who knows, there may even be a position for you somewhere in the set-up. What with the war and everything, things are always changing and there is so much scope.' He was taken aback by how easily she released his hold on her wrist.

'No thank you, Mr Westow, I have plans of my own now. I can assure you, though, that our paths will be entirely separate and there will be no competition.'

'Okay, then let me give you my other option.'

'If you must,' she sighed, 'but you'll be wasting your time.'

He glanced all around and drew even closer. 'In addition to working with Swinger, I have a little sideline all my own. It's quite profitable but it could do a whole lot better and with your help I think I could double it. Interested?'

'Go on.'

'First of all, what is your job at the moment and what is your pay?'

'I work on the Auxiliary Fire Service switchboard. It's an easy enough job because there are hardly enough fires to keep the regular brigade occupied so I don't know how much longer it'll last. As for wages, they vary with the hours but they average out about fifty bob a week.'

He reached over and ran his fingers over the fox-fur coat. 'If you can run to a coat like this on fifty bob a week, perhaps you should be chancellor?'

'Look!' she hissed, as she twisted his fingers away from the fur and slid back her chair. 'Let's leave it at that, shall we? You can be everlastingly grateful to me and I'll never see you again, how's that grab you?'

'Calm down, calm down,' he soothed. 'Let's not lose our temper. I'm going to offer you a job for which I'll need to trust you implicitly. Therefore I'll need to know more about you.'

'Okay, in that case I'll tell you all I think you need to know and no more, fair?'

He gave an exaggerated sweep with his arm. 'Pray continue.'

'I'm twenty-nine years old, I'm very much my own person. I doubt if I've ever spoken two words to anyone in my block, so they know next to nothing about me. I cycle to work; I'm not looking for romance; I keep well physically . . . oh yes, I hired the coat for twenty-four hours for two pounds from Berman's in the West End. Anything else is my business.'

'I'll settle for that,' he grinned. 'So here's my proposition. Since this war began, the port of London has never been so busy. The government have been stockpiling everything they think may become in short supply in the event of a U-boat blockade. Because of this the docks have been full of ships from all over the world. Even fifty extra ships a week will mean anything between one and three thousand extra crew members ashore. Many of these come from countries which are still neutral and many of them have all sorts of goodies to sell or barter. The police and customs can't possibly cope with such traffic and by now I have a reliable pipeline set up anyway. I do well enough as it is but, with a good-looking wench like you, I could at least double my take.'

'If you think I'm seducing half the Merchant Navy so you can deal in a few goodies, you've another think coming, sunshine.' She rose to her feet. 'No deal.'

'Last week I made forty quid on five hundred torch batteries alone,' he said casually.

'*You what!*' she exclaimed with sudden interest. 'You couldn't possibly!'

'Ah, but I did,' he replied smugly. 'Oh, I admit it wasn't an everyday deal, the crew had almost as many batteries in their bunk as the ship had timber in its hold but it still gives you some idea of the potential. Still not interested?'

She almost fell back into her seat. 'I'm interested,' she replied, flashing him her easy smile. 'But why do you think you need me?'

'Because what with the tides and everything, I can't always be at the docks at the best time. There are other people in this business beside me, you know. With you working shifts we could cover most of the day between us.'

'So what's actually involved?'

'Well, firstly, have you any commitments for the rest of the day?'

'None in the next couple of hours that take preference over forty quid,' she responded.

'Good, because there's no time like the present. We'll leave here separately; it's less conspicuous. See you outside St George's church in five minutes – okay?'

She had risen and gathered up her fur before he had finished speaking.

Minutes later, as he followed her across the busy Borough High Street, he realised what a striking-looking woman she was when he found himself fascinated by just the simple swing of her coat. Okay, so it wasn't actually *her* coat but, hired or not, he thought there would be few who could wear it so well. Though Arnold had always fancied himself with the opposite sex, he had to say he had never been very successful. He suddenly had a feeling that this time his luck could have changed. Running his thoughts over the pleasures of her body, he began to compliment himself on his good fortune. What was that she had said – 'I'm not looking for romance'. That probably meant she was still coming to terms with the loss of her husband. Even though she had doubtless drowned him, she probably still felt a sense of loss, women were funny like that. Well, he would soon cure her – after all, wasn't he now financially solvent? Even at wartime prices, he could well afford to wine her and dine her. More importantly, he could even take his time. This was something he had never been able to do with a woman before. All his previous relationships seemed to have been a race to bed the woman before his cash ran out. It was a dilemma that had always caused him to rush everything, and which he was convinced was the real reason for his lack of sexual success.

On the debit side, of course, was the question of her eyes. Yes, they were indeed a problem. Her eyes had made him feel just a little uncomfortable. No matter how much her mouth smiled, her eyes never did. There was a coldness about them that he had never experienced before. Oh, but what the hell, everything else about her was as good as it could be – and her legs were a knockout!

She was looking up at the church clock as he came up behind her and slid an arm confidently around her waist. 'This way, sweetheart,' he said, in what he thought passed for a lover's request. 'We'll get a cab from London Bridge station.'

The firmness she used to remove his arm was even greater than that she had shown when removing his fingers from the fur coat. It just went to show how distressed she still was, he thought. This poor kid could prove even more difficult to break down than he had first realised. Never mind, he would be benevolent, she'd like that.

Half an hour later the taxi had dropped them on the quayside of Limehouse Basin by the mouth of the Regent Canal. Here some ten acres of water provided good anchorage for at least a dozen small ships. A nearby greasy café hardly looked inviting but it was to there that Westow led her. The stares that followed her were not altogether ones of admiration; if a classy-looking woman in an expensive fur coat was not commonplace on those coal-dusted quaysides, then one about to enter Dick's Café was as rare as a nude hedgehog.

She frowned apprehensively. 'Are you sure?' she said, as Westow reached for the door.

'Of course,' he chuckled. 'Some of my best deals have been struck in here but if you ever find you're making a trip here on your own, you will find it advisable to be more discreetly attired.'

'Don't let that worry you,' she said. 'The coat goes back this evening.'

The smoke in the café attacked her eyes almost before she had set foot in the place. Westow nodded in recognition to a grotesquely fat woman seated behind the counter and made straight for a table in the far corner. There five woollen-hatted men were involved in an intense-looking card game. Westow reached out and shook hands with one of them. 'Good to see you, Sven,' he said. 'I'd like you to meet a partner of mine. This is Rita.'

Sven did not say a word but took the woman's hand and held it for some moments whilst he blatantly stripped her with his eyes.

Swinging around she faced Westow. 'Is this scum deaf as well as dumb?' she asked curtly. 'Because I want him to hear what I'm about to say to him.'

'No!' cut in Westow sharply. 'You're not down the local market, you know. This is a cut-throat business in more ways than one and don't forget it for a moment.'

'I theenk I go to like thees woman,' said Sven as he smiled through a set of horrendous teeth. 'Probably veer much.'

'Now look, sweetheart, Sven here is your go-between. You'll need him because very few of the sailors speak any English. Many of them are Lascars. You'll find him in or around this café for most of the time. If he's not here, Bertha behind the counter will usually know where he's to be found. God only knows what he *officially* does, but going to sea never seems to be a part of it.'

'Can I trust him?'

'Good heavens, no! But on the other hand there's little you can do about it and he knows that more than we do. Just assume that everything he tells you is a lie and cut any price he mentions by three hundred per cent and you'll be about right.'

She looked across at the still smiling Swede. 'Should you be saying this in front of him?'

'Why not?' shrugged Westow. 'He knows it . . . and don't be misled by that dreadful accent, his English may not be brilliant but he understands every bloody word, even rhyming slang.'

'So how am I supposed to know the going rates for this contraband?' she asked.

'I'll give you a list but you'll soon pick it up because there are only about a dozen different items at the moment. But with any luck the war will get worse and the list will get longer.'

'And the profits greater?'

He smiled. 'I'm superstitious, so remember you said that, I didn't.'

'I'm not a bit superstitious, Mr Westow. I believe that in life we make our own luck and I tell you now, I'm going to make mine.'

There was a coldness in her tone that caused him to stare at her intently and, for the first time since he'd met her, her face was as cold as her eyes. Familiar with scum and cut-throats though he was, what he saw in her face made him feel decidedly uncomfortable. 'Okay, now you've some idea of the works, are you in?'

'Of course, Mr Westow. When do I start?'

'Well, if you're working for me you start now and your first job is to stop calling me Mr Westow. Arnold or Arnie's the name. I'll give you all the griff on the journey back. Where d'you want dropping off?'

She glanced at her watch. 'The hop wharf in Clink Street will be fine.'

The late afternoon traffic around Tower Bridge was its customary confusion, which caused a fifteen-minute taxi journey to take an hour. For someone whose demeanour was normally so cool, Westow was surprised at Rita's increasing agitation. Although she did not speak, she sighed regularly and glanced at her watch almost every few seconds. Finally, as they passed the shadow of Southwark Cathedral, she gave a final sigh and adjusted her coat. Westow handed her a calling card that he took from his top pocket. 'I'm away for a few days but call in and see me Friday morning . . . and of course, not a word to anyone – okay?'

'Okay,' she sang, now back to her old self.

As the taxi turned into Clink Street, he made to kiss her cheek but she turned sharply away. 'Bye then, see you Friday?'

'See you Friday . . . Arnie,' she echoed.

He watched her as, with yet a further glance at her watch, she trotted briskly around the corner. He stared thoughtfully for a few seconds before leaning forward to the driver. 'Give me a minute will you, cabbie?' Alighting from the cab he strode the short distance to the junction of Stoney Street. Crossing its cobbled surface was a woman in a fur coat, running. The only other person in the street was a coatless, slightly built, fair-haired girl who was standing in front of some factory gates. Even at that distance she looked cold. On reaching her, the woman threw open her coat and enveloped the girl, whilst embracing her fiercely. Burying her face in the girl's neck for a full minute, Rita finally came up for air. The girl had almost wiggled her way into Rita's coat before the pair kissed with an almost animal intensity that Arnold Westow had never experienced in his forty-two years of life.

6

The winter of 1940 was the coldest anyone could remember. On 17 January the Thames had frozen over and the biting wind seemed to get colder and colder right through until spring. Shortages really began to bite, as much caused by the weather as the war. Arnold Westow did not much care what had caused the shortages just as long as the deficiencies were there to be exploited. Rita had proved so efficient that he had practically left the day-to-day running of the wheeling and dealing to her.

Duncan Forbes' winter, on the other hand, had been anything but harmonious. Winter is not a period that anyone would ideally choose for a four-month officer's course, not even a *normal* winter, but that winter was anything but normal. During some late February manoeuvres on Salisbury Plain, he was convinced he would never be warm again. The course certainly confirmed one suspicion, that was how easily he could swing between extremes. When he was out in the field making decisions and leading his men he was totally in his element, but when he was trying to justify to them inferior equipment or regimental incompetence he was anything but. 'I appreciate bluntness as much as the next man, Corporal Forbes,' said his company commander, 'but there is such a thing as diplomacy.'

'Sir, Hitler is winning this war through diplomacy. Everybody else in Europe is talking diplomacy while he's cutting off their balls ... with respect, sir,' he added dutifully.

During a students' assessment meeting, more than one

instructor raised this point. 'I've rarely met a better soldier,' said one sergeant-instructor, 'and if I was a platoon-sergeant in a unit led by him I'd follow him anywhere, but he has a vendetta against Whitehall and the war office, about which he'll let rip at the slightest provocation.'

There were nods all around at these words. 'Anyone have differing views?' asked the commander.

'I don't think he'll ever make an officer, sir,' said another sergeant. 'He just doesn't seem capable of accepting . . .' he paused whilst he searched for the appropriate words to describe Duncan's tactlessness.

'Fools gladly, Sergeant?' suggested the commander cynically.

The sergeant coloured in embarrassment. 'Well, I suppose there's an element of that in his make up, sir,' he blustered, 'but he's never going to have a unit that is staffed totally by geniuses, is he sir?'

'No in the army, he willnae,' cut in an anonymous Scottish voice.

'Let me put a hypothetical situation to you all then,' said the commander. 'Supposing, as a sergeant, you were cut off – say with a dozen assorted men – deep behind enemy lines, unarmed and hungry, you only had the barest notion of your location, you were on foot and Forbes was your officer. What then?' He glanced expectantly around the gathering.

'In that situation,' said the Scottish voice quietly, 'I doubt if I've ever seen any man gae through this establishment I'd trust mair.'

'I thought as much,' nodded the commander ruefully.

Duncan, being Duncan, had been pretty much impervious to these matters. Other than the weather, he had quite enjoyed the course, with the added advantage that he could reach Waterloo by train in forty-five minutes and in another forty minutes he could be in Julia's bed at Streatham. The result was that his romance with her had been on its best footing for years.

The end of the course was approaching fast and Duncan had already invited Julia to mark her calendar for a celebration after the results were known.

'But you don't even know if you'll pass,' she said. 'Personally, I think it's tempting fate.'

'But you have to book annual leave from the hospital so long in advance,' he said.

'I know, but let's wait and see. I'd be happier if we did.'

He gave a long and rather weary sigh. 'Oh, sod it!' he finally exclaimed. 'Look . . . I was trying to keep it secret so I could surprise you but . . . well, you really need to book that date because . . . well, I've got some tickets.'

'Tickets?' she queried. 'Tickets for what?'

'For just about the greatest event there's been in London for years. I thought it would be nice if we could invite a group of our friends. You know, Billie, Elsie, Queenie, Grace and their menfolk. We could make a great night of it. We could celebrate my passing out and get married at the same time. I've got eight tickets and I tell you they're going to be like gold-dust.'

'Duncan Forbes!' she said, shaking her head in bewilderment. 'Just what the blazes are you on about? Correct me if I'm wrong, but I've just understood you to say you've got eight tickets for our wedding! Of which, up until now, I've known nothing about. What have you in mind, an arranged marriage?'

'Oh now come on, Julia,' he pleaded. 'You've been giving me a hard time for years about our marriage – or lack of it. I thought I'd surprise you, that's all.'

'You've done that, right enough! Look, I know this may come as a total surprise to you but if a person is getting married to someone, there's a tiresome old tradition that says they're supposed to know something about it – and up to this moment I've known sod all about it. And another thing' – her voice rose as she really began to give vent to her feelings – 'just why the hell are you selling eight tickets for it? Will we be giving away groceries or something?'

'Selling eight ti—' he began before putting his hand to his forehead in feigned despair. 'The *tickets*, you dopy cow, are not for our wedding, they are for the cinema. In three weeks' time – according to the papers – one of the greatest films of all time is due to open in the West End. It's called *Gone with the Wind*. It's swept the board in America and it'll do the same here.'

'Okay, let's forget the fact that you omitted to tell me about our nuptials, but let me ask you one question. Did you think of all this by yourself?'

'Course I did.'

'About our wedding, I mean?'

'Whoa!' he said, raising his hand. 'You said *one* question.'

'It is only one question, it's a continuation, that's all. Well, did you?' He made no attempt to answer but the hint of a smile played briefly around his lips. 'You didn't, did you? I knew it, you bastard! Someone put you up to it, didn't they? All you thought about was the film – and you only did that because whenever you see Vivien Leigh you get a tingle in your groin! Then someone suggested we should get married, didn't they? Who was it . . . was it Billie Bardell? It was, wasn't it!' she exclaimed triumphantly. 'I knew you'd never think of it on your own. God, Duncan Forbes, but you're bloody transparent.'

He raised his hands in mock surrender. 'It's a fair cop, darlin',' he mimicked. 'But you must be a witch to have worked that out. I reckon you should apply for the Intelligence Corps, you'd make a better job than the lot we've got at the moment.'

'Oh come on,' she insisted. 'Now I've got it out of you I

want to know why you've had this sudden change of heart . . . about marriage, I mean.'

'Well, Billie pointed out to me I've had more of your life than any man has a right to take from any girl and she said it's time I made an honest woman of you. She also pointed out that no one knows what's in store for us and we should make the most of life while the chance is still here. I suppose you could say she pricked my conscience.'

As her eyes narrowed he realised she was still unconvinced. 'Tut tut,' she said acidly. 'And there was I thinking you kept your conscience hidden in your testicles.' She stared at him for a moment. 'Sorry Duncan, I'm not buying it. I just can't believe that concern for me was your only motivation. There has to be something else that caused this change of heart,' she said suspiciously.

'Well, of course there *is* the marriage allowance,' he admitted reluctantly. 'D'you know, if we marry, you'd be worth seventeen bob a week to me.' He had barely finished before the first of the armchair cushions came winging towards him. Cowering into his own armchair he only partially stifled his laughter. 'And once you present me with our third child I'll collect another ten bob. That's, let me see now . . . one pound seven shillings in total. What with my thirty bob a week wages,' he added, 'Christ, I'd feel like Lord Nuffield.' Ducking down even closer to the chair he called out through a covering of arms, 'Am I to take this bombardment as a refusal?'

'Not on your life, you bastard, this time we really *are* getting married. I've been down a similar path too many times before with you. This time I'm dashing downstairs to fetch up Queenie and Jim as witnesses.'

The difficulty with arranging anything involving more than two people on some future date in wartime was that it was impossible to take everyone's commitments into account. By

virtue of their ages, Billie Bardell and Elsie were not too much
of a problem, neither was Queenie who was a voluntary tea-
lady in a large anti-aircraft battery. Arrangements started to
get more complicated with Jim's duties as a wartime Scotland
Yard telephonist, then there was Grace's machining in a factory
that made flying suits and David's duties in the constabulary.
Yet all faded into insignificance besides Duncan's own problem
with the Military College at Sandhurst. Especially on an
emergency 7 a.m. parade four days before the wedding. *'Now
pay attention!'* Regimental Sergeant Major Bristow had
boomed, as if it were possible to do anything else when six
feet and eighteen stone of bristlingly aggressive brawn was
bellowing in a voice that could be heard in the next county.
'All leave an' course work is cancelled from this minute an'
for the foreseeable fu-char! You'll be given breakfast and then
you are to report back here at 8.15 a.m. sharp in your full
service marching order for a temporary attachment to a special
force. That's army language for a right balls up. You are to
write no letters. You will make no phone calls. You are to speak
to no one. After inspection, you'll board motorised transport
at 8.45 a.m. without fail.' Tight-lipped, he then glowered at
the three ranks as if daring an interruption. There was, of
course, none. After eyeballing every man with the speed of a
Gatling gun, the RSM then tucked his cane beneath his arm
and threw back his head. 'PARADE!!' he roared. 'Wait for it!
Wait for it! DIS-MISS!'

Minutes later as the queue jostled through the cookhouse
door the rumours as to their destination spread thick and fast.
'The Germans have landed paratroops at Southend,' was the
first one.

'Oh God, I hope not,' exclaimed Duncan on hearing it.

'Wassamatter, mate?' said a cockney voice behind. 'Yer
got family there or something?'

Duncan shook his head. 'No, but I'm supposed to be getting

married to my girl for the umpteenth time and she's never going to believe it. Southend's only thirty miles from London and if she hears about this she'll be there before we are and she'll slaughter me!'

'If she gets there that quick perhaps she'll fight Jerry for us,' laughed the cockney hopefully.

'If she gets there that quick you can take it from me she bloody well will!'

By this time suggestions for their destination were coming in thick and fast. There are few more fertile grounds for rumour-mongers than an army that hasn't the faintest idea of its destination. It was only two hours later, as they assembled at St Pancras station, that the first clue emerged. The sight that greeted them was a battalion of Irish Guards, Welsh Fusiliers and an escort of military police. The Fusiliers claimed their destination had been leaked to them before leaving their camp. Ayr racecourse was the surprising location. '*Ayr racecourse?*' was the widespread and incredulous reply. 'Why the blazes would Hitler want to land at Ayr racecourse? Or any other course for that matter.' To that there appeared no satisfactory answer.

The train had barely stopped at Ayr station before the familiar tones of the regimental sergeant major could be heard reverberating throughout its length. 'ALL OUTSIDE IN THREES . . . ON THE DOUBLE!' Under the command of RSM Bristow, the battalion climbed onto the line of lorries that waited by the concourse. Within minutes they were thundering their way east towards the racetrack. As the vehicles drew into the track site, Duncan groaned as he saw the array of tents and huts. He had served in India with the army and, as far as he was concerned, canvas tents should not be used any further north than Bengal. In midsummer in the Indian foothills they were tolerable, in winter on a flat Scottish racetrack they were loathsome.

After a meal the men had been instructed to assemble for a briefing. The buzz of expectancy that awaited the arrival of the commanding officer told its own story. Eventually, a large bluff colonel appeared clutching a sheaf of notes. Although his hair was only tinged with grey, his moustache and side-whiskers were almost white. 'I'm proud to address you,' he said in a surprisingly soft voice, 'as a part of the North West Expeditionary Force. Mark my words, this Force will be an army that Hitler will come to dread the day he heard of it.'

'North West Expeditionary Force?' side-mouthed a voice next to Duncan. 'Who do you think we're invading, America?'

'First thing tomorrow,' resumed the colonel, 'you will draw special equipment from the stores and we will head north to Greenock. There you will be told of our assignment. This whole operation is top secret and you will neither speak nor write to anyone. Do I make myself clear?'

'Clear as cow-shit,' whispered another anonymous voice. 'So who's at Greenock that we don't like – Rob Roy?'

'I suggest you men all get a good night's sleep because you all have a long day in front of you tomorrow. Oh yes,' added the colonel, 'I know some of you men may have had domestic commitments but I'm sure your families will understand. After all,' he smiled, 'there is a war on.'

'This war that he's on about,' said Duncan to his neighbour, 'am I the only bugger inconvenienced by it? Because I'm convinced this is now a personal thing between me and Hitler.'

Disenchanted as he was by the colonel's speech, Duncan knew from experience that the suggestion of an early night had considerable merit. He had prepared as much as he could for the morrow before deciding to go down to the NAAFI canteen for a last cup of tea before turning in. As he entered, raised voices told him he had run into no ordinary argument. Two chairs had been turned over, a table broken and two Irish Guardsmen were in the process of exchanging blows. Though both of the same height, they were not of the same build and it was generally presumed by those around that the heavier of the two would have the best of the battle. Surprisingly, this fact did not appear to be obvious to the slimmer of the pair. He evened the odds immediately by exploding his opponent's nose with a head-butt of such ferocity that it caused the heavier man to fall to the floor and the fight to end. The sinister gurgling that now came from the floored guardsman indicated that he had sustained an injury that no wet sponge was going to remedy. Duncan ran to the man and immediately turned him on his side. He was assisted in his action by a young, pale-faced Welsh Guardsman who had such an air of calm authority about him that Duncan instinctively left all treatment to him.

The young man called over the counter to the NAAFI manageress for the first aid box. 'It's up that flight of stairs in the office,' she cried, pointing to a staircase in the corner of the canteen. 'But I won't be able to reach it. It's on top of a cupboard.'

The young man then looked questioningly at Duncan who, without further ado, sprang to his feet and raced towards the closed door. The office was something of a mess with papers and files seemingly everywhere. He scanned the room quickly and soon saw the large brown box on top of a tall cupboard with the cross of St John emblazoned upon its side. The box, however, was not the only thing that registered. There, at the end of a long lead and half hidden by papers was a shiny black telephone. Even as he stretched up to the top of the cupboard, the sight of the telephone tantalised him. A few minutes alone in that office and he could at least leave a message for Julia. Okay, so they were all sworn to secrecy but at that moment he was in greater fear of Julia's wrath than of any regimental court martial.

Warding off temptation, he seized the box and ran back

to the canteen, where the young Welshman was busy wiping blood off the face of the prostrate soldier. 'He'll need hospital treatment immediately,' whispered the Welshman. 'I'd say he's sustained a smashed nose and cheekbone at the very least.'

The regimental police were soon on the scene and the perpetrator was led sheepishly away. Someone had obtained a stretcher from the sick bay and soon the only indication of the turmoil was a trail of blood that led out through the door. The general hubbub had subsided with latecomers being regaled by witnesses to the fight with every exaggerated, sickening detail. The queue at the tea-counter had lengthened considerably and the manageress and her deputy were certainly well occupied.

Lifting the box Duncan called over, 'I'll put this back for you, shall I?'

'If only you would, my bonny lad,' said the manageress, 'I'd be very obliged.'

Duncan took the staircase three at a time and it required only seconds to push the box to its place on top of the large cupboard. It then took even less time to dial 'TRU' on the telephone dial. 'Trunk number please,' sang out the operator. Her response had been so quick that he had not had time to look it up in his diary. 'Oh er—' he fumbled as he dropped the diary to the floor. Quickly glancing around him he flicked through the pages. 'Trunk number, please,' repeated the operator with a hint of impatience. 'Oh er . . . Streatham . . . seven-four-six-one and can you hurry please, operator, it's urgent.'

'I can only work as fast as the equipment will allow,' she replied haughtily. After numerous clicks and other muted sounds, there was a final distinctive ringing and the familiar voice of Queenie Forsythe answered. 'Streatham seven-four—'

'Queenie,' he cut in urgently, 'I only have seconds. Tell Julia that—'

'You can tell her yourself, she's here. Just a minute, I'll fetch her—'

'No!' he snapped. 'There's not time!' but she had already left the telephone. He could just hear her voice as she called up the staircase, 'Julia love! It's Duncan. He sounds miles away. Hello Duncan?' she continued. 'She won't be long, she's just coming down the stairs. Are you well?'

No, Duncan was not well. He was not well because though Julia may have been coming down the stairs in a Streatham house, someone was now coming up the stairs in an Ayrshire NAAFI. 'Listen,' he hissed, 'can't stop. At Ayr racetrack. I'll write. Bye.' He dropped the telephone onto its base and heard the click a split second before the office door swung open and Second Lieutenant Fyffe – the orderly officer – stepped smartly into the room.

'I'm sorry dear,' said Queenie. 'It was Duncan . . . but the line's gone dead.'

Julia snatched the telephone from Queenie's hand. 'Duncan! Hello Duncan! Duncan, speak to me!' she persisted. 'Speak to me, you bastard. Where are you?' But there was no Duncan there, just the all too familiar whir of the dialling tone. Julia placed her hands on her hips and stared at Queenie. 'Just what the hell's he playing at?' she demanded. 'D'you think he's feigning insanity to get out of the army?'

'No dear,' laughed Queenie. 'He's in Scotland and he's obviously rung to tell you as much and—'

'Don't make excuses for him, Queenie,' said the young woman furiously. 'He doesn't need it. He's the biggest bleeding liar I've ever met and I wouldn't believe anything he told me now no matter what it was.' She paused for a second. 'So okay, what was it?'

'Well, as far as I was able to understand, dear, I could have sworn he said he was at Ayr racecourse and he would write. I know I must have misheard it but that's certainly what it sounded like.'

'Ayr racecourse?' echoed Julia. 'But there is no racing at the moment and he's not a horse-racing man anyway.' She shook her head slowly in disbelief. 'It's not my imagination is it, Queenie?' she asked. 'He really *is* the most maddening person in the world, isn't he?'

Queenie placed a comforting arm around her young friend. 'Well, I must say that he does tend to be a little unpredictable, but then you've known him long enough to realise that part of him will never change. I mean, I'm sure you wouldn't like to spend the rest of your days with a quiet, boring old fuddy-duddy, now would you? If you really want him, I'm afraid it's just something you're going to have to live with, dear.'

'I appreciate what you say, I really do, but to the best of my knowledge, I am due to marry in another seventy-two hours and now I find my groom is in sodding Scotland and he's going to write to me *sometime*! You say that's unpredictability? I say it's insanity!'

'Look,' said Queenie as she searched desperately for comforting words. 'These things happen in wartime and he is a regular soldier, after all. Look at me for a minute.' She put her fingertips under Julia's chin and tilted back her head. 'Be honest, you wouldn't really want him any other way, now would you?'

Julia gave the deepest of sighs. 'Perhaps not. But d'you think I could possibly borrow that quiet, boring old fuddy-duddy? Nothing permanent, you understand, just for a year or so?'

'Corporal Forbes,' snapped Second Lieutenant Fyffe. 'Did you see anything of the fight in the NAAFI? I understand that one of the men is quite seriously hurt.'

Duncan instantly realised that the newcomer must have missed seeing the telephone being replaced by a whisker.

'Well, I certainly don't know what led up to it, you understand sir, and my original guess was that the one with the nose would well and truly stuff the other man. But it seemed this other man had a different idea. As much as it's possible to admire a head-butt – and I've seen a few – I'd say it was the neatest I've ever seen. One butt and five seconds and it was all over.'

'Are you saying this man should be applauded then, Corporal?' asked the orderly officer tersely.

'Not at all, sir,' replied Duncan. 'But what I will point out is that we are all front-line troops here and, if it ever comes to hand-to-hand fighting with the krauts, I wouldn't object too much if whatever-his-name-is was alongside me.'

'Hmm,' murmured the orderly officer thoughtfully. 'Good point, good point.' He then glanced around him as if he was seeing the office for the first time. 'Good God, what a state! It may only be a NAAFI office but it is a Guards unit, after all! Dreadful condition, dreadful! Lock up the damn place and tell the manageress to get her finger out. I'll inspect it tomorrow and there had better be an improvement.'

'I thought we were leaving early tomorrow, sir,' pointed out Duncan.

'Eh? Oh yes, so we are, so we are. Well, tell her I'll inspect it when we return.'

'Er,' murmured Duncan tentatively, 'return from *where*, sir?'

'From where?' retorted the orderly officer crustily. 'Why, from Norway, of course. We leave from Greenock tomorrow morning.'

'Er, this Norway, sir,' he persisted. 'It's going to be a bit cold at this time of the year, isn't it? I mean, I wouldn't have thought our ordinary issue clobber is going to be much use?'

'You're right about that, Corporal,' muttered Fyffe as he

began to open up. 'It'll be bloody perishing, if you really want to know. That's why Lord Nuffield is helping out.'

'Lord Nuffield?' repeated Duncan incredulously. 'He's coming?'

'Good God, no!' chuckled the second lieutenant. 'But he's providing much of our extra material. You know, string vests, pigskin boots, gloves, that type of thing.'

'But why?' Duncan almost exploded. 'Why is Nuffield providing this extra gear?'

'Because it's bloody cold, man! Why else do you think he's doing it?'

'I don't mean that, sir,' responded Duncan, his anger rising, 'I mean that if we're in the British Army, why is Lord Nuffield providing us with clothing? What has happened to the Whitehall Warriors?'

Realising he had already disclosed far more than he should, Fyffe then threw caution to the wind and really let rip. 'Look, you're a regular soldier, Forbes, so I can trust you. Both you know and I know that the Whitehall Warriors, as you call them, are fucking useless. Intelligence says that the Germans are almost certain to invade Norway tomorrow – yes Corporal, tomorrow! The war now looks like it's actually starting. We are therefore leaving Greenock in the morning for God knows where in Norway. We've no tanks, no artillery, next to no air support and, unless we can anchor at a quayside, no means of landing. Our clothing is unsuitable and our weapons are inferior. On the other hand, we have a very impressive name, we are the North West Expeditionary Force whom Hitler is going to regret he heard of. Does that make you feel good?'

Duncan gave a low whistle as he fell back into a chair. 'Well, I admit I wanted to get into the war but I must say a Norwegian winter in a string vest and pigskin boots wasn't actually on my short list.'

7

The troopship *Showbury* was more than two days out of Greenock. Though little more than an old coastal steamer, the title 'troopship' was pretentiously used if for no other reason than it was packed to its gunwales with soldiers. Like the rest of Britain that winter, Scotland had been bitterly cold but it was almost tropical compared to the rapidly closing north shore of Norway. Any location two hundred miles into the Arctic Circle would render string vests and pigskin boots inferior accoutrements at the best of times, but when goggles, ski-suits and furs could barely cope, they were worse than useless.

As the journey lengthened, Duncan found himself constantly remembering his pre-war return from army service in India. On that trip even the shortest stint on a breezy deck had been a supreme luxury. But similar exposure on the *Showbury*'s deck would probably have resulted in loss of an ear. As cold as it was, though, the great twin threat came not from the weather but from the skies above and sea below. With no aircraft support, the low cloud cover that had followed them since Greenock had been a blessing, although they wondered just how much longer it would last. The other fear was the sea itself. Just how long a man could survive in it could be measured in seconds. It would certainly be for less time than the speediest of rescues. This, of course, posed the additional question; that without air-cover, would any skipper be mad enough to attempt a rescue? Of the mass of dangers they were now approaching, it was the sea Duncan dreaded most of all. In every other hazard there was always a possibility of survival. In the sea there was none. Duncan by nature was a brave man, even foolhardy, yet for the first time in his life he knew real fear. It knotted his stomach, destroyed his appetite, loosened his bowels and obsessed his thoughts. Even Julia was forgotten once the ship had entered the sinister waters of the Norwegian sea. Of the two thousand men on board, most were professional front-line troops. Many had trained for years for such an occasion, yet it was possible that one bomb, one torpedo, or just one piece of rotten bad luck, would plunge them all to the icy depths without a shot fired back in anger.

Their two briefings had done little to inspire them, either. It was now a fact that the Germans had staged a carefully planned attack on Norway with just about every arm of their services. They had bombed, torpedoed, shelled, mined, para-chuted, and landed divisions at every major Norwegian port. On Duncan's first briefing they were told that in order to combat this well equipped army, several other brigades of string-vested men were also at sea in tubs similar to the *Showbury*. At the second briefing they were told that the Germans had already occupied most of the country so their new destination would be in the very north of the country at a port called Narvik. Finally, after what seemed like months but in effect was barely three days, Duncan saw the stone wall of a harbour gradually nearing. Though his relief was partially offset by the now clearing skies, he felt that once onto dry land he could take on the entire German army with a catapult.

Queenie leaned forward from her armchair and rolled another log onto the blazing fire. The embers from the previous log threw up a burst of sparks in protest before settling down to embrace the new arrival with a flurry of small blue flames. Spreading out her palms she then rubbed them vigorously together. Sitting opposite her in the other armchair, relishing a weekend off from her nursing duties, Julia Giles stared motionless at the flames.

'It doesn't get any warmer,' shivered Queenie. 'I think this winter's lasting forever.' It was not an observation that required a great response and as such it received none from the subdued Julia. The older woman looked at the girl for almost a full minute. She felt the urge to speak but did not really know what to say. 'Penny for them?' was her rather uninspired choice.

Julia finally jerked into life and, tearing her gaze from the flames, gave Queenie the most rueful of smiles. 'I'm sorry. I was just wondering what Duncan is doing right now. He won't be as comfortable as us, that's for sure.'

'Well, at least you know where he is, dear,' said Queenie. 'That's one blessing. Have you had a letter yet?'

The girl gave a brief, ironic laugh. 'Letter? From Duncan? You're joking, aren't you? I doubt if he's written to me three times in ten years! If he can't write from Sandhurst he's hardly likely to take up the pen in Narvik. Especially with the battle that's going on there at the moment. The newspapers say there is particularly heavy fighting.' She shook her head and gave a worried sigh. 'Every day I look at it on the map and wonder what lunatic sent them there in the first place. I do honestly try not to be negative but for the life of me I can't see how any of them are going to get out alive. I just pray that he will be taken prisoner.'

'Oh, he'll be all right,' Queenie assured her optimistically. 'Your Duncan is a natural survivor. He'll pop up like a cork, you'll see. Anyway, you don't know if he's actually in Narvik, do you? If you haven't heard from him, he could be anywhere.'

'Oh, he's at Narvik, right enough, at least he was until a week ago. I had a phone call at the hospital from a Lieutenant Fyffe this morning. He was injured in the fighting there and is now in a military hospital somewhere near Aberdeen. He said

Duncan told him to tell me that he was safe and well and was now at some place called Harstad. I've also found that on the map. It certainly looks a very cold place.'

Harstad was indeed a cold place but that was not the only reason that Duncan was furious. After just eight weeks the poorly planned action by the North West Expeditionary Force was now in danger of collapsing into chaos. True, it had not had the best of luck, especially when the Polish destroyer that was being used for a meeting of most of the allied senior ranks was struck by a bomb. A bomb which, by a hundred to one chance, went straight down the chimney stack and blew the ship and almost everyone in it to pieces. Even that disaster did not excuse the landing of the allied transport at Harstad. Though little more than thirty miles from Narvik, Harstad was on an island and to all intents and purposes, as Duncan claimed, 'Might as well be back in bloody Greenock.' So, in addition to an absence of air-cover, there was virtually no motorised transport. Many of the reinforcing troops that began to arrive from Britain were poorly trained and arrived just in time to be taken prisoner as the Germans finally overran the country. If there was now one sure thing, it was that the Expeditionary Force had all but disintegrated and was going to have to retreat swiftly if it was not going to be completely destroyed. At this stage a regiment's discipline is always severely strained because the basic instinct of every man is to make a rush for anything leaving. The prime task of every NCO, therefore, is to make sure that that does not happen. Although in this case the NCOs' task was made easier by the thought that even securing a boat meant a thousand-mile trip across a freezing, hostile sea and being attacked at every opportunity by people who were determined to put you at the bottom of it.

With so many officers killed, NCOs like Duncan assumed

various local commands. With a responsibility now for some sixty men, he began to seek the safest means of their evacuation. Having formed a defensive post half a mile from the port, Duncan began to order small groups to make their way to the quayside to try for any boat leaving. Mostly these were local fishing craft that would hopefully transfer them to larger British ships off-shore. The plan was successful, until by dark, he was left with just six men at a well-concealed strong point at a bend in the road. The problem then facing him was that if all six were to simultaneously leave, who would provide covering fire for their withdrawal? If the Germans realised that Duncan's patrol was retreating, they would massacre them before they were anywhere near the harbour wall. To offset this risk he quickly arranged for the six men to rig up an elaborate system of water buckets, some empty, some full. Then, copying an evacuation plan he had read about from Gallipoli in the First World War, he ran a length of string from the empty buckets to several rifle triggers. Punching a hole in the full buckets, he made funnels to ensure the water ran out into the empty ones. As these empty buckets filled, the weight increased, the string tightened and the triggers would be pulled and the guns fired. The fact that they never actually hit anything was of no consequence. As far as the Germans were concerned, guns were firing and bullets flying, so someone was pulling the trigger.

There was, of course, a limit to how long this bluff could work, particularly as he could hear the ominous sound of tanks, but with the enemy in such close proximity, even seconds were valuable. As one by one the six men vanished into the darkness, Duncan gave a farewell burst from a Bren gun before he too raced after his colleagues.

Twenty minutes later they were on a small fishing boat, crewed by two Norwegians, and fading into the gloom of a blessed mist when enemy fire opened up around them. At first they threw themselves to the bottom of the boat before realising they were not the targets. They could not actually see the Germans and it was now clear the Germans could not see them. It seemed they too were banging off their rounds hopefully. To be on the safe side, however, the fishermen cut their engine and allowed the boat to drift silently on the out-going tide.

'Do we know where we're goin', Corp?' asked Lance Bombardier Albie Shinn hopefully.

'Nope,' replied Duncan calmly, 'I just thought it might be a bit quieter sitting out here in a boat than squatting in that dug-out with all them bloody tanks approaching.'

'No bleedin' warmer, though, is it?' muttered the ungrateful bombardier.

The older of the Norwegians then tapped the bombardier's arm and put his finger to his lips to indicate silence. As the soldier raised a hand in acknowledgement, German voices could be clearly heard carrying across the still waters of the harbour.

The big problem then facing them in that crowded, small boat was that the channel to the open sea was over a hundred miles long and, if the mist should lift, they would be sitting targets for anyone on shore. Duncan would not have admitted it but he thought the best they could hope for was to reach some German-free part of the mainland and strike out across the mountains to Sweden. The one thing that amazed him most of all was the needless risks being taken by the two crew members. Apart from the obvious danger of losing their boat, they would be shot immediately on capture. In addition, there was no way this small craft with nine people on board could possibly make its way to Scotland. All they could do was to hope they would be picked up by one of the British ships covering the evacuation.

The two Norwegians suddenly exchanged a few quick words

and the older man indicated to Duncan he was not happy with the direction they were drifting and it was time to take a few extra risks. Indicating they should all lie flat, he started the engine and within seconds a churning white foam rose from the rear of the boat in perfect contrast to the gloom of their surroundings.

All too soon the short night evolved into a grey mist, then into a light haze. Even worse, visibility was increasing swiftly before their eyes; it must have been a hundred yards by now. It was the roar of engines overhead that finally caused Duncan to make his decision. If it was in the sky, then whatever it was, it was bad news. If the Royal Air Force had not been seen at any time of the campaign, then they were hardly likely to be up there now, a thousand miles from their nearest base. Their choice would now simply have to be overland to Sweden; anything else was too great a risk. He was wondering how best to break the news, particularly to his two Norwegian allies, when one of them cut the engine and swiftly held up a hand for silence. As the noise faded, the sound of engines many times greater than theirs suddenly filled the dawn air.

The older Norwegian stretched out his arms as if describing a huge fish. 'Boat!' he cried.

'The question is,' whispered the bombardier, '*whose* bloody boat . . . ours or theirs?'

'I tell you this,' muttered Duncan. 'Whoever's boat it is, it's too sodding close for comf—' Further words were rendered unnecessary as a grey hull suddenly leaped from the mist on their starboard side like a lion through a paper hoop. In comparison to their modest craft, it was like the *Titanic* but in reality it was a medium-sized destroyer. The immediate problem was the name featured clearly on its side – *Stord*.

'Blast! It's German!' exclaimed Duncan, instinctively raising his rifle. 'Of all the rotten luck!' He glanced quickly to the Norwegian and gestured port side. 'Quick, that way. We still may be able to lose them,' he snapped unconvincingly.

To his surprise both Norwegians were smiling broadly. But why? It was never a British ship, so, if it wasn't British, it had to be German. So why the smiles?

'It's a Norwegian!' yelled the lance bombardier. 'It's bloody Norwegian!'

The two crew members called and waved frantically to several sailors on the deck of the destroyer and, before it vanished once more into the mist, their enthusiastic response indicated their small boat had been seen.

'So what do we do now?' Duncan asked the older Norwegian. Although the man spoke no English, he well understood the question. He made no reply but pointed his finger straight down to the deck and pumped it up and down several times.

'We wait . . . *here*?' asked Duncan slowly.

The Norwegian nodded delightedly. In the distance, the sound of engines could be heard changing tone as the destroyer altered course and made to return. It was almost fifteen minutes before the throbbing of a small diesel engine could be heard closing out of the mist. Once more Duncan raised his rifle but the older Norwegian firmly pushed down his barrel and cupped his hands to his mouth and gave a brief call. Within seconds of the answer, a liberty boat with a three-man crew emerged some seventy yards distant and, changing course, headed straight towards them.

As the boat pulled alongside, it was obvious from the expressions of the three faces on board that there was little time to spare. 'Quick now,' said one in almost perfect English. 'The Germans are sweeping this channel regularly. They'll be here in a few minutes.'

The troops climbed aboard first, then the younger Norwegian. They all then waited whilst the older man hacked at the hull of his little boat with an axe he removed from beneath a seat. It took a surprising number of blows before water began to seep into it but it quickly became a torrent and he had hardly made the safety of the liberty boat before his small craft began to slowly sink. Soon there were only a few ripples to denote its grave. The older man was still staring at the fading ripples as the mist closed around them.

The English-speaking gunnery officer who had rescued them told them that a dozen of Duncan's colleagues were below decks having been picked up drifting helplessly in a boat they had confiscated. A boat, it transpired, that none of them had the remotest idea how to crew. Of the remaining forty-two men there was not a sign.

'Where are you bound for?' asked Duncan.

'Scotland,' came the welcome reply. 'We've done all we can do here and the mist will be lifting very soon. Once that happens it will not be an enjoyable trip.' The man shrugged. 'But don't worry, we will survive it. We have to, you see. We will return to throw this scum out of our country.'

He could not have been more accurate in his forecasts. Within minutes the sun began to break through and a cry from the deck drew their attention to several bodies floating on the surface. Duncan borrowed some binoculars and was dismayed to see that most of them were men from his unit. They had obviously stolen a boat and, without local knowledge, had been doomed from the start. Judging by what little of their bodies could be seen, it was not the sea that had done for them, though, but a machine gun.

A rating ran along the deck of the destroyer and spoke swiftly to the gunnery officer. 'It's a message from the captain,' said the officer. 'He says he's sorry we cannot pick up your comrades, it's much too dangerous and we would be placing lives at risk to salvage the dead. And in any case, if any of them *were* alive, once they fell into the water . . .' he shrugged and left the sentence unfinished.

The voyage to Aberdeen was all they had feared and every few miles they were attacked by Stuka dive-bombers. Everywhere there seemed to be traces of wreckage ranging from splintered rafts to ominously empty life-boats. Finally, as they passed the Girdle Ness and entered the mouth of the Dee, Duncan could barely believe they had made it safely. Had it really only been eight weeks since they had left Greenock? God, it had passed like a century.

Later, as he took his first step ashore, his feeling of gratitude and relief gave way to blinding anger at the entire operation. A so-called 'Expeditionary Force', idiotically equipped, appallingly escorted and naively planned, had been mauled like a three-legged deer in a tiger's cage. It must never be allowed to happen again. As he sat down for a meal later in the mess-room, the nine o'clock news on the radio made clear the real extent of the disaster. Whilst he and his mates had been busy losing Norway, it appeared that the rest of the army had lost Belgium, Holland and France.

Lowering his knife and fork he looked around in despair. 'I can't believe it,' he exclaimed. 'I've been away less than two months and it looks like we've lost the war. What's happened, for God's sake?'

'O' course, bein' in Norway ye would nae know, would ye?' said a heavily-bandaged, one-armed Gordon Highlander sitting opposite. 'They just steamrollered us in little mair than a couple o' weeks. They had tanks the like o' which we'd nae seen before and they dive-bombed us tae bits. Every bit o' equipment they had were better than ours and what little we did have we left behind at Dunkirk.'

'Dunkirk?' echoed Duncan. 'But that's on the coast! So we've really left France?'

'Left it?' the Highlander gave an acid laugh. 'We were thrown oot! Two armies were lifted off the beaches wi' barely a rifle or a pair o' boots between them.'

'How many got away?'

'In my battalion hardly any,' replied the Highlander bitterly, 'but yon radio says over three hundred thousand British and French were taken off by boat. But ye can nae believe a damn thing ye hear, it's all damned propaganda.'

Duncan momentarily buried his head in his hands. 'Well, Jock, I was impatient for it to start and now it looks like we've lost it before it's begun. The next thing we'll have is an invasion, but what're we going to fight with, rocks?'

'Aye, an' they'd be a damn sight better than some o' our guns,' muttered the Scot.

Next morning, Duncan was summoned with his fellow survivors to a parade in front of the local barracks. He soon discovered that of his original sixty men at the road block outside Harstad, just twenty-two had survived, although serious injuries amongst these survivors were surprisingly few. He had expected to hear a pep talk from the CO about new equipment and how, given time, it would help win the war. To his surprise the talk was short and frank.

'Jerry has given us a hell of a pasting,' said the CO with unusual honesty. 'And with little or no equipment, there is no way we will be able to meet them on even terms for a long time to come. However,' he paused and glanced swiftly up and down the small group, 'if we can't yet fight a big war, that's no reason not to fight a small one. Therefore it has been decided to form a special unit of men called Commandos whose aim will be to strike at enemy bases and installations throughout the coastline of Europe. You will need to be specially trained and equipped. It will be tough, risky and dangerous; for the first time in this war we will be making offensive moves instead of waiting to see what the enemy does first. You men have the dubious honour of being some of the few survivors of the Norwegian fiasco that may be suitable. All volunteers take one pace forward.'

* * *

For Duncan this felt like an incredible release. At long last, and after his aborted course, he felt he was on his way to do a job that he thought the army was for – fighting an enemy. He was so elated even Julia slipped from his mind.

Two months earlier, when he had left London for Greenock, the journey had been relatively easy. They had just climbed aboard the train and it had wound its way north. The return journey, to Aldershot, was a nightmare. Every few miles his train seemed to be shunted into a siding, detoured or rerouted. Finally, as it tortuously arrived at King's Cross station after almost a day and a half, he could never recollect being so weary in his life. It seemed as if every exertion he had made in the last two months had finally caught up with him. Whilst crossing London to catch his connection from Waterloo to Aldershot, he took the opportunity to ring Julia's hospital. Although he could not speak to her he left a message but omitted to say he was at Aldershot. Of necessity his message was brief but hopefully she now knew he was alive. She in turn was to spend most of her week in a futile effort to trace him.

If Duncan thought as a result of the interview he'd had in Aberdeen he was on his way to the Commandos, he was wrong. It was nothing more than a step to the next stage. A stage which involved interviews, followed by physical and aptitude tests and then more interviews. By the end of the first week he felt he had been interviewed by half of the staff officers of the British army and been screamed at by three-quarters of its physical training instructors. Each night he collapsed into his bunk and slept the sleep of the just, or perhaps that of the totally exhausted. Finally, by Friday, he discovered that together with Lance Bombardier Shinn, he had been accepted for the course and was to report to Portsmouth training depot on Monday. The other seven men from his unit had failed and would be returned to the Guards.

'I'm not sure I want ter do it now,' grumbled Shinn. 'I've never been so knackered in me life and I was only makin' inquiries!'

'Shinny boy,' said Duncan, ruffling the lance bombardier's thinning hair, 'I've not only been waiting for this but I tell you now, you and I are going to survive this bloody war. We didn't come through all that shit at Narvik for nothing.'

'Well all right,' agreed the bombardier reluctantly. 'But only as long as they send me somewhere warm. I've had me fill of icebergs and snow.'

'Well, we don't have to report to Portsmouth till Monday, Shinny, so I definitely intend to go somewhere warm this weekend,' said Duncan optimistically. 'Providing she's got a few hours' leave, my plan is to curl up with a good rounded nurse, in a comfortable bed, with a lapful of warm bum and two handfuls of bristol.'

'This nurse,' said the bombardier inquisitively, 'the one wiv the bum and the bristols, she know yer comin'?'

'Well, not yet she don't,' conceded Duncan. 'I thought I'd surprise her.'

'I don't like surprises meself,' said the bombardier mournfully. 'I ain't done ever since me missus came 'ome early and found me in bed with the landlady.'

'Bloody hell,' said Duncan. 'That sounds fraught. What'd she say?'

'Well, she weren't 'appy about it. But she was bloody livid the followin' week.'

'The following week?' echoed Duncan. 'But why?'

'The old cow put our rent up.'

'So are you going to go home this weekend and get your own back by hopefully surprising your wife?'

'Nah,' said Shinn, shaking his head. 'She still thinks I'm in Aberdeen. We get on better when we're four hundred miles apart.'

'So what're you going to do with yourself?' persisted Duncan. 'Because I don't think we'll be getting much leave for the next few months.'

Lance Bombardier Shinn gave a thoughtful sniff. 'I think I'll just pop round and see the landlady. All this talk of a warm bum has made me feel quite nostalgic.'

Before he went to bed that Friday evening, Duncan decided that perhaps surprises might after all be dangerous, so running down to the call box by the camp gates he joined the queue for the telephone. Half an hour later, as Queenie Forsythe sighed with relief at hearing from him, she told him that a birthday party had been arranged for her husband Jim for Sunday afternoon. Julia was nursing over the weekend but had promised to be present for three hours on Sunday. 'Only three hours,' he groaned to himself, 'and all of it at a birthday party. It's a criminal waste of a warm bum.'

8

During the next few weeks it became a cause of great regret for Duncan that his only excursion to London in months had been to Jim Forsythe's birthday party. Whilst he had nothing but admiration for Jim, the floods of real war had now finally surged in the shape of air raids on every airfield in the south of England, and were threatening to engulf every town and city as well. He had certainly enjoyed seeing Julia again and he could hardly believe how radiant she had looked that Sunday tea-time, but on returning to his unit he needed something more tangible to lock away in his memory than three hours of playing footsie under the table and family small talk. On those long aching days of rock climbing, under-water swimming, firing at and being fired upon, assault-courses, five-mile runs, ten-mile walks, blisters, aches, sprains and pains, a man needed a memory that he could repeatedly relive at moments of great stress and despair. A memory of happy talk with friends over tea and wartime cakes was indeed pleasant but that was all it was – pleasant. Whereas a memory of a loving Julia stretched out in a big warm bed would have been a hundred times more pleasurable and a thousand times more memorable. Standing on midnight guard on a lonely, windswept cliff, the memory of Julia's body could repel weariness far more easily than any recollection of a discussion on the merits of rationing.

To rub salt into his wounds, Albie Shinn had achieved everything on his rogue Sunday that Duncan had not. A matter which, on the slightest provocation, the smug Albert would, to Duncan's increasing fury, wistfully recall. 'My Gawd, but the ole landlady was magnificent, Corporal. Shame about your day though, especially seein' as it was you put the thought in me head,' was a statement he would make at least four times daily. Duncan did try to tell himself that the bombardier was greatly exaggerating the experience but the scratch marks on his back did tend to confirm his story.

In spite of his disappointment, Duncan had to admit that, as a result of the visit, his relationship with Julia was back on an even keel. This was mostly because he had the opportunity to regularly telephone her. She had bought herself a cycle and although she found the forty-minute ride from the hospital to her room in Queenie's house tiring and risky during blackout hours, she slept better and with fewer interruptions than in her tiny room at the nurses' home. She had given him a copy of her duty rota and, for the first time in their entire association, they had almost developed a routine. She knew it could not last, though, and by late August Duncan had finished his course, the air raids had reached the suburbs of London and she was ordered to return to the nurses' quarters nearer the hospital. Though these raids posed no immediate threat to the centre of the metropolis, with most of the attacks being aimed at distant places like Croydon, vapour trails from dog-fights would range high and wide across the city skies.

If there was one section of the population who seemed to rise above these tribulations, however, it was the children. The schools, which had reopened in the spring, had closed once more. The need to ensure that children did not now run wild threw an additional burden on the parents. In the main, Rosie, Freddie and Benjamin were happy to devote their days to an endless quest for German spies. So when Julia, returning a day early from a serious burns course, courageously suggested taking a dozen or so kids from Queen's Buildings on a picnic to Battersea Park, they leapt at the opportunity. Not that any of them had the faintest idea as to the location of Battersea. Indeed, for bewildering reasons only known to himself, Freddie Foskett thought it was in Ireland. Because no other child on the trip held differing views, it was generally accepted that Ireland was their destination. Julia did consider pointing out that this was not actually the case, but as her head was still in a whirl from her course, she decided if they thought it was Ireland, then for today at least, Ireland it was.

She had chosen Battersea Park because of the ease of travel and, to every child's delight, Saturday 7 September dawned into a really beautiful day. A No. 12 tram from outside the buildings would take them the five miles to the park. Few of the children possessed satchels and in the main, an assortment of newspaper-wrapped sandwiches were stuffed unhygienically into the recesses of litter-strewn pockets. After a few minutes of childish chatter at the tram stop, a great cheer arose from the group as the swaying monster rolled around the bend by the fire-station and groaned to a stop in the middle of the road. After warning them not to get too excited, Julia shepherded them safely aboard and fifteen chattering kids climbed the steps to share the top deck with a solitary sleeping drunk.

As soon as the last child had settled on his seat, so the wrapping came off Freddie Foskett's sandwiches. The rest of the group did not fail to notice this crass indulgence because it meant Freddie would now be on the cadge from the moment they reached the park. 'The pig! 'E ain't 'avin' mine' seemed to be the general verdict. Of course this was easier said than done because Freddie possessed a niggling persistence when food was involved. Past experience had also taught Benjamin and Rosie that on such outings with Freddie, it was not advisable to carry food of any sort about your person. It should either be left with a grown-up or carefully hidden. Half an hour later, the tram rattled to a halt in Battersea Park Road.

As the group raced through the park gates their excitement was intense. Apart from several anti-aircraft guns, there were trees, bushes, grass, row-boats, a lake and even a river. It may have been the very same Thames that each of them were familiar with a few miles downstream but from the viewpoint of the park it all looked so different. Just like Ireland, in fact. Before they could enjoy the view, Rosie and Benjamin had an immediate priority, namely where to hide their sandwiches. As she was wearing only a frilly summer dress, Julia's custody was soon rejected. She had only a handbag and Freddie would sniff that out in seconds. The most obvious landmark was the park lavatories but tucking sandwiches safely on top of the cistern somehow had no appeal. There just must be somewhere better. Whilst Benji was exploring the rear of the park-keeper's hut, Rosie noticed a particularly leafy bush, beneath which the soil was cool and damp. Glancing quickly about her, she saw that everyone else was suitably distracted and, as soon as Benji returned, they scooped out a hole in the soil. Lining it with grass, they carefully buried their sandwiches in their *Daily Mirror* wrapping.

'Tell yer what, let's 'ave one afore we leave?' suggested Rosie.

'Okay,' agreed Benji.

'Wot yer got in yours?' she asked, patently intent on a little swop.

'Raspberry jam,' replied Benji, also feeling the pangs of hunger.

'I'll swop yer one of mine,' she offered generously.

'What've you got?' he asked suspiciously.

'Black puddin',' came the devastating reply.

'Er – well,' faltered Benji, whose knowledge of the culinary delights of black pudding was nil but who did not fancy the sound of it at any price. 'I think black puddin'd make me sick.

114

Anycase I'm not really hungry now. We'll leave 'em till later, shall we?'

Feeling the door had not been totally closed, Rosie agreed and after a couple of hours exploring the park, they made their way back to the rest of their party. There they were met by the wheedling Freddie. 'You two 'ad your sandwiches yet?' he asked with as much indifference as he could muster.

'Nah, we're goin' fer another walk first ter see if we can find some more spies,' replied Rosie, swiftly changing the subject. The word 'walk' usually caused Freddie distress so, leaving them to their spy patrol, he decided to rejoin several of the party who were naively beginning to unravel their lunch. The rustling of so much paper, however, had begun to play havoc with Benjamin's digestive juices.

'I say, you two,' came Julia's tired voice. 'Why aren't you picnicking with the rest of us? I thought that was what we came for?'

Seeing that Freddie was preoccupied a few yards away, Rosie quickly confided her predicament to Julia. 'Well, you should have given them to me. I would have looked after them,' she laughed. 'Run along and fetch them back here to eat. I don't want you straying all over the place in case of an air raid. What have you got in them that's so precious, anyway?'

At the mere thought of Rosie's sandwich filling, Benji again faltered but when the girl shrewdly cut in with, 'I've got some really smashin' warm crusty bread, an' it smells a treat,' his hunger beat his resolve and even the thought of black pudding no longer daunted him. Pausing only long enough to ascertain the whereabouts of their friend Freddie, the pair raced off in the direction of the bush. Rosie was the first to expose her savoury delights to the fresh air. 'Mmm,' she kept repeating as she hungrily munched into the crusty bread. Benji, on the other hand, was experiencing some difficulty in removing his wrapper. There appeared to be a slight hole in the corner of his package and the sports page of the *Daily Mirror* seemed quite tangled. Eventually, removing the last of the wrapping, he raised the jam-stained bread to his eager mouth. The very first taste caused him to hurl it to the ground in terror. Someone was already enjoying the eagerly anticipated feast – a thousand ants had beaten him to the punch.

'Wassa matter wiv you?' exclaimed Rosie as she stared at the abandoned feast. 'Ugh. What're they – bugs?'

'No, they're ants,' shuddered Benji. 'My aunt's got some in her back yard. They're deadly poisonous and I'm sure I ate some. I reckon I'm lucky I ain't been killed. Can I have one of yours, Rose? It'll help take the taste away,' he added, blatantly playing for the sympathy vote.

Rosie shook her head firmly. 'Nah, you said they make yer sick,' she reminded him with more than a hint of triumph. 'An' yer wouldn't be able ter go back on a tram if yer was sick nah, would yer? Didn't Julia say that we mustn't get excited in case we were sick?'

'Yes I know but . . . well,' he faltered, 'I shouldn't think just *one* sandwich would make me sick.'

She again shook her head, this time with a dramatic intake of breath. 'Nah, I daren't,' she said with her most considerate expression. 'I mean, what would Julia say if I was ter make yer sick? Especially after wot she told us. It's more'n I dare do.'

For a fleeting moment – but no more – Benjamin seriously considered jumping at her and seizing at least one black pudding from the clutches of her filthy mitts. The big trouble with that idea was that Rosie could be a tigress when annoyed. She had almost killed Freddie once when he had pushed her into a paddling pool. 'Come on then,' he said sullenly, 'let's go back to Julia and tell her what's happened.'

On their return across the park Rosie cheerfully gulped down the final traces of six slices of burnt crusty bread and half a pound of black pudding. Benjamin then blurted out the loss of his sandwiches so dramatically to Julia that she thought that Rosie had also lost her picnic. This was an assumption that Rosie did nothing to dispel. After a quick rummage in her purse, Julia gave them each sixpence to run to the tea bar and replace at least some of their losses. Freddie Foskett suddenly had this recollection that his sandwiches had also been purloined by ants. Julia, however, countered this claim by pointing out that of all the known habitats of ants, she knew of none that included the top deck of a No. 12 tram.

Both Rosie and Benjamin made long deliberations at the tea bar before each deciding on two stale sticky buns and a biscuit. On their arrival back at the group, they were surprised to see a white-faced Julia bending anxiously over a prostrate Freddie. As usual he was yelling out his complaints to anyone he thought might listen. As the rest of the group unfolded the happenings to the newly arrived pair, they felt quite deprived. Two stale buns and a biscuit seemed a poor recompense for what they had actually missed.

As an after-lunch pastime and in an attempt to settle excited young stomachs before the tram-ride home, Julia had begun to teach them all how to make a daisy-chain. One boy had proclaimed that when he smelt a daisy it reminded him of cat's piss. Freddie had been surprised at this claim and after one sniff stated that in his opinion daisies had no smell, cat's piss or otherwise. The boy persisted. Freddie tried again to smell the aroma, again no luck. By this time others began to claim they too could clearly discern cat's piss. Freddie was nothing if he was not persistent so, expelling all the air from his ample frame, he screwed up his nose. Gathering momentum in a series of short sharp inhalations, he gave one great last despairing sniff. The tiny flower had quivered for a second, then promptly rocketed straight up his right nostril. Now whilst the kids had been singularly impressed with this trick, Julia, to say nothing of Freddie, was distinctly alarmed.

'Hold him still – I can just see it!' said the peering Julia to the rest of the group. This was not the wisest instruction she could have made to a collection of heads all vying with each other to see up Freddie's right nostril. 'Don't crowd him, let him breathe,' she shouted. 'I've some tweezers in my bag, get them for me someone, please!'

There was now a concerted rush from the tip of Freddie's nostrils to the handbag. Benjamin looked elatedly at Rosie, this was terrific! With luck he might even die! The more the squiggling, screaming Freddie protested the more intriguing the whole situation became. Rosie later claimed she would not have missed it for a whole bag of buns. Sadly however, with the assistance of the tweezers Julia retrieved the offending daisy and the patient recovered. A great sense of disappointment slowly settled on the group.

Minutes later, fun now over, a group of fifteen dirty, sunburnt kids made their way to the No. 12 tram stop. As a parting feature for a day well spent, they were provided with yet another sleeping drunk on the top deck of the tram.

Julia was just beginning to think what a success the day had been when the sound of distant air raid sirens overrode the rattle of their tram. She glanced anxiously at the conductor. ''S all right, Miss, don't worry,' he assured her cheerfully. 'We won't be stopped by a little thing like a siren. Anycase, ain't no Jerries yet been on our route. You'll be okay.'

'It's not me I'm worrying about,' she said, nodding towards the children. 'It's them. Their parents will be worried sick.'

'Well, if yer asks me, I don't think yer've much ter worry about with that lot. There ain't one of 'em takin' a blind bit of notice of the siren. Tell yer what though,' he added thoughtfully, 'just in case, why don't yer get 'em ter sing? Kids like a bit o' singin', y'know, perhaps a school song or somethin'?'

Any doubts she had about the suggestion were instantly

dispelled by an almighty *crump crump crump* as the tram vibrated from the trio of anti-aircraft guns that had just opened up in Battersea Park. One or two of the younger ones looked particularly alarmed.

'Tell you what, kids,' she called, holding up her hands for silence. 'Who knows a song? You know, one we can all join in . . . anyone?' She looked around despairingly. The solitary hand raised belonged to Rosie. 'I knew you wouldn't let me down, Rose,' she smiled. 'What is it?'

' "Little Boys a Penny", Miss,' replied the child.

Three more great *crumps* reverberated along the Nine Elms Lane. Julia stared anxiously up through the window at the sky. There were at least a dozen vapour trails ranging in a line from Victoria through the city towards the Tower of London. 'Oh, er – I don't think I know that one, dear. Stand up so everyone can see you and go ahead and perhaps we'll pick it up as you go along. Off you go, dear.'

Rosie climbed to her feet and, after a fair sized sniff, began:
'Dahn Horney Lane, there are some dirty women
An' if yer want ter sees 'em, yer 'as ter pay a shillin'
Soldiers half-a-crown; sailors half-a-guinea;
Big fat men two pound ten; little boys a penny.'

A burst of clapping broke out from the children. ' 'Gain!' demanded Freddie.

'I 'opes ter Gawd she didn't understand it,' muttered the conductor, shaking a disapproving head.

'Oh, I've a feeling she did,' replied Julia. 'That kid might look a scruff but she's as bright as a—' she cut her words short as a whistle that began as a distant noise suddenly roared louder.

'*Down, kids! All of you! Now!*' The tram rocked and braked to a halt as the explosion caused glass to cascade everywhere. There was a moment's silence before the first of the youngest began to cry. 'Shall I sing it agin, Miss?' asked Rosie helpfully.

'Yes, Rose, yes! Right, come on all you kids, join in with Rosie.' She did a quick count and then waved her hands and willed them to sing. 'Right . . . *Down Horney Lane, there are some dirty women* . . .' The words were only falteringly taken up at first but by the last line everyone, the conductor included, came in fiercely with, '*BIG FAT MEN TWO POUNDS TEN; LITTLE BOYS A PENNY!*'

'Again, Miss!' demanded several voices.

'Okay, sing it again,' she ordered. 'I'm leaving Rosie in charge whilst I get off the tram to see what's happened. Shan't be a moment.'

As she jumped from the tram she immediately realised how lucky they had been. There, seventy yards in front of them and slap in the middle of the tram lines at the foot of Lambeth Bridge, was a smoking crater. Glass and roofing tiles were scattered around like leaves in a forest. Every window and door on both sides of the road had vanished and people were sprawled and sitting haphazardly, either dazed, injured or dead. This included their tram driver who had been blown from the tram after having taken a sizable portion of the blast. One thing was sure, their tram was now going nowhere. Her first priority as a nurse should have been to the casualties that were strewn around, but the sound of the explosion would have easily carried to Queen's Buildings and the hovering cloud of dust and smoke would indicate its location. Even at that moment there would be some twenty parents beside themselves with worry. Other than a cursory glance to ensure she could not obviously save a life, she began the dash to get the children home. Mentally mapping out the route that would pass the least carnage, she ran back to the tram.

'Right, gang, listen carefully,' she snapped. 'We'll each hold hands because I don't want stragglers. The walls and houses are dangerous and everywhere is covered with glass. Do as

you are told and do it quickly. Understand?' She did not wait
for a reply but instantly began to count them from the tram.

'I don't see why I 'ave ter 'old Rosie's 'and,' grizzled
Freddie. 'She wouldn't give me a sandwich.'

Julia resisted the urge to cuff him but quietly said, 'Fred!
Just do as you are told for once,' and bundled him into the
road.

The children were surprisingly resilient. At one stage they
even had to step over what looked like a dead body but, because
they had a hand to hold, even the youngest was no longer
distressed. They hastened past the Imperial War Museum
where, for some unaccountable reason, Rosie suddenly asked
if they could all go for a paddle in the children's pool at its
rear.

'I ain't 'arf 'ot,' she complained. 'Just a little splash, please
Miss. We'd all like ter go.'

'No, we *all* wouldn't,' announced Freddie firmly. 'Last time
we went in there yer beat me up!'

'That's because yer pushed me in, yer fat sod!' yelled Rosie,
her blood rising at even the memory of it.

'*Rosie! Freddie!*' snapped Julia, as yet another explosion
followed by a pillar of smoke arose over towards London
Bridge. 'Will you please stop squabbling and of course you
can't paddle! Don't be so ridiculous.'

'It'll be safer in the water, Miss,' persisted the child. 'We
couldn't catch fire.'

Before Julia could reply the sound of a hooter drew her
attention. An army lorry had pulled in to the side of the road
and a familiar figure was waving frantically from its rear.
'What the hell are you doing with all those kids in a bloody
air raid?' called Duncan.

Her delight at seeing him instantly evaporated. 'Oh, don't
be so stupid, Duncan! There wasn't an air raid when we started
out. What're you doing here anyway?'

'Quick,' he commanded. 'Get them on board and we'll drop you all off. Come on kids, sharp now.'

The children could not get on the lorry quickly enough. What a day it had been! First the park, then a daisy up Freddie's nose, guns, bombs and now a ride in an army lorry! Wouldn't that be something to tell when they arrived home! As the last of them climbed aboard the Bedford three-tonner it roared away eastward.

'You still haven't told me what you're doing here,' said Julia as she tried to keep her balance and recover her breath.

'We're on our way to London Bridge,' he explained. 'Albie and me have been posted to Dover and we cadged this lift from a couple of ATS girls who're driving to Woolwich with the internal despatch. As we've got an hour before our train leaves Albie and me were going to drop in on Grace and scrounge a cup of tea, or whatever else is going.'

'Oh, so you had no intention of seeing me?'

'Oh, come on, Julia, how could I?' he protested. 'What would you have said if I'd arrived unannounced and told you I could only spare you an hour? That's even if I'd been lucky enough to find you in the first place! You'd have slaughtered me and you know it. Now be fair, how could I guess you'd be busy taking a dozen kids for a picnic in an air raid? Anyway, this is no way to greet the man in your life – give me a big smacking kiss!'

Seizing her around the waist he lifted her off her feet, much to the delight of the children. 'Put me d—' she began but it was only token resistance.

A plump but pretty young driver smiled knowingly at her colleague, then glanced quickly over her shoulder into the rear of the truck. 'When you've finally finished eating that woman, Sergeant,' she said, 'perhaps you'll tell us where we're supposed to be dropping you off?'

'Eh? Oh, er, yes,' replied Duncan, reassembling his

thoughts. 'Straight across the junction, left under the railway bridge and second on the right.'

'What's all this "Sergeant" business mean, then?' queried Julia, turning him around as three new gleaming white stripes instantly caught the eye. 'My oh my! What a bright lad you are! Sergeant now, are we? And what's this?' She pointed to his shoulder flash that showed the name COMMANDO. 'Is this the new you?'

'Uh huh,' he agreed.

'Well, I suppose anything must be an improvement on the old one,' she said casually, yet failing to hide the pride in her voice.

'This the place, Sarge?' called the plump lass.

'That's it and thanks a lot, sweetheart. C'mon kids, we're here. All off.'

'Any time, Sarge. Don't forget, Sally and me do this run every day,' she said pointedly. 'You can pick us up any time, always the same route from the barracks. Ta-ta.'

Duncan nodded a goodbye and winked a sly acknowledgement as Julia, eyes narrowed, glared up at him in the expectation of a leading reply. Instead he smiled almost to himself and began to lower the children down to her on the pavement. A group of anxious adults, who appeared to have been in the process of a meeting by the gates of the flats, broke ranks and ran towards them. To Julia's surprise, amongst the forerunners was Billie Bardell. 'What on earth are you doing here, Miss Bardell?' asked Julia.

'I'd come up to town for some shopping but got caught in the raid. As most of the transport had stopped I thought I'd pop in and see David and Grace but neither is in. I was just leaving when David raced back from work to ask if I could claim Benji. Now suddenly you lot've arrived. Are the kids all okay?'

'The kids are just fine,' Julia assured her. 'It's me that's a wreck!'

By this time the last of the children had vacated the lorry. 'George,' 'Olive,' 'Topsy,' 'Renee,' – name after name was anxiously called as the children were claimed by their parents and guardians.

Julia was soon making her apologies to each of them. 'Oh, I'm so terribly sorry,' she began, 'but the raid was all so sudden and unexpected.'

'Not to worry,' assured Polly Foskett, 'not now they're all back safe and sound, it's not your fault, darling.' She pointed skyward. 'It's those bastards up there.'

'*I* wasn't safe an' sound,' moaned Freddie. '*I* 'ad a daisy up me nose.'

'Oh I'm sure you did, dear,' smiled Polly, without the faintest idea what the boy was talking about. 'Did you thank Julia nicely for it?'

Within minutes all the children were claimed except Benjamin and Rosie. 'What's happening about these two?' asked Duncan. 'Don't anyone want them?'

'I was supposed to be responsible for them,' confessed Julia. 'Rosie's dad is on air raid duty, Benji's dad is busy coppering and his mum is on late shift at the factory, but Billie said she'll take them under her wing until their parents return. Meantime I think I should be getting back to the hospital. After this raid they must be needing me.'

'Oh, and how about *my* need for you?' asked Duncan.

She turned towards him with her hands on her hips. 'You, Sergeant, by your own admission, now have considerably less than an hour for anyone. The hospital's need is greater than yours. Not only that but they need me for more than an hour. So, while you still have the time, perhaps you should head for the train?'

He turned immediately to his companion. 'Bombardier

Shinn,' he said, 'do you think your landlady would oblige a poor, lonely soldier like me with an hour of female company before he goes off to fight the kraut? Or do you think she'd be an insensitive cow and tell me to bugger off and catch my train?'

'I 'ave absolutely no doubt at all what she'd say, Sergeant,' said the bombardier emphatically. 'She's an intelligent sort o' gel, so she'd say piss orf an' get yer train.'

'There you are, you see, Julia,' he said haughtily. 'See what you've done. You've caused a good woman who's never even met me to malign my character. Shame on you.'

'Good God,' exclaimed Billie Bardell. 'You're not still at each other's throats, are you? You've been like it since you were kids! I've never met anyone quite like you two. I've never seen a pair more suited but I've never seen a couple who deserve each other more. For heaven's sake, Duncan, marry the girl and give us all some peace.'

'As soon as me and old Shinny here have won the war, I'll not only marry her, I'll ensure you're the maid of honour,' said Duncan. 'Can't say fairer than that, can I?'

Whether Billie would have taken up the offer he never discovered because suddenly a ferocious barrage began and, as they looked up, the whole sky seemed to be full of aircraft, most of them German. 'Bloody hell!' cried Duncan. 'They mean business this time. Quick, take cover, everyone.'

'No, I must go,' said Julia. 'I've been away far too long as it is. Billie can take the kids to the shelter. Grace should be home in an hour or so and Jackie Blackwell will probably be back when the raid is over.' She was already running when she called over her shoulder, 'I love you Duncan . . . so write to me, you bastard. Goodbye!'

Duncan's gut instinct was to run after her, but he knew she was right. Her route was north for the hospital, his was east for the station. He glanced at Billie and, although she could hardly believe it, she could have sworn she saw the hint of a tear. 'One day, Billie,' he muttered, 'one day . . . me and that girl are going to find ourselves running in the same direction. Now won't that be something?'

9

Duncan stared out of the train window. He had long given up any idea of guessing where he was. The train that was due to leave London Bridge at three minutes past the hour had left two-and-a-half hours late and the tortuous route it had taken gave only a small idea of the confusion that the Southern Railway now found itself in. He guessed they could be somewhere near Dartford; if that was the case then they were twenty miles from the fires that were lighting up the early dusk. Even at that distance the light from those fires made a mockery of the blacked-out streets. He had never felt so helpless in his life. Somewhere back there in that inferno was the woman he loved and the people he cared for. Part of him wanted to jump from the train and race back to show support, to help them, to suffer with them, or simply be with them. Yet he knew he could not; he was a professional soldier and after years of griping, he had now to prove both himself and his loyalty. All he could do was to stare out of the window and swear that one day someone would pay dearly for this inferno.

Julia Giles meantime had not a moment to think about anything except the matter in hand, which in her case was the constant stream of casualties that were flooding into the emergency department. It was strange that even though she was surrounded by windows, glass partitions, high ceilings and all the other dangers that people had learned to avoid during raids, she felt no fear. Not that a children's hospital carried immunity of any sort. How could it when it was in the centre of a city and anything in that city was considered fair game? It would therefore be the luck of the draw where obliteration would strike next. It could be a factory, church, barracks, hospital, or hopefully the middle of the river. The location was irrelevant; just as long as there was death, destruction, maiming and fear, the raid would be deemed a success.

At this precise moment Billie Bardell would have given worlds even for a share of Julia's resolution. Instead she was sitting quietly in a corner of a Queen's Buildings shelter bored out of her mind. In fact sitting quietly in a corner was most of the problem. She had probably never sat quietly in a corner in her life. The shelter was crowded but most people had prepared themselves for it. A bag, box, sack, or other receptacle would be placed by their street door and contain food, precious belongings, reading matter and sleeping gear. As soon as they left for the shelter they would pick it up as instinctively as they would pick up a child. Some folk took so much junk with them it looked like they were preparing for a medieval siege. Not so Billie. She had been caught out miles from home without as much as a coat or a newspaper. The ironic aspect was that when she was at home, she did not shelter at all. She would simply go to bed with a book and a bottle of gin, muttering, 'Sod everyone.' Her only concession was to pull the bedclothes over her head if the raid appeared extra heavy. Oh, how she now wished she was there, instead of this dingy, stinking cellar.

Outside, the raid was happening in fits and starts. There would be the whistles and hisses of bombs and the loud reply of the guns. This would frequently be followed by a deceptive lull. But just when everyone thought it was over for the night there would be a sudden resurgence. It was after midnight when she thought if the raid was to go on much longer she would be in serious danger of losing her mind. She stared about her for the umpteenth time in a desperate attempt at interest. Most of the children were either asleep on laps, or dozing at their mothers' feet. Benji sat with his back to the wall, slumped sideways like a vagrant drunk, but with an unread comic lying limply across his legs. Meanwhile Rosie was playing with a sleeping boy's lead soldiers and had executed her fifth German spy of the night. Many women knitted, some read, others dozed. There were few men and most that were present stood just outside the door, exposed to the night air. This was not to give the women privacy but simply because they felt uncomfortable at being in the shelter when others were outside risking their lives. To stand outside that door placated their consciences and took away their feeling of impotence.

Queen's Buildings air raid shelters were something of a misnomer. The seventy-year-old six-storey tenements actually had no purpose-built shelters at all. What each block did have were two basement flats that had been condemned as unfit for human habitation years earlier. These flats each had a bricked-up twenty-four-inch window that faced out at pavement level and a criss-cross of wooden beams that had been inserted between floor and ceiling. If the building were to take a direct hit and collapse, no one knew if those few beams could take the weight of the six floors that would then be resting above them. If the beams could not do the job, then the tenants sheltering there would not have the slightest worry – they would all be dead.

It was a point that did not totally escape Billie's mind as she looked for something tangible to occupy her thoughts. 'Billie!' exclaimed a voice. 'What the hell are you doing here?'

She glanced up to see Grace Diamond, tall and elegant as ever with a bag slung carelessly over her shoulder, in a style that would have taken anyone else months to acquire. Billie had forgotten just how attractive the young woman had always been, yet tonight she looked tired. But then why the hell shouldn't she? If she had been working at that factory for the last twelve hours it was a wonder she wasn't out on her feet. Billie edged along on the seat. 'Here, come and sit down, love,' she said. 'You must be whacked out.'

'Oh, I'm all right,' replied Grace wearily. 'I thought David would be back by now.' She nodded at the slumped figure of her son. 'I think it all went wrong today, didn't it?'

'Yes,' agreed Billie. 'Julia feels terribly responsible. Apparently they had a lucky escape.'

'It's not her that's to blame, it's me, I'm responsible. I'm Benji's mother and I wasn't here. I *should* have been.' She shrugged. 'It's as simple as that.'

'You can hardly blame yourself when you're working a twelve-hour stint at the factory, now can you?' comforted Billie.

'That's the point, I'm not. I haven't been for some time.'

'But—' began Billie. 'I don't understand. If you're not at the factory, what've you been doing?'

'I just couldn't stand the work. The repetition sent me crazy. If I thought I had to do it until the end of the war – whenever that's likely to be – I'm sure I'd have a breakdown. So I joined the Auxiliary Fire Service. I'm now only working part-time at the factory whilst I'm training for the AFS. When I'm qualified, sometime next week, I'll be out of that factory like a shot.'

'What does David think about this?' asked Billie.

'That's my current big problem. He doesn't know.'

'*He doesn't know?*' exploded Billie. 'How in heaven's name can you possibly be a firefighter in the middle of a blitz and your husband not know?'

'Oh, I shall tell him when I'm qualified. It's just that he would do everything to dissuade me if he found me out now.'

'Well, I can understand that,' said Billie. 'There are few

130

husbands worth their salt who want to see their wives fighting such fires as we've seen today.'

'But that's exactly what I want to do!' persisted Grace. 'Look, we've all got to do something in this bloody war. I know that I could never give my best in a factory, no matter how vital the work, but I also know I could do much better out there at the sharp end.'

'But David will go mad when he finds out, surely?'

'Well, he certainly won't like it, I concede that. But he'll get over it.' She gave a weak smile. 'I'll just remind him there's a war on.'

'How about the boy? What with his father in the police force and his mother in the brigade, the poor little sod'll feel just like an orphan.'

'Polly and Ted Foskett have said they will look after him; they are only over the road and they usually care for Rosie when Jackie Blackwell's on duty. They have an Anderson shelter in their back yard and that'll just about accommodate two grown-ups and three kids. Besides, the youngsters all get on well together . . . I wouldn't do it otherwise,' she added as a rather desperate afterthought.

'Well, I don't like it,' said Billie, 'but I must say I admire your guts. I'd like to think I would have had the same courage if I had been in your situation. Tell you what, if ever you need me, just say the word. There's not a lot I can do now at my age, so if nothing else it'd make me feel useful.'

'Excellent,' laughed Grace. 'Everyone has a badge nowadays to state their role in the war. How about I make you one, you know, perhaps, "Useful Old Lady"?'

'You do and I'll kill you. Anyway, now you're here I can make tracks for home.'

'Don't be silly, you'll never get home at this time of night. There's no transport running out there. You couldn't get a taxi to Hampstead to save your life.'

'All right,' said Billie. 'Now I've handed Benji over to you, give me your key and I'll go upstairs on his bed. I can't stand this place a second longer.'

'No, it's not safe,' Grace protested. 'It's far too high. Besides—'

Billie cut her short. 'Look, if I'm ever going to help you out I'll need some practice, so I'm starting now.' She held out her hand. 'Key, please.'

Still Grace refused.

'Grace, if you don't give me that key, I swear I'm leaving here immediately and I'll walk to sodding Hampstead . . . I mean it!'

Grace nodded wearily and after a quick fumble in her handbag finally handed over the key. 'I'm too tired to argue,' she muttered.

'Good,' said Billie as she slipped into her shoes. 'But I'll tell you one thing – if you're coming down here in the future, fetch some bedding with you. It's the only way to see this place, with your eyes shut and the clothes over your head.'

There had been a lull from the bombing for some forty-five minutes and as Billie climbed the stairs to the fourth floor she wondered if the raid was finally over. As she reached the third floor, she could see out of the landing window, over the row of terraced houses opposite. The sight that greeted her took her breath away. There, in an arc, sweeping from Tower Bridge round towards Woolwich, was a wall of flame, frequently higher than the steeples. 'My God,' she murmured, 'the whole world's on fire!'

Minutes later, in the kitchen, she parted the curtain around Benji's bed and fell exhaustedly onto it, removing neither coat nor shoes. Before she lost consciousness, a barrage of guns started again and the sound of hundreds of bombers droning their way over the Thames to feed the flames with high explosives could be heard. As the first of the bombs crashed down, Billie Bardell pulled the clothes up over her head, closed her eyes and was asleep in seconds.

Billie may have slept but almost everyone else in the metropolis was woken either by bombs, clanging bells or roaring engines, as every conceivable vehicle that could be used to transport rescue services, raced to the heart of the apocalyptic horror that was once the docks of London.

Grace tried to make herself at ease on the bare wooden bench but with little success. She began to envy her son who, whilst looking completely uncomfortable, was obviously so soundly asleep that neither bell nor bomb woke him. 'Here, love,' said a female voice, 'take these.' Turning her head in the direction of the speaker she saw Rita Roberts sitting up in a sleeping bag and unfolding two blankets she'd been using as a pillow.

'Oh, I wouldn't think of it,' protested Grace.

'Then do so,' commanded the woman. 'I don't particularly need them and you look as if you could do with some sleep, and you're never going to get any sitting on that bloody bench. I know, I've had some.'

Grace smiled. 'You're certainly right there. Thank you, on second thoughts I will take them, if you don't mind. It's kind of you.'

'Only paying back a debt,' said Rita. 'Your husband did try to help me once when I was getting a terrible pasting. At the time he probably thought I was an ungrateful bitch, but it was the only way I could play it then. Perhaps you'll tell him when next you see him?'

'I'll certainly do that for you . . . and thanks again.'

'That's okay, us fire service girls must stick together.'

'Er—' began Grace, 'I don't understand?'

'I work on the switchboard at Brigade Headquarters at Lambeth Bridge. I've seen you in the canteen a few times lately. I take it you've joined the AFS?'

'Ah,' winced Grace, 'look . . . well . . . I'd rather you didn't say anything about that at the moment. You see—'

Rita Roberts suddenly leaned forward and with an exaggerated squint said, 'Sorry dear, I've got you completely mixed up with someone else. You're the lady from up at ninety-one, aren't you? Must be the light in here. Now I come to think about it, I've never seen you outside of this block.'

'Thank you,' murmured Grace. 'It's not nearly as dubious as it sounds but it seems like you understand anyway.'

'You know,' sighed Rita as she wriggled down into her sleeping bag, 'if you don't stop talking, you won't get a wink of sleep. Not a wink. Goodnight.'

'Goodnight.'

If there were two people who were certainly not going to get a wink of sleep that night it was Jackie Blackwell and David Diamond. Although they worked for different sections of the civil defence their paths had consistently crossed during the previous twelve hours. Earlier both had been on the flat roof of Queen's Buildings, battling with incendiary bombs. The roof of the old tenement was a perfect spot for incendiaries, sprawled as it was over three streets. On the face of it, if it had nothing to ignite, a bomb should burn itself out, as many a charred stain on road and pavement would show. But even on the best-kept roofs – and Queen's Buildings had by no means a best-kept roof – there would always be something that would burn. Boxes, pigeon-lofts, hopping-equipment, washing, rope lines and door frames. Although the building was of a sound enough structure, with three thousand residents and such narrow staircases, a serious fire could result in a slaughter.

A little after midnight a 'breadbasket' of incendiaries had burst a thousand feet above the tenement. The angle of their fall ensured they were scattered over a square mile of streets but a dozen or more found their way down to that vast, flat roof. These thermite incendiaries were little bigger than a large wine bottle and weighed just over two pounds, but in the wrong location they were lethal. If the fire-fighter was lucky, these bombs did not immediately ignite but lay for some seconds as if savouring the destruction they were about to cause. This meant there were a few priceless moments when they were at their most vulnerable. Anyone without fear could make a score of them safe in as many minutes. But to hesitate, even for a moment, could result in a drenching from its skin-melting contents. An inverted bucket of sand was usually the most effective manner of dealing with them but there was a limit to how many buckets of sand could be carried up and stored on a six-storey-high roof. The second preference would be a pail of water but for that the bomb would need to be picked up and submerged. Throwing it down into the street was the third and least viable option. After all, there was no point in removing its threat from a roof, if it was to land on – or even worse *in* – someone's outdoor lavatory.

When the incendiary raid faded, somewhere around three in the morning, the two smoke-blackened neighbours paused in their task and looked across at a similar scene to that studied by Billie Bardell an hour or so earlier. Being two floors higher they could see further and realised the fires ranged not just to Woolwich but at least as far as Barking Reach. 'Bloody hell, Jack!' panted David as he shielded his face from the eye-melting heat. 'It's like a volcano that's going to burn forever.'

As the two men wound their weary way down the staircase, it was on David's mind to look in at the shelter to inquire as to the welfare of his family, but a yell from a passing heavy rescue truck directed them both to a little street off the Marshalsea Road where an unexploded parachute mine was giving cause for concern.

'They want all the help they can get down there, mate,' called the voice. 'Your guv'nor said to send anyone we see, sorry.'

'You'd at least think the bastard would've given us a lift there, wouldn't yer?' complained Jack.

'Probably wasn't going that way,' muttered David wearily. 'But I tell you this, Jack, I'm not looking forward to this. When those bloody things go off they can take four streets with 'em.'

'Wiv luck it'll go orf afore we get there,' replied Jack with waning enthusiasm. 'Then all we'll need is a shovel.'

Although they had not been told the exact location in Marshalsea Road it was soon obvious as a cordon of rope could be clearly seen stretched from pavement to pavement. Station Sergeant Ted Andrews appeared to be in charge until the bomb disposal team arrived, a fact that gave David some hope. 'Davy boy,' he called, 'got a little job for you. Right now we should be putting a 600-yard exclusion zone around this little lot but I can't do that otherwise nothing will be moving over London Bridge in the morning, so I'll have to shorten it. While I'm doing that I want you to call on a Mr Reggie Stubbins and wake him up and give him a message. Think you can do that for me?'

'Don't sound the most difficult task, Sarge,' replied David. 'Where's he live?'

'Well, that's the problem y'see, Davy. He ain't at home at the moment, he's at work. So you'll need to go there but you'll need to be a bit delicate about it.'

'Delicate, Sarge?' queried the puzzled David. 'Why delicate? Where's he work?'

The sergeant put his arm around the constable's shoulder and pointed down the street to where a parachute was swinging gently to and fro from a warehouse wall crane. 'I'm afraid he's in there, Davy, Richardson's Bonded Warehouse, and from local inquiries afore you got here, he's probably pissed. Now take this axe and carve your way in if you have to, but whatever you do don't clout the bloody mine.'

David took the axe and glanced swiftly at the half dozen or so policemen who were milling around. 'What's so special about me that I'm selected for this job?'

'Nothing personal,' assured the old sergeant, 'just the fact that someone has to go and you arrived last.'

'I only arrived last, Sarge, because me and Jack Blackwell, the ARP warden, were putting out a dozen incendiaries on the roof of Queen's Buildings,' pointed out the constable tersely.

'Brave lad, brave lad,' repeated the sergeant, 'and so I'd like you to be brave for a few minutes longer and find Reggie Stubbins, okay?'

David stared at the swinging parachute. 'How long d'you reckon I've got?'

'You've got all the time in the world. Unless, of course, that mine swings against the wall. Then you've got about a tenth of a second. But if it's any consolation, so have we. Though it's not all bad news.'

'Why's that?'

'Well, if you set that mine off, we'll be in a terrible mess, but you won't.'

'Why not?'

'Because no one'll be able to find you – *now get going!*'

David's first instinct, like so many others, was to tip-toe up to the mine but it was not noise that would set it off but impact. His approach was nevertheless cautious in the extreme. The biggest problem with these parachute mines was their unpredictability. They were by origin sea mines and had been designed to blast battleships out of the ocean. They were black, cylinder-shaped objects almost three yards long and one yard in diameter, packed with explosives. Because their fall was broken by the parachute, they did not bury themselves in the ground but exploded on impact level causing a colossal blast-wave at the scene and for some quarter-mile around. As opposed to the fall of a bomb, their descent was almost silent.

Usually the first any householder knew of the bomb's arrival was when it blew him to bits or demolished his home or factory. In this particular case, the parachute had entangled itself in a small crane and the mine swung gently in the slight breeze, missing the wall by a hair's breadth on each swing. There was a small, green-painted door at the side of the main factory gates with a doorbell with the word DELIVERIES at its side. David pressed on the bell repeatedly but had no way of knowing if the thing was working. Other than the noise of the raid, the only other noise he could hear was the flapping of the parachute. He quickly examined the building for its weakest point, to gain entry.

Richardson's Bonded Warehouse contained a vast store of wines and spirits and the deterrents it set for a determined burglar would prove just as difficult for a courageous constable. Well, there was no point in being subtle. The best way was to whack a window with the axe and hope the noise roused the sleeping watchman. With guns and bombs exploding almost every few seconds, David did not rate his chances very highly. The wire-reinforced glass proved tougher than he had imagined. After the first few whacks he turned quickly to stare apprehensively at the swinging mine but after a dozen or so blows he no longer bothered with anything else but smashing the glass.

It was a full ten minutes and a blunted axe later that he managed to loosen enough of the pane to wriggle through the window without ribboning himself. He fell into a corridor and suddenly found himself blessing the fires for lighting the building enough for him to move around freely without danger. '*Reg!*' he yelled repeatedly. '*Reggie Stubbins!*' There was no response. Deciding to search systematically, he raced to the top of the four-storey building and, ignoring the stacks and rows of crates and cases, sought out every intriguing-looking recess and partitioned floor space. He was down to the first floor when he saw a small door that carried the notice THUNDERBOX. He threw open the door and had almost closed it again before the scene before him quite registered. The thunderbox was the warehouse lavatory and there, sitting on the pan, mouth wide open, reeking of booze, trousers at his ankles, cap on his head, and a cold clay pipe on his lap, was the sleeping – or dead – figure of Reggie Stubbins. David seized the man's right arm and shook it vigorously. '*Reg! Reg!* C'mon, wake up! Wake up, for Christ's sake!'

'Eh?' grunted the rotund middle-aged watchman. 'Wasamarrer? Wasamarrer? Who are yer? What's 'appened?'

'Quick,' snapped David, reaching to pull up the man's trousers. 'We've only got seconds before the place blows up. There's a mine swinging outside on your crane.'

'My crane?' asked the bewildered Reg. 'What crane? I ain't gorra crane, I've gorra bike.'

'Oh not *your* bloody crane, you fool,' corrected the exasperated policeman. 'I didn't mean *your* bloody crane. It's your firm's crane. If we don't get out of here soon we'll both be swinging on it.'

Reg then leaned back, opened his mouth wide, closed his eyes and gave quite the largest yawn David had ever seen. 'Can't go yet,' he said finally, as he blasted David with the stench of stale tobacco and even staler rum.

'Can't go? Can't go?' exploded David. 'Why ever not, you old fool?'

'Ain't finished,' announced the watchman, jerking himself back onto the lavatory pan.

David threw the axe to the floor and seized the man by the scruff and began dragging him through the doorway. 'Ain't finished?' he echoed. 'Ain't bloody finished? I don't care if you've shit yourself, we're going out now – this bloody second!'

'I've got yer number!' yelled Reg. 'I know me rights, you see if I don't!'

'Shut up, you drunken sod,' grunted David as he bounced Reg down the flight of stairs to the street door. 'Now give me the key!' he snapped.

'Won't,' said Reg defiantly.

David's first instinct was to threaten Reg with the axe until he realised he had left it on the floor of the lavatory. 'Look!' he said, pointing to the broken window where he had gained entry. 'See that window?'

'Oi! Who's broke that?' cried the watchman indignantly. 'Heads'll roll for that, you mark me words.'

'The chances are, mate,' growled David, 'the first head to roll will be yours because unless you come up with the key in three seconds, it won't just be your *words* that are marked . . . it'll be your bloody *throat*, as I put you through that window. Now give me the bloody key!'

The alcoholic haze through which Reggie Stubbins had been viewing the world suddenly began to fade. 'What's that?' he said, pointing up at the broken window. 'There, that white thing swingin' about outside? What is it?'

'Well, it's not a ghost, if that's what you're thinking,' David almost screamed. 'It's a bloody great mine, you prat. I've told you once, it's swinging on your crane. Now will you find the key?'

'A mine!' echoed Reggie. 'Oh my good Gawd! I could 'ave been killed as I slept. Oh, it's wicked it is, attacking innocent civilians like this. Especially as I done me bit in the last war.'

'Never mind about that,' snapped David as he began to search the man's pockets. 'Just get the key.'

Reg thrust his hand down the top of his trousers and pulled out a long leather boot lace. One end was tied to his braces and the other to a large iron key. David dragged him to the door and a few seconds later they had practically fallen out into the street. As David made to move quickly away towards the distant police cordon, so Reg stood staring up at the flapping parachute.

'C'mon, man,' called David. 'Don't stand looking at it, run! It could hit that wall any moment and send us both to kingdom come. Run! Run!'

At last his words seemed to finally sink into Reg's psyche. With a great roar the watchman clutched at his waist-band and, swivelling his head every few seconds to look up at the parachute, he limped rapidly off in the same direction as David, with his trousers falling further down his legs at each step.

'My God,' exclaimed Station Sergeant Andrews to no one in particular, 'what the hell have we got here?'

'One complaining watchman, Sarge,' panted David, 'but he stinks a bit.'

'By the look of him and where he's been, I'd say he stinks a lot,' said the sergeant. 'How'd you get him out?'

David briefly recounted the chain of events.

The old sergeant nodded. 'Okay, Davy boy, well done. We'll leave it to the Royal Engineers to take it further. Now go home and unless you hear any different stay there for at least twelve hours. Off you go.'

David did not require a second telling. A warm feeling grew inside him. He had known Sergeant Andrews for almost ten years and that was the first time he had ever heard the man give a compliment. 'Well done' eh? Bloody hell, but he would sleep well now.

The distance from the swinging mine to number 91 Queen's Buildings was well within the six-hundred-yard radius of normal evacuation but evacuation was a word that never entered David's head. All he could think about was sleep. He was so tired he had begun to hallucinate. Oh lovely, warm, blessed sleep. Just to flop down on a feather bed and let the clouds of sleep flood over and wake up in unmeasurable time with a beard, a grown-up son and a peaceful world. He could not remember climbing

the eight flights of stairs. He could not remember turning the
key, checking the blackout, turning on the light, unbuttoning
his filthy tunic, though he would always remember seeing the
fully-dressed woman on Benji's bed. At first he thought he
had entered the wrong flat, but if anything she looked as tired
as he did. It was a condition he knew only too well. He was
beginning to think the whole bloody world was sleep starved.
He squinted, peered, rubbed his eyes and finally recognised
the slumbering figure. What the hell was she doing here and
where was his son? Of course, in the shelter, that was it, he
had to be there, he'd be furious if he wasn't. To be sure he
glanced quickly in the other room but the large double bed lay
made up and empty.

As he stepped forward to wake Billie Bardell, the awful
truth dawned on him. If his wife and child were in the shelter,
he would need to know they were safe before he could collapse
into his own bed. But to ascertain their safety he would need
to go down and then up that blasted staircase once more! He
groaned in self-pity and, turning round, did not even bother to
close the door as he began his descent. The dingy staircase
was still lit by the distant fires as, muttering to himself, he
finally reached the basement shelter. Too tired to speak, he
passed through the four men standing at the door without a
word. On entering the shelter, his first reaction was one of
envy, everyone was asleep! True, few of them looked
comfortable but not one was awake! Grace was one of the first
he saw. She lay most awkwardly on a bench and was screwed
up like a dormouse. 'Grace! Grace!' he whispered.

'Eh?' she muttered, before opening her eyes. 'Oh, my back's
killing me. What is it? . . . Oh David . . . it's you.'

'Of course it's me,' he snapped irritably. 'Who were you
expecting, the Grim Reaper? Where's Benji and why is Billie
Bardell in his bed? I would have thought he's a bit young,
even for her.'

She sat up, rubbing her back with both her hands. 'Oh Davy, it's been pandemonium. Pick up Benji and let's all go to a proper bed, please?'

'But the raid is still on and there's an unexploded mine in Marshalsea Road.'

'Quite frankly, darling, I don't care if it's hanging in our kitchen. I'd sooner die than spend another minute in this place. I've never been so uncomfortable in my life – and it stinks.' She glanced quickly around the room. 'There's a few in here who have an allergy to soap, I can tell you.'

'Right, I'll pick up the boy. Where is he?'

'There against the wall. You carry him and I'll carry Rosie, they are both out to the world.'

David nodded. 'Okay,' he agreed, 'but if that bloody mine goes off I hope it doesn't wait until we've reached the fourth floor before it kills us. That'd be just too unkind.'

Ten minutes later they staggered into their flat and dumped both sleeping children alongside Billie Bardell. It coincided with a particularly close blast. The buildings rattled but the windows stayed in. 'That wasn't the mine . . . not big enough,' panted David.

'You know,' whispered Grace as she fell back into a kitchen chair, 'I could never have carried . . . that kid up those stairs . . . if I'd been fully awake.'

'Why not?'

'I'd have . . . known what I was doing . . . and collapsed.'

He began to throw off his clothes and probably for the first time in his life did not bother to hang them up. Grace did likewise. As his head hit the pillow he was almost asleep – but not quite.

'David,' whispered Grace, cuddling up to him, 'you still awake?'

'Eh?' he groaned. 'Just about. What's the matter?'

'I've got something important . . . must tell.'

'Oh Gawd, gel . . . can't it wait till tomorrow?'

'Davy, it's already tomorrow . . . and no, it can't wait.'

'What is it then?' he muttered through a mouthful of pillow.

'I'm goin' . . . be a fireman.'

He slipped his arm around her waist. 'Yes sweetie . . . course you are,' he soothed. 'Goodnight.'

10

The ferocity of the daylight air raids began to fade in the face of the Royal Air Force's increasing strength. This was just as well because no matter how heavy these daylight raids were, people seemed determined to carry on their normal life. Somehow Germans in the daylight seemed nowhere near as sinister as Germans after dark. Of course there were still small daily attacks but in the main these were little more than nuisance raids. Nevertheless, people still needed to shelter from them. This meant that a few enemy aircraft could cause the warning sirens to operate and vital work to stop for hours on end. By the end of September a new system was tried in which people did not go to their shelters as soon as the siren sounded but instead were alerted by roof spotters who would warn them with whistles or klaxons whenever an attack was imminent.

It was an effective system but it meant that when the spotter did give a warning, time was very short indeed. If the daylight raids had faded, the night raids had increased greatly in intensity. No spotters were needed then as, night after night, waves of bombers would attack from dusk until dawn. Explosion would follow explosion and the only thing that seemed to matter was the location. How far away is it? Is it our house; our flat; our factory; is it damaged? Can we still live there? Can we still work there? Who are the injured; who are the dead? People can get used to anything, and people did. Each night those who were not at work, or in the defence services, would go to their shelter, or the safest place in their house. There, mole-like, they would hide and not emerge again until daybreak.

It had taken David some time to accept, as he patrolled the streets or searched for survivors at one incident, that his wife might be wrestling with a fire-hose at the next. The people who took it most in their stride were undoubtedly the children. This was providing there were other children with them. Indeed another child could be more reassuring than a parent. The shelter might vibrate, cracks would appear and dust fall in clouds, yet, as long as the light stayed on, children would rise above it all. Because of this tendency, David, Grace and Jack decided that, whenever all three were collectively on duty, Benjamin and Rosie should stay with Freddie's grandparents in their back-yard Anderson shelter. These shelters were little miracles. They were made of steel and no bigger than a small cellar. Half-buried in the ground and away from the house, they were covered with a thick layer of soil. Other than a direct hit they could survive almost anything. Anything, that is, except perhaps a torrential downpour, when they could flood within minutes. But with care, many made them extraordinarily cosy.

In truth, the children quite looked forward to the nightly raids. Bedtime in the shelter was much later than normal bedtime. Then there was also grown-up conversation to be heard through the pretence of sleep. Of course, it was not always understood, particularly when a character-assassination of a neighbour was being performed. 'And that eldest of hers is no better than she ought to be either,' or 'The tally man was round there three times last week! You can draw your own conclusions from that.' All such similar grown-up pronounce-ments would be followed with a folding of the arms and a wise nod.

It was well into October when Rosie developed a cough

that she seemed unable to shake off. Within a day or so both Benjamin and Freddie had also contracted it. It did not seem too disabling and all three children seemed cheerful enough but the nightly chorus of children coughing, interspersed with high explosives, did little for the sleep of Ted and Polly Foskett. In normal times the children would have been taken to the Evalina Hospital where someone in a white coat would have prescribed brown medicine. The taste of this medicine was a guaranteed cure for any disease known to medical science and within days all would be well again. But these were not normal times and with the Evalina bursting at the seams with injured children, it did not seem right to burden the hospital with coughing kids.

When Julia called in one Sunday afternoon she recognised the cough immediately. 'It's gone through our hospital like wildfire,' she told them. 'I've contracted it myself. It lasts about ten days but doesn't appear too serious for youngsters, although it is a bit more debilitating for adults. In fact I've been placed sick for a few days. But it's not TB, if that's what's bothering you.'

'Well, I've certainly been concerned about it,' agreed Grace worriedly. 'Being in that damp shelter doesn't help.'

'Tell you what,' said Julia, 'make up a bed for the children under Polly's kitchen table and I'll sleep alongside them for a few days and we can do all our coughing together. Meanwhile Polly and Ted can get some sleep in their Anderson shelter.'

'I wouldn't dream of it,' protested Polly. 'It's far too dangerous for you all.'

'Strangely enough it's not,' said Grace. 'Judging by the times we've found people alive under a table when the rest of the house has collapsed, I'm beginning to think it must be the safest place to shelter.'

At first the elderly couple totally refused to entertain the idea but finally the combined arguments of Grace, Jack and

Julia, to say nothing of the children, persuaded them to agree. The almost fiendish delight of the children did cause a momentary doubt in Julia's mind but then she told herself it would only be for a few nights and their coughs and chat would be as nothing against the usual sound of bombs and guns.

Sometimes this chat would take on a surprisingly serious air. Julia was particularly impressed when a discussion arose amongst the children on the effects of the bombing. Only the most cursory details of raids were given on the radio. The announcer would merely say something nondescript, such as, 'Enemy planes last night attacked targets in the London area. They were repulsed with heavy losses and bombs were dropped at random.' Benji pointed out to Freddie how lucky they were to live in London and not in Random. That unfortunate town seemed to be bombed at least three times each day. Freddie replied the thing that puzzled him most was just *where* Random was. He assumed it must be somewhere near London, yet until the start of the blitz he had never even heard of it. Benji, who was always quite knowledgeable on these things, said he was sure Random was a town in Essex – somewhere near Southend – and as he had an aunt who he didn't like much who lived in Southend, he was rather glad it kept being bombed. Rosie said she didn't think Random could be much of a town anyway because by now it must have been blown to bits. All three then weighed up the evidence and mutually decided that perhaps Random was a bigger place than they had given it credit for and they were just very glad they didn't live there.

Grace and David had not been the only ones to decide to vacate the basement shelter in Queen's Buildings. Rita Roberts had arrived at the same conclusion, though for differing reasons. Her telephonist job at the Fire Brigade HQ was proving to be more and more of a nuisance. Though war work for married women and widows was not yet compulsory, and in theory she could have left the service any time, it was not quite as simple as that. All sorts of perks existed for serving women that would not be available to their less patriotic sisters.

However, her black market work with Arnold Westow was taking up more and more of her time and seemed to be expanding each day. Not only that but she was tiring rapidly of both his attention and his tendency to delegate to her the day-to-day running of the racket. She felt she was taking the majority of the risks but receiving the minority of the rewards. Her plan was to gradually remove herself from the Fire Service in order to work the black market full time. To do this she began to take days off from the Service, she arrived late, pleaded sickness and ensured she was rarely at her own address when anyone called. This, of course, necessitated changing her air raid shelter because, at that stage of the blitz, people were expected to be in one place or the other.

For over a year she had been friends with Wanda Williams, a pretty but rather sad wisp of a girl. Wanda had been married to a merchant seaman who had perished on the *Athenia* which had been torpedoed on the first day of the war. Since that day Wanda had retreated into her shell. Her only real friend was Rita, on whom she relied more and more. By mid-October Rita had practically moved in to Wanda's second-floor flat which was also situated in Queen's Buildings but at the opposite end of the street to her own. Strictly speaking, she should have notified the local warden to prevent rescue services wasting their time searching for potential victims who were safe elsewhere. However, this anonymity suited her well and indeed was a vital part of her ploy to become more elusive.

Her plan, however, began to get complicated when she realised that Wanda Williams was not just dependent on her but had obviously fallen in love with her. Such a possibility had simply never entered her head. True, they shared a bed but so did thousands of others at such times. Wanda would also cuddle up tightly when the bombing heightened but yet again so did many others. It was a week or more before Rita finally realised that she herself had begun to look forward to Wanda's nightly embraces. It was only then a question of time before she finally threw off all pretence and the pair became lovers. It had to be said that the real love mainly came from Wanda; Rita was in it simply to enjoy the experience. Night after night they would lie blithely curled in each other's arms as if they had divine immunity from the nightmare outside. Rita once asked Wanda if she wished to take shelter in the basement but the girl declined. For more than a year she had believed she would never know love again but now that it was here she was not going to relinquish it, and certainly not for a nightly twelve hours in a smelly basement.

Of course Rita did not share Wanda's bed every night, sometimes she needed to be at the Clinkside Club until the early hours. On such nights, alone once more, Wanda would know an obsessive terror she could not even bring herself to speak of until Rita's safe return. At such times, no matter how late the hour, she did not even undress until Rita walked in the door. This despair peaked when a large bomb fell on a row of nearby shops in Southwark Bridge Road just before midnight. The incident gave Queen's Buildings its greatest blasting to date. It broke gas and water mains, took out hundreds of windows, blocked Southwark Bridge Road and blew up Jackie Blackwell's old boots.

When Jack was not an air raid warden, he was a porter in Billingsgate Fish Market. Because of the aroma, his wife had been adamant that his boots must never be kept inside their flat or on their balcony. With only two rooms, the front windowsill was the only alternative. Even though she had long died, Jack still kept faith by placing the boots in a battered old biscuit tin on the ledge five floors high. The tin was secured firmly enough against the strongest of breezes but could not cope with a 500-pound bomb and as a result its contents were now at street level and covered with broken glass.

It was the tin that Rita first noticed as she picked her way over the pavement debris on her return to Wanda some ten minutes later. A further quick search soon revealed Jack's boots. Picking them up she held them at arm's length as she made her way to Wanda's flat. The girl, hysterical with fright, opened the door almost before Rita had finished knocking. She threw her arms around Rita in relief before she even noticed the boots. 'Oh darling, darling!' she cried. 'I was worried sick that something had happened to you.'

'Whoa!' laughed Rita. 'Give me a chance to get in the door!' She dropped the boots and returned the girl's embrace.

As the pair finally broke away from a passionate kiss, Wanda finally noticed the footwear. 'Whatever are they?' she cried.

'Jackie Blackwell's boots,' said Rita dismissively. 'You must know about them, surely? He keeps them on the windowsill because of the smell. I saw the tin in the street and found one boot halfway down the road and then searched around until I found the other. I picked them up because he'll need them for work.'

Wanda, her relief changing to incredulity, suddenly stared at her. 'What? D'you mean to say that while I've been waiting here terror-struck and half out of my mind because I thought you were dead, you've been searching the street for a pair of stinking boots?' She shook her head as if in a frenzy. 'No! No! I can't believe I heard you say that. I can't, I can't!'

Rita's face changed instantly, the laugh that had played around her lips moments before transformed into a snarl. '*You* can't believe it?' she mocked as she repeatedly slapped the girl's face backward and forward. '*You* can't believe it? And just who the hell are *you* not to believe anything *I* say or do? Don't you *ever* speak to me like that again . . . understand? I do what I want to do and I say what I want to say, or I'm out of this door. Do you understand me?' She slapped her face again, each slap emphasising her last three words. '*Well . . . do . . . you?*'

The girl covered her stinging red face with her hands and fell sobbing to her knees, then, locking her arms tightly around Rita's thighs, she buried her face into them. 'I won't, I won't . . .' she mumbled. 'Oh, I promise I won't, Rita . . . Oh my God, please don't go! Please don't leave me, not now you've come into my life . . . I love you, Rita. You mean so much to me I couldn't stand it.'

Rita seized the girl by her hair and dragged her to her feet. 'Get up and get yourself to bed. Your snivelling disgusts me,' she hissed.

'I'm sorry, I'm sorry,' Wanda whimpered, tearing off her clothes and scrambling naked into bed. 'You won't leave me though, will you? Promise? I'll do anything you want, Rita, honest I will. Just don't leave me, please.'

Her words suddenly caused the snarling Rita to revert to the smiling woman who had knocked at the door minutes earlier. 'D'you mean that, Wanda?' she said in a sudden soft tone.

'Of . . . of course I do,' said the girl a little apprehensively. 'I . . . wouldn't have said it otherwise.'

'Good,' said Rita slipping out of her dress and shoes and sliding into bed alongside her. She began to gently stroke back the shock of sweat-streaked hair that had fallen damply across the girl's stinging cheeks. She lowered her face until their lips were almost touching. 'You do trust me, Wanda, don't you?' she whispered.

'Of course,' replied the girl.

'How would you like to ensure that we never fall out again, eh?'

'Just tell me what I'll have to do,' whispered the girl as she reached up and put her arms around Rita, 'and I'll do it. But don't go, please don't g—'

Rita put her finger against the girl's lips to cut off her words. 'Shush,' she murmured, 'let's have no more talk of leaving, shall we? We're going to be friends forever, you and I, aren't we?'

'Yes,' breathed the girl, as Rita placed the kiss for which Wanda was aching fully onto her lips.

As they finally broke off Rita whispered, 'You know the club I work at from time to time?' Wanda nodded. 'Well the guv'nor, a Mr Baxter, has made me a particularly good offer. To get the best out of it, I need someone to work with me. Someone I can trust and someone who trusts me. She needs to be pretty and' – Rita eased back the bedclothes and ran her hand over the girl's naked, trembling body – 'she needs to look good. Of course you could do with putting on a few pounds here and there but then some men prefer the little-girl-lost type. You wouldn't be with just anyone, though, there'd be no rough slobs in my set-up, so you needn't worry. In fact, I'd choose them for you.'

'Rita, I don't underst—'

Rita placed another kiss full onto the girl's mouth and then began to move her own mouth down Wanda's neck and shoulders. 'Of course you do, Wanda,' she soothed, 'of course you do. All we need is to work at the club for the duration of this bloody war. Then we can move out of this dump and have our own little place anywhere you fancy. A little country cottage, maybe? You know, just the two of us. You'd like that, wouldn't you?'

Wanda nodded eagerly. 'Oh Rita, you have no idea how much I'd like it. I'd give anything, anything!'

'So you agree?'

'You want me to be . . . to be . . . a whore? Is that it?'

'Well, that's being a bit coarse, sweetie,' corrected Rita. 'Let's just say you'll need to be nice to people from time to time and leave it at that, shall we?'

'I don't know if I'll be any good at it, though,' frowned Wanda. 'I don't think I could show love for just anyone and—'

'Good God, girl,' laughed Rita, 'love doesn't enter into it! I'll teach you what to say and what to do. Or even more importantly, what *not* to say and do. Sometimes we could even work together, you'd like that, wouldn't you?'

'If that's what you really want me to do, I'll do it,' she said simply.

'Good girl,' murmured Rita as she began to ease out of her underslip. 'Now where were we?' Before Wanda could reply a loud whistle filled the room. Rita instinctively pushed the girl from the bed and onto the floor and rolled over on top of her. The building trembled and the glass that had survived the earlier blast finally succumbed. The curtains were ripped from their fixtures and a gigantic wind swept through the room for a few seconds, followed by another of less intensity a few seconds later. Outside, the rattle of falling slates could be heard crashing down from the roofs of houses opposite. 'Christ, but that must have been close. I think there were two of them. I wonder where they were?'

Along the length of the entire street everyone cowering in their shelters was saying the same thing. Everyone, that is, except Polly and Ted Foskett. The claims made for the Anderson shelter had been proved correct. They were indeed bomb proof for everything except a direct hit. Likewise Grace's prediction of the safety advantages of a solid kitchen table. It had certainly stood up nobly to a bomb barely twenty yards away. Unfortunately the entire house had collapsed over it and anyone who was alive beneath it looked like being there for a very long time.

Twelve thousand feet above Queen's Buildings, Josef Frinker was in all sorts of trouble. His Heinkel had been struck twice by anti-aircraft fire, his rudder was jammed and he was losing height fast. In addition, flames were spreading along the fuselage and he could get no answer from his crew on his intercom. Just to round off the entire proceedings he was caught in twin searchlight beams and knew he had more chance of walking back to his airfield in Boulogne than flying there. Minutes ago he had dumped his last two bombs and had had the satisfaction of seeing them explode somewhere down there, just south of the river. This satisfaction was rather spoilt when his rudder and fuselage damage caused the plane to fly in circles, which made him virtual target practice for the gunners below. He had already realised he would not be returning to his home town of Liebenau for some time, if at all. His priority therefore was to ensure that when he did bale out, he did not land in the vicinity where his bombs had just fallen. In the main, civilians who had been bombed night and day for two months were not known for their tolerance towards bomber-crews unfortunate enough to land amongst them. Whatever plan he might have formulated to avoid this was abandoned when his control panel exploded and the flames leaped out around him.

Two minutes later, with his clothing partially ignited, he had jumped from his plane and was cascading rapidly down towards St Paul's Cathedral. He pulled the cord and, as his parachute billowed above him, he saw he was drifting towards the river. As a non-swimmer he was now in something of a dilemma. He had no desire to drop into the Thames. With all the activity going on down there, most of it of his own making, he knew the rescue services would not have his welfare at the top of their priority list. On the other hand, he had a feeling that his welcome might be even more uncomfortable if he landed anywhere near the two smoking ruins he could now clearly see in the moonlight.

It would have been of scant consolation to him to have known that Jack Blackwell, who had just arrived at a large hole in the ground that had once been an Anderson shelter, had spotted him swinging in the moonlight. As far as Jack was concerned, bits of Polly, Ted and the three kids were now scattered generally around north Southwark and the bastard who did it was about to land a few streets away. With a terrifying roar Jackie ploughed through the broken glass that lay everywhere and ran in the direction of the parachute's drift. As he passed various shelter entrances, he called to the men at the doors who were thankful at last to be able to do something useful – namely string up a kraut airman.

Although the parachute did not drift far, by the time it landed in the park by the Imperial War Museum, Josef Frinker had more followers than the Pied Piper. As Josef landed on the front lawn, the driver of a passing fire engine swerved in to the side of the road as if he could not believe his eyes. There, clearly illuminated in the moonlight, was an airman disentangling himself from his harness. There was also a policeman climbing the fence and a small army running down the main road some hundred yards distant. He called to his crew, all of whom were smoke-blackened and exhausted.

'Looks like they want ter kill 'im,' said leading fireman Tug Wilson indifferently. 'I don't think it's anythin' much to do with us, d'you? Drive on, Bert.'

'No, wait!' cut in a female voice urgently. 'That's my Davy there!'

'What, in the parachute?' said Wilson sarcastically.

'You are a pig at times, Tug! That copper's my husband. Stop, Bert, we've got to help him. That's a lynch mob there.'

'If you want ter help him, love,' said Wilson, 'then you'd better talk him into takin' a short walk round the park for the next ten minutes.'

'He won't do that,' she said anxiously. 'He's a stubborn bugger at the best of times. If he thinks he's right he won't give an inch.'

'Well, he's *not* right, is he?' moaned Wilson. 'But I suppose we'll have to help him. But I tell yer this, Grace, if he wasn't your old man, I'd say fuck him, let them string him up as well. Come on then, Bert, what yer waiting for?'

In all, five fire-crew reached the pilot just about the same time as the policeman. 'Grace!' exclaimed David. 'What on earth are you doing here?'

'Saving your life if you're about to do what I think you're about to do,' she said acidly.

The pilot, by now free of his harness, turned and looked fearfully at the advancing crowd.

'You speak English?' asked David sharply. The German stared back blankly. 'Er—' faltered David. 'Sprecken ze English, ya?'

'Ah!' said Josef, the penny finally dropping. 'Nix! Nix!'

'Davy!' cried Grace. 'Look! It's Jack, Jackie Blackwell, he's leading the mob. It's not like him. I wonder what's happened?'

Surprised at seeing both Grace and David, Jack Blackwell was obviously taken aback and made no attempt to speak. 'We're gonna 'ang 'im,' cut in a female voice from the rapidly assembling crowd. 'So yer might as well let us 'ave 'im now. We've got nothing agin you six, but this fuckin' Jerry is ours.' She turned to the forty or so people behind her. 'Ain't that so?' she asked. They roared a cheer of approval.

'I'm sorry,' said David quietly, 'but that's not on. It'd be murder and you know it. I can't let you do it and neither can they.' He nodded towards the fire-crew. 'He looks like he's a bit burnt down one side so what you say we take him to the local nick? You can follow us if you like but don't worry, he won't escape.'

'Listen,' said the woman who, because of the silence of Jackie, seemed to have taken over as leader, 'a few minutes ago the guns were tryin' ter blow this scum out of the sky and there 'e was, up there trying ter kill us all. If he'd been blown

157

ter bits we'd still be cheerin'. So you tell me, what's the big change?'

'The big change,' said Grace, 'is that he's no longer up there trying to kill us but he's now down here with us.' She pointed at the terrified pilot. 'I hate him and I wish he was dead but could you' – she pointed directly at the woman – 'could *you* kill him on your own? Forget this lot,' she said, waving her arms towards the group. 'Anyone can do anything sheltering in a mob. You're a woman so how would you feel if your son was captured by the Germans and they wanted to tear him apart?' She then turned to Jackie Blackwell. 'Come on Jack, this is not like you, you know I'm right, don't you?'

Jack was in mental turmoil and found himself totally unable to speak. Whether the German lived or died no longer concerned him in the slightest. What did concern him was how to tell his two friends that the Anderson shelter had sustained a direct hit. Several times he opened his mouth but nothing came out. All he could see was that smoking crater and his beloved daughter.

'Jack!' said David sharply. 'Are you all right, mate?'

Jack just stared and stood gaping and silent, which made the background of crackling guns sound even louder. He slowly shook his head and suddenly burst into a fit of trembling and would have fallen if one of the fire-crew had not caught him and lowered him gently to the grass. David realised that this was now the vital moment. Whatever happened in the next few seconds would dictate the fate of their prisoner. It was essential that the fire-crew did not carry Jack to their engine. It had to be part of the mob. It was vital they were given a function, if they didn't then the pilot was as good as dead.

'Right, you group, Jack here needs attention urgently. I've seen this sort of thing before. Now, six of you take a bit each, because he's a big lad, and carry him to the fire tender. I also want another four to help carry the prisoner. He looks like he has a badly burnt leg. I then need a few more to run down to the nick and tell them we've got a prisoner and we're taking him and Jack to hospital on the tender. Got it? Good, now off you go and mind the shrapnel, it's falling like rain at the moment.'

To his surprise the woman who had had the most to say was the first to lead the way. 'The copper's right, old Jack's the salt of the earth and worth more than any fuckin' kraut. C'mon you lot, let's git movin'.'

The fire tenders used by the AFS were cramped at the best of times but with the two casualties plus the policeman this one rolled alarmingly as Bert took the bends and corners at St George's Circus ten miles per hour too fast. At one stage Josef Frinker was convinced he had survived his destroyed Heinkel and an imminent lynching, only to be killed by a lunatic fireman doing his best to be helpful. The only one who did not seem alarmed by the drive was Jack Blackwell. In fact by the time they arrived at the casualty door of Guy's Hospital he was quite tranquil.

'Jack, sweetie,' said Grace, putting an arm around his great shoulders, 'how are you feeling now? You certainly look better.'

The warden made no reply but gave her a weary smile and then stared straight at the German.

'Still not talking to me?' she chided gently. 'I must be losing my charm.'

The pilot was closest to the door so he was the first to be removed from the tender. He had already been met with his escort and gone through the heavy blackout screen at the casualty entrance before Jack even began to make a move.

'Come on, Jack boy,' said Grace encouragingly. 'Show 'em what you're made of.' Jack reached up and pulled the woman down beside him. 'The war's finished,' he said simply. 'It's over.'

She looked at him worriedly. 'Jack, love, what do you mean?

You know it's not over, listen to it.' She gestured out towards the street.

'It's over for me ... all gone ... all gone,' he repeated.

'What's all gone?' she asked in a puzzled tone. Then suddenly a cold fear struck her. 'What's all gone, Jack? Tell me ... you mean the kids, Jack? *Well, do you ...?*' She seized him by the shoulders and shook him as hard as she could. '*Do you, Jack? Tell me, for God's sake ...* TELL ME.'

He gave just the slightest nods as she slumped slowly to the floor.

11

The row of terraced houses in Collinson Street was indeed in a sorry state. Although the bomb that had fallen was by no means large, the little row of houses were hardly fortified castles and the damage was therefore enormous. The first two houses had completely disappeared into a pile of smoking rubble. The rest were blasted out of use. One moment, in those first two houses, the hopes, dreams and possessions of six families – twenty-six people – had been anchored there, the next there was nothing but a hole in the ground and a pile of broken debris. In the crater were remnants of twisted steel, three items of bloodstained clothing, a white clay pipe and an intact bag of knitting.

In addition to a team of assorted helpers, the Heavy Rescue Unit had also arrived and, after consulting with Willy Brolly, a warden from Jackie Blackwell's post, decided they could be better employed on more vital incidents elsewhere. About the only good aspect was that the casualty rate was relatively low. In the first house, the Fosketts and the three children were dead. In the second house, a woman was killed by the blast, though four others, only inches away in the same shelter, were unharmed. In the remaining houses a total of four adults sustained moderate cuts from glass splinters and roofing tiles.

'No one appears trapped, Will,' said the leader of the heavy rescue team, 'and we've still got another three incidents to attend, so we'll leave the clearing up to your mob, if you don't mind. You're quite sure there was no one sheltering in this house, though?'

'Oh yeh,' said Will confidently. 'The families on the first and second floor take shelter over the road in Queen's Buildings but Jackie Blackwell's young daughter usually sheltered 'ere and Jack was always poppin' in to check on 'er. He would have kept our record bang up to date.'

'Oh, I'm sorry to hear about that,' said the heavy rescue leader. 'She was a smashing kid, that one. Right saucy little cow, but you couldn't help liking her. Jack'll be in a state, though, she was the apple of his eye. By the way, where is he? He wasn't caught up in it, by any chance?'

'No, someone said they saw him chasing a German airman coming down in a parachute. No one's seen him since.'

'Hope he cuts the bastard's throat before he hangs him,' muttered the leader as he put the vehicle into gear. 'By the way,' he pointed back to the smoking debris, 'get someone to check the scullery table when you get a chance. You never know what you'll find. If nothing else, you can sometimes get the family cat crawling under there. Poor little buggers, it ain't their war.' He gave a brief wave. 'See you.'

The truck was barely out of sight when Will was suddenly assailed by doubts. 'Take nothing for granted,' Jack had drummed into him when he had first joined the post, but that was exactly what he had done. Supposing there *was* someone in that house, what then? They could have gone back into the house to make tea, use the lavatory or collect a blanket, in fact any of a dozen reasons. Well, if they did they would be dead for certain, no one could have possibly survived that explosion because the house was nothing other than a pile of debris. There was no doubt the debris had to be searched so he would need to organise the helpers into a team of sorts. Oh, how he wished Jack were here, he was good at that type of thing, was Jack. It was whilst he was contemplating his various options that he heard the brash voice of young Peter Marsh, who was filling in as a warden for a few weeks before joining the army. 'What 'o, Brolly boy,' said the young man cheerily. 'I've been sent from the post ter solve all yer problems. They reckoned they needed a reliable bloke down here so they sent yours truly. What needs doin'?'

Will had never liked the youth and, for reasons he could not fathom, neither did he trust him. 'Well, there's the scullery at the back of the house,' said Will. 'You could take some of these helpers and start digging there, I suppose.'

'Why there?' asked Marsh.

'Well, there ain't no kitchens in these places so most folk keep their kitchen table in the scullery. The heavy rescue leader reckons there's always a chance you might find something.'

'No point diggin' there,' said Marsh dismissively. 'Folk'd never keep their valuables under a kitchen table. They'd either keep 'em wiv 'em in the Anderson shelter, or they'd bury 'em in the coal cupboard or such like.'

'Valuables?' echoed Will. 'What's valuables got to do with it? This ain't a bloody treasure trail. We're supposed to be saving lives, or didn't you know?'

'Of course I did,' protested Marsh. 'It's just that yer gits a lot of people gittin' a bit funny about valuables, they make accusations and things. I think it's better if yer finds the valuables first and stores 'em for safety, like. Yer know what I mean, don't yer?'

'Oh yeh,' said Will emphatically, 'I know *exactly* what yer mean and that's why I want yer to dig over that scullery. If I see yer anywhere else I'm ordering yer off this site and back to the post – and I'm tellin' Control why, got it?'

Marsh scowled but made his way over the debris towards the back of the house.

Grace Diamond had regained consciousness within seconds

of fainting and although she felt she was taking part in a dream, she was still aware of the reality of the situation. Jackie Blackwell had just told her her son and his friends were dead and she realised she had probably saved the life of the man who killed them.

'Jack,' she called, 'please tell David what's happened. I'm all right now and I'm not going in that hospital. Bert will drive us to Collinson Street, won't you, Bert?'

'Of course, love, don't worry,' replied the driver. 'As soon as Davy comes we're off.'

Jack Blackwell returned within a few minutes with David and a protesting nurse in tow.

'Mr Blackwell!' cried the nurse. 'You really must come into casualty at least until a doctor can examine you.'

'I'm all right now, nurse, don't worry. I've got to find me Rosie.'

Grace seized hold of David's tunic. 'It's my fault,' she sobbed. 'If I hadn't agreed to them leaving the shelter they'd have been in with a chance. Why was I so stupid! It's as if I care more about this war than I do about my own child.'

David put his arms around her and kissed her forehead. 'You can't blame yourself, darling, it wasn't your fault, it's just . . . it's just the war.'

'Of course it was my fault!' she cried. 'Polly never wanted the kids to leave the shelter in the first place. It was my agreeing with Julia that finally swung it.'

'Wait, wait just a minute,' said Jack. 'I've not quite got this. What are you saying about the kids?'

'Oh God, I'm sorry Jack, but you don't know about it, do you? They . . . they all had these terrible coughs and—' with that she broke down into a flood of tears.

'The kids all had coughs,' continued David, 'and Julia suggested they should all sleep under the table in the scullery with her. It wouldn't be so damp and Ted and Polly might get some sleep, for a change. Forgive us, Jack, we should have told you but you weren't there at the time and . . .' he shrugged as his voice trailed away.

'Look, I'm sorry but I'm still not gettin' it,' persisted Jack, almost frightened to believe that there was still a chance for his child. 'Are you sayin' . . . are you sayin' that the kids were in the *house* and not . . . not the shelter? Is that it?'

Grace, who was the first to realise that there was a note of hope in Jack's voice, looked up sharply. 'Yes, Jack, that's *exactly* what we're saying. Why?'

'Then there's still a chance!' he exclaimed. 'The Anderson got a direct 'it an' it's blown ter kingdom come and the 'ouse is certainly wrecked, but if they *were* under the table . . . then . . . well, who knows?'

'Bert!' yelled Grace. 'Ignore the craters, Collinson Street as fast as you can!'

The big problem facing Julia Giles was dust. She knew exactly what had happened and, as the joists had fallen from the rooms above, they had sloped from the edge of the table to the floor like a sloping roof. Plaster and masonry had followed them and whilst some had slipped through the joists – hence the dust – in the main there was a large cavity under and around the table in which she and the children could just about shelter. The big trouble was that they were in a virtual air-lock and, with four of them in it, the air could not last forever. The children had not panicked but they were waving and blowing like mad to clear the dust. 'No, don't, kids!' she said sharply. 'You must all lie as still as you can – and no talking, Rosie, understand me?'

'But I've got lots of stuff up me snitch,' complained Rosie.

'I know, love, we all have, but we must keep still. Someone will come to dig us out soon, so I suggest we're all nice and quiet and listen for the diggers.'

'But if we all lie nice an' quiet,' said Rosie, ''ow are they gonna know we're 'ere?'

'Be *quiet*, Rose, please!' emphasised Julia. 'And listen hard.'

There was something in the tone of her voice that finally transmitted to the children the seriousness of the situation, that was until Rosie suddenly asked, 'Can I 'um then?'

Deciding that it was the lesser of two evils Julia finally conceded, 'Okay Rose, you can hum. But quietly, mind.'

The child was about two-thirds through 'Bobby Shaftoe' when she was interrupted by a great 'Shush' from Julia. 'Listen, kids,' she said urgently. 'Can you hear anything?'

'I can,' said Freddie. 'Sounds like a sort of scratching noise.'

'It's someone digging!' exclaimed Julia.

'Shall we all shout?' asked Freddie.

'No!' replied Julia sharply. 'I'll tap, they'll hear it better.' She gingerly levered two portions of a broken gas-ring through the sloping joists and began banging them together. After a few bangs she paused briefly before resuming. She carried out this drill three or four times before she thought she could hear a response. She turned to the children to tell them the news and was appalled when she saw they were all breathing heavily and lying quite still. Her first instinct was to scream for help at the top of her voice but she knew that would only worsen the situation. She crawled over to them and realised that in moving that short distance the temperature had increased. That meant if there was any air coming in at all, then it was from her side of the table. The question was, just how much was there? She banged again with renewed vigour before realising she was becoming dreadfully sleepy. In a desperate attempt to help the rescue she began to tear recklessly at some of the larger debris covering the joists. The whole covering slipped a few inches and the rest of the gas-stove fell onto her arm, pinning it to the floor. Before she could even begin to struggle she closed her eyes and lay still.

Just above her, Peter Marsh stopped digging and sat on a cross-beam and lit a cigarette. He had never wanted to become a warden. He had been hoping to obtain employment in a munitions factory or somewhere where his work could be considered of national importance and he could avoid army service altogether. He had thought his chances of such employment would be greater if he became a warden for a couple of months and did not continue his civilian job as a bookie's tout. He glanced towards the docks as a particularly large explosion indicated that some building had just disintegrated. Oh well, he thought, should be safe enough here, lightning never strikes twice in the same place.

'Marsh! Yer lazy bastard!' came the voice of Will Brolly. 'There could be people down there, get fuckin' diggin'.'

He looked around him and all over the ruined houses, illuminated clearly by a wickedly bright moon, scattered figures were digging frantically with picks, shovels and bare hands. Bloody fools, he thought, resuming his dig, what does it matter how quickly you reach them if they're dead when you get there? He had been scratching lethargically for some ten minutes when a large piece of chimney stack slithered, causing him to leap back. Having assured himself it was now safe he glanced casually at the spot where it had been. There was nothing there other than a broken gas-stove lying on its side. He made a mental note to put it somewhere safe a little later when there were not so many people about. The last one he had taken to the scrap dealer had been worth half-a-crown. This one looked at least comparable.

As he was mentally pricing it, he realised that lying immediately beneath him was a hand. Not just a hand but a female hand with two rings on its fingers! He had no means of working out their value but they certainly looked neat enough. He glanced quickly around and ensured everyone else was otherwise engaged before slipping his hand into his pocket for his knife. If he could slip the rings off easily, so much the better, but he couldn't afford to be seen struggling. He had found it quicker and safer on previous occasions to cut off the fingers. After all, when so many mangled bodies are pulled from wreckage no one pays much attention to individual fingers. He raised the hand slightly and began to tug at the rings. Neither moved an inch. He changed his position for a better grasp and tugged again, this time much harder. Still nothing moved. Cursing, he transferred the knife from his left to his right hand but in doing so it slipped from his grasp and slid down the side of the gas-stove. He swore again and released the ringed fingers whilst he felt in the crevice for the blade.

His attention was suddenly taken by a fire tender skidding to a halt on the loose debris in the road. Excited voices told him time was shortening fast. He then heard Will Brolly clearly say, 'I've sent a lad where the scullery might be and he's diggin' there now, Jack, but I don't think there's much—'

That was all Peter Marsh could absorb because a sudden gut-wrenching scream swept across the ruin. It was a scream that races down the spine of the hearer and disappears into the ground, leaving just a cold shudder in its wake. It was only a second or so before Marsh realised the scream was his own. He had been so intent on looking at the newcomers that he had failed to see his own knife and had run the entire palm of his hand firmly across its razored edge.

Four figures from the tender raced across the debris and there, just above where they thought the table might be buried, was a tall, slim, young man staring at what was left of his right hand. Jackie Blackwell pulled out a torch and shone it down into the debris. 'Poor sod!' he exclaimed. 'Look, 'e's caught it on that knife while 'e was tryin' ter rescue 'em. That looks like a hand down there and it could just be Julia's.'

Bert the driver half-led, half-carried the young warden to the tender to search the first aid box for a dressing large enough for the wound. Once out of earshot Will Brolly muttered, 'I'll need to take back what I said about 'im. I'd clocked 'im as a lazy, untrustworthy git. Poor bugger, 'e'll be lucky if 'e don't lose that 'and.'

As sympathetic as they felt for the young warden their interest had not deviated from the search for the scullery table. 'It's Julia, right enough,' panted David, forcing the gas-stove aside with his feet, 'but she doesn't look good.'

Grace was the first down to the girl's face where she remained impassive for almost a minute. 'Davy! I think she's still breathing. She was being held in place by that gas-stove, but the rest of her seems fairly free. Do you think – oh I daren't even ask . . . do you think . . . the kids could still be . . . ?'

'We'll soon find out!' yelled Jackie Blackwell, as he began to rip apart the largest pieces of wreckage.

'Careful, Jack, careful,' warned David, but Jack was beyond advice and all they could do was to help him in his frenzy. Finally they uncovered what resembled a small cave; it was, of course, the table. There, curled up on the far side and to all intents and purposes asleep, were three dust-covered children. Before they could make a move to carry them out, a groan from the still-unconscious Julia told them at least one was still alive. It gave them renewed hope as each little figure was carried out and laid on the pavement. 'Jack! Davy!' sang out Grace. 'They are all breathing! Not very well, perhaps, but they certainly are breathing. Isn't that wonderful? Oh, I'm never letting Benji out of my sight again!'

Jack Blackwell picked up Rosie as if she were a doll and murmured a prayer of thanks as she began to groan. Then, bending down, he picked up the now-groaning Freddie. 'Amongst all the celebrations, don't let's forget this little lad,' he said, 'because we won't be findin' Ted and Polly quite so easy.'

'Oh yes yer will, Jack,' said Will Brolly sadly. 'I've already found 'em, at least what's left of 'em, in the back yard of the hardware shop in the next street.'

'Who's goin' to tell Freddie?' asked Jack. ''E's got no one in the world now.'

'Oh yes he has,' corrected Grace. 'He's got us. He's got us for just about as long as he wants us. Isn't that right, Davy?'

David, who was cradling his own son, replied, 'Five minutes ago I had no son, now I have two. I think we're grateful enough to settle for that, don't you, Grace?'

'We'll be back to nil again unless we get them to hospital a bit sharpish, but we mustn't forget that brave young man who saved them,' she replied. She glanced towards the fire tender where Bert had finally finished bandaging the ashen-faced Marsh. 'And as for you, young man,' she called, 'I'll never be able to thank you enough. When Julia is fully conscious again I'll tell her she owes you her life.'

The young man, still in agony, gave the weakest of smiles in return. ''S all right,' he panted nobly. 'Only doin' me job.'

'Speaking of doing a job,' said David, 'they'll be wondering down at the nick whether I've been doing mine. No one has seen me since I followed that parachute what seems like days ago.' He took Grace's hands. 'Look, love, you go to the hospital with the kids and I'll go back to the nick and put them in the picture. If there are any complications when you reach the hospital, give the station a ring and I'll be with you as soon as possible, okay?' He kissed her lightly on the cheek as he handed her the dozing figure of Benjamin.

He waved to them as the fire tender pulled away, and then turned towards the police station. Glancing up to an angry sky he saw a renewed wave of bombers sweeping through the searchlights to attack the nearby Surrey Docks.

As he approached the east end of Collinson Street, through the noise of an increasing barrage he thought heard a call. 'Up here,' it said. He looked up and on the first floor he saw two female figures at a window. 'Where were those two bombs, officer?' said a vaguely familar voice. 'They must have been close. They've buggered up everything here except our floors and walls.'

'The first was nasty,' he called back. 'A direct hit on an Anderson shelter at the end of the street, but the second weren't so bad. Apparently it simply made a mess of a few empty barges down by Southwark Bridge. Here,' he said, peering into the dark. 'Is that Rita?'

She peered back. 'Blimey! You're the copper who lives up at ninety-one, ain't you?'

'That's right. But what are you doing here? I thought you'd be in the shelter?'

'What, that stinking hole? Not so bloody likely. I'm staying here with Miss Williams for now, it's safer than my flat, not so high up.'

'Hope you've told the warden you've moved,' he said disapprovingly, 'otherwise he'll have the entire rescue team looking for you if the buildings get a whack.'

'Well, there's always Tibs, my cat, she'll probably be at home. She don't like the shelter either. See you, mate!' She waved a goodbye and closed the window. 'Blast!' she exclaimed.

'What's the matter?' asked Wanda. 'If you didn't want him to know where you were why did you call?'

'It's not that, you stupid cow,' snapped Rita. 'It's the barges. If they are the ones I think they are, we could have trouble.' She stood for a moment staring at the mantelpiece clock. 'Get dressed, quick!' she commanded. 'C'mon! Look lively!'

'Why? What for? Where're we going at this time of night?'

'We're going to the river, that's where we're going, and we're going there because everything I've worked for could have just been blown sky high, so get moving, you dopy cow!'

Although Southwark Bridge was no more than a few

minutes' walk away, because of two craters and one unexploded bomb the journey took them a good half hour. They reached the bridge as the first chink of dawn filtered through the pall of black smoke that now hung over the Surrey Docks. As they picked their way down the glass-strewn steps that led from the bridge down to Bankside, Rita had her first view of the wrecked barges. 'It's not as bad as it could have been, I suppose,' she muttered. 'At least they're still in the shallows.'

'Who're those men?' asked Wanda. 'They don't look much like police or wardens.' She pointed beyond the furthest barge where two men in a dinghy had just appeared.

'They're a couple of Swinger Baxter's heavies,' murmured Rita quietly. 'Georgie Jinks and Jimmy Tyler. Wonder what they're doing there?' She thought for a moment, then called to them, 'Morning, boys! You're up early. What's the attraction?'

At first they appeared alarmed, then, seeing it was Rita, waved back cheerily and began to make for the river steps. 'Got a big surprise for yer, Rita,' laughed Jinks as the dinghy bumped against the stone steps.

'I don't much care for surprises,' she replied suspiciously, 'unless they're expensive, that is.'

'Oh, this one was certainly expensive,' he said, reaching down to a tarpaulin that lay in the bottom of the dinghy. 'In fact yer might say because it was so expensive is why it is now such a surprise . . . Hey presto!' He pulled back the sheet to reveal the soaking wet corpse of Arnold Westow.

Rita did not flinch a muscle though the same could not be said for Wanda, who spun on her feet and buried her face into the older woman's shoulder. 'Did he fall or was he pushed?' asked Rita.

'Well,' said Jinks matter-of-factly, 'seeing as the barge was hit by a bomb I'd say he overbalanced and fell, wouldn't you?'

'Oh, without a doubt,' she agreed. 'I always did think it was his balance that would prove his undoing in the end. Tell me, is Swinger still awake? If he is I'd like to speak with him.'

'You know Swinger,' said Tyler. 'Hardly ever sleeps, except in his chair. Pop in and see him while we ring the law and tell 'em about poor Arnold who fell off his own barge.'

The two women made their way down the alley that led to the Clinkside Club. The door was propped open with a chair as two cleaners in turbans and overalls were already at work polishing the dancefloor. As they entered, the all-clear siren wailed its message. 'Ah, my dear,' growled a breathless voice. 'What could be more appropriate? The enemy flees, the dawn rises and two charming visitors honour me with their presence. Pray sit down.'

'Morning, Swinger,' said Rita. 'On another day and another hour, I'd say that little recitation was charming, but at five o'clock on a morning when I've had sod all sleep, I'd say it was pure bullshit. Anyway, meet Wanda Williams, my flat-mate.'

'Wanda, my dear!' said Swinger. 'I've heard much about you. How delightful you look.' The voice came from a large, fat man who sat half-covered in blankets and surrounded by cushions in an armchair. He had a fat fleshy face with an horrendous scar running from his jawbone to the front of his hairline. Although he was in late middle-age, there was not a trace of grey in his thick hair and his centre parting was so straight that it could have been made with a ruler. What clothing could be seen above the blankets comprised a thick thornproof jacket and a cricket club tie. At first glance it was easy to see the man was an invalid of considerable disability.

He turned his attention to Rita. 'I too have had a poor night's sleep, my dear. Still, what can one expect when one's old friend has such a nasty accident. Er – you have heard about poor Arnold I take it?'

'Yes,' agreed Rita. 'Slipped on something, didn't he?'

Swinger nodded a reply. 'His greed, some might say.' He

drummed his fingers on the arm of his chair for some seconds. 'Strange thing, greed. Most folk who have it don't have any excuse to have it – if you know what I mean. Take Arnold, for example. He had a good job here, he also had his own little sideline – the one he shared with you, my dear – then he became incapable of sorting out his priorities from mine. I expect he rushed out there too quickly when the barges were bombed. You'll probably find it was something simple, like slipping over the side because of the wrong footware. Oh well, it's water under the bridge, as you might say.' He gave a slight smile. 'No pun intended, of course.'

'Swinger,' said Rita sharply. 'I'm tired, we both are. I've come down here to see what the score is. As far as I can see, at the end of the game it's Swinger Baxter one, Arnold Westow nil. So will you please tell me what happens now? Is the competition finished, or can I sign for a new team?'

'If you remember, my dear, I have already offered you a position in my team. Although I was quite happy for you to remain with poor old Arnold, I thought you might like to earn the odd groat with me, that's all. Nothing has happened to change that.'

Rita cut in sharply, 'Ah but it has! In fact a whole new aspect has opened up. Look, I can now run Arnold's old business standing on my head, I know all the contacts. I could also take on whatever you offer me. Unlike Arnold, I have no intention of getting out of my depth. Er – also no pun intended.'

'If you're telling me you want to take over where Arnold left off, then of course I must ask you, what's in this for me? Otherwise it could put me back where I started.'

'Well, two of the barges look beyond repair, but the third doesn't seem so bad. They are virtually on your doorstep and I could continue to operate buying and selling under your protection for, shall we say, a twenty per cent cut?'

'Fifty per cent cut,' he corrected.

'Wait, you've not heard me out yet. Twenty per cent cut and not only will I agree to take your other offer of work but Wanda here will be my assistant. How's that grab you? Two for the price of one, you might say.'

Swinger drummed even more quickly on the arm of his chair. 'Stand up, Miss Williams. Turn around . . . hmm, okay, sit down.' He turned again to Rita. 'Twenty per cent it is, but my work has the priority, agreed?'

'Almost,' she said, 'but I want your assurance that we are not in the frame for being just another couple of cheap brasses. We'll do whatever we have to do for the right sort of money but we are not going to get the right sort of money with Friday night stokers. And a couple more things, we'll need two rooms to operate. We'll continue to live in Wanda's flat but we'll work entirely from here.'

'Two rooms?' he queried. 'Why two?'

'One room for us to change and prepare, the other to work in.'

Swinger pointed at Wanda. 'And she's prepared to go along with that?'

'She'll do whatever I want her to do.'

'You said there were two more things, what's the second?'

'We'll work only three weeks in each month. We are definitely not working through our periods. Oh, it's all right, I can answer your next question, there is usually only a day or so's difference between the two of us.'

'We're in business then.'

'Do you think your blokes can fix that third barge for me?' she asked.

'Well, as you seem to be in the market for miracles this morning, why not the other two barges?' he asked acidly.

'Because they are a perfect cover for the third. If you look at them they appear total wrecks. It's only when you have a close look that you see the third is nowhere near as damaged as the first two.'

'True, but I do have a slight reservation about the Thames Police,' he said thoughtfully. 'Surely it is only going to be a matter of time before they examine all riverside wreckage.'

'I can see you haven't been out on the river lately, Swinger,' she said. 'Between here and Tilbury there are literally hundreds of wrecked craft scattered all over the river. Many of them good-sized vessels sunk in mainstream. Wrecked and burnt out barges are ten-a-penny between here and Limehouse Basin. Even if the whole of the London police decided to search every one it'd take years.'

'Deal done,' he said briefly. 'Pop back Friday evening and we'll finalise terms. Meanwhile, go home to bed, you both look as if you could do with it.' He slumped back into his chair, pulled up the blankets and closed his eyes to denote the audience was over.

As the two women stepped outside into the now bright, if smoke-laden dawn, he called after them, 'And there had better *only* be a day or so's difference between the pair of you . . . or there'll be big trouble, very big trouble.'

12

All night there had been a steady stream of casualties into Guy's Hospital but it seemed to peak with the arrival of Julia and the children. 'Look,' said Bert as he clapped eyes on the number of people waiting to be seen, 'I appreciate it's been one emergency after another but we *are* supposed to be a fire tender and, if you remember, HQ control thinks we are on our way to the docks to assist the local brigade. From the moment we were given that assignment we've been a bleedin' ambulance. I suggest me and Tug take the tender back to Collinson Street to drop Jack off, then we'll shoot off to Surrey Docks swift like, and you can stay here and look after the kids.'

'But—' began Grace.

'Don't you go givin' us any of your "buts", gel,' said Tug Wilson wearily. ''E's right. We may 'ave been doin' this runnin' around for the best of reasons but fact is there're other services better equipped for it and we're not where we're needed most.' He reached forward and took her wrist. 'Look, love, Hitler ain't goin' ter win the war just 'cos you're stayin' behind ter look after Benji and Freddie, now is 'e? Bert's right, you stay 'ere for just as long as yer needed.'

Grace found she was unable to muster a word of thanks to her colleagues. Instead she settled for biting her bottom lip and giving a brief but tearful nod.

Jackie Blackwell also agreed and, giving his Rosie another

177

hug, he said, 'I'll be 'ome before you, kid, don't worry.' There was a chorus of goodbyes as the grey tender then pulled away from the front of the hospital.

Jack glanced back as the children reached the hospital doorway. Turning to the two firemen he murmured, 'I don't think that poor little sod fully understands yet he has lost both his grandparents.'

Bert laid a sympathetic hand on the warden's arm. 'I know, yet it can sometimes be a mercy when they are so young. I really think that the kids are the most resilient of us all.'

To assess some category of priority, a staff nurse briefly examined each new arrival almost as soon as they came through the hospital door. Those with only superficial injuries were referred down the street to the First Aid Post. By the time she reached Julia and the children, other than all being filthy dirty and Julia having a badly grazed forearm, all four certainly looked like imposters. The children were chatting loudly and Julia was engrossed in deep conversation with a fellow nurse whom she recognised from student days. In fact they had not shared a cough between them since they had been pulled from the wreckage half an hour earlier.

'Look,' said the staff nurse, 'because you seem to have been unconscious, I think you should all see the doctor. I'll take your details but I'm afraid it's going to be some time before he gets to look at you. It's been a hell of a night and the hospital is swamped with a whole variety of casualties. The WVS have a canteen down the corridor. If you're sure you have no other injuries you may be able to get yourselves a hot drink.' She then glanced anxiously at Grace. 'And that goes for you too, my dear. In fact, you most of all, I'd say.'

Twenty minutes later all five sat on a wooden bench, each nursing a steaming cup of Oxo. Welcome though it was, its aroma still failed to dispel the strong smell of antiseptic that wafted strongly down from casualty. Grace slipped her arm from Freddie's shoulder to lean forward and whisper to Julia, 'I've just thought, when we walk out of this hospital, I haven't the faintest idea where we're going to live. Our flats are still standing but they've taken a terrific blasting. I doubt if we have a window in place and four floors up in late October is not going to be fun.' She dropped her gaze and, staring at her cup for a moment, began to swirl it slowly. 'You know, Julia, I don't think I can take this much more. I really feel I'm going out of my mind. Where is it all going to end? Is it going to continue until there's nowhere to live and no one to live there?'

Julia took Grace's hands. 'Most of your problem eventually comes down to Benji and now of course Freddie. They must leave London and get out of this hell hole. It's not fair on them and it's not fair on you. You'll be so much more relaxed when you know they are safe each night. They have an evacuation officer round at the school, why don't you go there tomorrow and get their names put down? Once Jackie Blackwell knows the two boys are going he'll probably agree to Rosie joining them. They all get on well together, it's an obvious thing to do.'

Before she could answer, the call 'Nurse Giles!' echoed down the corridor. The staff nurse who had examined them when they arrived was hastening towards them.

'Ah nurse! I've found you.' She glanced down at the notes she held in her hand. 'I've given Dr Rawlings a brief run-down of your history and he wants to see you. Will you follow me, please?'

'How about the children?' asked Julia.

The request appeared to cause some indecision. 'Er – well . . . oh yes, I suppose so, although he made no mention of them. If they're with you, then you'd better take them along.'

Julia rose to her feet and with a half turn, glanced quickly at Grace and gave a puzzled shrug. 'Come on gang, this way,' she called.

When the group finally arrived at casualty, Dr Rawlings was sitting in a cubicle with the curtains open studying a memorandum. On their approach he rose to his feet and gave a tired smile. He was slightly above average height and quite powerfully built. His thick, jet-black hair started in neat tiny waves from the top of his forehead but seemed to lose interest halfway over his head and changed into a ruffled thatch. He had a square, solid-looking face with a strong jaw, wide mouth and a thick but tidy black moustache. His eyes were of a faint grey that looked as if they could comfortably close at a moment's notice.

'You must be Nurse Giles and these young folk are your . . . ?' he left the question unfinished, inviting a reply. His leisurely deep voice gave an impression of total dependability that made her feel that she could lean on him and go to sleep.

'Oh well,' replied Julia, 'for want of a better term you can say they are my niece and nephews. Needless to say they are not quite that,' she added, then immediately wondered why she had added it.

'And this lady?' Again a tired smile but this time a nod towards Grace.

'Oh, er, this lady here, is the mother of' – she turned and gestured at Benjamin – 'that lad there.'

'Uh huh,' he murmured. 'And I understand you are a nurse from—' he glanced down again at the papers in front of him, 'Evalina Hospital, correct?'

'Um, yes, yes, that's correct.' He had not asked her a thing that was difficult to answer yet she knew she had yet to give him one straight reply.

'I'm afraid I'm about to ask you to commit one of the most serious wartime offences. Think you're ready for it?' He grinned.

This time she did not even attempt a reply but gave a weak smile by way of response.

'Good! It's called "Queue-jumping".' To forestall any response he solemnly raised his hand and continued, 'There is a good reason for it. I have here a memo from London Emergency Services; it says we are to give priority to any member of the civil defence who – well, at this stage it uses a ream of jargon – but basically it's saying, if we can patch 'em up and send 'em back, do so. Can you be patched up and sent back, Nurse Giles?'

'What's 'e talkin' about?' Rosie asked Freddie in a tone loud enough to be a stage whisper.

'Dunno,' said the uninterested Fred.

'Shush, you two!' cut in Grace. 'Don't be so rude.'

The doctor chuckled. 'They're right, of course. I understand you and the children were buried and you suffered from a lack of oxygen but other than a rather nasty graze, you seem to have recovered well enough by yourselves. Is that correct?'

There was silence at first then Grace nudged Julia who gave a slight start before replying. 'Er – yes, well that's about the sum total of it.'

'Well, I'll sound you all out and if you seem okay you can all toddle off as soon as you like. But you, Mrs' – he glanced down at the notes again – 'Diamond, I'd say watch the children closely for the next few days and don't hesitate to return here if you're at all worried.' He then turned to Julia. 'And as for you, nurse, I think a solid forty-eight hours' sleep could be the making of you.'

She closed her eyes and gave a long, weary sigh. 'Forty-eight hours' sleep,' she echoed nostalgically. 'Whatever is that?'

'I think it's what you get when you're dead,' muttered Grace.

'Well, that's something to look forward to,' said Julia in a tone that made Grace feel uncomfortable.

Though the children had recovered every bit of their chirpiness, the doctor still gave them a thorough, if swift, examination. Then, once Julia's forearm was firmly bandaged and he had checked her breathing and pulse, they were free to go.

'So other than lack of sleep, are you sure you're all right, nurse?' he asked as she buttoned her dress.

'I'll be fine,' she assured him. 'None of us have as much as spluttered since the house fell in.'

'There must be a cure in there somewhere.' He smiled. 'Goodnight and take care of yourselves.'

As they left the hospital, dawn was just about breaking somewhere behind that mile-wide curtain of black smoke that was winding its way up, thousands of feet above the docks. Grace stared at it for a few moments. 'I wonder how Tug and Bert are coping,' she murmured. 'They must be in there somewhere but it looks like hell itself.' Breathing in their first lungful of smoke-laden air, they each realised just how tired they were. 'You sure you're all right, Julia?' she asked anxiously. 'You seemed half-dopy in there.'

Julia smiled. 'It was that doctor. I was okay until he spoke, then I just wanted to curl up and sleep with him.'

'Julia!' cried Grace, glancing quickly at the trio. 'The children, please.'

Julia laughed, 'No, Grace, I really did mean sleep. I am so dog tired and that man was so relaxing, that if he'd invited me to bed with him I'd have been asleep before he took off his socks.'

'And if he didn't take off his socks, what then?'

'In that case,' she said wearily, 'then there's nothing to worry about. I couldn't possibly sleep with a man who goes to bed in his socks.'

'Speaking of socks,' said Grace, 'if there's one person who must have slept in his socks for a week at least, it's Jackie Blackwell. I just don't know how he manages on so little sleep. I bet you he hasn't been in a bed this week, with or without his socks. I know people think he's bossy but for my money he's the best air raid warden in London.'

'I agree,' laughed Julia. 'He takes every bomb dropped on this city as a personal affront. But you're right, I've never known the man sleep.'

'I must find a telephone box,' said Grace. 'I need to leave a message for David. I also need to tell the brigade that I won't be in tonight and finally ring the ARP Control to tell Jack that Rosie will be staying with us for at least the rest of the day. Then we'll have to decide what we're going to do about you. If you don't mind roughing it you can sleep on our kitchen floor.'

'No bloody fear,' replied Julia. 'The last time I slept on a kitchen floor with this bunch we got blown up! I'll see if I can get a tram to Streatham and sleep at Queenie's house. At least I'll be in a bed.'

'You'll never get a tram at this hour,' pointed out Grace. 'There won't have been time to clear the debris from the tramlines. It'll have to be our kitchen floor, I'm afraid.'

'Is this all you have to do at this time of day?' said a familiar voice. 'Standing around gabbling on the pavement? Respectable people have been in bed long ago.'

They looked up to see Rita Roberts and her friend Wanda purchasing some milk from a Jenkins' Dairy milk float.

'The same might be said for you,' replied Julia.

'Ah, but then we're not respectable, are we, Wanda?' Wanda did not seem too sure so she settled for a smile instead. 'So come on,' added Rita, 'what're you and the kids doing here?'

Julia gave them a brief rundown of the night's events and the dilemma in which she found herself. 'Then sleep at my place,' suggested Rita. 'It's in the same block as Grace's and as I'm currently staying with Wanda, providing you give this milk to my cat you can sleep there as long as you like, or at least until the Germans blow it up – there you are, easy!'

'I'll admit it's tempting,' agreed Julia. 'The way I feel at the moment I could sleep on the pavement.'

'Okay,' said Grace. 'Discussion over! Now for God's sake can we all get to bed, wherever it is because I'm fit to drop.'

As the group strode along it was obvious to both Grace and Julia that neither Rita nor her friend were going to divulge the reason for their presence, so the matter was not raised again.

As they neared Queen's Buildings, Julia was the first to turn the corner. 'My God,' she exclaimed. 'Look at the state of it!' Parts of the building did indeed look a sorry mess. The bomb that had killed the Fosketts had also blasted almost every pane of glass out of the west end of the buildings. The result was that the windows of forty-eight flats looked like a mass collection of eyeless sockets. 'As I suspected,' sighed Grace, 'all my windows have gone, for a start.'

'And mine,' said Rita. 'So we're none the worse off, are we? Everyone at this end of the buildings is in exactly the same boat.' She turned to Julia. 'Here you are, love, here's my key. When you leave drop it into Wanda's letter box, flat three, far end of the street.' She then cut short Julia's gratitude with a brief wave and a curt, 'Sleep well and don't forget the cat.'

As Julia, Grace and the children climbed the dusty staircase, Grace said, 'She's a strange girl, that Rita. Sometimes you feel like killing her, yet other times . . .' She shrugged. 'To be perfectly honest I haven't the faintest idea what to make of her.'

'I know exactly what you mean,' agreed Julia. 'I can never imagine her having any emotions. It's as if she's an automaton and her life has been programmed for her. I'd hate to have her for an enemy.'

'How do you feel about sleeping in her bed?'

'Strangely enough, I'm not bothered. In an odd kind of way I'm quite looking forward to it. Perhaps it may give me an insight into what sort of person she is. Anyway, I tell you this, unless it's a bed of thorns I shall be out like a light within seconds.'

They had reached Rita's flat and, after a brief tussle with the key, Julia said goodbye to Grace and threw open the door. Like all flats in the tenement it consisted of just two rooms and a lavatory. The kitchen-cum-living-room was sparsely furnished and immaculately tidy. Before the windows had blown in, it was doubtless spotlessly clean but with dust and glass everywhere she could only surmise that fact. She lifted the eiderdown and pillows and shook off the worst of the debris. Then pulling the heavy blackout curtains across the yawning window socket, she kicked off her shoes, shed her coat and dress and fell into the bed in her underwear. The last thought she had before oblivion overcame her was how the war had changed so many things. A year ago she would have died sooner than go to bed in this state. Now she felt she would die if she did not.

A common yet illogical feeling that most survivors of bomb blasts felt, was that they were now bomb-proof. It was as if they had had their allocation of destruction and now it was someone else's turn. After all, if lightning did not strike twice in the same place, why should bombs? This, of course, completely overlooked the fact that unlike lightning, bombs were *aimed* at the same place. Yet a feeling of pure fatalism would take over the most sensible of people. So it was with the residents of Queen's Buildings. There had been one blasting so there was hardly likely to be another, therefore folks could now get on with the rest of their lives with impunity. Even though the night raids actually increased in ferocity and Grace and the children all sought the safety of the formerly dreaded basement shelters, the question of evacuation had not risen again.

Julia too had returned both to work and her flat at the nurses' quarters. Even though at first hand she could clearly see the increase in the number of casualties, she too had acquired this feeling of immunity. Meanwhile, Wanda and Rita, unless they were whoring at the Clinkside or supervising the alteration of the barge into a black market store, would spend most nights curled in each other's arms in Wanda's flat, regardless of the intensity of the raids. Even Jackie Blackwell seemed to share this delusion. Whereas he had spent earlier weeks looking after his sector as diligently as a shepherd with a flock of particularly wayward sheep, he now did not hesitate to work further and further afield.

The children, of course, had adapted most easily of all. There was not a school in the borough that was open, so every morning after breakfast they would scour the local recreation ground for shrapnel pieces. Not that these pieces had any value but each child was determined to find the largest piece of these jagged, razor-sharp shell fragments, with a nose-cap being the most valued prize of all. Because of the relative absence of daylight raids, at least some sort of routine to people's lives could at last begin to take shape. The night raids would last for some ten to twelve hours so the Civil Defence Forces were still required to work at least twelve-hour shifts. This, of course, threw enormous strain on their families, particularly those with children and living in just two rooms. In such cases sleep would become the most desired acquisition of all. Many settled for sleeping at their place of employment, regardless of wherever that might be. Firemen slept at fire stations, policemen at police stations, nurses at hospitals and factory workers at factories. The whole philosophy appeared to be to keep society going any way possible.

Society, though, did not appear to include the children. Once the early morning shrapnel collection had finished the problem arose of what to do next. In the case of the trio, it was the eternal quest for German spies. The fact that there were German spies out there to be caught went without saying, but how did they get here? It was that question that puzzled Freddie most. It couldn't be by parachute because they would be seen coming down. It could hardly be by train because where would they buy their ticket? In any case, half the trains weren't running, so Benjamin was probably right when he suggested they came up the Thames by submarine. The trio had suddenly stumbled on this proof by accident one autumn morning when the search for shrapnel had been particularly fruitless. They had found themselves down by Bankside and saw two men working furtively in the river mist on some damaged barges.

'Told yer,' cried the triumphant Freddie, 'they must've come up on the tide.' Benji suggested they should perhaps look for the submarine, seeing as it would be a far more important capture than a mere spy, but Rosie said she thought submarines 'Wouldn't 'ang about in case they got whacked by one of their own bombs in an air raid.'

There was a certain logic in this observation so therefore the threesome directed all their attention to spying on the spies. The two spies, alias Georgie Jinks and Jimmy Tyler, had spent several days scouring various bomb sites for planking and panelling and, even though they said so themselves, had made a reasonable job of a false floor in the bottom of the largest barge. As the mist began to lift and the first of the city workers began to filter across the bridge above them, they decided to vacate the scene until the cover of the following evening's blackout.

The pair's departure was the signal for the threesome to pull back the tarpaulin sheet and inspect the barge. At first they were particularly disappointed. Except for its new floor it seemed to be like every other barge and a new floor hardly indicated a proof of espionage. It was Rosie who eventually found the handle which pulled up a trap door that led down to a hold that was lined for its whole length with triple racks of shelving. *Empty* shelving, it is true, but shelving nevertheless.

'I reckon they're goin' to make this their base,' said Benji thoughtfully. 'I'll bet this'll soon be full of guns an' tanks an' things.'

'I think yer right,' agreed Rosie. 'Let's shove the sheet back and see what they do tomorrow.' It seemed the most sensible suggestion and so within minutes they were back on the shore.

The discovery had given the spy-catchers the boost they so desperately needed. For over a year now they had searched endlessly for spies and in truth they had not been enormously successful. Freddie had been complaining for weeks about their lack of success and suggested instead that they visited the various WVS locations where dedicated ladies handed out food and hot drinks to the homeless. It was true that none of them were actually homeless but the qualifications of ten- and eleven-year-olds were rarely queried. Benjamin was uncomfortable with this and thought it was little short of treasonable, though Rosie had kept an open mind on the subject. But now, with the discovery of the barge, they had satisfied themselves that they really could catch spies and so set to work with renewed vigour. It seemed that once they really applied themselves there were spies to be found all over the place and who were really quite easy to spot.

Cinema posters of the time regularly featured an actor named Conrad Veidt. In his films the long-nosed, sharp-featured Veidt would invariably play spies dressed in dark raincoats. It therefore followed that any sharp-featured, long-nosed man would bear watching. If he was sharp-featured, long-nosed *and* wore a dark raincoat – well that was virtually a confession. The friends began to patrol the riverbank just to examine clothes and faces. In fact Freddie became so keen on this counter-espionage, that he almost caught them a master spy. Not only did his suspect feature a long nose, sharp features and a long dark macintosh but he was also extremely furtive. He first came to Freddie's attention one Sunday afternoon by flitting from doorway to doorway along the wharves and warehouses that lay beneath Southwark Bridge. The next week he was at it again. The trio followed him closely until they noticed that he was completely preoccupied with some activity in a distant doorway. In this doorway were two other figures. In the gathering gloom, the trio could see they were a man and a woman. Perhaps accomplices? On closer examination this did not appear to be the case because the woman lay on a large wooden pallet and the man lay on top of her. Freddie said she could possibly be asleep because he was sure her eyes were closed. Benji said he didn't think she was asleep because he thought he could hear her moaning and the man on top of her seemed to be whispering in her ear.

'Perhaps 'e's tryin' ter wake 'er up?' suggested Freddie.

Their spy became so absorbed in the couple that he forsook his cover and edged so close to the pair that Freddie said he thought he was going to whisper in her other ear.

Suddenly Rosie, who had been uncharacteristically thoughtful during the entire proceedings, gave forth a dramatic yell. ''E ain't a spy! 'E's a dirty old man!' Once more she had astounded her friends with her perception.

The man who was whispering in the lady's ear scuttled quickly to his feet, buttoning his trousers as he did so. The lady, meanwhile, was frantically pushing down her skirt which was up somewhere near her waist. There was no doubt Rosie was right. Somebody was a dirty old man. But who? Was it the man who was peeping, or the man with his trousers undone? And how about the lady with her skirt up? Was there such a thing as a dirty old woman?

Conrad Veidt took just a second to assess the situation, then was away like a whippet. He even fell once but he was so quick he had outpaced the cheering kids before they had reached the street corner. Disappointedly they ceased their pursuit and returned their attention to the couple.

The lady was close to tears but the man looked so angry

that Benji said he thought they should all go home before the evening raid began. In view of the circumstances it seemed a sensible suggestion. Whether they had disturbed a spy or just a dirty old man they never did discover. But if it *was* a spy, then before the next twelve hours were through, Hitler was to wreak on them a nightmarish revenge.

13

Though it had been only a few weeks since the Fosketts' death, it seemed like a lifetime to Julia. Whether it was the closeness of her escape she was not sure but she knew it was time for her life to change direction. Since Duncan had left with the Commandos, she had received just two letters from him. Being Duncan, they consisted of a couple of fairly placid pages in which he certainly mentioned he loved her but that was about the sum total. In neither did he mention anything at all about their future. He was still in the country, of that she was sure, so why then did he not telephone and just where was he spending his leave? Typical of the bastard. It was when she saw a recruiting poster for military nurses that she finally decided to make her move. She knew she was doing a priceless job at the children's hospital but she also realised she had a gap in her life that even the most deserving child could never fill. She felt she needed someone – if only occasionally – to make a fuss of her, to look after her, to show concern, or simply to bloody telephone.

The transfer was easier and quicker than she expected. The first wave of British casualties were reaching London from the Italian advance into Egypt and she was posted to Millbank Military Hospital just a stone's throw from the Houses of Parliament. The daylight raids had waned and whenever possible a Sunday tea-time meeting would be held at Queenie's house where Jim, Billie, Grace and David – duties permitting

– would be in attendance. The problem was that each of their homes were in a different part of London and most of them worked shifts of one sort or another. Still, it was something she enjoyed immensely and, other than sleep, there was little else to look forward to at that period.

Billie Bardell, being the most outspoken, was the first to broach the subject. 'How's that randy lad of yours, Julia? Still seeing him?'

Queenie glanced swiftly across and raised her eyebrows in disapproval. 'Mother!' she hissed. 'Don't ask the girl that sort of question in company. It's not nice.'

'Since when is having a healthy animal like Duncan around "not nice"?' asked her mother. 'I used to find it bloody marvellous!'

Before Queenie could respond Julia cut in with a rueful smile. 'Billie,' she said wearily, 'you know what he's like, he'll never change. I did get the impression that he was finally thinking of settling down but people who are thinking of settling down don't usually bugger off and join the Commandos, do they?'

'Did you tell him?' asked Billie. 'That you were thinking he might be settling down, I mean?'

'Well, I hinted we weren't getting any younger, if that's what you mean.'

'That's not what I mean and you haven't answered my question,' persisted Billie.

Julia looked exasperated. 'Oh, I don't damn well know!' she snapped. 'How do you tell that oaf anything? If he doesn't want to hear it he simply lets it go in one side and straight out the other.'

'Y'know,' said Billie, 'I never thought I'd hear myself say this but I admit I am now an old lady.' She put her hands up to forestall a protest that never came. 'I realise that you are of the modern generation. However, some things never change, namely men like Duncan. Or should I say *boys*, because that's what he really is, a boy. He has never really grown up. Now I have no doubt at all that he really loves you, or at least as much as he could love anyone. But he is never going to do anything about it until you are practically walking up the aisle with someone else. Only then will he stir himself. You see, you're partly to blame for this, you're an attractive girl and you're not short of admirers but it's like he has you on elastic the way you bounce back to him each time. I know you find it surprising but there really are *other* men in the world, so go out and grab one of the sods.'

'Haven't I done that? Well, haven't I?' cried Julia, looking at Grace for support. 'And every time I do so he jumps back in my life like a genie from a bottle!'

'Yes,' murmured Grace, 'but who loosens the cork for him by tumbling into his arms every time he does it?' She put an arm around the protesting Julia. 'You do, kid, you really do. The maddening thing is, he is such a great bloke, but then you are a great girl and as such you deserve to be treated a whole lot better.'

'Is that it?' asked Julia acidly, as she looked around the room. 'Anyone else got anything to say?'

David rose out of his chair. 'Only me, sweetie,' he said with the straightest of faces. 'Tell me, if I poison Grace, will you run away with me?'

She smiled a reply and fell silently into his arms, whereon he kissed the top of her head. 'We're not having a go at you, kid, honestly we're not,' he said softly. 'We all love you dearly but Grace is right, you *do* deserve better.'

'Perhaps I know it myself,' she replied. 'That's why I have changed direction. I thought I would never give up child nursing but when it came to it I was surprised at my own determination. Anyway,' she said, glancing up at the clock, 'it's time I was getting back to Millbank.'

Everyone, it seemed, had to be getting back to somewhere or other and as they gathered at the door Julia asked Grace about the children and if she had given any more thought to their evacuation. 'Not really,' replied Grace. 'I just feel we've survived the worst and things can now only get better. The buildings were in an awful state but we knuckled down to tidying them up and once the workmen patched up the worst of the blast damage, we simply got on with our life again.'

'Where are the kids today?' asked Julia. 'I was hoping to see them.'

'Yes, I'm sorry about that,' replied Grace, 'but it is a bit of a dilemma. The three of them get on so well and there isn't a lot in life for them at the moment. What with the winter coming and the evenings drawing in, we thought they'd rather play out than be cooped up with a lot of boring adults on such a nice afternoon. Benjamin did say they were off to catch some German spies.' She laughed. 'They are absolutely obsessed with spies. Still, Jackie Blackwell's off duty today so he's keeping an eye on them.'

'What are you doing about an air raid shelter? Are you still going into the basement?'

'Yes, just me and the three kids because David is usually at work. Though both he and Jack pop in regularly. It's one blessing of them both being local.' There were kisses and embraces all round before each party moved off in their different directions.

By this time the nightly raids had become such a routine that many people no longer waited for the sirens to sound their warning. They just assumed a raid would always take place and, instead of going upstairs, downstairs, or in the other room to bed, they simply went to the shelter. This was usually in or on the same bunk, chair, floor-space, corner, passage or step. Grace had managed to obtain a narrow canvas lounger and the children usually lay in sleeping bags on the floor on either side of her. The noise from outside indicated that the raid was heavy and twice the floor trembled as explosions took place nearby. Both David and Jackie Blackwell had popped in but stayed only briefly because of the sheer intensity of the bombing.

The usual banter had ceased as, one by one, the residents closed their eyes. Even the three old men who played cards until dawn had tapped out their pipes and slipped fearfully down into their blankets. From a small hole in the ceiling, a twisting brown wire looped down to a naked, dim bulb that only partially lit the shelter. The streaks of deep shadows that snaked into every recess were easily preferable to the depressing yellow light that bathed the centre of the basement. An optimistic spider sat fruitlessly at the corner of a cobweb that stretched triangularly from the bulb-socket to the ceiling, its quivering threads marking each explosion like an earthquake on a seismograph. Here and there a cough would be heard and occasionally a few indecipherable words as someone conversed in their sleep. Though the aroma of carbolic did little to screen body smells, the odour was still inescapable.

Grace guessed she was the only inhabitant still awake. She turned and looked down fondly at the children, who, having frustrated yet another spy, were sleeping the sleep of the just. The heavy, pulsating drone of the bombers was broken only by the guns and the explosions. On every explosion she glanced anxiously up at the ceiling. With six floors being supported by just a few beams and supports, she never felt relaxed in that basement.

On the tenement roof, eighty feet above the basement, Jackie Blackwell tilted his head and squinted apprehensively into the night sky. 'I tell yer this much, Davy boy,' he confided, 'I ain't missed many of these nights since this blitz began but I've never seen such a bright moon. We must be as clear as daylight ter those fuckers up there! The river's a complete give-away; we must be reflectin' more light than the front at Blackpool.'

'Cuts both ways though, Jack,' replied David. 'They can see us and we can certainly see them.' He pointed to where three waves of Heinkels were coming up via the estuary. The anti-aircraft guns opened up against them with renewed vigour. 'Getting a bit hot on this roof though,' he added. 'Reckon we ought to go down?'

'Just a minute!' exclaimed Jack, pointing up excitedly. 'They've got one of 'em, look!' Just visible against the silvery background was a swinging parachute. He gave a loud cheer. 'Hurrah! I'd let them 'ang this bugger this time if I was you, Davy, that's unless yer want another chase. Oh! Fuckin' hell, Davy . . . run!'

David did not want a second telling, he had recognised it as soon as his friend had spoken. At the end of the parachute was not some petrified German pilot but an eight-foot-long mine, packed with high explosives, that was capable of demolishing four streets and, if it kept on its current course, would strike the very spot they were standing on in something less than a minute. Time, it seemed, had finally run out for Queen's Buildings.

They raced east across the roof, avoiding mangles, washing lines, chimney stacks, low brick walls, old bikes and hopping boxes, until they reached the blessedly open staircase door of the last block. They had barely tumbled into it when an explosion occurred that David felt must have taken off his head. At first he could neither see nor hear. The blast wave had hurled him down the first flight of stairs without even touching the sides and had finally crashed him into the brick wall on the landing ten feet below. Jack followed him to the exact spot.

The mine had exploded on the west end of the building

where the first two blocks crashed instantly to ground level. The reinforcing beams in the basements of those blocks held up for all of forty seconds before dropping the entire six storeys down onto the shelterers therein. In the third block, the flats also dropped down, but even though the shelter walls cracked, the beams moved and the whole basement groaned ominously, everything just about held. Throughout the street, the basements were less damaged the further from the explosion they were situated. In the eighth and last block, Wanda and Rita were showered by ceiling plaster but the rest of the block remained intact, with the basement showing no damage at all.

After the initial explosion in basement three, there was complete blackness and a few seconds of total silence. This was followed instantly by a crescendo of calls and screams. 'Where are you, Benji?' 'Are you all right, Sid?' '*Mummy!*' 'Here, in the corner, George!' 'What the fuck—!' Grace instinctively reached out to feel for the faces of the three children. Once having established their location she needed to know if they were alive. From two she received an instant acknowledgement but from the third, nothing. 'Freddie! Freddie!' she repeated. In the absence of a response she fumblingly ran her hand quickly down his body. The first thing she discovered was another hand moving up. 'Freddie! Freddie!' cried Rosie.

Grace gripped the girl's hand. 'Is that you, Rose?' she cried.

'Yeh, I was seein' if Freddie's all right.'

Before they could say another word Freddie's dozy voice could be heard as he emerged from sleep. 'Oi,' he said wearily, 'who's ticklin' me?'

One of the old card players struck a match. A tiny flame danced momentarily before someone yelled, 'Don't strike matches, you old fool. There may be gas escaping!'

'Who has a torch?' called Grace loudly. There was a great deal of swearing as shelterers fumbled in the pitch blackness for a safe means of illumination. Eventually five torches of variable brilliance lit up the basement. 'Let's just have one to start with,' suggested Grace, 'we don't know how long we'll need them to last.' Instantly all five were extinguished. 'No, please,' she cried. 'You . . . the one nearest the door . . . try yours first.' There was a click and a reasonable beam slowly swept around the shelter. Every set of eyes followed its travels and none of them cared for what they saw. The west wall had a pronounced bulge and so did part of the ceiling. The beams seemed to take it in turns to creak and groan and the whole room looked out of alignment. 'Oh me Gawd,' sobbed a female voice. 'We're all gonna die! We'll never get out, never.'

'Course we will,' snapped Grace, pulling the three children tightly towards her.

'Where can we get out when we're trapped an' the 'ole fuckin' buildin' is comin' down on us?'

'We can get out either there or there,' said Grace, pointing to a white-painted square on each of the two side walls. 'We'll do it through one of those.'

'We can't walk through the fuckin' wall, yer dopy cow!' screamed the voice. 'It's brick, it's fuckin' brick!'

'No, she's right,' said one of the old card players. 'Each shelter has a small, thin section of wall. We can knock it through and get into the next basement. That's providing we can find the tools – they should be in a box here somewhere. In theory we could tunnel through all the basements right to the end of the street.'

'Okay,' said Grace, 'then let's look for the box.'

'What colour d'yer say it was?' asked a young voice from the edge of the darkness.

'I didn't,' said the card player, 'but it was yellow. You shouldn't be able to miss it, must be here somewhere.'

'No it ain't,' said the young voice. 'It's not 'ere an' it ain't been for over two weeks. You gonna tell 'em where it is, Maggie Tozer, or do I?'

Maggie Tozer was obviously the woman who had announced they were all going to die, but she now had to announce exactly why she had removed the box to give to her husband for a job he was doing for Sid Pavey in the Winchester. ''Ow was I ter know?' she wailed.

An elderly woman with a black shawl could just about be seen in a particularly dark section of the basement. 'You have condemned us all to death, my dear,' she said softly. 'I hope the job was worth it.'

'Can't we start, though?' said Grace. 'You said it was a *thin* wall. Better to try it than just sit here waiting for the buildings to fall on us.'

'I've got a knife and fork,' called a voice.

'I've got hobnailed boots and a penknife,' said another, and suddenly several other voices added various implements to the collection.

'Wait!' said the old card player. 'How do we know what wall to dig at? For all we know we could be taking away the very wall that's keeping this lot' – he pointed at the ceiling with his thumb – 'off our heads.'

'Well,' said Grace. 'Ideas, anyone?'

Before 'anyone' could reply the sound of knocking could be heard close by. 'Oh bless 'em, the Rescue's comin' for us,' cried Maggie Tozer. 'I knew it, I knew it.'

'No they're not,' said another of the card players. 'They couldn't have got here this quick anyway.' He pointed to the white square on the east wall. 'It's them . . . them in the basement next door. They're digging to us thinking it's their way out!'

'Then let them,' said Grace. 'It at least doubles our chances. If we scratch away from this side it shouldn't take too long.'

It was the spurt they needed and everyone clustered around

the painted square on the east wall to scratch, carve, knock, or just offer advice. Everyone, that is, except Rosie whose attention was drawn elsewhere. She discreetly tugged at Grace's sleeve and pointed to the west wall. There, the largest of the cracks had appreciably widened but more importantly, gathering momentum every second was a steady trickle of water. Suddenly a chunk of plaster fell away and water began to pour into the basement. A basement that was below ground level, a basement without drain or exit – a basement that was now a tomb.

David Diamond was vaguely aware someone was slapping his face. As the curtain of mist faded from his eyes his first sight was of a steel helmet with the words ARP WARDEN emblazoned on it. His gaze travelled down to a concerned bearded face. 'Davy, c'mon, wake up, wake up, son!'

David blinked several times before his vision came into focus. 'What happened, Jack?' he muttered. 'No, don't tell me, I remember now.' He looked about him. 'I thought the buildings got hit. Why are we still here?'

'We just about cleared the worst section of it afore we dived down this staircase,' explained Jack. 'I'm afraid I walloped into you. How d'yer feel?'

'Oh I don't feel too—' he began wearily. 'Jack!' he suddenly yelled. 'Grace and the kids! Where are we? Where are they? Come on, man, we've got to find out!' He began to struggle to his feet.

'Steady, steady!' cried Jack. 'We've got ter see if yer can walk first, you've 'ad an 'ell of a whack.'

'I'm okay, bit stiff and bruised, but come on, let's go.'

They picked their way down the rubble-strewn staircase and eventually emerged into Collinson Street. 'Oh my God!' cried David. 'Look at it! Just look at it!'

Jack, who was a pace or two behind, stood aghast as he

surveyed the scene. There at the far end of the street, in beautiful moonlight, a six-storey block of flats was spread out into the road like a small mountain of builders' hardcore. 'My wife and boy are under that lot,' sobbed David, as he sat down on the kerb and just stared as if unable to take in the full horror of it all.

'C'mon,' urged Jack, pulling the policeman to his feet once more. 'Me daughter's there too. Let's see what we can do.'

The first of the rescuers had already arrived at the scene and the most obvious danger was the bulging walls. There could be no possible survivors from the flats themselves but if anyone had survived in the basement shelters – and that offered barely the remotest of hopes – then they had to be dug out. However, to dig them out would mean working beneath an eighty-foot wall that looked like the first breeze or explosion would make it collapse like a house of cards.

Amongst the first of the official rescuers were the fire brigade from the Southwark station two minutes up the road. The senior fire officer immediately made a pronouncement. 'I don't care who is beneath that lot but no one is to go near that rubble. That exterior wall is going to come down any minute and I'm not losing any of my men needlessly.'

'But I can't just stand by here and do nothing!' shrieked David. 'My wife and kid are down there!'

'Control yourself, man!' ordered the fire officer. 'Look, see that?' He pointed at two gushing pipes. 'These are only two but there are another half-dozen scattered around somewhere and they are all flooding those basements. If the poor devils are not dead already then they'll be drowned within minutes. It's an impossible task.'

''Ow about the panels?' said Jack. 'We could try 'em.'

'Panels?' queried the fire officer. 'What panels?'

'Each basement shelter 'as a small, thin section o' wall,' explained Jack, 'so it can be cut into from next door.'

'I didn't know that!' exclaimed the fireman. 'Quick, Percy,' he called to a firemen standing close by. 'Go with this warden and copper and see what you can do about cutting through from one of the basements further down the street. Take all the tools you think you'll need, but hurry, man, hurry!' As a burst of shrapnel suddenly cascaded down so the three men raced down towards the first undamaged basement.

The water level in Grace's shelter indicated the fire officer had not been too pessimistic in his prediction. It was almost hip deep and the children had been lifted onto the bunks. At the rate it was going, another ten minutes would see it at ceiling level. Suddenly a rumbling noise caused them all to stop and stare at the panel. A hole appeared and the tip of a pickaxe emerged; their neighbours had finally made it through. Their cheers were stifled, however, when they saw the spurt of water that accompanied it. As the section of wall fell away they could see the water level next door was marginally higher than their own and flowing in fast.

Maggie Tozer let out a terrible scream. 'I knew it, I knew it,' she sobbed.

'Wait, listen!' cried Grace. 'We must all go through the hole and try to escape through the opposite panel. The wall behind us is going to fall in any minute so we have no choice anyway, we must vacate this shelter. Come on, at least we now have some decent tools. Let's all have a go at that panel.'

The shelterers in the fourth basement were mortified when they realised they had been digging in the wrong direction, but everyone now realised the urgency of the situation.

The children were passed through the hole and one by one the adults began to scramble after them. Grace was just squeezing through the hole when a great rumbling from behind her told its own story. The bulging west wall had finally succumbed and the water in the shelter was forced across the basement and almost catapulted her through the hole into the fourth shelter. '*Block it! Block,*' someone shouted, '*or we're all dead!*'

Ignoring the cries of the dozen or so left in the third basement, mattresses, coats, bedding and anything else that could be stuffed into the hole were not just pushed into it, but actually held in place. Within thirty seconds the cries from beyond the rising water changed to gurgles, then ceased. 'Hold the children's heads above the water level,' shouted Grace. 'And we *must*, we *must* knock that other panel down!'

She had barely said the words when a great thumping could be heard coming from the panel to basement five. 'Someone's trying to get through,' screeched a female voice. 'Oh holy mother of Joseph!'

'Well, they'd better make it double quick,' said a slow-speaking man from the shadows, 'because unless I'm mistaken . . . I smell gas.'

Grace sniffed deeply. Gas? Yes, of course there was gas! If the water pipes had burst then the gas pipes would obviously follow. They had all been so preoccupied that they had not noticed it. She closed her eyes and prayed silently. 'Oh God! If you let us out of this I'll send the kids away, I swear I will. I swear it!'

A loud rumble from behind her indicated that great sections of the basement they had just vacated were on the move and at the same time the panel fell in and a filthy-looking trio of faces peeked through the hole. One sweat-covered fireman, one bearded warden and a particularly dirty policeman.

'Kids first, quick!' ordered the fireman.

Grace passed the children through with surprising speed but just as she prepared to follow, the whole basement shook as if in an earthquake. To be the wrong side of the hole would mean instant death and of the two dozen people remaining, two, perhaps three, might conceivably make it. Within a split second the law of the jungle took over. There was a screeching, clawing and fighting but suddenly Jackie Blackwell's great arms reached in and snatched her like a doll from a pram. She could feel the skin being torn from her legs as she was dragged over the sharp edges of the hole. Before she fainted she was also aware that one other person had followed her. Mercifully she did not see, nor did she hear, the death-throes and curses of the remainder.

She was gradually aware of a bewildering rocking and bumping as she began to reassemble her wits. She felt feverishly hot, yet the clothes that hung on her were icy and wet. In fact everything about her seemed wet and her legs hurt like hell. But where was she? She opened her eyes wide and discovered she was slung over a fireman's shoulder, a panting, running fireman. On either side of them and also running were David and Jack. David had slung Benjamin over his left shoulder whilst Jack had the still dozy Freddie over his right shoulder and Rosie, kicking and complaining, under his left arm. But why were they running? She lifted her head and instantly saw the reason. Slowly disintegrating behind them were huge sections of Queen's Buildings that had originally appeared to have survived the explosion. Finally clear of the immediate danger, all three men wheezed to a stop and breathlessly lowered their charges to the pavement.

'Where we goin', Dad?' asked Benjamin, as if he were discussing a walk up the park.

'School, son,' said his gasping father. 'Charles Dickens School, to be exact. You're all going to stay there until we can get you out of this hell hole and send you somewhere safe in the country. All three of you can go together. You'd like that, wouldn't you?'

'Not much,' sniffed Rosie.

'Why ever not?' cried the now distraught Grace.

'I think it's too quiet. Besides, I'm frightened of earwigs,' said the girl sulkily.

'You think it's too—' began an incredulous David. He put both hands on his head and shook it vigorously. Looking up at the sky it appeared full of planes, shells, searchlights and smoke. With raised eyebrows he turned to Jack Blackwell. 'She's frightened of earwigs,' he said disbelievingly. 'Well . . . I can understand that, can't you, Jack?'

'Yeh,' replied Jack, matter-of-factly. 'She takes after 'er muvver – she didn't like 'em either.'

14

Sergeant Duncan Forbes stood rigidly at attention in front of the CO's desk. Lance Corporal Albie Shinn stood equally stiffly beside him. They had been in the room for some ten minutes and the lieutenant-colonel had yet to lift his head from the papers in front of him. When he did so he appeared preoccupied.

'Eh?' he said, as if seeing them for the first time. 'Oh, sit down, sit down.' He waved them each to a chair. He then rose from his desk and walked across the room to a large wall map of Guernsey. 'Right, gentlemen,' he said in a sharp clipped tone. 'Before we start let's get one thing clear. You are not expected to fight the war on your own. I want no heroics. I want no Victoria Crosses. I just want you to do the job you are sent to do and return back safely. I look for nothing else. This is not for your welfare, believe me. You have been trained at great expense and the army would like to recoup some of its expenditure. Got that?'

The double 'Yessir' spoke for itself.

'Apparently Mr Churchill does not like inactivity. Therefore, we are mounting dozens of small raids on enemy installations up and down their coastline. Clear?'

'Yessir!'

'Good. Your target is the ammunition dump here,' he thrust a stubby finger into the map as if destroying it himself, 'and the petrol storage depot there. It's a half-mile inland from Petit

Port on the south coast of Guernsey. You'll be landed by submarine and picked up same time twenty-four hours on. Got it?' This time he did not even wait for an acknowledgement. 'This country cannot yet mount an offensive of any size but we must not vegetate. I'm fully aware these small raids are nothing more to the enemy than pin-pricks. *But* – he doesn't know when they are coming and he doesn't know where. Twenty men in ten pairs can cause a huge reaction in a defending force, out of all proportion to what they actually accomplish. If you succeed in this venture, for the next few weeks every kraut sentry will be a bundle of nerves. Guards will be doubled and they'll fire at anything that moves. False alarms will be commonplace, whilst you'll be back here with your feet up eating egg-and-chips in the NAAFI. Any questions?'

'Will we be getting any help from the inhabitants, sir?' asked Duncan.

'No, Sergeant. There's a reason for that. At this moment in the occupation we don't know whom we can trust. Of course if you balls things up and are stuck, it may be worth a chance. But don't assume because they are British they are on your side. Life's not as tidy as that. Go in, do the job, get out.'

'But it won't take us a whole day to cover the distance from the shore to the targets, sir,' pointed out Duncan. 'We could do the whole thing in two hours.'

'No you couldn't,' contradicted the lieutenant-colonel. 'The tide wouldn't let you, for starters. The sub will drop you half a mile off-shore and meet you in the same place. I suggest you don't blow the dump immediately you arrive because Jerry will be awfully annoyed with you and you'll still be on the island for another twenty-two hours. We'd like you to reconnoitre a few other installations while you're in the area. Better do that first and blow both the dump and the storage depot on your way out. Agreed?'

Duncan felt that it would have mattered little whether he agreed or not, so he responded with as brief a 'Yessir' as he could make it.

'Okay. Report to Company Sergeant Major Beatty who'll fill you in on the technicalities. Good luck.'

And so it was, five days later, the two Commandos found themselves in the cramped cabin of the captain of HMS *Terror*, a small, 'T' class submarine, thirty feet below the suface of the Atlantic and two miles off Jerbourg Point, Guernsey. 'You'll get your marker from here.' He pointed at the chart. 'It's called Dog and Lion Rock. Go straight in with it on your port side and you should be able to climb the rocks at the end of the inlet. It's all quite clearly marked there on the map. You're blessed with luck because the barometer is set fair for the next twenty-four hours, although after that a gale could blow up. It'll be dark in thirty minutes so I'll surface then and return at the same time tomorrow. Two of my men are now inflating your dinghy so you should be under way without too much delay. If anything does go wrong I will also return once more at the same time the following day but that will be final. Have you got everything?'

'Think so, sir,' replied Duncan, blacking his face. 'If not we'll send you a letter.'

'Lousy idea, Sergeant,' said the straight-faced captain. 'Once at sea we never open the door to strangers.'

The inflatable dinghy had been purloined from one of the vast army stores in Didcot where it had been stowed away as unused gear of some long disbanded army survey team. 'Bit ancient,' said the captain apologetically, 'but it's the best your mob could do. They claim that anything more modern has been grabbed by the Fleet Air Arm. Don't know what it's like, it's still in its container.' He turned to the sailor who was in the process of unwrapping it. 'Okay, Crookston, inflate the thing.'

Crookston began to do so but it did not take long for the

captain to realise one very important difficulty; once inflated, a dinghy that was specifically designed to explore the upper reaches of the Zambezi River would not go through the exit from a 'T' class submarine. 'Good God,' exclaimed the skipper. 'It's bloody enormous! It's like building a ship in your front room! Didn't it have a bloody size shown on it, man?'

'No, skipper,' said Crookston almost tearfully.

The captain sucked his teeth for a moment. 'Right!' he said finally. 'Well then, there's two choices. Firstly, we abandon the whole thing and return to Devonport. Or secondly, we take it up on the surface only partially inflated and finish blowing it up on deck.'

'Well then, we must take the second option sir, surely?' pleaded Duncan.

'Hmm,' muttered the captain. 'The trouble with that option is that while we're blowing up the dinghy, some bloody Jerry might be blowing *us* up.' He stared at the partly-inflated craft. 'Only the British army would be disorganised enough to send me a dinghy half the size of Wales to be launched in the dark in enemy waters from a submarine only marginally longer than a punt.' He paused again and stood back thoughtfully. 'Okay then, let's do it . . . but I tell you this, it's *not* coming back on *my* boat. Once we pick you up tomorrow, we'll cut it loose. With any luck the German navy will pursue it, thinking it's an aircraft carrier.'

A 'T' class submarine is not the most spacious craft at the best of times but manoeuvring a rubber dinghy with a will of its own was, as Able Seaman Crookston aptly observed, 'Like pushing a greased hippo through a swing-door.'

The carefully arranged timetable was soon thrown into disarray and it was almost an hour before Duncan and Albie sat in the dinghy and watched as the submarine slipped slowly back under the waves. The dinghy was certainly much larger than the pair had anticipated and Duncan was relieved the sea was mill-pond calm. The night, though moonless, was only partially cloudy and the cliffs at Jerbourg could just be discerned against the starry sky.

'Our big problem is going to be,' said Duncan, 'where to hide this bloody thing for the next twenty-four hours.'

'Couldn't we deflate it?' suggested Albie. 'We could fold it up then.'

'Oh yes,' said Duncan acidly, 'and supposing Jerry is on our tail and we need to leave in a hurry, what then? Don't forget they had a decent inflator on the sub. You and me would need a bloody transformer.' He shook his head. 'No, we'll just have to chance it. We'll look for some suitable rocks. Hey, look, over there to the right, they must be the Dog and Lion. Well, we're dead on course, that's one blessing.'

It was indeed a blessing. By good fortune as much as anything else, they had come to the exact spot on shore and could step onto a small boulder without as much as dampening their feet. After stacking their explosives and ammunition above the high-tide mark, they looked around for a suitable hiding place for the dinghy. After a few minutes they seemed to have found one. A large rock partially screened a short blind cave. It was not a perfect location, by any means, but it could only be seen from the sea and was better than they had dared hope. 'We'll need a marker for this spot,' said Duncan. 'It may be a lot darker when we come back tomorrow.'

They both looked hopefully around until Albie pointed at two rather odd-shaped rocks just a few yards away. 'There,' he cried, 'that'll do it. We'll remember them all right, won't we?'

'Will we?' asked the puzzled Duncan. 'What's so special about them? They look just like all the other rocks to me.'

The lance corporal gave a weary sigh. 'Lack of imagination, I'm afraid, Sarge. Look, can't yer see it? Stand 'ere.' He took his colleague by the shoulder and turned him slightly. 'Now tell me what yer see.'

Duncan did as he was bid and stared at the rock for some seconds. 'Nope,' he said. 'Still looks like every other rock.'

'That first rock's pointing in a straight line, yeh?'

Duncan nodded.

'Very well, now look at the second rock. Don't yer see, the middle of it curves into a deep vee. If it was possible ter push this rock into that rock, you'd have sexual intercourse between rocks. So all we'll need ter do is ter look fer two rocks 'avin' it off.'

'God but you're a pervert, Shinn,' said Duncan. 'Still, it's not a bad idea. Come on, what're you waiting for? Give us a hand.' After a few oaths and scraped knuckles the dinghy appeared to be reasonably well concealed and the two men picked up their backpacks and hurried from the shore.

They had barely climbed over the escarpment when a small slither of stones rolled down from a thick bush some twelve feet up the more gently sloping part of the cliff face. A blacked-up face slowly appeared, followed by a man in a thick jersey and seaboots. He made no further move until he was sure both Commandos had left the scene. Finally satisfied, he slithered down the slope and looked into the cave. On seeing the dinghy he gave a little whistle of surprise. He began to examine it closely. Curiosity satisfied, he pushed it even further into the concealed recess and made his way thoughtfully up the cliff face, picking up a large fishing net on his way. Once at the top he delved into some gorse bushes and pulled out a rusty old cycle. Squeezing through a gateway Charles Dupre then cycled away over a narrow path towards a distant farmhouse.

In the farmhouse the lovely Roselyn Dupre had only slept fitfully throughout her husband's absence. He had been gone for some hours now and although their relationship was by no means harmonious, she was always on edge during these nocturnal trips. She heard the squeaking of the front gate which was followed by footsteps on the gravel at the side of the house.

The rattle of the key in the back door was the final indication of his return. His footsteps on the stairs caused her some surprise. It meant that he had not removed his heavy fishing boots. But why? He never wore them in the house, she would never allow it. He would kick them off as soon as he entered the small lean-to conservatory. She gave a sigh of exasperation and, as the footsteps reached the landing, she turned to face the bedroom door.

'Rozz,' he called almost before he was in the room. 'Roselyn, you awake?'

'I'm hardly likely to be anything else with you clumping all over the place, now am I?' she replied tersely. 'So what's the excitement?'

As he sat on the edge of the bed, she put a match to the small night-light that stood on a saucer on the bedside locker, then swung her long legs down and faced him. The shadows danced for a moment before settling down into their respective places. In spite of his eagerness to recount the last thirty minutes, and also of the abrasiveness of their relationship, he still found himself impressed by her beauty. How, he wondered, could someone who looked so angelic be so mean in almost every respect? For almost the entire eight years of their marriage he had been the classic henpecked husband. He had carried out her every wish, as far as he was capable, yet it had never been enough. He knew the remedy had always been in his own hands but he also knew it was now too late. He should have drawn the battle lines long ago; now he no longer had the will or the inclination. Even at this moment he was excited by her, the wispy pink nightie she wore covered everything yet concealed nothing. Every curve, every hollow, every slope of her body mocked him. He was a thirty-year-old man, with all the desires, lusts and fantasies that absorb thirty-year-old men. Part of him wanted to reach out instinctively to touch, feel and caress her but there was an invisible barrier. The barrier was her mean, selfish nature that had long before destroyed his love. Now it had also put paid to his passion.

'Okay,' she said curtly, 'what is it this time? One of these nights you're going to break the curfew once too often and some eager German sentry is going to put five rounds into your arse before you've even fallen off your bike.'

'I was down at Petit Port with my nets when I saw a dinghy coming ashore. The voices were English and they hid the dinghy behind some rocks. I assume by that they will be returning for it. It was quite a large one and I was thinking . . .' his voice trailed away as if he were almost afraid to finish the sentence.

'Well, go on,' she ordered. 'The fact that you were actually thinking is a step in the right direction. What were you thinking?'

'Well, if they are returning for it, they are hardly likely to do it in daylight, so . . .' he faltered again for a moment. 'Well . . . if they return, say, tomorrow night, I'd like to join them and go to England. I'd be more useful there than I am here . . . to the war effort, I mean.'

'You!' she sneered. 'What use are you going to be to anyone? In any case, they are hardly likely to have arrived in a dinghy to organise a recruiting drive. Be sensible for once in your life. Are you sure they were English and there were only two of them?'

'Positive!'

'The question then is why are they here?'

'Perhaps they are carrying out some raid or other,' he suggested.

'What, just two of them? I hardly think so.'

'Well, it could be a little raid,' he persisted. 'There are enough small targets scattered around the island.'

'If anyone hears you talking like that, Charles Dupre,' she snapped, 'you'll be up before the Military Tribunal and deported – if not shot.'

'I've a suggestion,' he said in a tentative tone. 'Why don't we wait to see what happens in the next couple of days? You know, an explosion or fire or such like? If that happens, I could go to the dinghy and wait for their return and ask to join them. The dinghy is big enough for a dozen people, it's huge.'

'And where does that leave me, pray?'

'I don't understand,' he said in a puzzled tone. 'You want to come too?'

'No, you fool,' she said. 'I mean, what happens to me when the Germans find out my husband has gone off with a British army raiding party? They are hardly likely to make me the Guernsey Queen, are they?'

He rose and walked to the window. Moving back the curtain an inch or so, he gazed at the first rays of dawn coming up over the distant Sark. 'I never thought of that,' he admitted, 'but it makes no difference, I'm going anyway.'

'But you'll more than likely be killed, you idiot . . . me too, if they find out.'

'I couldn't think of a better reason for going, then,' he said quietly as he walked out of the room.

Her mind raced as she watched him go. A whole combination of thoughts ran through her head. She could betray him to the Germans and they might even catch the two Englishmen in the bargain. She cared little for them one way or the other but then again the Germans had made life so much more difficult that she could not see why she should help them either. No, he was acting out a little boy's fantasy, he had obviously not thought it through. He saw himself as some hero instead of the rabbit he really was. If the English soldiers didn't kill him the Germans probably would. Well, good riddance; once he was gone she could reshape her life.

She quite liked the idea of being a widow. Perhaps even a merry widow. At twenty-nine she had most of her life still before her and when this war was over, whoever won, she had a house, some land and the potential for expansion. A potential that her husband would never have the ambition to exploit in a million years. Yes, that was it, she would simply let matters take their natural course. She had a feeling that in the next day or so things would change and it would be a change for the better. She looked in the dressing table mirror and, turning her body first one way, then the other, liked what she saw. Slipping back into bed, she shivered as she found the sheets had chilled, but that was a small thing when your life was about to change. She hugged herself and drew her knees up tight and, with a serene smile on her lovely face, went soundly to sleep.

Her guess that her husband was living out a boyish fantasy may have been closer than she realised. He suddenly felt that for the first time in his life he could make a mark. He could actually be somebody, do something. Perhaps in years to come people in St Peter Port would speak of him in awed tones as the one who rescued the English soldiers and escaped with them to Britain. Who knows, perhaps his old school might put his name on a plaque?

The first thing to do was to make preparations. He must not carry any identification; after all, this was his personal sacrifice, he did not want his wife to share it. He went to his shed at the end of the garden. It was here that he would usually seek solitude, it was here that he would frequently close the door and shut out the world. He lay on the bunk staring at the ceiling and thought of all the adventures that were now before him. Though dawn had long broken and he had not been to bed, sleep was the furthest thing from his mind.

Suddenly he realised that although he might be leaving, there were many animals on the farm that would still require attention. Perhaps he should take Dan Duquemin into his confidence – after all, he seemed a trustworthy sort of bloke. Dan had been employed as a part-time dairyman for some twenty years. Firstly by Charles' father, then three years ago, when the old man died, by Charles himself. Dan would come in every morning and deal with the milking and feed the poultry. He would then busy himself around the place until eleven o'clock. Yes, that was it, he would speak to Dan and ask if he would take on the running of the farm for the duration of the war. Dan could keep the profits but would simply be required to hand back the reins when Charles made his heroic return. He was not sure what Roselyn would make of it but, what the hell? Who cared? Rising from the bunk, he wandered down to the cattle stalls where Dan was already busy milking. 'Mornin', Dan,' he said. 'I've a proposition to make to you.' He pulled up another stool and sat by the curious dairyman.

Meantime, matters had not been going too well for the two Commandos. Their good luck with the weather seemed to have deserted them when they discovered they had run into a German garrison unit carrying out manoeuvres. Far from being able to reconnoitre the German installations, their greatest difficulty had been to avoid colliding with them. They had spent most of the time since they landed crawling through one hedgerow after another.

'We'll have to cut our losses, Albie,' whispered Duncan. 'The reconnoitre'll have to go by the board. We'll lie low till dark. We need to be in this vicinity, though, because it's central to the targets and the boat. We'll look for somewhere as secluded as possible and stay there until midnight, okay?'

Albie pointed to a small wood at the end of their hedgerow. 'Looks as good as any, wouldn't yer say, Sarge?'

Duncan nodded and sliding in behind his lance corporal, followed him along the muddy ditch. They were just yards short when a stage whisper came through from the other side of the hedgerow. 'Don't shoot!' it hissed. 'I'm a friend. Can I speak to you?' Before the sentence was finished the barrels of two .45 tommy guns were directed at the solid chest of Charles Dupre and two fingers had already curled around the triggers.

217

Duncan glanced meaningfully at Albie and silently pointed to the newcomer.

Albie nodded and called, 'Okay, friend, step forward – but slowly.'

Duncan then turned apprehensively and scanned the area behind them whilst sweeping it with the sights of his gun. 'It's all right,' hissed the voice, 'there's no one around except my dairyman in the cowshed and my wife in bed – no one at all.'

'Well, if no one's around,' replied Albie, 'what's 'alf the bleedin' German army doin' on the other side of the road?'

'They are on local manoeuvres on the strip of land between the road and the coast. They'll not come here,' he assured them.

'Okay,' whispered Duncan. 'Slide slowly – very slowly, mark you – into this ditch and tell us what you want.'

'I want to join you,' said the newcomer. 'I want to join you in your dinghy and return to England with you. If you agree, I'll get you out of this mess, that's a promise.'

'How d'you know about the dinghy?' asked Duncan sharply.

'I was fishing during the curfew when I saw you come ashore,' answered Dupre. 'I didn't know who you were at first but now I know I'm sure I can help you. By the amount of Germans milling around, you certainly could do with it,' he added, playing a trump card.

Duncan's instincts told him to ignore the offer but at the same time he knew the man's local knowledge would be invaluable. He came to a rapid decision; he would partially accept Dupre's offer but only later tell him they would not take him to the submarine. 'Who are you?' he asked curtly.

'Charles Dupre, that's my small farm beyond that field. I want to get away to England to fight.'

'D'you know a place we could hole up till dark then, Charles?' asked Duncan.

'Yes,' answered Dupre eagerly, 'my shed, it's comfortable

and close by and no one goes there except me.'

'Lead on, then,' said Duncan, 'but remember we're right behind you and as yet we're still not sure of your story. Off you go.' He gestured with the barrel of his gun and Dupre nodded and led them into a field of kale which was of sufficient height to cover their crawl.

The shed was far better than Duncan had expected, and he took the opportunity to interview Dupre at length. On their arrival at the farm the dairyman had gone but Roselyn Dupre later stumbled onto them when she entered seeking some logs that were kept at the rear. Albie promptly seized her and forced her to sit whilst Duncan carried out a brief interrogation.

Her enthusiasm for her husband's departure certainly surprised Duncan: he suspected she had ulterior motives but he dismissed it as a domestic matter and not of his concern. However, when he told her she would not be allowed to leave the farm until long after the three had vacated the premises, her mood changed. 'Why ever not?' she demanded haughtily. 'I have a right to come and go as I please.'

'Not whilst I'm here, you don't,' said Duncan quietly. 'When I'm here you will do as *I* please. What you do after we go is of no consequence to me.'

'I tell you I *will* go,' she persisted.

'Madam,' he said icily, 'believe me. You will not.'

There was something in his tone that made her shiver, but it was not out of fear, she was not a fearful person. No one had spoken to her like that since she was a child. For the moment it seemed to disorientate her and for the first time since Charles Dupre had known her, she seemed to be at a loss for words. Charles quite enjoyed her discomfort.

As dusk approached, the trio prepared for their departure and Charles gave a stilted and embarrassing farewell to his wife. Duncan thought this was the appropriate moment to tell them of a change of plan. 'Charles, what time does your dairyman arrive?' he asked.

'Usually a little after dawn,' replied Dupre.

'Does he ever enter the house, or just the cattle stalls?'

'Just the stalls. Why?'

Ignoring the question he continued, 'Do you have a telephone here?'

'No, look, what's all this about?'

'Good,' said Duncan. 'Well I'm sorry, Mrs Dupre, but I cannot risk you wandering around. So I intend to tie you up in your bedroom and leave a note for the dairyman to release you when he arrives at dawn.' He glanced at his watch. 'Say in some eight hours. By then we should be well clear. So if you wish to avail yourself of the lavatory, do it now because you'll find it difficult for the next few hours.'

'*What!*' she screamed. 'It's disgusting! You'll do no such thing!'

'Madam, I have three lives at stake here. Set beside that, your disgust doesn't matter a toss but if it makes you happier I'll write you a letter of apology after the war.'

Albie wondered how Charles Dupre would take this, but if anything he seemed to be enjoying it. 'Charles, do something,' she pleaded.

'I'm sorry, my dear, but he's right; we can't afford the risk. But don't worry, one day you'll look back on this and laugh, mark my words.'

'I'll mark your throat!' she hissed. 'You gutless swine.'

'Do you wish to use the lavatory of your own accord or do I "pot" you, ma'am?' said Duncan curtly.

She snatched up a coat and strode briskly towards the kitchen door. 'This is unpardonable!' she cried. 'Even the Nazis would never do this!'

'Lance Corporal Shinn,' he commanded, 'escort the young

lady to the outside toilet. She is to go straight there and come straight back.'

'Sergeant!' acknowledged the lance corporal, barely able to conceal a grin.

Ten minutes later, Duncan had finished securing Roselyn Dupre to the bed with an assortment of scarves and sheets. She could move around the bed, but couldn't escape. 'And supposing the dairyman doesn't come here in the morning. What then?' she demanded.

'Then there's a chamber-pot under the bed, ma'am,' replied Duncan. 'You might just about reach it, it'll be okay, no one will be looking. Anyway, it's now time for us to go. Farewell, it's been a pleasure to meet you.'

'I hope the Germans shoot you . . . *All* of you!' she snarled.

As they left the house Duncan took hold of Charles Dupre's arm. 'Listen,' he said, 'Albie and me both have on our uniforms beneath our denims. Once we've hit our targets we'll take off our denims, which may just possibly stop the Germans shooting us as spies. You have no uniform, so they'd shoot you without question. Still sure you want to go through with this?'

'Of course.'

'Right! Enough said,' snapped Duncan. 'Take us first on the quickest route to the petrol storage depot, then secondly to the ammunition dump. Whatever you do, though, don't talk. If you want to communicate give us a sign. Off you go.'

The calm weather had faded and a strong south-westerly was beginning to announce its presence. Sloping rain stung their faces they bent even lower to traverse the kale field. Duncan viewed the storm with mixed feelings. There would certainly be less chance of being spotted than on a moonlit night but the thought of handling that dinghy in anything other than a friendly sea had no appeal at all.

It was all nearly too easy. They set fuses at the first place, then scampered to repeat the procedure at the second. They had reached the shoreline before the first explosion occurred and they had extricated the dinghy before the second. It was then that their luck ran out. The only German patrol venturing out that night had just climbed a rock at Petit Port neatly in time to see two men trying to launch a large dinghy. The patrol leader called to them to stop but one of the men turned and, tommy gun in hand, raced towards them, firing frantically. At first the patrol was taken by surprise but as they took up defensive positions, the overall picture became clear. The first man was holding them with his tommy gun, whilst the second was trying desperately to launch the dinghy.

The dark and the rocks were preventing a clear shot so the patrol leader tossed over two grenades. The first instantly killed the man with the tommy gun and the second appeared to fall short of the figure who had finally launched the dinghy. However, it landed on a rock that disintegrated with such force that it virtually took off his head, which fell into the sea whilst his remains hung over the side of the dinghy. Two of the Germans then stepped over the dead lance corporal and advanced cautiously towards both the gory remains and the dinghy. When they were barely three yards away, a wave, slightly more vigorous than its predecessors, tugged the dinghy into the swirling shallows. One of the soldiers waded into the water but before he could reach out, the dinghy was tugged away yet again and, gradually gathering momentum, swirled away into the darkness.

Duncan Forbes had sat crouched behind a rock with a jammed tommy gun for the whole of the forty seconds the attack had taken. As he saw it he had three options. The first was to launch a surprise attack of his own – but his gun had jammed. The second was to surrender, but he had no doubt they would kill him. The third was to keep quiet and put as much distance as possible between him and them and see what happened. It was really no contest. He eased the useless tommy gun into a spot where it should hopefully be seen and slowly inched himself away from the place. The rocky ground blessedly left no tracks and he was a hundred yards away from the immediate area when excited German voices indicated that his tommy gun had been found. They now had two guns and two bodies; he hoped they would not come looking for a third. He was not too far wrong in his assumptions. The patrol did make a cursory search of the area but basically were so pleased with their night's handiwork that they longed to get back to base to recount it.

He had reached the kale field and paused to bury his denim overalls before he really gave thought to his destination. It would be light in an hour and he knew little or nothing about the surrounding countryside, except for the Dupre farm. It was true the dairyman had probably not yet arrived but Roselyn Dupre was hardly likely to welcome him with open arms. Perhaps if he could shelter there for the day, he could then ask the woman the best place to steal a boat at nightfall – after he had told her she was a widow!

As he passed the cowshed he remembered the note left for the cowman. He retrieved it and had soon secured an entry to the house. He had no wish to frighten the woman in case she screamed, so he called, 'It's okay, we're back,' as cheerily as he could and pretended he was having a conversation as he climbed the stairs that led to her bedroom. On opening the door, the dishevelled state of the bed told him she had made a vigorous if unsuccessful attempt at escape. It seemed his Boy Scout knots had held better than he had hoped.

'Changed your mind and come back to gloat, have you?' she muttered. 'I heard the explosions. I suppose you're pleased with your handiwork? I don't imagine you've given much thought to what the Germans will now do to us civilians. And what was that shooting? You've never let that useless husband of mine loose with a gun, surely?' she added bitterly.

He sat beside her on the bed and began to undo her bindings. 'I'm afraid your husband is dead, ma'am,' he said quietly. 'It's of scant consolation, I know, but he died bravely and instantly without knowing what had hit him.'

She sat furiously rubbing her shins and forearms as the last of the bindings were removed. 'Pity,' she snapped, 'my prayers were not fully answered after all.'

'Ma'am?' he queried.

'I knew the fool would not survive but I was hoping he would die slowly for all the distress he's caused me. Still, you can't have everything, can you?'

He said nothing at first, then offered her the glass of water that stood on the locker by the side of the bed. He watched her as she drank so quickly that part of it ran down her face and spilled onto the front of her crumpled blouse. 'Hah,' she panted, 'that's better, much better.'

'Not really,' he said calmly. 'You've spilt some of it down your clothing. Here, let me help you.' He reached forward but, before he could do anything else, she had grabbed the neck of her blouse, and shredded it from her shoulders. Her crumpled peasant-style skirt was ripped off in the same way.

She then seized her knickers with one hand and her bra with the other. Her breasts tumbled out as the bra undid easily but her knickers resisted. As she tugged them fiercely, Duncan, recovering from his shock at her shameless reaction, finally wrenched them from her and spanked her plump bare buttocks with a series of stinging blows. 'You cow!' he hissed. 'You unfeeling cow!' She twisted back to face him again, now naked except for frayed and ripped stockings. Though tears welled up from the pain in her buttocks, she placed her hands on her hips and, leaning forward, put her face almost to his. 'Am I supposed to feel remorseful?' she snarled. 'Because I don't.' With that she clawed at his face and drew blood before she kissed his mouth with an intensity that evoked a passionate mix of anger and hunger from deep within him. Four hands tore frantically at his uniform until somehow it parted from his body. He even managed to kick off his army boots without ever recollecting how he did it. He penetrated her with a ferocity he never dreamed he possessed but, no matter how hard he thrust, her nails, mouth, and teeth never once relented. At the peak of his passion he suddenly wondered how long he could do this for before he died. Or even how long he had been doing it, because he had lost all sense of time. Whether it was two minutes or two hours he knew not, but suddenly it felt like someone had painlessly removed his skeletal frame as he flopped back onto the bed. He opened and closed his eyes several times whilst his chest heaved like the ground swell of an earthquake. 'Bloody hell,' he finally panted, 'I think I've been raped!'

'Not yet you haven't, sweetie,' she smiled, as she suddenly twisted over and sat astride him. 'But you're about to be.'

15

Because of the volume of casualties that night, most civilian hospitals and First Aid Posts were packed with patients so a Royal Artillery gunner, on sick leave from his unit, decided he might be better served at Millbank Military Hospital, a mile and a half distant. Once he told of the carnage at the old flats, the matron gave Julia leave, in the hope that she would find Grace and the children. Running through the shrapnel-showered streets, she reached the tenements at a time of mass confusion. Most of the wardens who would have known the casualties were either dead, or themselves buried beneath the buildings they had tried to protect. There was nothing to see at the scene except dozens of uniformed people digging over a vast pile of smoking rubble. In addition a few stumbling figures wandered vaguely around asking everyone – plaintively and repeatedly – if they had seen their family or friends.

'D'yer know what's happened to the family from thirty-two?'

''Ave yer seen a tall woman and a blind old lady?'

'Ain't seen a black-an'-white mongrel, 'ave yer? Dark patch over 'is left eye. Friendly little thing. Won't bite . . . honest. Name's Wilf . . . but 'e'll come if yer calls 'im Stinks.'

She found herself seizing a shell-shocked old man sitting on a kerbside staring at the ruins. 'What's happened to the survivors?' she demanded. At first he ignored her but after she repeated the question twice, he muttered, 'If they're alive, they're either at the hospital or the school rest-centre. If they're dead, they're either under there,' he pointed at the rubble, 'or they're scattered over every street between 'ere an' the river . . . an' they're the lucky ones.'

A feeling of nausea surged over her as she felt sure that if they were not in the school, she would never see them again. White-faced and tearful she ran blindly from the scene, hugging the walls of the houses as closely as possible because of the falling shrapnel. 'Don't walk there, you dopy cow!' called a distant male voice from heaven knew where. 'Look at the wall!' She glanced up and saw the front wall of the three-storey house bulging over the pavement like the pregnant belly of a vast prehistoric ape. She leaped from the pavement, half-falling half-staggering the remaining four streets to the school.

Charles Dickens Primary School had been built in 1877. One of the first Board Schools, it was neat and compact, built to replace scores of tiny slum dwellings in the heart of Dickens' London. Yet it was doubtful if even Dickens would have envisaged the scene that confronted Julia as she fell breathlessly in the school doorway. Like all schools, the windows were large and no matter how conscientiously the blackout was applied, chinks would still appear. To counteract this, the lighting was dim, bordering on poor. As she peered across the assembly hall, she saw scores of people of all ages, sitting, standing up, lying down and queueing. There were two queues, the first for tea, where the angels from the Women's Voluntary Service performed their customary miracles in impossible surroundings.

The second was longer and it led to a trestle table that was piled high with used clothing and shoes of every sort. Because of the hour, many people, mostly children, were still wearing their night attire and probably shoeless into the bargain. The supply was hardly limitless, so any garment that covered any shape, irrespective of size, colour or condition, would be eagerly seized. Even at a superficial glance Julia thought it was an advantage that the lighting was poor. There was clothing on display there that she would not want to touch in total blackness, never mind place next to her skin. She began to look for an organiser, someone who might have a list of names, anything that could at least help begin her quest.

Suddenly a familiar young voice cut loudly across the hall. 'Oi, Benji! Oi, Freddie! Look, it's Aunt Julia! She's over there by Miss Jones' classroom.' At the sound of Rosie's voice she wheeled round in time to see the three children jumping over the prostrate figures and colliding with many others. At first she barely recognised them, they looked like participants in a grotesque fancy dress ball. Both boys were wearing long stained jerseys which came down well past their shorts. Their socks were ridiculously long with Freddie's pulled up almost until they reached the bottom of his jersey and Benjamin's so baggy that they hung around his ankles like small blankets. It seemed Benjamin had certainly come off worst for footware. Of his two grimy brown plimsolls, the left was laced with string and the right had a hole in the front that showed a great gathering of sock. Still, he had at least bothered to roll his sleeves back to his cuff, whilst Freddie's just flapped about an inch or two beyond his fingertips. On the other hand, Rosie was dressed in a boy's shirt which was of reasonable fit and ankle-length trousers that suited her tomboyish demeanour perfectly and gave her an almost sophisticated appearance.

They each leaped at her like puppies at feeding time. Grasping each one gratefully to her, she closed her eyes in silent thanks and summoned her resolve to ask, 'Where's Mummy ... Daddy and ... er,' she never really knew what title to use in poor Freddie's case, '... your daddy, Rosie?'

'Me dad's gone with Uncle David ter dig fer people in the buildin's,' explained Rosie, 'and Aunt Grace is getting her cuts on her leg mended by the nitty-nurse.'

'The nitty-nurse?' said Julia incredulously. 'The nitty-nurse wouldn't be in the school at this time of night and she'd hardly be attending to Auntie Grace even if she was!'

'I tell yer it *is* the nitty-nurse,' said the indignant Rosie. 'I ought ter know, she's always searchin' me 'ead.'

'Show me,' requested the disbelieving Julia. 'Where is she?'

The children pointed as one to the staircase that led up to the headmistress's room. Rosie promptly led the way as if determined to prove the truth of her utterances. The door was wide open and several people queued at the door. Before they entered Rosie turned to Julia and said, 'Penny bet it's the nitty-nurse?'

'Penny bet,' agreed Julia, stepping into the room.

There, sitting up on a couch and squinting with pain, Grace Diamond was in the process of having two enormous grazes, easily the length of each shin, painted with iodine.

'Sorry, Mrs Diamond,' apologised the nurse, 'but iodine's all we have left. It'll sting for a bit but it'll kill all the germs.'

'There!' exclaimed Rosie smugly. 'Told yer, didn't I?'

The sound of the child's voice caused Grace to open her eyes and, on seeing Julia, shriek with delight. She held her arms wide and Julia fell sobbing into them. The nurse stepped back for a moment but soon interrupted. 'I'm sorry, my dears, but I have several people waiting—'

'Of course, of course,' said Julia. 'Look, would it help if I finished dressing her wounds over there?' She pointed to a second couch. 'I am a nurse ... and family,' she added needlessly.

'An' this lady's the nitty-nurse,' cut in Rosie, 'ain't yer, Miss Evans?'

Miss Evans smiled. 'Well, usually I am, Rosie, but tonight I'm wearing my other hat. That's why I'm trying to mend your Aunt Grace's legs.'

''At? What 'at?' asked the bewildered child. 'Yer ain't got an 'at!'

Julia put one hand on the girl's shoulder and with the other she presented her with a penny. 'She's actually got two hats, Rose,' she said, 'but she's forgotten them both. You win.'

With that she turned to Grace and, as she helped her to the second couch, bombarded her with questions as to how they had survived; how were David and Jackie; what were the plans for the children's evacuation; could they obtain better clothing for them and finally, what could she do to help?

'They will be clothed properly sometime tomorrow,' answered Grace. 'I'll be given a chit in the morning and I can take it to the local shops and rig them out. But first of all I'll need ration cards and money because, other than what we're left standing with, we've lost everything. They tell me I'll get a small allowance from the National Assistance Board but you have to queue most of the day for an interview. Also I'll need to see someone from the council about the children's evacuation. There is no question they must go now, we can't stay here any longer.'

'You said "*they* must go now" but then you said "*we* can't stay here",' queried Julia. 'Don't you propose going with them?'

'Only to see them safely housed,' replied Grace. 'I can't just leave it to David, there is far too much to do. Once the children are settled I'll come back and try to make a home of sorts for their return. Don't forget, David and Jack will need to live somewhere and with the hours they are working they will hardly have time to set up another home ... always providing they could find one, of course.'

'Why don't you let me take the children for you?' asked Julia. 'To the country, I mean. I have some leave due and our military hospital is not as busy as the general hospitals are at the moment. I could probably get a week, or at least a couple of days. Once they are settled, I could return and perhaps you could visit them for a weekend or bank holiday?'

'It would certainly be a great help,' agreed Grace, 'and you'd probably be the only one whose judgement I'd trust enough.'

'Good!' exclaimed Julia. 'Now I'll finish bandaging your shins, then we'll get those kids settled down to sleep. Once we've achieved that I must return to the hospital. I'll call tomorrow evening and see what you've managed to accomplish.'

The next few days were a nightmare for Grace. On the first day she spent six hours queueing for a cash grant at the National Assistance Board. The destruction at Queen's Buildings alone had caused homelessness for some two hundred families but besides that there had been many other houses similarly destroyed throughout that horrendous attack. But the real problem came during the night raids. In the school there was no air raid shelter to speak of and most of the windows were huge affairs and the only protection for those sleeping beneath was to pull the blankets over their heads. Most adults managed this without too much fuss but the children were different. They either slept restlessly, throwing clothes off in every direction, or did not sleep at all, complaining that sleep was impossible with a blanket-covered face.

It was exactly a week before Grace had an evacuation date. Seven days and seven nights, each of which she was convinced would be their last. When she thought of the instant collapse of the solid old tenement and compared the fraility of the school classroom walls, she seriously wondered if they would not be safer sleeping outside in the playground. The idea was only dismissed from her mind when Benjamin, after his regular morning hunt for shrapnel, returned from the playground with five jagged pieces that would have ribboned elephants.

Finally, after the last tearful farewells from their respective parents, some twenty children, together with an escort of a few adults, climbed aboard a three-ton truck that was parked outside the school. 'Where are they going?' was the question most asked. To this obvious query there did not seem an answer. At least not one that anyone knew. 'The children must affix these labels and wear them at all times. Once they have reached their destination, they will be instructed to write, telling of their safe arrival,' recited an important-looking bowler-hatted man with EDUCATION OFFICER emblazoned on the sleeve of his tightly-belted trench-coat.

'Well, if yer think that, yer know sod-all about me daughter . . . or any of the kids, fer that matter,' complained Jackie Blackwell as he tied a label to his daughter's lapel. 'Why can't yer tell us now, before they go?'

'I am not allowed to divulge transportation details. It's more than me job's worth. Remember, careless talk costs lives,' chorused the man, parrot fashion.

'Are yer tryin' ter tell us that where these kids are goin's a national secret?'

'Well they are going to Liverpool Street station,' said the man with a condescending wink, 'but that's purely between ourselves.'

'And if I promise faithfully not to tell 'Itler,' said Jack sarcastically, 'where do they go from there?'

'Norfolk, Dad,' whispered Rosie.

'Norfolk?' asked her father ''Ow'd yer know that, gel?'

'I saw it on that bit of paper 'e's got in 'is 'and.'

'Oh dear,' cried the education officer, as a worried crease crossed his brow. 'This could be a breach of the Official Secrets Act,' he added, thrusting the papers into a battered brown satchel.

'Good,' exclaimed Jack. 'Then perhaps you'll shove my kid in the Tower? It'll be cheaper than visitin' Norfolk.'

Now that the cat was out of the bag, everyone was trying to recollect anything they had ever heard about Norfolk. The consensus seemed to be that they made rather nice dumplings and the King went there for Christmas. Jack remarked that he did not see this as a twin threat to national security and as such he would not mind overmuch if Hitler did hear of their departure. Then, just as the worried Grace was about to pull the children off the truck, Julia arrived on the back of a motorcycle ridden by an army despatch rider.

'I got a lift,' she explained breathlessly and, seeing the children on the lorry, panted, 'That our truck?'

''Tis indeed,' said Jack, tossing her bag up over the tailboard. ''An yer goin' ter Norfolk. But it's a bit 'ush 'ush, so fer Gawd's sake don't tell anyone.'

To a chorus of goodbyes, a profusion of waves and floods of tears, the lorry clunked into gear and rattled off round the corner through the appropriately named Sanctuary Street.

Liverpool Street station in wartime was one of London's grimiest stations. Soot festooned the walls and the smell of smoke and railway engines pervaded every corner of the vast complex. Like all wartime railway stations it had an aura all its own. It was a place of transition where people paused just before their whole lives were changed, sometimes for better, sometimes for worse. The children seemed to take it in their stride but Julia felt life would never be quite the same again. A door was definitely closing, the test would be whether another door would start to open. On the concourse was a stall, not unlike that of a paper-seller but it had two kindly-looking elderly WVS ladies in attendance. It was there that all evacuees were required to report. The mass migration of the early part of the blitz had long passed and only occasional bursts of evacuees would flood the station. As the Charles Dickens contingent queued to be processed, Benjamin tugged at Julia's coat. 'What's your other name, Aunt Julia?' he surprisingly asked.

She gave the child a puzzled look. 'My other name? If you mean my surname, it's Giles. Why d'you ask?'

He did not reply but pointed to a notice that was attached to the framework of the stall, still a yard or two in front of them. It read URGENT MESSAGE FOR NURSE GILES. They were now so close to the counter that it did not seem worth breaking ranks so it was some ten minutes before Julia introduced herself to one of the ladies. 'Ah yes, m'dear,' she said, 'it's here somewhere.' She scuffled some papers, then read from a small note. 'It says "Telephone ward sister at Millbank Hospital urgently".'

'Nothing else?' asked Julia.

'That's all, my dear,' replied the lady sympathetically. 'Here, see for yourself. It was delivered by a despatch rider barely fifteen minutes ago.'

Julia closed her eyes in frustration. 'Blast!' she said. 'There goes my leave, first of the war, too!'

'Oh what a shame, m'dear. Look, I'll tell them they must have missed you, shall I?'

'No,' sighed Julia reluctantly. 'If they need me, then they need me. You can't just be a nurse when you feel like it. Where's the nearest call box, please?'

After finding the box and sorting out her tuppence, she was finally connected to the ward sister. She was prepared for the disappointment of a cancelled leave but not prepared for the news that a telegram awaited her. 'I'll read it to you, shall I?' offered the sister helpfully.

An involuntary shudder passed over Julia as she suddenly realised it was the first telegram she had ever received. 'Er – yes . . . yes please.' There was just the faint sound of rustling paper before the voice came back. Julia did not hear the first or the last words, but the middle section came over with icy clarity. '. . . regret to inform you that Sergeant Duncan Forbes of the No. 3 Commando unit is missing presumed killed in action . . .' There was also a telephone number which she somehow scrawled on the corner of the WVS lady's note.

She stared through a mist of tears as everything began to blur. Composing herself, she wiped the corners of her eyes with her fingertips and dialled the number. After a brief explanation she was passed to a male voice who said matter-of-factly, 'He had nominated you as his next of kin. He was one of a two-man party. Both Sergeant Forbes and Lance Corporal Shinn were killed instantly.'

'But ... but it says in the telegram ... it says missing *presumed* killed?'

'Yes, that is because we cannot establish death from the presence of the body. However, there were only two men sent on this mission and only two men were killed. Officially Sergeant Forbes is "missing"; in reality he's dead. I'm sorry.'

She stood motionless and slowly lowered the telephone onto its cradle and left her hand resting lightly upon it. How long she was there she did not know but suddenly she was aware of an angry, fat man tapping on the door and pointing sharply at his wrist-watch. 'Oh ... I'm ... I'm sorry,' she murmured as she sidled past him into the bustle of the busy concourse.

She wanted to scream and run to the nearest person and shout 'My Duncan is dead!' but the piercing cry of Rosie cut through her grief. ''Urry up, Aunt Julia, train's goin' in a minute.' Yes, of course, the children had already suffered enough; the last thing she wished to do was to add her distress to theirs. She bit her lip and – as much for her own comfort – she slipped a reassuring arm around the child's shoulder. 'C'mon then, Rose,' she murmured hoarsely, 'let's spit-spot.'

The roof of the station had long been blasted away and the rain that had now begun to fall steadily gave everything an appropriate sombre, wet, black look. She followed the children into the train and, after much slamming of doors, shouts and whistles, there was a rapid tattoo of muffled power as a cloud of white steam billowed past the window and the train creaked into movement. Slowly at first, but then with increasing momentum, the train rounded the east bend out of the station. Soon bomb-damaged roofs began to slip rapidly past, their broken slates shining in the steady falling rain. Julia felt almost glad that the sun was not shining. It would not seem right if the world was brightly lit when its brightest light had just been extinguished.

By the time they reached Tottenham, there was hardly a child that had not undone their lunch pack, and the rhythmic playing of the wheels over the rails had edged Julia into the numbness she desperately needed to remove her mind from reality. Already, throughout this war, she had experienced so much misery she wondered if she could ever be really happy again.

Although there was now little doubt their destination was Norfolk, exactly where in the county was a mystery. No matter who was asked, no one seemed to know.

'D'yer think the driver knows?' asked Rosie with mild curiosity.

''E don't 'as ter know,' replied Freddie. ''E just 'as ter follow the rails. 'S easy, anyone can do it.' He pronounced this with such an air of authority that no one felt confident enough to question him. If the train really was driving itself then it made a pretty fair job of it. At least it did until it reached Enfield when the first of their unscheduled stops was made. Delay then followed delay, as rumour followed rumour. Each stop the train made – and there were many – these rumours became wilder, each one more garnished than its predecessor. 'They've bombed/machine-gunned/blown up/set fire to the track. The guard, who told me, told me not to tell anyone else. So don't pass it on, it's an official secret.'

At Cambridge they were shunted into a siding for forty minutes. The constant stream of children queueing for the now disgusting lavatory was approached by the same guard who had been such a mine of alarming and confidential information for the previous fifty miles. 'Yer can't flush the lavatory when the train's in a stationary position,' he announced firmly. 'Once it moves, though, yer can flush all yer like,' he added unhelpfully. He passed through the train repeating this instruction on latrinal abstention at every carriage. Within the space of a few minutes, the first thin jet of a small boy's pee arced its way out of an open compartment window. The idea caught on rapidly. Even little lads who had 'just been' felt obliged to give it one more go. Some boys even held impromptu competitions as to who could do it the highest. The guard may have banned the lavatories but there was not much he could do about the windows. Convenient as this was for boys, it threw a decided strain on the girls. Those that did try achieved only minimal success. Adjacent to the immobile train was an undergrowth of tangled brambles. Soon an ever-increasing number of females was seen leaving the train, either alone or clutching the hand of a tight-kneed daughter.

The resumption of the journey was sudden, with no indication at all that they were about to move off. The train had travelled some sixty yards down the track before a chorus of protests drew the driver's attention to a half-dozen crouching females. The train jerked instantly to a halt. The guard was then in his element. Not only was Hitler now waiting to pounce on them all but, by flushing the toilet, peeing in the blackberry bushes and high-jetting from train windows, evacuees in general and Charles Dickens School in particular had practically assured our defeat. Three hours and another fifty miles later, to the relief of the passengers, the disgust of the guard, and seemingly the impotent fury of Adolf Hitler, the train rolled successfully into platform two at King's Lynn railway station.

The reception committee at Lynn were almost as tired and irritable as the passengers. They too had been waiting half a day. Four times a train had rounded the approach curve to the station and four times they had surged forward to greet it. The first had been the 3.59 p.m. local from Swaffham; the second was a goods train laden with cattle food; and the last two were forty trucks of sugar-beet. Once they finally had the right train, they quickly herded the passengers into a fleet of Eastern County buses and transported them to the village school at Wootton, some three miles distant. Though everyone was ravenous, with dusk already falling, there was simply no time to eat. The good ladies of Wootton therefore were obliged to use their best culinary efforts for the next day's pig-meals. At Wootton the whole influx was split into groups of varying sizes and quickly bused out to distant villages. There appeared to be no system to keep the children together and the Charles Dickens contingent were immediately broken up. If it had not been for Julia claiming Rosie, Freddie and Benjamin were of the same family, they would have certainly gone to different parts of the county. Instead they were in a party of eight children to go to the small village of Whicham Marsh that lay in a hollow ten miles east of King's Lynn. The same bus that had taken them from King's Lynn now dropped them at Whicham school gate. Julia was now the only remaining adult and the added responsibility helped ease her grief.

As they alighted from the bus, the smiling village dignitary was more than taken aback to hear Rosie exclaim, 'Blimey! It ain't 'alf bleedin' dark!'

Though Julia's reprimand was instant, she had to admit that it was indeed 'bleedin' dark'. Somehow London, even at its darkest, never quite matched the solid blackness of a misty Norfolk night. As the group entered their third school of the day, they felt the tempo had appreciably slackened. They were given tea and a selection of cakes and sandwiches and actually invited to sit down. It was indeed a strange feeling. From the moment they had struggled from the ruins of Queen's Buildings, they had been *told* to do everything. Now someone was giving them a choice! 'Would you like cake or a sandwich?'

may not have seemed much of a decision to make but it served to remind them they were still human.

This feeling of humanity was unfortunately premature. After finishing their tea, the children were asked to stand in line. Wearily they climbed to their feet and several people who had been sitting chatting in the rear of the classroom came forward to stare at each child. One by one they approached a short, rotund, tight-suited woman who sat at a desk with a register in front of her and a breast label with the word ORGANISER boldly displayed. They would point at one of the children and whisper to the tight-suited woman. She would then nod and ask the name of the child to whom they had pointed. 'Kingston, Miss' came back the reply. 'Very well, Kingston, you have been billeted with Mrs Easter here. Pick up your haversack and go with her.' She made a brief note in her register, then, looking up again, called, 'Next?'

All children except Rosie, Freddie and Benjamin were eventually allocated in this manner before Julia suddenly snapped out of her self-pity. 'Just a minute!' she exclaimed. 'What's going on here? This isn't a billeting allocation, it's a slave auction. You'll be looking at muscles and counting teeth next.'

'We were just trying to match each child with a suitable person,' explained the tight-suited woman. 'It is particularly important to make the correct match.' She paused, before adding pointedly, 'You know, placing like with – shall we say – like?'

The thought that flashed through Julia's mind was the fascinating task of anyone using a 'like-with-like' system to place Rosie, but she decided to gloss over that. 'Madam,' she snapped, rising to her feet, 'these children have been through hell these last two weeks. I think at least you could spare them this indignity!'

'Er, and just who are *you*, m'dear?' asked the tight-suited woman condescendingly. 'I don't seem to have you here on my register of names.'

'You don't need to worry about me,' replied Julia. 'I'm not staying. You could say I'm only here to look after the children's interest and see fair play. By what I've just heard, it's as well I came.'

'But where do you propose sleeping tonight?' persisted the tight-suited woman. 'There are no hotels for miles.'

Julia could feel her hackles rising. 'It's the countryside, isn't it? There are barns and stables, aren't there? I'm a strong healthy lass, I'll survive.' She walked the few yards to the table and whispered quietly in the tight-suited woman's ear, 'But don't you *ever* patronise me again.'

An icy silence hung momentarily over the classroom. It was only broken when Rosie whispered to Freddie, ''Ere, I think Julia's gonna slosh 'er!'

Suddenly an elderly, silver-haired lady, with a remote air of elegance, rose to her feet. 'Are these three chillun all together?' she asked in a gentle Norfolk accent.

Grateful for the interruption, the tight-suited woman agreed they were.

'I'll take both boys, then,' said the elderly lady, 'and my neighbour, Mrs Bumpstead here, will take yon gal. They may not be in the same house but they'll at least be next door. Providing that suits the young lady, that is?' She looked pointedly at Julia.

'Thank you, ma'am,' acknowledged Julia quietly. 'Would you mind if I came with the children? Just to see them settled before I leave, you understand?' she added hastily.

'I'd be bitterly disappointed in you if you didn't,' smiled the elderly lady. 'By the way, my name is Maclure, Clara Maclure. Bit of a mouthful I'm afraid, but I'm sure the lads'll manage.'

'Well, thank you, Mrs Maclure,' said the tight-suited

241

woman, rising to her feet. 'That concludes billeting for today. All worked out rather well, don't you think?'

No one replied as Julia and the children followed Clara Maclure and Mrs Bumpstead out into the dark Norfolk night.

'You'd better stick to me closely,' said Clara. 'The village pond lies atween here 'n' my cottage. Can't 'ave yer afallin' in when I'm supposed to be alookin' after you, now can I?'

On the walk to the cottage, Julia discovered that Clara was in her late sixties and was a widow of some years. Her children had long moved away and with two spare rooms she felt guilty when she heard of so many homeless children in the cities. June Bumpstead, on the other hand, was a fair-haired, plump, lively young woman and the wife of a serving soldier in the Royal Norfolks, and was eager for an evacuee for the extra ten shillings and sixpence per week to supplement her income. As a pair they were poles apart yet they appeared good enough friends. As to the cottage, it was impossible to see the outside in such darkness but an oil-lamp glimmered in the kitchen and Clara busied herself for a few minutes by turning up the glow and then lighting a few candles. The rooms were tiny but seemed full of comfortable chairs, drapes and cushions and the glowing ashes of a log fire still slumbered peacefully in the grate. Julia thought she had never seen such a comfortable-looking house in her life. 'It looks like a house Christopher Robin would live in,' she said. 'I'm sure the boys will be very happy here.'

'Well, if you'd just care to pop next door and see June's place,' suggested Clara, 'I'll stoke up the fire and be cookin' a little supper for us.'

The structure of the two cottages was identical but June Bumpstead's place was as sparse as Clara's was cluttered. There was certainly a fire laid but it was not lit and, though it was spotlessly clean, Julia had no doubt at all which she preferred. Still, though Rosie could not share with the boys, she could

have hardly been closer. 'She'll have this room next to mine,'
pointed out June, 'so she'll be fine. Clara'll probably do most
of our cooking, she usually does, she's like a mother to me.'

On their return to Clara's house, she had already organised
the children into preparing their room and laying the table.
'Now, me old darlin',' said Clara, 'we don't have another bed
but I can fix you up good and proper down here on the sofa.
With a good fire acracklin' away, I reckon you'll be cosy
enough, don't you?'

Julia smiled and shook her head in an act of disbelieving
gratitude. 'I'm so pleased I came, Mrs Maclure. I know the
children's parents will be settled in their minds once I tell
them of you.'

'Well, I think once you've all eaten, you should be agettin'
yourselves to sleep, 'cos I think we've all had a very long day.'

'I agree,' sighed Julia. 'Can you tell me how best to get to
King's Lynn station tomorrow? I understand a train leaves for
London around late morning.'

'As long as you're up a bit early, thas no problem, m'dear.
Ole Bill Raspberry, the village carter, will be agoin' to Lynn
market. If you don't mind sharin' with a bit of livestock, he'll
drop you off at the station for a sixpenny piece.' Seeing as the
bus to Lynn only ran two days a week, Julia felt she had little
choice. It was therefore with great delight, at 7 a.m. next
morning, that the children watched her climb about the carter's
pony and trap and struggle to find a seat amidst two dozen
chickens, four geese, six rabbits and a ferret. They waved till
she was out of sight.

Bill Raspberry was good company and the ten miles to
King's Lynn passed quickly enough. He dropped her outside
the booking hall where she was disappointed to find the train
was running an hour and a quarter late. There was no cafeteria
in the vicinity but the booking clerk directed her to a nearby
tea-room. She was not remotely hungry but she thought she

might be able to dawdle for a while over a cup of wartime tea and flood her mind with thoughts of Duncan. There was only one other occupant at the counter and he was buried behind a newspaper. 'Tea please,' she requested. The unsmiling, heavily made-up woman behind the counter did not say a word but poured out a cup of brown liquid that appeared to have stewed for hours.

'I'll have another cup of that enamel-remover, if you don't mind,' said the voice behind the paper as he slid an empty cup onto the white marble counter top.

She shivered as the woman filled the cup. She knew that voice, in fact she would never forget it. She leaned one way, then the other in a vain attempt to peer around the newspaper. 'Thank you,' said the voice, as a hand reached out and slid the cup back out of sight.

It *is* him, she thought, but how can it be? She could contain herself no longer. 'Excuse me,' she said, 'but do you have the correct time?'

16

Although much of the old tenement had been destroyed, part of it, furthest from the explosion, seemed to have offered up its wounds to be dressed, and carried on. This certainly applied to Wanda's block. Doors and windows had gone or were hanging by a screw. Ceilings cracked and flaked and the simple act of turning a tap or switch, be it gas, water or electric light, proved a greater gamble than choosing the first three horses in the Grand National. Yet in spite of this, with a bit of tarpaulin, plywood, hammer and nails, oil-lamp and candles, people adapted. 'You can get used to anything,' became the philosophy of the day. Yet no matter how many times the two women cleaned the flat it was always dusty. Somewhere there seemed to be this inexhaustible supply of dust that was just waiting to replenish all the smaller pockets that were removed by industrious women.

'I didn't know there was so much dust in the world,' Wanda would complain. They were in the midst of their daily clean-up, when there was a rattle against the plywood screen they used for a door. Rather than climb down from the chair on which she was standing, Wanda called, 'Who is it?'

'Air raid warden,' came the gruff reply.

At the mere mention of the title, Wanda gave an instinctive glance at her window, or rather the hole where the window used to be, before realising that it was still broad daylight and the blackout was not in operation. The next step was to remove the extension lead that hung from the central light socket. She was a customer of the Fixed Price Light Company and for one shilling and ninepence a week she was allowed all the electric light she could use from two 60-watt bulbs. However, a local electrician had rigged up a Heath Robinson socket arrangement so she could also run a radio and, in emergencies, a small one-bar electric fire. This functioned surprisingly well but it did mean that in the event of an unexpected knock on the door, the whole thing had to be tiresomely dismantled in case it was a caller from the light company. She quickly unplugged the lead and kicked it under an armchair. Ensuring it was well out of sight she then slid back the plywood screen to reveal the burly figure of Jack Blackwell.

'Got a message from—' he glanced down at a note he held in his hand, 'a Mrs Roberts. It says next time I'm near, would I call . . . so I've called,' he announced.

Wanda leaned over and, after satisfying her curiosity by reading the note, called, 'Rita! Bloke at the door wants you.' She turned to Jack before adding, 'Come in, she won't be long, she's cleaning the balcony.'

As he stepped in the room from one end, Rita did likewise from the other. 'Oh blimey!' he exclaimed. 'I didn't realise it was you, ma'am! It was the "Mrs Roberts" bit that threw me. That plus the fact that yer used to live down the street at eighty-seven. It's nice ter see yer again, Mrs Roberts, I always assumed yer were killed in the shelter wiv all the other poor bleeders.'

'No, Mr Blackwell,' she smiled. 'They can't get rid of me that easily, I'm a survivor. Besides, that land-mine obviously didn't have my name on it.'

'It's not the one with me name on that bothers me, Mrs Roberts,' he muttered, 'I can accept that. It's the one that reads, "To whom it may concern." That's the bugger that keeps me awake at night.'

Rita's smile evolved into a short laugh. Jack, who had not

shown the slightest interest in women since his beloved Jean died three years earlier, began to stare at her with more than his customary indifference. With an old pair of fire service slacks, a tightly-tied, dreadfully patterned pinafore and her hair dragged back in a ragged headscarf, she could not have been more plainly attired, yet she still managed to be attractive enough to make him feel uncomfortable. But his interest faded when his gaze reached her eyes; with Rita they were always the giveaway. Her greeting was warm but her gaze was chilled.

'Anyway,' he chirruped with false bonhomie, 'what can I do for yer?'

Rita wagged a finger at him and laughed again. 'No, Mr Blackwell, it's what I can do for you this time. Wait there a moment!' She turned and stepped out onto the balcony and rustled around in a stout wooden coal-box for a moment. 'Here!' she finally exclaimed, holding up a pair of quite filthy boots. 'Yours, I think?'

'Bloody 'ell!' he cried. 'They are indeed! Wherever did yer get 'em? I thought they blowed away weeks ago.'

'They did,' she agreed. 'But I knew *you* were the only person in the buildings who kept his boots on the windowsill and, seeing as they practically brained me, I thought I'd better take care of them and return them to you. I'll confess in view of all the drama lately, I did tend to forget all about them. Anyway, you're here now. I'll put them in a bag for you.'

Jack was practically speechless, but he eventually blurted out his thanks and only in the nick of time did he refrain from saying that he never thought such a hard woman would make such a thoughtful gesture.

'We were just making some tea,' lied Rita. 'Will you join us in a cup before you go? You can update us about your daughter and her friends. What's happened to them? I haven't seen them around for some time.'

'That's kind of yer, ma'am,' said Jack. 'And yer certainly

right about the kids, they've all gone off ter Norfolk. I've 'ad a couple o' letters from 'er already,' he added proudly. Removing his warden's helmet he made himself comfortable in the armchair. Rita seemed to be unusually interested in Jack's family news and he seemed more than happy to speak at some length of his daughter and her friends. He said he was quite looking forward to visiting the children and confessed that, until the children had gone there, all he knew about Norfolk was that it was the home of the Yarmouth bloater.

Wanda, into the spirit of her new occupation at the brothel, thought a 'Yarmouth bloater' was some form of sexual deviation and could hardly wait until Jack had gone before asking Rita for the definition.

'It's a herring, you idiot,' said Rita curtly. 'What the hell did you think it was?'

Wanda gave a slight shrug. 'I wasn't sure, but sometimes some of our clients ask me for some strange things. I feel such a fool when I don't know the answer.'

'Well, now you can get in first and turn the tables on them.'

'I don't understand,' frowned Wanda. 'How?'

'Well, you can wink knowingly and say, "For another two quid you can have a Yarmouth bloater." I'll bet none'll query it and a good half'll probably want it. At least they will until you present them with a smoked herring and a sprinkle of vinegar.'

Wanda was never sure when Rita was serious and responded with just a weak smile and changed the subject. 'It's getting late,' she said. 'I'll cook our tea while you're washing, okay?'

Rita nodded, and carrying the kettle from the stove, poured out a bowl of hot water. Within a minute she had slipped out of her clothes and was standing naked on her creased pinafore at the sink, rubbing soap vigorously under her armpits. Wanda always felt strange at these moments. Since she had known Rita she had done things with her and with her customers she would have never once dreamed of, but there was usually that first split-second when she was confused. This was now one of them. She felt she should say something trivial, if only to prove how irrepressible she was feeling. 'I don't much care for that Jackie Blackwell, do you? I think he's a bit common.' In truth she did not know why she said it and the moment she did she regretted it.

Rita spun around with eyes even harder than usual. 'You think he's common, do you?' she hissed. 'What gives you, you of all people, a five-quid Bankside whore who doesn't even know what a fucking bloater is, the right to come out with such claptrap? I grant you the man's uneducated and a bit thick at times but common he most definitely is *not*! Do you know, before now, he's been up on that roof slinging incendiaries over the edge with his bare hands – with his *bare hands*! For no other reason than to save stuck-up, toffee-nosed, small-minded little cows like you from burning to death? That's why I said he was *thick*. If he had any sense he would have said, "Fuck you, you little snob – you can burn to death." I know I would!'

Wanda was suddenly panic-stricken. She rushed across the room and threw her arms around the glaring Rita, though she did check momentarily when she felt a coldness that somehow had nothing to do with the woman's nudity. 'Please, please stop, Rita, I'm sorry. I don't know why I said it. It was a stupid thing to say. I take it back, really I do, honest. I didn't know he was a friend of yours.'

Rita angrily pushed the girl away. 'Jackie Blackwell a friend of mine? No! No man is that!' She had finished washing and had draped a large white towel around herself before she spoke again. 'Listen to me, you dopy cow. Jackie Blackwell may not be a friend of mine but he is just about the most dependable man you'll ever meet and in my book that makes him worth his weight in gold. Other than being a man, I have nothing against him, I'll always give credit where it's due. But in ten minutes sitting down here with a cup of tea I've found out more about what's currently going on in these buildings than I have in the previous ten weeks, and that's important to me, understand – *important*! And do you know why it's important?'

The bewildered girl shook her head.

'It's important because you and I are running two separate lives here and we can't pretend forever. This is our haven, this is where – on the face of it – two quiet, law-abiding, not over-bright, young women live. This is our home, with no doors and windows. With strip-washing at the sink, mice and bed-bugs, dirt, poverty and cold. This is a guise, a front, if you like. We must do it if we ever want to get out of it. The better we do it now the greater will be the reward in the end. If we play our cards right, we can be the first ones out of here. Until then, if anyone comes creeping round putting their nose where it didn't ought to be, well, we're just two very ordinary girls who can't do war-work because we're not fit. Get it?'

'Oh, I didn't know that . . . that we're not fit, I mean,' she whimpered.

Rita went to the kitchen drawer and lifted out a cutlery box, beneath which lay a manila envelope. She said nothing, but opening it, laid its contents in front of Wanda. The first one was a certificate and stated that Wanda Williams suffered from severe psychiatric problems and was not suited for war-work. The second was also a certificate and stated that the lungs of Rita Roberts were seriously impaired by tuberculosis and she too was unfit for war-work.

'But I know nothing about this,' protested Wanda. 'It's really saying I'm mad, isn't it? Where did it come from?'

'It comes from that regular Monday evening stint we used to do for that tall, grey-haired bloke, remember?'

'Oh yes, I remember now! Nice-looking fellow. That reminds me, we haven't seen him lately, have we?'

'No. He was a consultant and was killed when a bomb fell on St Thomas's Hospital. Pity really, I know he was a bit quirky but he was spotlessly clean and a good payer. Fortunately I got these from him a week before he was killed.' She slipped the certificates back into their place. 'Now forget this conversation because they are our insurance in case anyone starts prying around. All you have to do is to do everything I tell you. Nothing could be easier, understand?'

'Well . . . yes,' mumbled Wanda sullenly, 'but I'm not happy about what it says on that certificate. Why am I the one who has to be mental? Why can't you be mad and I have tuber-whatever-it-is, instead?'

'Because, my dear,' hissed Rita angrily, 'the fact that you even have to ask that question explains it all! Now speed up or we'll be late for work.'

Within the hour they had both washed and eaten. Because they had a changing room at the Clinkside, they did not have to dress too sharply when they left for work each evening. This proved just as well when they were surprised at the early return of Jack Blackwell, who stood at the door clutching an old canvas bag. The light fixture was fortunately still dismantled. 'Why, Mr Blackwell,' exclaimed Rita with a distinct lack of enthusiasm. 'Twice in one afternoon! My my, what *have* we done to deserve this pleasure?'

'I'm just returnin' yer kindness, ma'am,' he said, thrusting his hand down into the bag. 'Oh sod!' he exclaimed as he jerked out a scratched, bloodstained wrist considerably more quickly than he had put it in. Rita looked at Wanda and gave a bewildered shrug. He made another attempt, this time more circumspect. 'Ah, that's better,' he murmured. 'C'mon, me little beauty.' So saying he pulled out a medium-sized black-and-white cat that was minus part of a left ear. The cat looked quickly around as if to take in the surroundings before letting out the most plaintive of cries.

'It's Tibs!' cried Rita. 'It's Tibs! But I thought you were dead, darling!' She gently took the cat from the pleased-looking warden and hugged it close to her body. 'But . . . how?' she asked, looking expectantly at Jack.

'Gawd knows, ma'am,' he said, 'but if cats 'ave only nine lives then this one must be a carnation 'cos I'm sure it needed more'n nine lives ter git out of that lot!'

'I think you mean reincarnation, Mr Blackwell, but I get your point.' She smiled happily. 'Anyway, take my word for it, she's the real Tibs. Where was she?'

'I found 'er up on the roof a few days after the mine exploded. She was trapped under some boxes. I reckon she must 'ave climbed up there before the mine went off, probably she was after some pigeons. At first I didn't recognise 'er as your cat, and we kept 'er at the wardens' post because we've got enough mice there for a dozen cats, but seein' you again triggered it off, like.'

'Mr Blackwell,' she cried, giving him a big kiss on the cheek. 'You're wonderful.'

Jack reddened considerably and, shuffling his feet in embarrassment, mumbled something that sounded like, ''S all right, no more'n I ought . . . goodbye,' and left.

'I'm not losing her again,' said Rita, 'not now she's been through so much.'

'That's easy to say,' said Wanda, 'but what do you propose to do with her? You can hardly keep her locked up here, when we don't even have any doors or windows.'

Rita thought for a moment before almost shrieking, 'Of course, the barge! It's the perfect place. She can have the run of all three barges and she can't get away. Other than getting a direct hit, she'll be safe from the raids and she can catch pigeons, gulls and the odd rat to her heart's content!' Pivoting on one foot, she swirled around in delight. 'I tell you, Wanda, things are looking up. Hold out the bag and I'll drop her in.'

Though Wanda did not seemed fired with the same enthusiasm, she did as she was told and a few minutes later both women and Tibs set off for the river. 'I feel just like Dick Whittington,' chortled Rita. 'D'you reckon Swinger Baxter's going to make me Lord Mayor of London?'

It had become the habit of both women to visit their barge before reporting to the Clinkside each evening. There was no doubt that Georgie Jinks and Jimmy Tyler had made a first-class job of renovating the old barge. The woodwork classes they had attended in prison had obviously not been wasted. By now the shelving was best part full and Rita had known for some time now that they really had no need to work at the Clinkside any more. Though this was a sound idea in theory, she knew it would be tremendously risky in practice because of the close proximity of club and barge. She was only too aware of what had happened to Monkey Westow and she had no intention of following him into the river. Her big problem was that the success of her black market operations took place mainly slap in front of the club. Even worse, so was the river. The temptation could prove too much for old Swinger. Perhaps she should speak to him; a little discreet negotiation might go a very long way. The obvious drawback with this plan, though, was that he could then become aware of how well she was doing. Gang bosses in general and Swinger Baxter in particular loved to get their fingers in any successful pie that was being made on their own manor.

After paddling the little boat the few yards to the barges, she released the bewildered cat onto the craft and returned to the riverside steps near the Clinkside. There were few customers in at this time of the evening and the few staff who were around were mostly playing cards in the corner of the foyer.

'Swinger around?' asked Rita.

No one actually spoke but at least two heads nodded towards

the office in the opposite corner. Rita knocked and following the 'C'm in' both women entered the room. Swinger was in his customary pose in his favourite chair with a blanket around him. 'Ah, come in, my dears. Always nice to see two attractive ladies after some of the scruffs who frequent this place. What can I do for you?'

'I've come to do a bit of negotiating,' said Rita.

'Oh dear,' said Swinger quietly. 'That bad, eh?'

'Er – no,' replied Rita with some apprehension. 'Nothing *bad* about it at all. I . . . that is we – Wanda and me – wondered if we could reduce the time we spend here? Originally we came in for two or three evenings a week but now it seems to be every evening and recently we were here for the best part of two weekends. You see—' She paused as she realised he was not fully taking in her case. 'You see, well . . . what with the buildings being bombed and everything, it does become particularly difficult at times for us—'

'You mean you are doing so well with your other sideline you would like to ease out of our arrangement, is that it, m'dear? Hmm, now let me see—' She appeared to be about to protest but he raised his hand to forestall her. 'No, no, m'dear, as you say let's negotiate. Now to the best of my recollection, we did negotiate once before. If I remember correctly *you* approached *me* with an offer. You were even kind enough to offer the services of Mrs Williams here. "Two for the price of one," I believe your exact words were. When I suggested a fifty per cent divide you suggested eighty per cent for you and twenty per cent for me and I believe that was agreed *providing* I had priority for both your services at this establishment?' He gave a wide but humourless smile. 'You will correct me if I'm wrong, won't you, m'dear?'

Rita's apprehension began to give way to anger. 'You know full well you're not wrong, Swinger. It's just that circumstances change, that's all. Because of that I'd like us to come to an agreement based on those changes. I'm not reneging on our agreement, I'm just trying to amend it slightly.'

'Let me get this straight,' he said, now not even bothering to use the false charm with which he usually cloaked his conversation. 'Because your sideline could now become your main line, I'm supposed to cheerfully say that's all right, m'dear, you go ahead. Even though I've invested heavily in the pair of you I'm expected to lose out? In other words, because your market has expanded it has the right of way and everything else can go to pot?' His smile had vanished and her anger had shaded into fear as a transformation appeared to come over him. 'Well, Mrs Roberts, my market has also expanded and as it so happens I was going to ask – no, I was going to *tell* you that, starting from this very evening, I shall be requiring your services a great deal more in future. You will only spend time on your other business when I say you can and at no other period. If your work here is satisfactory then fine, so will be your free time.'

'But you can't do that,' she protested. 'That's tantamount to slavery.'

'Nonsense!' he exploded. 'Since when did a slave get more salary than a minister of the crown!'

Rita was silent for a moment, then she shrugged and said resignedly, 'Looks like you win, doesn't it?'

Swinger, who had just picked up a glass of whisky from a table at his side, slammed it down again, spilling it in almost every direction. 'Don't you give me that Little Bo-Peep act,' he snarled. 'I know you, Mrs Roberts, for the very dangerous and calculating woman you are. I didn't buy that "Misadventure" bollocks from the coroner for a moment, so let's be quite frank with each other. My point is this, if this war goes on for say, another two years, you could make enough money with your two rackets to ensure you never need work again. But to do that you need me on your side. One thing's for sure, if you don't get my approval you're back working that Fire Service switchboard again. Very well, at the moment you've still got me on your side but now, because of your bloody greed, the rules have changed. I want you both here for three weeks in every month and, if need be, at weekends. You can carry on running your business in the barge but the instant I feel I haven't got your entire attention, the barge is finished – and so are you. Get it?'

Her eyes blazed with fury but she nodded quietly.

'Of course it's not all gloom. As a show of good faith I intend to up your salary to a hundred pounds a week and your assistant's to sixty pounds, and all tips, gratuities or any little extras that customers give you are yours.'

'And the sales from the barge?' she asked.

'Fifty-fifty,' he said.

'I see,' she said quietly. 'The old game, give it with one hand and take it back with the other, eh?'

'It's still a blindingly good deal,' he pointed out.

'Okay,' she agreed, 'but you said you were requiring my services this very evening. What is it? If it's that little fat greasy Greek diplomat you inflicted on me last week then forget it, the deal's off!'

'No, no!' he laughed. 'This is much more civilised. In fact it could make you famous and open up a whole new career for you.'

'I already don't like it,' she sighed. 'There's too much of me been opened up already. But go on, tell us the worst.'

'Films, m'dear, films. That's where the money is now!'

'Films?' she echoed. 'But there are cinemas on about every half-dozen streets. We can't compete with those. Anyway, this place is not big enough to be economical.'

'No, no, you don't understand. We're not going to *show* pictures, we're going to *make* them,' he said. 'And what's more, you'll be the star! How's that grab you?'

'If you're talking about what I think you're talking about, it don't grab me at all.'

'Nonsense!' he cried. 'Look, nearly every army, navy and air-force unit has a film-projector now, agreed?'

She nodded. 'Go on.'

'Most of the people watching these films are men. Men, I might add, who frequently haven't seen a woman for weeks, in some cases, months. What are they showing these red-blooded males at the moment? I'll tell you – war films and *Pinocchio*,' he roared. 'Bloody *Pinocchio*! If you were a red-blooded male and you hadn't had your leg over for six months what would you sooner see, some fatuous little story about a wooden doll and a cretinous cricket, or a couple of decent-looking birds like you and Wanda doing a few good tricks?'

'But how are you going to make these films? You have to have some sort of expertise, surely?'

'Of course you do and I happen to have the very man. With any luck he could make us all a fortune.'

'Who is he, Sam Goldwyn?' she said dismissively.

'Close,' he said with mock seriousness. 'Actually, it's your Greek, the greasy one you moaned about. It's a hobby of his and whatever country he's been posted to for his embassy, he usually manages to supplement his income by making "artistic" fifteen-minute films.'

'Swinger,' she said emphatically, tilting back her head, 'you can cut my throat right now but there is no way that I'm going to perform in a film, or anywhere else again with that horrible little shit.'

'But m'dear, you don't have to. He's not going to appear in the damn films! We need much more of a young stallion for that part. He's going to direct them.'

'I still don't like it,' she mumbled.

'How about you, m'dear?' said Swinger, turning to Wanda. 'You'd like to be a film star, wouldn't you?'

The question threw Wanda into an instant predicament. She had a gut feeling that Rita was not in favour of the project but without asking her she could not really be sure. After all, it may just have been one of her ploys to squeeze out extra money from Baxter.

'Well, wouldn't you?' he persisted.

'Er—' she faltered. 'Well . . . you see, Mr Baxter . . . I quite liked *Pinocchio*.'

17

Duncan Forbes had found himself in a whole new situation. Never before in his life had he ever been in a sexual relationship that he had not had control of, or at least not had a bolt hole into which he could quickly vanish. In some ways it could be said that in Roselyn Dupre he had met his match. Simmering beneath her eight years of passionless marriage, a whole volcano had come to the boil. When it finally erupted it was all consuming, and the indifferent Commando sergeant did not want to be consumed. At first he simply enjoyed it. After all, how much better to be the duty stallion for an attractive – if insufferable – woman than languishing in a prisoner of war camp, or even worse, dead. But gradually the novelty faded and a creeping feeling of helpless incarceration replaced it.

Of course, being Duncan, this did not happen overnight. Some days he would feel so desperate he would feel like swimming to England just to get away from her, yet on others he would be the first one up the stairs to bed. Occasionally his conscience would prick him. Not for the fact that he was in the relationship purely for his sexual gratification – he saw little wrong in that. No, it was for the fact that he had made a grand talk of carrying the war to the Germans and had even joined the Commandos for that very reason, but now found himself fighting a vastly different battle. During the days that followed he had slowly increased his presence around the farm. To do this, Dan Duquemin, the cowman, had to be taken into his confidence. Duncan did not find this easy; there was something about Duquemin that made him feel uncomfortable.

Apart from the fact that the man hardly ever spoke, he was particularly unconciliatory and yet Duncan had no choice but to trust him. In spite of this, he could placate his pricked conscience with the fact that he was in a helpless situation and could do little about it. If his identity was revealed to the Germans now they would almost certainly shoot him as a spy. He had almost come to terms with being a 'kept man' for the duration of the war when Roselyn dropped her bombshell. 'I've been thinking,' she said one night as they lay quietly in the afterglow of a particularly passionate session. 'I'm a widow and you're single so there is no reason at all why we can't get married and start a family. After all, we are extremely compatible.'

Duncan had not the courage to tell her that compatibility was just about the last thing they had in common so he concentrated his defence on the proposed nuptials.

'We can hardly do that, can we?' he protested. 'I mean, I can hardly wander down to the register office at St Peter Port on a sunny Saturday and say, "Hello, I'm a British Commando and I've popped ashore to marry a local widow and put her in the family way. Make it quick, will you, I've a dinghy waiting." The bloody krauts would have shot me before you'd cut the cake. No, sorry love, we'll have to give that a miss until the war's over.'

She propped herself up on her elbow and, leaning over him, glowered down. 'Why the delay? So you can do a runner?'

'How can I do a runner?' he protested. 'We're on an island, aren't we? I couldn't possibly get off without you knowing, now could I?'

'Well, you managed to get on all right!'

Duncan knew her well enough by now to sense the change in her voice patterns and immediately realised he was heading for one of her periodic blastings. For his own security he tried to keep these to a minimum. Unfortunately there was only one thing that could forestall them and he was by no means sure he was up to it.

Still, it was worth a try. 'You know,' he said, gazing up at her, 'I love looking at you from this angle, you have such symmetrically perfect nipples.'

'Don't you soft-soap me, Duncan Forbes. I'm well aware of your—'

'It wasn't soft-soap I had in mind,' he whispered as he began to circle the halo of her nipple with his fingertips.

Her voice changed instantly to a softer tone. 'You know that curls my toes,' she said, 'so why start something you can't finish?'

He pushed her over onto her back. 'And who *said* I can't finish?' he asked as he slid his hand down her belly and began to gently caress her vulva.

'Mmm,' she purred. 'Oh I love this . . . this is esstasy.'

At her pronunciation of 'esstasy' he closed his eyes in frustration. It was the one word he had hoped she would not say. He knew he was being illogical because the word was a great favourite of hers and she used it on frequent occasions during their love-making, but for some reason her pronunciation always irritated him beyond measure.

'Ecstasy!' he suddenly snapped. 'The word is *ecstasy*, it is not esstasy. *Ecstasy* and it's spelt E–C–S–T–A–S–Y. Got it?'

She sat bolt upright and swung a left arm at him which he only managed to partially parry. 'I don't believe this!' she cried. 'There I am thinking you're making love and instead you're giving me a fucking spelling lesson!' She then proceeded to pummel him off the bed. 'Well, you know what you can do, don't you?' she demanded. 'You can fuck off! Spelt F–U–C–K O–F–F. Got it?'

He might have been Commando trained but she was proving

quite a handful and the fact that they were both naked did not help matters. At first he had tried to ward off her blows defensively but this approach had simply not worked. So at the first opportunity he dived in and seized her left arm. Bending forward he tugged the arm over his head and lifted her up in a fireman's style lift almost before she knew what was happening.

The view of her naked buttocks slung over the shoulder of a still-aroused man was a sight that Dan Duquemin hardly expected as he entered the room.

'I suppose you know that you stupid pair can be heard halfway to Cherbourg?' he growled. 'And if the Germans come looking for the source of the noise they're hardly likely to believe I know nothing about it, are they?'

Duncan stood listening for a moment to what the man had to say before he remembered the naked Roselyn was still slung over his shoulder. He took two quick paces and dumped her on the bed with such force that the mattress bounced up and down for some seconds after impact. 'Yes, I'm sorry, Dan,' he said apologetically. 'It was stupid of me, should have known better, thanks.' Yet as he looked at the cowman he could see the man's attention was entirely taken up with the naked Roselyn who was now lying provocatively spread-eagled, face-down across the bed.

She glanced over her shoulder and deliberately raised herself up on the edge of the bed and faced him from a sitting position. 'Hand me my gown then, Dan, there's a dear,' she said demurely. Without uttering a word the man did so and continued to stare at her as she took her time slipping into it.

'If you're playing the jealousy card, don't bother,' said Duncan wearily. 'It never works with me.'

She smiled at the cowman as if Duncan did not even exist. 'Now Dan,' she said as she tied up the cord. 'What was it you were saying?'

'I said you must cut down on the noise because sooner or later some Jerry is going to come prowling around and the fat will really be in the fire.'

'Yes, you're right, of course. But seeing as you're here, it's only right you should be the first to know. Sergeant Forbes and I have decided to get married and start a family so I suppose . . . well . . . perhaps we were being a bit boisterous.'

Duquemin seemed to be taken aback at this news and glanced at Duncan as if seeking confirmation. Duncan, however, was still working on the best line to take. If he denied the news, Roselyn could really look quite silly and he could not afford to upset her too many times, but if he agreed, he was now somewhat concerned over Duquemin himself. Apart from the fact that he did not trust him, he now suspected the man was also jealous of his relationship with Roselyn.

He was saved from a decision by the swishing sound of bicycle tyres on the gravel outside the house. 'Someone's coming,' said Duquemin, making for the window. 'Oh it's all right, it's Ray Pusser from the nursery at the crossroads. Wonder what he wants?' He turned to Duncan. 'Does he know of your presence here?'

Duncan nodded. 'Yes, we've spoken a couple of times in the last few weeks. It should be okay. If he's on his own let him in while we get dressed.'

Duquemin descended the stairs and met the newcomer at the front door. 'Come in,' he said. 'Mrs Dupre and her friend won't be a minute, they're getting dressed.'

At first Pusser looked as if he was going to respond to this announcement but then appeared to think better of it. 'I've got some news,' he said.

'Keep it until they're both down,' said Duquemin curtly. 'That is if they can keep their hands off each other until then.'

Raymond Pusser was a small, almost tiny individual aged about thirty. He seemed to move in a series of quick jerks, almost like a darting ferret. In fact his thin but wide moustache would tilt up and down frantically as he fired out his words in staccato-like sentences. As Duncan and Roselyn finally entered the room he glanced rapidly from one to the other as if requesting permission to speak.

When it did come it came from Duquemin. 'Now you can go ahead,' he growled.

'Bad news, I'm afraid,' said Pusser. 'Cat's out of bag!'

'What d'you mean?' asked Duncan. 'What cat's out of what bag?'

'You, I'm talking about. Your presence here. Now pretty well known all over this part of the island.'

'How can it be? I've hardly been off the farm!'

'You may pass for Charlie Dupre for a short time,' said Pusser, 'but not indefinitely. It was only a question of time before someone passing put two and two together. Besides, rumours spread over this island like pestilence.'

'What are they saying?' asked Roselyn.

'Depends who you talk to,' shrugged Pusser. 'Some say you have a dozen men holed up here, waiting to perform some dramatic raid. Others say you only have one man here and he's trying to organise a resistance movement, and some . . .' his voice trailed off.

'And some?' persisted Roselyn. 'What do these "some" say?'

'Well, they say he's not a soldier at all but just some fancy bloke from Sark.'

'Bloody cheek!' she exploded 'Who said—'

'Never mind who said it,' cut in Duncan sharply. 'The fact that I'm a cause for discussion means I'm on borrowed time. Sooner or later someone is going to grass to the Germans and you'll all be in trouble. I'll have to go.'

'No one would do that to us,' said Roselyn indignantly. 'Guernsey people aren't like that. We're all British.'

'Oh yeh?' laughed Duncan ironically. 'I've met British people who would have sold their mothers for a brown ale, so let's not get too carried away with other people's integrity.'

'Guernsey folk are not "other people",' argued Roselyn. 'They're different.'

'Without being too adamant,' said Pusser apologetically, 'I think it's near time you left the island.'

'So do I,' agreed Duncan.

'There is just one thing I'd like to suggest,' said Pusser. 'This occupation is still so new. To be honest I don't think many of us have a clue what to do. We don't want to be seen to cooperate, but we've nowhere to hide if we don't. I suppose passive resistance might be our only role. There are a dozen of us who'd like to do something about it. Will you give us some help before you go? None of us are military men. All we know about fighting is what we've seen at the cinema. It would at least mean your trip here wasn't wasted. What d'you say?'

Duncan laughed. 'Good! I've been looking for something I can tell my CO that I've accomplished during my time here. If I don't do something soon he'll think I came here on holiday.'

'Ah,' said Pusser, sucking his teeth thoughtfully, 'then you don't know?'

'Know what?' asked Duncan, his eyes narrowing.

'The news bulletin said that both British soldiers were killed in the raid. The body of one was on the rocks and the other was decapitated and washed away by the sea. The Germans think you're dead. By now, it's pretty certain your own side does too.'

'Well than, that's a real stroke of luck,' said Roselyn. 'It means they won't be searching for you, doesn't it?'

'True,' agreed Duncan, 'but it also means that my next of kin will be told that I'm dead and as far as the bureaucracy on the island is concerned, Charles Dupre still lives.'

'If all this is correct,' interrupted Duquemin, 'then I'd say you have a few days at the most. At the moment I'd say the Germans do not know you're here but sooner or later it's inevitable they will.'

'That's nonsense,' said Roselyn. 'If they believe both British soldiers were killed, why would they come looking for him?'

'They wouldn't be actually *looking* for him, but they are currently doing so many bureaucratic checks that sooner or later the deception is bound to come to light. Also, if there is anyone local who doesn't care much for you, well . . .' he shrugged and left the sentence unfinished.

'I can't see that myself,' she said haughtily. 'I haven't an enemy in the world!' At this, all three men exchanged rapid glances, with Duncan and Pusser each giving a silent whistle.

'Dan's right,' said Duncan. 'That settles it – for all your sakes I must leave. The next problem is how? What's the chances of stealing a boat?' He looked at both men.

'Almost none,' said Duquemin adamantly. 'The Germans have listed every boat capable of making a Channel crossing. Nothing moves along this coast without their permission and if it does, they'd sink it.'

'Well, the sea's a big place,' said Duncan dismissively. 'If I left at dark I'd be halfway across before anyone woke up.'

'There's more to it than that,' replied Pusser. 'For example, what d'you know about boats and tides? Have you sailed or navigated these waters before?'

'No, but it's simple enough surely?' said Duncan confidently. 'You just point the sharp end north and off you go. That way, sooner or later, you'd be bound to hit the south of England. With luck I'd probably sail straight into Plymouth Harbour.'

'Huh,' snorted Pusser, 'you'd be lucky to clear the rocks at Alderney. Even if you did, you'd be almost certain to land on Cherbourg.'

'So are you telling me that it's impossible for me to travel eighty miles across the Channel to England? Bloody hell, man, Captain Bligh sailed three thousand miles across the Pacific in an open boat!'

'With respect, Sergeant,' replied Pusser, 'Captain Bligh was a *seafarer* and he knew about *water*. I suspect you'd have difficulty crossing a damp flannel.'

'Okay, okay,' said Duncan irritably, 'so you tell me my alternative.'

'Well, I've a proposition,' replied Pusser. 'Come to address our meeting tomorrow night and I think I may be able to help you with a boat.'

'But that's no good if he can't sail or navigate the thing!' snapped Roselyn. 'I'm sure he'd be much better off staying here with me.'

'Nevertheless, I think I may help with your problem, agreed, Sergeant?'

'Well, sort of,' said Duncan half-heartedly. 'You see, it's the meeting that bothers me. It would need to be held here because at this stage I don't particularly want to go wandering around the island.'

'Then if it's okay with Mrs Dupre let's have it here, then,' agreed Pusser. 'How about six o'clock tomorrow evening? It'll give everyone a chance to get home comfortably before curfew.'

'Oh yes, of course,' said Roselyn testily. 'Let them all come, I'm no one, I'm only the bloody owner of the place. Invite the Germans as well, perhaps we'll have a party. They can amuse themselves by shooting me at dawn if they like.'

'No, the Germans won't shoot you at dawn,' said the straight-faced Duncan. 'That's milking time and they won't want to frighten the cows. Stick around till lunch, though, they might do it for you then.'

She glowered at him before hissing, 'Sod you, you bastard!' then spinning on her toes, she ran from the room.

Pusser watched the door slam before turning to Duncan. 'You shouldn't upset her like that. It achieves nothing and she could be dangerous.'

Duncan nodded in agreement. 'I know, I'm sorry. It's just the frustration of being cooped up here, I suppose. Everyone will be better off when I leave.'

'That's for sure,' muttered Duquemin almost under his breath.

The following evening, some fifteen local people drifted into the Dupre farm under the pretext of making a rota for the use of communally owned farm machinery and all listened intently whilst Duncan instructed them in the basics of civil resistance. They were particularly limited as there were no natural hideouts such as swamps, forests or mountains on the island. In fact, until the whole pattern of the war changed, all they could offer would be passive resistance and non-cooperation. Communications with England were essential, if only so British intelligence could be aware of developments on the island. However, at the end of the meeting Duncan had the impression that the fact that he was present as a Commando sergeant helped lift morale, so the evening had not been totally wasted. People drifted away singly until there was only Duquemin, Pusser and Duncan remaining.

It was not until that moment that Roselyn made her entrance. There was no doubt she had made a real effort. During the whole time that Duncan had been on the island he had never seen her look quite so attractive – even beautiful was not too strong a word. As he watched her walk across the room and drape herself on the settee, there was a fleeting moment when he thought that leaving the island might not necessarily be the best idea. On the other hand, if he did not make his break soon he knew he might never be able to make it at all.

'So,' he said, looking at Ray Pusser, 'I've kept my part of

the bargain, what have you got to tell me, Mr Pusser?'

'How much notice would you want to leave the island?' asked the little man.

'As little as you wish,' replied Duncan. 'I have no ties here.'

Pusser shot a quick glance at Roselyn before continuing, 'How about two hours?'

'Two hours!' she cried. 'He can't possibly be ready in two hours. Whose boat is it and what's the rush?'

'The rush is,' answered Pusser, 'that the weather and tides will be as perfect for the trip in two hours as they are ever likely to be again, perhaps for years.'

'What's so special about the weather this evening, then?' asked Duquemin.

'A fog's closing in. It will be dark soon. The sea's dead calm and the tide's right. It'd be hard to better that,' said Pusser confidently.

'And just how the bloody hell do you think that this bloke here,' Roselyn pointed at Duncan, 'who you yourself said would have difficulty crossing a flannel, is going to navigate eighty miles of sea in a fog and probably cross mine-fields?'

'Mine-fields we can't do much about,' conceded Pusser, 'but as to the rest, I think I can manage.'

'*You!*' she exclaimed. 'You're not going, surely ... or is everyone on this island going mad and I don't know it?'

'I have a motorboat and it's well hidden at the moment,' said Pusser. 'Fuel could be a problem but the fact that the sea is so calm is a help. Two people could just about make the crossing. Even if we did run out of fuel we should be fairly close to Weymouth by that time. Close enough to take a chance, anyway.'

'But what does your wife say about it?' persisted Roselyn.

'She's said nothing so far,' replied Pusser, 'but that's probably because she knows nothing about it.'

'You mean you haven't told her?' she asked incredulously.

'Why ever not? What is it with you blokes and your women-folk? Just the shock could kill her!'

He stared at her for a moment, as if deciding if he wished to pursue the conversation any further. 'I doubt it,' he said quietly. 'I haven't told my wife, for one very good reason. She is having an affair – and with a German. You see, if I stay around here much longer no one is going to trust me anyway. But if I go now the Germans may even suspect her of complicity.' He gave an unusually broad smile before adding, 'I quite like the thought of that. Perhaps I could leave little notes scattered behind me such as, "Thanks for the boat, darling," or, "I couldn't have done it if you hadn't kept him occupied." That's a pleasant thought, isn't it?'

'So tell me exactly what you need me to do,' said Duncan, now aching to get their move under way.

'Well, I need to check the fuel and give the engine the once-over,' said Pusser. 'Then I have to remove some panelling in my shed which is screening the boat. So if you find some warm clothing, a torch, make a few sandwiches and a flask of hot something-or-other, I'll call back for you and we'll be off in just under the two hours.'

Roselyn now turned to Duquemin for support. 'Please, Dan, tell them, for Christ's sake, tell them! It's insanity, isn't it? They haven't a snowball in hell's chance of making it, not in a tuppenny boat in a fog and a mine-field!'

Duquemin, who suddenly saw the best chance to date of removing Duncan Forbes from the scene, was having none of it, though. 'They're either leaving or they're not,' he said. 'And if they're leaving, it has to be now. That's all there is to it.'

Roselyn suddenly threw herself face down on the settee. 'Oh, why is it every time things start to go well in my life, a bloody man comes along and spoils it?' she groaned. Picking up one of a pair of glass ashtrays from the small table at the head of the settee, she threw it hard towards Duncan. She missed by inches and the missile smashed harmlessly on the floor. 'And you can forget about sandwiches,' she screamed, 'I'll see you starve first!'

'Okay, sweetie, just do me some cake, then,' he said, ducking for cover as the second missile flew over his shoulder.

Ray Pusser, deciding that now would be as good a time as any to make his departure, slipped quietly out of the door and looked up at the evening sky. A bank of fog was rolling in and though it would mean navigation would be tricky, the chances of being spotted in a small boat would be remote. Pedalling hard he was back in his nursery within minutes and noticed a German army cycle propped against the front of his house. With his kitchen being at the rear he was able to enter the larder and help himself to an assortment of bits without anyone else in the premises being aware of his presence. Tip-toeing out, he hurried down to a small inlet about a hundred yards away where he kept a small rowing boat in a waterside shed. At the side of the shed he unscrewed a large false panel and there was his pride and joy, a small 14-foot clinker-built motor-boat with in-board engine. Quickly greasing two planks of wood he slid the boat into the water with the minimum of splashing. He topped up the tank and made sure that the two spare cans were also full. Throwing his bag of food and spare clothes into the boat he tied it quickly to a mooring post and doubled back to the Dupre farm, noticing as he passed that the German cycle was still in place.

Duncan was sitting on the back doorstep waiting for him. 'Everything okay?' he asked anxiously.

'About as okay as it's ever going to be,' replied Pusser, 'but I'd be misleading you if I didn't tell you it's a risk. Are you still keen?'

'Keen?' echoed Duncan. 'I tell you this, if your boat doesn't start – I'm walking!'

Both men trotted quickly away down the gravel path towards

the Pusser nursery and the sea. Two figures watched them go. The first was Dan Duquemin who was hidden in the hayloft of the cowshed. The second was Roselyn Dupre, who stared hatefully at them as they started to fade into the mist. Then, without taking her eyes from them, she reached for the telephone and dialled the operator. 'Give me Gestapo headquarters . . . quickly,' she hissed.

18

The man lowered his newspaper, at first unaware from where the question came or even to whom it was addressed. Seeing that there was only one other person present, he slipped a pocket watch from his waistcoat and glanced down. 'It's almost ten o'clock,' he said, retreating behind his paper screen.

She felt a little shiver run up her body, yes, it was him! But what was he doing here? Suddenly the newspaper was slowly lowered, the man leaned forward inquisitively and stared across at her. 'Don't I know you?' he asked. 'I never forget an attractive woman so I can't believe I'd forget you.'

She smiled at the predictable compliment but enjoyed it nevertheless. 'We have met,' she agreed, and then gestured around her, 'but not in a tea-room.'

'Of course! I remember you now, you're Nurse Giles! It's all coming back to me! You were the nurse who had a niece and nephews who were . . . now what was the term you used?' He tutted twice before continuing, 'I've got it! "They are not quite that," was what you said at the time and I've been trying to fathom out what "they are not quite that" meant ever since. Julia is your name, at least that was the one on the casualty card. You had a badly grazed arm and your so-called niece had a whisper that could be heard three streets away.'

'Very good, Dr Rawlings, I'm impressed. Now perhaps you'll tell me what you are doing in this tea-room a hundred miles from home?'

'But it's not a hundred miles from home, at least not *my* home. I come from a village called Gayton, about seven miles from here.'

'You don't speak like a Norfolk dumpling,' she said.

'That's what a posh education does for you, I suppose. Though to be fair, I did leave here some years ago.'

'When you say you come from here,' she persisted, 'is this your permanent home?'

'Not really, although since the war I spend all my free time here. It helps me unwind, particularly when we've had periods at the hospital similar to the night of your visit. I am soon transferring to King's Lynn general hospital anyway. I've just been to make final arrangements. So now it's your turn. What brings you to this greasy spoon tea-room, a hundred miles from home?'

She briefly recounted her reasons but really let rip when she spoke of the evacuees' selection system.

'I know,' he agreed, 'but there really are two sides to this whole question. My father has just retired from his village practice and he can recount some hair-raising stories of some real genteel country folk whose lives have been turned upside down by some real monsters – children and adults – who have been billeted upon them. Many of these evacuees are ignorant of even the most basic rules of hygiene and suffering from scabies, septic sores and bed-wetting. Some were so bad, that one old countryman swore that no lice could ever live on them. It's bound to happen, I'm afraid. I think we'd better just call it a clash between town and country and let it go at that.'

At first she felt like taking issue with him on one or two points but was soon persuaded that there really were two sides to the question. They chatted for some time and she was surprised when he suddenly looked at his watch and said, 'We'd better get along to the station in case the train really does leave at 11.15 a.m.'

She could not believe it was that late. Slipping back her cuff to check with her own watch, she suddenly realised he was smiling at her deception. 'It's been broken for a while . . .' she bleated, 'and, er . . . I've recently had it mended.' She gave a little shrug. 'Got out of the habit of looking at it, I suppose,' she said weakly.

'I never doubted it for a moment,' he said reassuringly, as he picked up her bag and ushered her to the door. A strong image of Duncan suddenly flooded her mind and it was not without a momentary pang of guilt that she allowed herself to be shepherded from the café.

'Train's in, platform one,' grunted the inspector, as he examined their tickets at the gate to the concourse. As he clipped their tickets she saw a blackboard notice that read, 'Owing to enemy action, the 10 a.m. train to Liverpool St station, due there at 1.15 p.m., is now leaving at 11.15 a.m. It will now travel via Peterborough and will arrive at London at King's Cross station at approximately 5.15 p.m.' She could hardly believe her luck! A four-hour delay! That meant she would have him to herself for at least another six hours! She could see it all, as the train rolled out of King's Lynn station he would talk to her in that dreamy voice of his and she would lean on his shoulder and doze gently all the way to London. On the very night she had met him she had told Grace that she was filled by the desire to sleep with him, but she had never really thought it could happen. Well, now it was about to and at a time when she felt she needed someone trustworthy and dependable. Perhaps her life was changing for the better, after all.

'Oh dear!' It was this 'oh dear' that first hinted her fantasy could be going awry. She looked up at him, then followed his gaze. She was appalled by what she saw. 'Oh dear' was the understatement of all time. The train was standing at the platform, right enough, the trouble was half the British army looked as if it was already on board, whilst the other half was trying to gain access. 'What on earth are we going to do?' she asked helplessly. 'Is there another train?'

'There certainly should be a later train,' he agreed, 'but who's to say it would be any better than this one? Or come to that, even if it would actually get to London today? At least we *know* that this one's going to King's Cross. I don't think we have a choice. I'm afraid it's this or hitch-hike. Anyway, you won't have a problem. No matter how crowded it is those soldiers will open up like the Red Sea. My difficulty is going to be staying with you.'

'I don't understand,' she said. 'Why won't I have a problem and why will they open up?'

'They'll open up because the idea of squeezing you tight for the next six hours will doubtless be infinitely preferable to the bloke they are currently squeezing tight. Blokes do like to cuddle up to attractive women, you know. I thought you would have discovered that by now.'

'Oh that!' she sighed wearily. 'Oh, I'm only too aware of it. Trouble is you usually get your bum felt. But okay, let's say I get on the train, how about if I tell them you're my husband? They may even make room for you. At least we'd both be on board?'

'I think it's a great idea, and I'm all in favour.' He smiled. 'Then if anyone feels your bum, well . . . it might just be me. Conjugal rights, and all that.'

'Okay!' she cried determinedly. 'Cling to my coat-tails, we're going in.'

His forecast about a Red Sea style opening was certainly correct. The big trouble was that the opening did try to close rather swiftly behind her. But by sticking as close to her backside as possible – a task he found particularly easy – they finally made it aboard the train corridor. The train could have hardly been more packed. In every compartment soldiers were sitting sardine-tight with kitbags, rifles and field-packs hanging from luggage-racks or propped between knees. In the corridors, burly greatcoated men were at least two deep for the entire length of the train. Everywhere cigarette smoke hung in dense blue clouds, so still and unmoving it seemed to be painted there. Suddenly a distant whistle blew and there was a thunderous roar from the engine and much to Julia's surprise, the train actually began to move. Once under way, the crowd in the corridor began to ease slightly, probably because those standing no longer puffed themselves up to preserve a breathing space. At first Julia and the doctor were lined side by side but, as the train jolted, a few deft shuffles and a couple of quick turns soon brought them face to face and much closer than a last waltz at any New Year's Eve ball. Gradually, as one arm crept tightly around her, she leaned into him with her head on his chest. She was by no means asleep but was certainly dozing when she gave a little jump. She opened her eyes and saw he was trying to peer out of a window streaming with condensation. It was his right arm that was around her whilst his left was holding their balance against the corridor walls. 'How far d'you reckon we've travelled?' she whispered.

'About twenty miles, I'd say, why?'

'Someone's just stroked my bum for the third time.'

'Well, it wasn't me, unfortunately,' he said with mock sadness.

'I know,' she again whispered, 'but the last one was definitely an improvement. If you see him doing it again, tell him a little higher next time, will you, I'm beginning to like it.'

He looked her straight in the eyes and held her gaze for some moments and slowly ran his lips down from her hairline via her cheeks until he reached her lips. This time she did not jump when the fourth stroke of the twenty-mile journey caressed her right buttock.

The train seemed to stop at every station and signal, though the condensation was so heavy that most of the time no one knew just where they were. If it was possible to see a tiled roof she guessed it was a station, if it was just a tree, then it was probably a signal. Most of the time she did not even bother to open her eyes, that was until a distant voice called, '*Peterborough! Peterborough!*' As the train rolled into the platform a general hubbub broke out amongst the soldiers and commands were heard from the length of the train. 'Four company outside on the platform, at the double, now!'

'Hey,' he shook her excitedly, 'guess what! They're getting off! They're all getting off! The train will be nigh on empty.'

She looked around in disbelief but it was true. Doors were opening and banging, oaths and curses could be heard but finally, throughout the entire train, just a handful of people remained. As the men lined up on the platform the doctor opened a window to ease the condensation, just in time to hear an anonymous voice rise from the rear rank. 'She's got a lovely arse, guv'nor, a real beaut!'

He turned into the compartment to where Julia was just about to luxuriously spread herself. 'There's a fellow out there who reckons you possess – if you'll pardon the anatomical expression – a lovely arse.'

'Only *one* fellow?' she asked. 'That's a disappointment. It felt like half the Berks and Bucks Light Infantry.'

The train stood immobile at Peterborough station for almost an hour. The troops had long gone and Julia lay along a compartment seat with her head on Dr Stuart Rawlings' lap. Both had their eyes closed but neither was asleep. 'Can I ask you a personal question?' he said.

'Providing I can ask you one in return,' she countered.

'I should have expected that,' he said ruefully, 'but here goes. Is there a – let us say – a someone in your life? I just can't believe that a woman like you is not spoken for.'

She did not answer at first. The question was hardly unexpected yet she found it difficult to explain. Perhaps if the telegram had read *dead* she might have found it easier to speak of Duncan. But what did *missing, presumed killed* mean and for how long is someone *missing, presumed killed*? Would he still be missing when she was sixty . . . or even eighty? If they did not know now, when would they know? Would the whole thing become an obsession with her? For the rest of her life would she look expectantly at every opening door, hoping the person entering would be Duncan Forbes? If so, what age would he be on that day? Would he be the age he was when she last saw him, or the age of the day he reappeared? Young man or old man, who's to say? 'No,' she said softly. 'There's no one . . . There was, until a short time ago, but not now. Duncan, his name was . . . They tell me it's the war . . . And you?'

'Well, there is . . . and then again there isn't,' he began.

She interrupted with an ironic little laugh. 'Why is it that when it comes to relationships, men can never give straight answers?' she asked. 'I don't want to hear your family history, I simply want to know if you're romantically involved. If you're not, you're not. If you are, say so. I'd sooner know now than when I'm in too deep.'

'Well let's say I *was* – as you so eloquently put it – romantically involved but I don't think I am now.' He raised a hand to forestall her obvious questions. 'You see, I was courting a young woman – a doctor, in point of fact – for some two years. At one stage we were at the same hospital. We became so close that we decided we should no longer work together. We literally tossed to decide who would transfer and she lost. She transferred, right enough, the trouble was she transferred to Hong Kong. I just don't think you can have a proper relationship with someone who is on the other side of the world for three years, do you?'

'Wait a minute!' she cried. 'It's happening all the time today.

279

Men and women are being called up and sent everywhere. Are you saying that they should not enter into a relationship until after the war?'

'No, I'm emphatically not!' he said firmly. 'If the government sends you away, then so be it. But when she decided to leave, there was not a war on. Oh yes, we write to each other and, unless she falls for some millionaire on a Far East cruise, I must assume she'll come back some day. In the meantime I work in London and I don't know from one day to the next if I'm going to survive the night. There must be more to life than that, surely? Especially when someone as wonderful as you explodes into it.'

'So where do you live whilst you are carrying out all these meditations?'

'I shared a flat with a colleague at Herne Hill. Typical bachelor flat, one big wash-up when you can no longer find a clean cup and one big laundry when you run out of clean shirts.'

'But you said *shared*?'

'That's right. He's been called up for the army and he's a medical officer in some regiment or other, I forget which. Most of his cases, though, seem to be crabs and the pox. He's still in England somewhere and providing he gives me sufficent notice of his leaves, I usually have a massive tidy-up the day before he arrives home.' He carried on speaking at some length after this but his voice seemed to just become such a warming, comforting sound that she gradually fell into a relaxing sleep that was only disturbed by him kissing her forehead and whispering, 'Come on, kid, we're pulling into King's Cross.'

She wriggled the back of her head down into his lap. 'Ooh! Let's stay on the train and go back to King's Lynn,' she murmured. 'I could sleep again.'

'You'd better look out of the window before you make requests like that,' he laughed.

Sure enough there seemed to be enough military personnel milling around to finish the war in a week.

'Oh well, perhaps not,' she groaned, as she sat up and stretched her arms in a long, satisfying yawn. 'I'm not sure if my bum is up to it again, anyway.'

'How much of your leave do you have left?' he asked, as they stepped down onto the platform.

She was still half asleep and blinked sharply a few times before replying, 'Oh, er – let me see, I've lost track of time.' She did a quick calculation and then said, 'Until tomorrow, I think, yes, 8 p.m. tomorrow night.'

'And where are you off to now?'

'Well, if I can find a telephone box I'll ring Queenie, a friend of mine in Streatham. She lets me stay from time to time.'

'Is she expecting you?'

'No, but that's the advantage of Queenie, you can just descend on her without a moment's notice and she doesn't get rattled or flustered.'

'Look, I know this sounds a . . . well, a cheek at the very least, I suppose, but well . . . would you care to—'

'Stay at your place for the night?' she cut in with a half smile.

'Oh dear, I'm that obvious?'

'No, but it looks like I am,' she said thoughtfully. 'You know,' she paused for a moment. 'I knew from the time we got on that train you were going to ask me that question and I've been thinking what my answer would be ever since.'

'And what is your answer?'

'I'm none the more forward,' she admitted. 'But listen, let me talk straight to you. There is no question in my mind that I want to spend this night with you but I am still haunted by the ghost of my Duncan. You could say he and I had almost a love-hate relationship but all our little battles – and there were a tidy few – just seemed to push us closer together. We actually split up a few times and during those times I certainly knew other men. Yet deep down, I always felt Duncan would coming toddling over the horizon and we'd pick up the pieces as if he'd never been away. So many times he would take me for granted and I hated him for it, but then I would always come running when he returned. Now that's either serious love or the height of stupidity.'

'It sounds pretty serious stuff to me.'

'I was hoping it would, because that leads me to my main problem. I felt that every man I knew, other than Duncan, would only be a short-term relationship, primarily because he would always come back. But now he's dead, so should that feeling be.' She gave a great sigh. 'But it isn't. I think what I'm trying to say is that it's *possible* I could become too intense for you to cope with. After all, we didn't properly meet until a few hours ago, so we owe each other nothing. I'm afraid of getting hurt, Stuart, it's as selfish as that.'

'But could we not try?' he asked. 'Without obligations or recriminations on either side, I mean. If you so wish you can pack your bag in the morning and never see me again, with absolutely no hard feelings.'

'Oh isn't that sweet?' she mocked. 'And spoken like a true man! Forgive me, Stuart, but if during the next few hours I find I'm falling in love with you, what then? Tomorrow morning you could say to me, "Great knowing you, kid. Bye." I might then throw a tantrum of unrequited love and you would look all bewildered and say, "But I thought we had an agreement?" So where would I be then . . . or you, for that matter?'

He placed a comforting arm round her shoulder. 'You're right, I suppose,' he murmured ruefully. 'It's this damn war. It rips people like you and your Duncan apart, then it throws people like you and me together. I'm sorry, I shouldn't have asked that.'

'But you *did* ask me, Stuart, and I'm pleased you did. I've simply pointed out the pitfalls. If in spite of them you still want to take a chance, then let's get a taxi because we're losing precious moments.'

His eyes narrowed. 'I've never met a woman quite like you,' he said, shaking his head in puzzlement.

'Aren't you the lucky one then?' she smiled.

'I'll let you know that in the morning. *Hey! Taxi!*' he yelled.

As the taxi negotiated its way through rush-hour traffic, it reached the huge complex at the Elephant and Castle where six main roads converge. During the daylight raids of the early autumn, it had been a perfect landmark for German bombers and it certainly showed. There was hardly a building upright. As they passed, Julia stared silently at the devastation. 'Where do you think this is all going to end, Stuart?' she asked sadly. 'There has to be a limit to what the population can endure, surely?'

'True,' he acknowledged, 'but I don't know what that limit is. Sometimes people bring themselves into casualty at night with injuries so bad I cannot begin to imagine how they have survived, never mind arrived. Their homes and work-places have been smashed and friends and relatives killed but they just plod on in a strange, sometimes frightening, way. Take the nightly raids we have now. Every night, about eight o'clock, the siren sounds. Minutes later the bombers come. They rain death and destruction down all night, then just before dawn, they leave. The only thing people on the ground can be sure of is that many of them will not see that dawn. Yet they emerge from their holes and shelters, not even knowing if their home is destroyed, to begin the day as if it is the most normal thing in the world. I don't know what it is; it's certainly not bravery, perhaps it's stoicism, but it's certainly beyond my comprehension.'

'Will we be coming out of our hole or shelter tomorrow morning?' she asked.

'No,' he smiled. 'I have a comfortable bed that I kid myself is bomb-proof and I insist on sleeping in it. My only concession will be to share it with a beautiful woman . . . and I promise you this,' he added, 'I will be neither brave nor stoic but I *will* be bloody appreciative!'

He directed the taxi to a block of elderly but neat Edwardian flats at the south end of Herne Hill and she stood looking around her as he paid the taxi fare. He pointed to a corner window on the second floor. 'That's it,' he said. 'I'll be glad to get home. I feel like I've been travelling for days.'

'I'll ignore the compliment,' she said, 'providing you have running water and a bathroom.'

'Oh, I didn't mean . . . ' he blustered. 'Er – yes, but of course. At least it was working when I left here a few days ago. But look, you surely didn't think—?'

'Stuart, shush! Just lead me to the bathroom, you can grovel as much as you like when I'm soaking my weary body.'

The idea of seeing Julia's body, weary or otherwise, soaking in a bath, concentrated his mind so wonderfully that he had gathered their baggage and was up the stairs and into the flat at such a rate it left her breathless. The flat was much as she had imagined. It was sparsely furnished with the breakfast china still soaking in a bowl of cold suds from the time he had left the place a week before.

'I see you weren't kidding about your washing up,' she said, nodding to the sink. 'And though I hate to ask you this, I feel I must . . . what do we do for food? That's not in the soapy water too, is it?'

He put his hands to his head in horror. 'Oh dear!' he exclaimed. 'I've got some tea, that's about it, I'm afraid!'

She shook her head in mock admiration. 'You certainly know how to spoil a girl, don't you? I'm too tired to eat anyway, just lead me to the bathroom and make me a nice cup of strong tea.'

A few minutes later, after a bewildering battle and two slight explosions with an enormous heater, a spluttering and intermittent stream of hot water began to cascade out of a greeny brass tap and swirl into the dull glazed bath. 'Will you want your tea in the bathroom, or out here?' he called from the kitchen.

'In here, of course,' she replied, lowering herself into the water. At first she just lay back enjoying the heat to her limbs. She then stretched her arms up in a great relaxing yawn.

'Good heavens, woman,' he exclaimed as he entered the room, balancing a cup and saucer in each hand. 'Fancy doing that when a fellow has his hands full. It could have given me a coronary. By the way, I don't have any bath salts but there're soap flakes on the windowsill.'

'You know, Stuart Rawlings, I think you're all show. You keep your soap flakes on the windowsill but sod all in your kitchen. I bet your neighbours pass by saying, "Cor, look yer can tell 'e's a doctor, 'e's got soap flakes on 'is windowsill." But it's just as I always thought, take away your white coats and underneath you doctors are just ordinary blokes.'

'If being an ordinary bloke means the view of you stretching your arms in a bath is the loveliest sight he's ever seen, then my white coat's in the dustbin first thing in the morning.'

'Flatterer,' she said, handing him the soap. 'Do my back whilst I drink my tea.'

'I'm not sure if I should,' he said, taking the soap. 'That's my best china there.'

She turned to him and, putting her mouth to his, whispered, 'Live dangerously . . . risk it.'

He was still risking it for minutes after she had drained the cup. So much so that she finally said, 'Okay, Dr Rawlings, you've proved your talent as a back-washer but how are you with fronts?'

'Fronts,' he said, carelessly slipping his hand over her

breasts, 'just happen to be my speciality. So too are tops, bottoms, aboves, belows and in-betweens.'

'Hmm, I'm not sure my nerve-ends could take all that,' she said, deliberately standing up in the water to face him, feet astride and hands on hips.

He slowly feasted his eyes up and down her naked wet form. 'D'you know,' he said, 'if this was a film, great clusters of foam would have gathered over the most interesting parts of your body. That proves to me this is not a film. So, if this is not a film then it must either be real, or it's only a dream. Therefore I'm going to touch you again, this time to test if you're only a dream.' He pulled her towards him and, sliding his arms around her slippery body, kissed her passionately. 'Nope,' he said, 'that was no dream. If it wasn't a dream then you must be for real. Thank heaven for that, move over, I'm getting in.'

They played, kissed, stroked and soaped until a distant siren and the cooling water fetched them down to earth again. He wrapped her in a large blue towel and said, 'Last chance, kid. The bombers will be here soon. If you want to shelter, we should be going now.'

She shook her head and tut-tutted. 'Dr Rawlings!' she exclaimed. 'You told me your bed was bomb-proof. You've not been misleading a poor girl, have you?'

'I don't think so,' he said, lifting her up in his arms, 'but shall we try it?'

She nodded. 'I can't see how we will know otherwise, do you?'

After carrying her into the bedroom, he laid her on the bed and turned out the light. The first bombs of the night followed a second later. He moved on top of her and eased her thighs apart with his knees. 'By the way,' he whispered, 'if the earth moves for you, it'll probably be a 500-pounder on the railway junction opposite, but don't worry, it's just that I don't want all the credit.'

In spite of his claimed recent celibacy, she thought him a very good lover. The foreplay had been good and they could not have been more compatible. Yet the longer he was inside her the more she knew it was all a mistake and she was relieved it was too dark for him to see her face. Because of the lack of a contraceptive, he pulled out of her before climaxing, an act for which she was more than grateful. She could now delude herself it had been little more than heavy petting. As he lay breathing heavily alongside her, she remembered the desire she had confided to Grace that night at the hospital. 'To curl up and sleep with him' was the phrase she had used. Well, now she could. She knew he was a fine man and felt relaxed and warmed in his presence, but she sadly now realised she could never share his passion.

He turned in to her and kissed her goodnight as the house shook from an explosion from the direction of Brixton. 'That's probably the couple next door,' he mumbled. 'Always at it, they are. Disgraceful, costs a fortune in windows.'

She smiled and returned his embrace and did not wake until the siren sounded an 'all clear' at 6 a.m. next morning. She stirred just as he was emerging from the kitchen, again with two cups of tea. 'I'll pop out in a minute and see if the bakers have anything before the queues start to form.'

She gave him a sleepy smile and in a quiet voice whispered, 'Thank you for last night, it was wonderful.'

He gave a smile in return and sat down on the side of the bed. 'Of course it was wonderful . . . you're a wonderful girl,' he said slowly, 'and if I didn't have such an affinity for you I'd say you might have got away with it . . . but you didn't, did you?'

'Stuart, I don't understand,' she said, with a note of concern in her voice. 'Get away with what?'

He made no reply at first but walked over to the window and drew back the blackout curtains. The early sun streaked across the room and rested on her naked torso. 'The instant I actually entered your body last night I realised the game rules had changed. I was effectively playing on my own, you were no longer with me. Even your orgasm was faked.'

'Stuart, I—'

He placed a finger to her lips. 'Shush now, darling, it's my turn,' he said. 'It may be too soon for you, or you may simply not want me sexually, but whatever it was, from the time when you should have been beyond recall, you were actually on automatic pilot. It's okay though, kid, at least we know now this heavy love-stuff is not for us. I'm prepared to compete against most rivals but your dead Commando has got me licked to a frazzle. One day you are going to have to let go of him. Mind you, I don't know when that day's going to be, but until it comes, you're going to have to be a chaste woman. Otherwise you're going to bewilder a whole lot of men. I like you a lot, Julia, in fact I could oh so easily love you but—' He broke off and, shaking his head, returned to the window in silence.

She seized a blanket and, wrapping it around her shoulders, followed him. 'You're right, of course. It was extremely adept of you to sense the fake orgasm but that was stupid and cruel of me. But I assure you, Stuart, that it was the only fake moment about the whole of last night. I wanted you, Stuart, I wanted your help to pick up the pieces of my life, but when it came to the crucial moment I knew that side of it wasn't going to work. I know I am seeking something new and I need to change direction but I just don't know how to do it. I'd like you to forgive me, but I feel I don't deserve it and I could well understand if you did not. Will you, though? Will you forgive me?'

He ruffled her hair. 'There's nothing to forgive, kid, really there isn't. I adore your company, you looked beautiful and I had the best night's sleep I've had since the war began. In fact I'm so relaxed I'm going to ask you something totally illogical, do you mind?'

'As long as I'm not required to give an answer, go ahead.'

He took her hands and stared at her for a moment. 'Come back to Norfolk and stay with me. I'm sure I could get you a transfer.'

'After what happened last night? Besides, you said a previous love of yours transferred because you were at the same hospital, now you want me to actually join you there! Are you crazy?'

'That was a mistake and we should never have split, but what's done is done. Yes, perhaps you're right, maybe I am crazy but this is going to be my only chance to ask you. I would curse myself forever if I let you go without pleading my case.'

'But last night was a classic example of what could happen. Besides, I think we both now know that I don't love you.'

'I understand that, but what is left for you in London now?'

She shrugged. 'Nothing, I suppose. Oh, I have friends, of course, but no family. Although I'm probably the eternal aunt to each of those three kids.'

'But they're not in London!' he cried triumphantly. 'They're in Norfolk. There you are, fate has answered for you!'

'But Stuart, it's not as simple as that. You're asking me to break my ties and come to Norfolk on little more than a whim. People just can't do that, our relationship would be doomed before it even started.'

'But our relationship has *already* started,' he persisted. 'Okay, tell me, what have you got to lose? If it works it's brilliant. If it doesn't neither of us is worse off than we are now.'

'But love's not a business arrangement that you can juggle around to suit the circumstances,' she protested. 'Love is an illogical mass of contradictions and confusions, that's why it's such a bloody nuisance.'

'You still haven't answered my question, Julia. Will you come?'

'I do hope you haven't just caught me at a low ebb,' she murmured thoughtfully, 'because I think . . . ' She paused. 'I think I'm coming to Norfolk.'

'Well, that's it then,' he said jubilantly. 'My world is now complete. Now come on, tell me, what more could anyone want?'

She squeezed his hands and glanced down at the now empty tea-cups. 'Breakfast?' she hinted.

19

Duncan Forbes' boots were much heavier on the gravel than Ray Pusser cared for. Ray knew every yard of the path, he knew where every patch of grass that could be trodden on safely at speed was rooted. Even though the Germans had not been in occupation long, inhabitants were already finding ways of moving around the island silently and unobserved. Duncan may have been fine crossing ground continually raked by shot and shell but he was pretty useless at scrambling along a gravel path and through a chap's garden, particularly when a German soldier could slip out any minute after frolicking with that chap's wife.

'You've got feet like pile-drivers,' hissed Pusser irritably at the Commando. 'Couldn't you make less noise?'

'Only if I could fly,' snapped Duncan, equally peeved. As the fog rolled in even more thickly, his confidence was losing a little of its potency and it showed. 'I think I'd be pushed to find the sea from here on my own and it's only yards away,' whispered Duncan. 'I don't wish to be unkind but I'm pleased your missus has fallen for a kraut,' he added undiplomatically. 'I'm sure I'd get lost on my own.'

'I hope you're not going to talk crap like that all the way to England,' said the islander tersely. 'If you do, I'll swim off and leave you.'

The problem was eased as the gravel gave way to sand and soon they reached the boat house. 'We won't be able to start up the engine for a while,' explained Pusser, 'because I have no idea where the German patrols might be. It'll be safer to paddle out quietly beyond Jerbourg Head. Once we're clear of the coast, the trick is to give it everything we've got and put as much distance as possible between us and the island before anyone realises we've gone.'

'How far out do you reckon they patrol these waters?' asked Duncan.

'Not all that far,' conceded Pusser, 'but then they don't need to, they can cover it easily enough from the air. That's why fog is such an asset.'

The two men agreed that Duncan should do the paddling whilst Pusser continued to prepare the boat and their provisions for the quick dash across the Channel. Every few minutes Pusser would look at his watch and his compass and slightly amend the direction of Duncan's paddling. As the minutes rolled by, their confidence grew and Pusser was just about to start the engine when Duncan gave an almighty '*Shush!*'

'What is it?' asked the anxious islander.

Duncan shook his head. 'Dunno, thought I heard voices, though I couldn't quite make out what they were saying. Be quiet and I'll listen again.'

Both men remained almost fossilised but only the gentle lapping of the water against the bow of their craft could be heard. Pusser shook his head. 'No,' he whispered, 'there's nothing out—'

'There it is again!' hissed Duncan. 'You must have heard that, surely?'

If it had been daylight Duncan would have seen the change in Pusser's colour. He had heard it, all right. 'It's German!' he whispered. 'They're speaking German! Not only that, they must be bloody close, because they are only conversing, yet I can hear them clearly.'

Duncan knew the man was about to panic so he leaned over

and grabbed him firmly by the arm. 'Listen,' he snapped
sharply. 'Even if they are searching for us, they have no idea
we're so close, otherwise they would be far more discreet.
That means they are still only searching. You can forget your
compass for the moment, because they'll assume we're heading
for England. Our first priority is to put as much distance as
possible between us and them . . . but quietly!'

His words calmed Pusser, who soon saw the sense of the
theory. Giving a weak smile the islander nodded and gestured
with his hands in a paddling motion. Both men then leaned
over the side and propelled the boat agonisingly slowly by
hand. The occasional voices became fainter and, after half an
hour, it was with relief that Pusser raised his finger in a gesture
to stop. They each rubbed their hands vigorously to promote
some circulation. Pusser in particular was wincing with the
cold. They paused in silence whilst they regained their breath
and warmed their hands beneath their armpits.

'I think we can now risk a paddle again, don't you?' asked
Duncan.

'We'll have to,' agreed Pusser worriedly, 'because if daylight
clears this fog, we'll be sitting ducks until we put more distance
between us and Guernsey.'

Both men then picked up their paddles and, on a nod from
Pusser, started off in unison. They had been paddling for only
a few minutes when the first call to '*Halt!*' cut the still air like
a knife.

They both looked around frantically, without success. 'We
can't see them so they can't possibly see us,' snapped Duncan.
'They're bluffing, keep paddling.'

'But they're so bloody close,' panted Pusser. 'If they do see
us then we'll never lose them. Their boats are bigger than
ours.'

Duncan rummaged through Pusser's knapsack and found
two tins of beans. Standing upright, he hurled one of them as

far as possible. The distant splash was immediately followed by the repeated cry of 'Halt!' but this time it was also followed by a burst of machine gun fire. Seconds after the burst ceased, he hurled the second tin in the same direction. Again the gun opened fire but this time the burst was double.

'They must only be yards away!' cried Pusser.

'We've got to chance the motor,' said Duncan curtly. 'With any luck we could be a quarter-mile away before they can work out exactly what direction we've gone in.'

In his anxiety to reach the engine, Pusser staggered and almost fell but once he reached it he was quickness itself. The engine exploded into life and the bow of the craft seemed to leap out of the water. Duncan wrestled with the wheel as a great white wave of foam streamed out behind them and they roared away into the murky blackness. In the distance, the roar of two other craft could also be heard accelerating in pursuit.

'Zig-zag,' commanded Pusser, 'but not too sharp otherwise we'll not be covering sufficient distance.' Suddenly a searchlight beam cut through the fog.

'Blast,' said Duncan. 'I wasn't expecting that. I didn't think they'd risk it because if we had guns we could blow them out of the water.'

'Perhaps they know we have no guns,' murmured Pusser pointedly.

'How could they possibly know that unless . . . of course . . . *Roselyn!*' he exclaimed bitterly. 'But surely not, though? She wouldn't do that to us, would she?'

'Who else is there?' asked Pusser. 'They obviously knew we were out here, they also seem fairly sure we're unarmed. Draw your own conclusion, soldier.'

'The cow!' exploded Duncan furiously. 'The bloody treacherous cow! She must have telephoned as soon as we left. I tell you, Raymond old son, I'm going to get out of this if only to come back when the war's over and spank that bitch's arse.'

'Huh,' replied Pusser, singularly unimpressed, 'from what I've heard of her, if she thought for one minute you'd do that she'd meet you from the boat.'

Further conversation concerning the moral scruples of Roselyn Dupre was adjourned as another burst of fire splashed into the sea barely forty yards ahead of them. This time the occasional tracer bullet could be seen lighting up the darkness.

'Wonder why they haven't used flares?' said Pusser thoughtfully. 'They must know there are no British craft in the vicinity. With a flare they would have us cold.'

'If they haven't used them then they haven't got any!' exclaimed Duncan. 'That still gives us a chance. They obviously still haven't seen us. Cut the engine, let's drift and take the risk. It's our only choice.'

Pusser was reluctant to stop the motor but he also knew it was probably the best, if riskiest, course to take. Once more the dead silence of the night took over. For the next hour a real cat and mouse chase took place. Sometimes the voices seemed miles away, other times they seemed just yards. Suddenly just ahead of them the rear of a German motor torpedo boat could be clearly observed; they were but yards from colliding with it. If the crew turned to look in their direction they were as good as captured. Duncan gradually steered the boat away from the searchers but Pusser panicked and chose that very minute to restart the engine.

This time the machine gun fire was directly at them. Duncan changed course numerous times and on one occasion felt the boat shudder as at least one bullet struck them. The firing then seemed to be moving further away from them. Duncan turned to the rear of the craft. 'I think we've lost them again,' he cried triumphantly, but his relief turned to distress as he saw Pusser slumped in the bottom of the boat.

'I've . . . been hit,' the islander groaned, wincing with pain.

The spreading bloodstain over his shoulder told its own story. The Commando knew he had to keep the man conscious at all costs; without him and in this fog he was done for. 'Stay with it, mate,' Duncan encouraged him. 'We've come this far, we'll do it yet, you'll see.'

Pusser raised himself on his good shoulder and called back, 'You must keep going . . . on this course. It's . . . our only . . . chance,' he panted.

Duncan divided his time between comforting the man and steering the boat. As he returned to Pusser for the third time, the islander shook his head and pointed to the stern of the craft where petrol was seeping everywhere. The tank had obviously been hit and, even worse, so had both spare cans. Even if everything else was perfect, there was now no way they could reach the English coast.

'No . . . matter,' said Pusser doggedly. 'Keep going. When . . . fog lifts . . . fifty-fifty chance . . . who sees . . . us first, British . . . or . . . Germans.'

Duncan increased the speed to get maximum distance before the fuel was finally exhausted. In the east the early sun was beginning to dissolve the fog. Visibility that had been barely ten yards had now increased to sixty and was lifting fast. At this rate and in another hour, they would be conspicuous for miles. Duncan examined his compatriot's shoulder and found the wound much worse than he had thought. Although it had almost stopped bleeding, it was such a mess that he decided to just make the man comfortable and hope for a miracle. It was whilst he was hoping for this miracle that the fuel finally ran out.

'How far d'you think we've travelled?' Duncan asked.

'Dunno . . . we've twisted . . . turned . . . so much . . . impossible . . . to say,' panted Pusser, 'but . . . still nearer . . . Guernsey . . . than . . . England.'

They drifted silently for the next hour as the visibility increased to well over a couple of miles, all the time the bloodstain on the islander's shoulder becoming wider and wetter. Suddenly an aircraft could be heard. They scanned the skies anxiously. 'It's not a normal sound, though,' said a puzzled Duncan. 'That's why I can't recognise it. Whoever, or whatever it is, sounds in trouble.'

It was the islander who spotted it first. 'There . . . look!' He nodded towards the south-east and Duncan could see a smoking twin-engine aircraft obviously trying to pancake in the sea.

'It's one of ours,' Duncan sighed. 'It's a Wellington bomber and it's on fire. If the krauts couldn't find us before they won't be able to miss us now.'

'Why?' asked the puzzled Pusser.

'Because the clever bastard who shot him down is up there too. Look, see him?' He pointed to a Messerschmitt fighter that was circling some two or three thousand feet up to the east. As the bomber finally splashed to a halt on the surface, so the fighter-plane, now sure of its location, made off towards France.

'Quick,' breathed Pusser. 'Let's . . . move off . . . in the other . . . direction.'

'No! Wait a minute,' said Duncan. 'It's time to take an awful big risk but in view of your condition we've got to chance it.'

'I dunno . . . what . . . you . . . mean.'

'The krauts will be sending someone soon to pick up the crew as prisoners but the Royal Air Force run an excellent Air-Sea Rescue service. If the pilot has managed to radio his position there is a possibility the RAF will arrive first. So let's paddle to the plane.'

'But that's where the Germans . . . will make for . . . first,' whispered Pusser. 'You're mad.'

'I know,' agreed Duncan, 'but you shouldn't use that in an

argument with me, it's not fair. Come on, we're going to join the Air Force.'

There was little that Pusser could do to oppose his colleague no matter how dangerous this new idea was, but he guessed his own time was limited if he did not receive medical attention soon. In addition he was now so weary that he no longer cared. 'Do what you . . . bloody well . . . like, then. I'm so . . . bloody cold . . . I don't . . . care any more,' he muttered fatalistically, as he slumped down into the bottom of the boat.

The floating bomber was by now little more than sixty yards away and Duncan could see that two men had clambered from the plane into an inflated rubber dinghy. He could also see that it was only going to be a matter of seconds before the aircraft sank. Already one wing was submerged and the plane was slowly turning over. Suddenly there was a loud crack as the fuselage split in two and both halves sank instantly. 'I can only see two men in the dinghy,' said Duncan sadly. 'I wonder how many other poor sods went down with the plane?'

Once the Wellington had disappeared, the men in the dinghy appeared to give thought to their whereabouts and suddenly saw the crippled speedboat. Duncan waved and called to let them know they were all on the same side. 'Who the hell are you and what're you doing here?' called the plumper of the two survivors.

'Don't worry about that right now,' replied Duncan sharply. 'Did you have time to get a location message off before you crashed?'

'Yes,' came back the reply. By this time the two boats were only yards apart.

'How many of your crew went down with the plane?' asked Duncan.

'None, they baled out ten minutes ago but we were losing height fast, we knew we'd never make it back but our 'chutes were burnt, so we had no choice but to risk ditching in the sea.

What d'you reckon our chances are out here?'

'Well,' said Duncan philosophically, 'that's easy. You two watch the north and we'll watch the south. If you cheer first we've won . . . if we boo first, we've lost.'

'Yes, but who's favourite?' persisted the airman.

'Well the krauts were already out here looking for us, but that was some time ago. So they may have either given up or returned to refuel. If they've done either of those two things, we're in with chances.'

'But if they didn't return to refuel, what then?' asked the airman.

'It means they are still out here somewhere and they will be here any time now with the milk and papers. In that case they'll make prisoners of you pair and shoot us. That's one thing you have to say about the Germans, they always let you know where you stand.'

'If we're hoping to be picked up by the Air-Sea Rescue,' said the plump airman, 'we should all share the same boat. After all, they will be looking for an RAF dinghy, not a civilian motorboat. In addition, in case it's a close-run thing, it will be easier to be picked up from one craft instead of two.'

'That's true,' agreed Duncan, 'but that's entirely providing my poor mate here can make it.'

'Well,' said the slimmer of the two airmen, 'I don't think that's something that need bother you any longer. Look at him.'

Duncan swung around and realised in the minute or so he had taken his eyes from him, the islander had died. 'Poor bastard,' he muttered. 'His womenfolk certainly didn't do well by him, did they? The only reason he was here was because his missus is kipping with a kraut. Then, to get back at me, his female neighbour has grassed him to the Germans. Poor old Pusser. He was brave and deserved better.'

'What shall we do with him? There's not much point in taking him with us if he's dead, is there?'

Duncan stared at him for a few moments. 'Have you got a pen?' he asked suddenly.

'Yes,' said the puzzled airman. 'It's a bit late for his will, though, isn't it?'

'I noticed some paper in his bag of goodies,' explained Duncan. 'If I can think of something that will incriminate a certain Mrs Dupre, I'll stick it in his pocket and cut him adrift. With any luck the Germans will find the boat and subsequently the note. It's certainly worth a try.'

'In that case do a partial letter. It's always better than a whole one,' said the airman. 'In fact a letter that's been torn up is even more convincing. It makes it look as though there's been a deliberate attempt to destroy it. That always makes it more plausible.'

'Why?' asked Duncan curiously.

'Because the reader feels he's worked it out for himself. A whole letter could easily be a fraud but a person only tears up something he wants no one else to read. So, for best results, write it, tear it up, then hide it – carefully but not too carefully. Got it?'

'Oh, I've got it, right enough.' Glancing up at the still-empty horizon he added, 'And if that rescue boat comes along while I'm doing it, tell him to drive twice round the park until I finish it.' He leaned down and closed the dead man's eyes, and whispered, 'One for you, me old son . . . one for you.'

Duncan quickly scrawled a note.

My Darling Roselyn,

  He has given me all the contacts on the island for you to meet. With luck we could have a resistance group up and working within a month. I suggest you sacrifice someone expendable in order to obtain a trusting relationship with the krauts, perhaps the army sergeant may be the best idea, after all we have no further use for him and his presence makes us vulnerable. Especially since they once believed him dead. I'm aching for you so much, my darling, that I can't wait to get back to you. Take care, though, because I want you to myself for the rest of time.

Yours forever, R.

'Do you think it'll work?' asked Tubby.

'We may never know, but we don't have the time for anything more subtle,' conceded Duncan. Tearing the letter into sections he slid them into a trouser pocket. 'But if nothing else it'll give them food for thought. The least it can do is put the fear of God into that devious cow for a time. Who knows, if we're really lucky, they might even shoot her.'

'I take it you don't like women,' said the slimmer airman as they collectively pushed the speedboat away from the dinghy.

'On the contrary,' countered Duncan, 'I love 'em, well most of 'em. In fact my greatest incentive now is to get home to see the loveliest little nurse who ever slipped into a starched petticoat.'

'Serious, is it then?' asked the airman.

'I never used to think so but the longer I'm without her the more I miss her.'

'You don't look the type to tell her that,' replied the airman.

'Good God no!' exclaimed Duncan. 'Once they know you feel like that, they've got you good and proper.'

With nothing to do except wait for a potential rescue, or in Duncan's case a potential execution, they began to discuss women in general and their own relationships in particular. Both airmen were married but the prolonged separations of wartime were obviously causing stress on both marriages.

'I don't think you can improve on the ground rule that my old grandad told me on my wedding day,' said the tubby airman seriously.

'That was?' asked Duncan.

The airman finished filling his pipe, then sniffed loudly and lit it before replying thoughtfully, 'Stuff 'em regular and shoe 'em poorly.'

'Sounds a reasonable philosophy to me,' mused Duncan, equally thoughtfully. 'Bit difficult in my case though. See . . . she's a nurse and the matron inspects her footware daily.'

'Hmm, I see . . . perhaps it doesn't apply to nurses then,' suggested the slim airman helpfully.

The mutual merits of a Commando's libido and a nurse's footware were instantly forgotten as the plump airman yelled, 'Look!' and rose to his feet, pointing to the distant horizon excitedly. 'Two boats! They're coming quick but they're coming from the wrong direction. That makes them krauts for certain!'

Duncan turned and scanned the opposite horizon to the boats but there was nothing to be seen but water. 'Well, soldier,' said the plump airman sadly, 'what d'you reckon? Do you think we could pass you off as a third member of our crew? At least you'd be classified as a prisoner of war and not a spy?'

'There are three problems with that,' replied Duncan ruefully. 'Firstly I have no uniform, secondly they probably know by now there were *two* people in the speedboat, but they will only find poor old Pusser. Thirdly, if they asked me anything at all about Wellington bombers, I wouldn't have the faintest notion what they were talking about.'

'But our plane was on fire, they must know that,' persisted the airman. 'We could say your uniform was alight so you had to shed it. You wouldn't have had time to put on anything else even if we'd had it. After all, no one hangs around in a bomber when it catches fire. Quick, soldier, whilst they're still four miles away, what d'you say?'

'That still leaves my lack of knowledge of aircraft in general and Wellington bombers in particular,' pointed out Duncan. 'A Boy Scout'd know more. Still, I suppose I've nothing to lose.' He began to un do his coat. 'Although I do hope they don't shoot me in the nude, there's no dignity in it.'

'If they are going to shoot you,' snapped the airman, 'convince yourself it's a jealous husband and you're climbing out of a window, I'm sure you'll feel better . . . but just bloody *hurry*!'

Duncan's heart was not truly in the subterfuge, which accounted for his great delight to hear the words, 'Aircraft approaching!'

He looked up quickly and on the distant horizon he saw an old biplane with sea-floats, skimming along just a few feet above the water. 'It looks like it's out of the ark. Whose side d'you reckon it's on?' he asked. 'Francis Drake's?'

'If it's out of the ark, then it can only be ours,' said the slim airman ruefully. 'They really do have some geriatric craft in the rescue service. As far as I can tell from here, I'd say it was a Walrus Amphibian. They fly just a bit slower than a duck but they're pretty manoeuvrable and they land on water like a seagull.'

'But he can't pick us up now,' pointed out Duncan. 'The krauts would be on us before he hits the sea.'

'I know,' murmured the airman solemnly. 'So he's got no alternative. He's got to take them on first . . . all we can do is watch.'

'It don't look much like a fighting plane to me,' observed Duncan worriedly.

'Well, it does have a couple of Lewis guns and carries a few small bombs so it can't be trifled with. If I was on those boats, I'd be as worried as if I was on that plane, so I'd say it's even-steven. Anyway, soldier, at least you can now keep your clothes on.'

Because of its low altitude, the German boats had not yet seen the plane. Guessing this, the pilot took the Walrus into a large curve and, instead of meeting the Germans head on, came in from the side.

'Why's he doing that?' asked Duncan. 'It means one of the boats will be unscathed even if his attack is successful.'

'He can now concentrate everything on the one boat,' said the airman, 'and if he's successful—' He shrugged. 'Well, how would you feel if you were in the remaining boat? It's a chance . . . and he's risking it. It's all he can do.'

'Then let's try to draw all their attention,' snapped Duncan. 'Do anything, even a second could be precious. The longer they look at us the less time they'll have to see the Walrus.'

'There are some flares here in the survival kit,' said the plump airman.

'Then let them off,' yelled Duncan, 'because there's not much else we can do in a rubber dinghy!' Within seconds there was a brilliant though brief firework display as the package of flares was ignited. Just before the last one had faded, they saw the starboard boat change course as it had obviously spotted the aircraft. It was undoubtedly a quick manoeuvre, though not quick enough. The first burst of fire from the Walrus straddled the boat and ignited it into a fireball. At least four of the crew, with flames leaping from their clothing, could be seen jumping into the sea. The second boat also changed course and, besides opening fire on the seaplane, instantly began to zig-zag.

'The old plane won't find the second boat such an easy target,' pointed out the plump airman. 'But at least he's halved the odds.'

To their surprise, the Walrus showed no intention of attacking the second boat. Instead it turned towards them and began to fly slowly around them. The undamaged German boat then began to make for the distressed, burnt men now waving frantically from the water. Like stretcher bearers in no-man's-land, both antagonists had now turned to assist their helpless compatriots. As the Walrus landed lightly alongside the dinghy, the gunner yelled from its cockpit, 'You've got ten seconds to clamber aboard, lads. Dive in here head first if you have to, otherwise they'll blow us to bits before we can take off. Leave everything in the dinghy or we'll never get off with the weight. *Now!*'

Ducking beneath the wide wings of the plane, Duncan pulled himself up by its struts before tumbling head first into the open cockpit. The other two airmen followed suit. The last of them was only in up to his waist before the plane began to move forward. It was a glorious tangle of arms and legs before they could sort themselves out. 'You're lucky we're a crewman short,' shouted the gunner over the noise of the Pegasus 750 hp engine situated just above their heads. 'We left the observer behind in case we had to do the rescue ourselves. Best idea we've had today.'

'You found us without an observer?' asked the slim airman incredulously.

'Yeh,' yelled the gunner, with a wink and a nod towards the pilot. 'Skipper likes doing things the hard way. He reckons our observer has difficulty finding France.'

Duncan looked anxiously at the German motorboat. It seemed it had picked up what remained of the survivors and had now turned and was heading full blast towards them, no doubt seeking retribution. They had to clear the water at first attempt otherwise the whole operation would be a disaster. 'Not out of the woods yet,' he muttered into the ear of the slim airman.

'We are if he gets off first time,' he replied confidently.

The engine certainly seemed laboured but nevertheless did not falter as the plane soared skywards and turned north-west for Devonport. 'Done bloody well to get out of there in one piece,' shouted the plump airman with obvious relief.

Duncan glanced down at the sea as something caught his eye. He stared at it sadly for some seconds before replying, 'There's one there who wasn't so lucky.' Both airmen peered curiously through the Perspex and there, three hundred feet below, a lifeless little figure sprawled face down in a gently drifting motorboat.

20

Though Duncan had been more than grateful to be rescued, he was the only one on board the plane who was not suitably dressed for flying and it did not take long for the cold to bite deep into his body. 'Shouldn't be long,' the pilot mouthed to him above the engine roar. It was only when he noticed the sun was not on his right side as he expected but facing him that he queried the aircraft's course.

'Had to change it,' shouted the pilot. 'There're enemy aircraft about and we're seeking a bank of cloud cover ten miles east.'

Before he could ask his question it was answered for him by the plump airman. 'Apparently they can't spare us any fighter escort at the moment so we're on our own and we'll hopefully make landfall through a cloud bank. The trouble with these planes is their lack of speed – elephants fly faster. Even the slowest German fighter could shoot us like fish in a barrel.'

'So where are we heading now?' asked the shivering Duncan.

'Portsmouth, probably.' Sure enough, after hugging the sanctuary of the Isle of Wight coastline, the Walrus left it at Bembridge and taxied to a halt near the slipway in Portsmouth harbour, barely thirty minutes later than planned. It was a thirty minutes that almost froze Duncan into hypothermia. Before his debriefing by the intelligence officer he insisted on a long soak in a hot bath. There, in the soothing water, he suddenly noticed the fading bite marks inflicted by the passionate – if treacherous – Roselyn. Though he found her subsequent actions unforgivable, the thought of those mind-blowing times with her certainly stimulated his libido. With his eyes closed and his brain in neutral, his imagination began to run riot over his desire for the absent Julia. He found it strange that no matter how many women passed through his life, always his thoughts returned to Julia.

Two hours later, kitted out with a uniform of sorts, he was shown into a room for a debriefing by a Colonel Baker of the Intelligence Corps. Duncan's first impression was one of disbelief. The colonel's desk was a total mess with papers, dossiers and files strewn everywhere. There were two large trays marked 'In' and 'Out' but very little correspondence rested in either. The man himself was middle-aged and fat with a Friar Tuck hairstyle. He was dressed in an assortment of tatty clothes, none of which looked like military issue. He glanced up with a frown that slowly changed into a welcoming smile. 'I know you, don't I?' he said in a flat accentless voice. 'No, don't tell me. Guards corporal, weren't you? Did some intelligence for me with the fascists before the war? Yes, I remember you now! Anyway, what've you been up to that requires you to be interviewed by me?'

He glanced down at the mess and rummaged for a few moments. 'Ah yes, I knew I had it somewhere, here it is.' He studied a report in front of him for little more than a few seconds. 'Think I've got the gist of that. Now what have you got to tell me about life in occupied Guernsey?'

It was only then that Duncan realised he knew the man. He also remembered him as being deceptively astute. He recounted his adventures from the time he had left the submarine to the time he had landed in Portsmouth from the Walrus.

'My!' exclaimed the colonel. 'You do seem to have been a busy little soldier.'

'I may have been busy, sir,' agreed Duncan, 'but I've certainly been neither useful nor economical. I had a submarine to get me there and an aeroplane to get me back. I've lost a dinghy and my uniform and all I've managed to do is to get three good men killed.'

'And to bed a Nazi informant, Sergeant,' interceded the colonel. 'Let's not be too modest about that. To ship you ashore in enemy-occupied territory for you to cheerfully fornicate with the natives is one of the few wartime successes we have managed to date.'

Choosing to ignore the remark Duncan continued, 'Wasting money and lives is not what I joined the Commandos for, sir, and I feel that this whole operation succeeded in wasting both. If we can't yet plan something better, then perhaps we should wait until we can.'

'Very profound of you, Sergeant,' said the colonel, 'but using your own measure, on the balance of value for money, this operation only cost the life of one soldier and two civilians. The submarine and the plane were doing little more than their normal patrol and you made at least one small section of the German war machine realise the war is not yet won. Not bad for a beginning, you know.' He leaned back in his chair and tapped his fingertips together. 'I understand there are other raids being proposed. You know, small-scale things, twenty or thirty men attacking coastal stations, gun emplacements, taking a few prisoners, bluff and counter bluff, that sort of thing. We have all the enthusiasm in the world but what we lack is experience. That is what you and others like you can provide. It's going to be a long war, Sergeant, so don't get impatient, you've plenty of time to get yourself killed.'

'Yessir,' acknowledged Duncan without too much conviction.

'If I remember rightly, you used to be heavily embroiled with a gorgeous little nurse. Did anything come of it?'

'I see her from time to time, sir,' agreed Duncan.

'Good, then take a seventy-two-hour leave and see her again because I'm sure the army is soon going to have all sorts of interesting little tasks for experienced men like you to do. Off you go.'

It was in Duncan's mind to tell him the army had already wrecked his chances by informing her he was dead, but he thought better of it and so saluted and turned to leave the office. As he reached the door the colonel called after him, 'And don't forget, pace yourself, man, or you'll never see the bloody war out.'

Landing at the headquarters of one branch of the forces and trying to obtain a uniform from another, was about as easy as seeking an audience with the pope. Nevertheless, he was finally kitted out and hastening through the barriers at Waterloo station. He made firstly for the telephone kiosks but the section of the building that housed them had been flattened by a bomb. He suddenly realised he had no set plan for finding Julia. With the constant changing face of wartime London, she could be anywhere. His only stroke of luck was to find a bed for two nights in the Union Jack Club opposite the station. This would at least give him a base and a place to leave his kitbag. The club was a hostel for servicemen passing through the capital and perfectly central for his purposes, being scarcely fifteen minutes' walk from Millbank Hospital in one direction and Queen's Buildings in the other.

He finally found an intact call box in a derelict street and telephoned Queenie. He could tell by her astonished reaction that she had considered him dead. She bombarded him with so many questions that he barely had time to ask any of his own. 'Look, I don't have much time. Tell me where I can find Julia,' he cut in finally.

'You'll give her a terrible shock if ever you do,' she said. 'After she received the telegram reporting you were dead, she was so upset that after taking the children away to Norfolk, she transferred away from Millbank.'

'Where to this time?'

'That's the strange part about it, we don't know. She said she was going away because she was tired, confused and needed to sort her life out again. She did say she would keep in touch but we've heard nothing since. We did get some information that she was living with a doctor somewhere but we only got that third hand. The raids have been so bad lately that there has been little time for anything other than surviving. Everyone is getting war-weary, I'm afraid. The whole country is in need of some good news, for a change. Where are you staying?'

'I have managed two nights at the Union Jack Club but I'll have to vacate after that.'

'Then stay here, you're always welcome, you know that. Besides, Jim would love to see you again for a chat.'

'I may take you up on that but in the meantime I'll call on Grace and David.'

'They don't know where she is either, neither does Billie. Look, I'll leave the invitation open. Take care, Duncan, it's wonderful to hear from you again.'

He replaced the receiver and looked at the devastated street outside. Where the hell should he begin his search? David might be as good a start as anywhere. After all, he was a policeman – if he didn't know then surely he could find out? It was only when he saw the ruins of the former home of Grace and David that he remembered Queenie's phrase, 'little time for anything other than surviving'. Just what do you do, he wondered, when everything you have in the world is a pile of dust? On seeing a passing postwoman, he pointed to the mountain of debris that once was the western end of the old tenements. 'How will I find what has happened to a family that used to live in there?' he asked.

'You could try the rent office in Scovell Road,' she suggested. 'Or the wardens' control office. Failing that, there's the local cop-shop. Though you'll need to be very lucky; so many people scattered to the far corners after that happened. Some say there are still families buried in there, poor devils.' So saying she crossed herself rapidly. 'Who are you looking for specifically?'

'Family named Diamond, used to live at ninety-one.'

'Oh, I remember them, very attractive girl, he was a bit tasty too. No, I don't know where they are now but there is a woman who lived close to them at number eighty-seven, she now shares with her friend at flat three, far end of the street. She might know.'

'Thanks, Miss, you've been a great help,' replied Duncan gratefully.

'Any time, Sergeant . . . any time at all. I'm around here every day,' she sighed hopefully, as she watched him turn about and stride manfully away.

He climbed the eight stone steps to the first floor and gave a rat-tat on the door of number three. Inside, Wanda Williams cursed as she clambered quickly onto a chair to disconnect the central light socket.

'Just a minute,' she called. Moments later she opened the door and was agreeably surprised to see Duncan standing before her.

'Excuse me, love,' he said, 'but I've been told to ask for the lady who used to live at number eighty-seven. I understand she could be staying with you. Shan't keep her long, she may be able to help me.'

'You're, er, not with the light company, then?' came back the perplexing answer.

Duncan, to whom 'light company' was entirely associated with the charge at Balaclava, looked particularly puzzled.

'Light company? No ma'am, I'm in the army and simply looking for a woman.'

'Ask for the lady', 'shan't keep her long', 'looking for a woman' were all responses that caused confusion to Wanda. Since she had been whoring at the Clinkside, these were the sort of code-like, double-meaning phrases that now meant only one thing to her. The problem was that Rita had made a particular point of never working from the flat, yet here was someone who looked for all the world like a client. Not only that, he was very good-looking and that was something that could not be said about many of their usual clients. Perhaps Rita had made an exception because of this and had simply forgotten to tell her he would call? The financial side of their business was always left to Rita, but unfortunately she was not at home. Wanda started to wonder if she had the expertise to strike a deal with the soldier herself. 'Er – come in, come in,' she requested. 'I'm sorry, but the lady who told you to call ain't here for the moment. But I think I can do most things that she does. Oh—' she cried as an afterthought struck her, 'unless you wanted both of us? In that case you'll have to wait because it's probably special rates and she won't be back for a little while.'

As Duncan removed his beret, he began to realise they were speaking on different levels. 'I think there's been a bit of a misunderstanding, love,' he said. 'I've never seen the lady before and the only reason I've called—'

He was interrupted as a key turned in the door lock. 'Oh good, she's back early,' smiled the relieved Wanda sweetly. 'She'll work the rates out for you, she does it quicker than me.'

Rita looked quickly from one to the other. 'What's going on here? You!' she cried as she recognised Duncan. 'What the hell are you doing here?'

'I know you,' responded Duncan. 'You're the fire-service

lady that rides a bike. Ah, now I've got it. It's you! *You're* the lady from number eighty-seven!'

'Okay,' said Rita, 'now we've established who we are, I repeat, what're you doing here?'

Once Duncan fully explained his mission her suspicions evaporated. 'I can't help you, but they would surely have all the information over at the police station? After all, David Diamond was a copper. Look, tell you what, we'll put the kettle on and you can update us on what you've been doing. After you've had some tea, you can pop over the nick, it's only at the bottom of the street, and ask them.'

As she spoke, Duncan remembered the impression the woman had made on their first meeting, when he had thought the children had fallen into the river. If anything, she was now even more attractive, yet he felt the hardness about her had perceptibly increased. 'Sounds good to me, love,' he agreed. 'I've not had a decent cup of tea for weeks.'

During the next half-hour, with the notable exception of his sojourn in Guernsey, they swopped their wartime experiences since that morning by the river. Their conversation began to develop a rapport that seemed to leave Wanda further and further behind. 'So what're you doing for the rest of your leave?' asked Rita.

'I'm looking for my Julia,' Duncan reminded her.

'Yes, but if you don't find her, what then? For example, you're hardly likely to find her tonight in the blackout.'

'I don't get what you're driving at,' said Duncan.

'Well, here you are, with a few days' precious leave,' she explained, 'and no young lady to share it. Why don't you join us at the Clinkside tonight? It's a lively enough club and if you ask for me – Rita Roberts – when you arrive I'll make sure your evening isn't too expensive. There's good entertainment, good decor and decent booze. Okay, so the food's a bit poxy but nowadays it's poxy everywhere.'

Duncan had a feeling that this visit would not be a good idea, which is probably why he jumped at the chance to attend. 'I've only got my uniform to wear,' he replied. 'I assume that will be okay?'

'With that Commando flash on your shoulder, you'll either get free drinks or a free fight, depends entirely who else is in there. Are you still game?' she asked pointedly.

He ran his eyes rapidly over her body. 'Well, if you two young ladies are present,' he replied, 'then count me in.'

Duncan left the flat a few minutes later with the feeling that the day had not been totally wasted and whistled a little tune as he strode across to Stones End police station. It was here that he received his first clue as to Julia's whereabouts.

'Yes,' said the station officer, 'Davy Diamond is still here and is in the canteen at this very moment for his meal break.' The sergeant then directed him to the basement canteen where he saw his old friend doing battle with two dubious-looking wartime sausages.

'Tripe in battledress, that's what these are,' David Diamond was complaining loudly. 'The soles of my boots would make a better sandwich.'

'Bloody hell! You're not still moaning, are you, Diamond?' whispered Duncan into the policeman's ear.

Wheeling around, David immediately let out a roar of delight as he threw his arms around his old friend. 'What's this then, judgement day?' he exclaimed. 'You're supposed to be dead, you fraud!'

'But I am,' joked Duncan. 'They gave me compassionate leave to get over it. They're thoughtful like that in the Commandos.'

After the initial greetings, Duncan explained his mission. Although David was unable to help, a young police colleague on the same table mentioned he was friendly with a nurse who had worked at Millbank Hospital. He was able to confirm that

Julia was somewhere in Norfolk and believed to be working on one of the many large airfields.

'I'd like to invite you home for a meal,' said David apologetically, 'but at the moment we're living in just one room in a friend's house. Every time we think we have found another place, the bloody thing gets flattened or blasted.'

'Don't worry,' Duncan assured him, 'I've already mapped out this evening.'

'Something good?' inquired David with only mild interest.

'I'll let you know,' responded Duncan. 'I've been invited by a couple of friendly wenches to the Clinkside Club.'

David seemed taken aback at this news. 'Oh, I don't think that's for you tonight,' he said unconvincingly. 'It's a terribly expensive place. A proper catchpenny clip-joint. We're constantly receiving complaints from those daft enough to go there.'

'I'm a big boy now, David,' replied Duncan cheerily. 'I can look after myself.'

David appeared about to take his point further, but they were joined at that moment by the duty inspector, which immediately restricted the conversation.

'Ah, Diamond,' said the inspector, 'just the man I've been looking for. Not interrupting anything, am I?'

Taking the hint Duncan glanced at his watch. 'Well, I need a bath and shave so I'll be making my way back to the Union Jack Club. Give my love to Grace and I'll try to see you again before I return to my unit.'

'Oh, you'll see me all right,' replied David in a surprisingly ominous tone. 'Don't you worry about that.'

Duncan gave the smile of acknowledgement that indicated he recognised an underlying message in David's words, but he hadn't the faintest idea what it was.

21

After his farewells Duncan walked briskly back to the Union Jack Club. There, after a shave, a regulation five-inch-deep bath and a dried egg and chips tea, Duncan felt in perfect condition to savour the fleshly delights of the Clinkside Club.

An hour or so later, the nightly sirens had sounded and, exactly on cue, the bombers rode a biting east wind as they followed the snaking river up from the estuary. Searchlights cut across the now starry sky and illuminated the dome of St Paul's like some ghostly surrealist painting. Duncan was pleased to escape from the wind as he pushed open the foyer door of the club. The first thing he noticed was the smell of the place. A cocktail of stale cigarette smoke, cheap perfume and inadequately washed parts, mingled together to test the determination of the newcomer. He had to admit that at first it did take his breath away but he soon became accustomed to it and, at the request for a fifteen-shilling admission fee from a heavily-painted pudding of a woman, he used the name Rita Roberts to great effect. 'Rita? Oh yes, sir, lovely girl you 'ave there,' she cackled. 'She said a nice-looking young man would be askin' for 'er ternight. Such a sweet young thing is our Reet, isn't she, sir?'

Duncan doubted if Rita had been a sweet young thing since she was twelve years of age but he decided it was a matter better left unsaid. 'Is she here?' he asked.

'Oh yes, sir,' replied the woman, 'but she's occupied, as you

317

might say, at the moment. She said you were to take a seat at the basement bar and she'll join you in a short while.'

Duncan then went through a door and saw the club proper for the first time. It was about a quarter full with great palls of blue smoke already hanging on the still air. He thought it similar to every other sordid club he had ever seen, even the characters seemed to be the same. The tariffs and the toilets definitely were. A five-piece band played in the corner of the room and some forty tables occupied a space that would have been crowded with twenty. In the centre was the tiniest of dance floors. He needed a moment or two to become accustomed to the poor lighting before making his way to the bar through the maze of tables. At the end of the bar were two girls in evening gowns deep in conversation with their bare backs half-turned to him. A huge bear of a barman looked at Duncan and promptly raised one eyebrow, which seemed an accepted substitute for 'What would you like to drink, sir?'

'Do you serve bitter?' replied Duncan, guessing the answer.

'We don't do beer of any sort. Got a nice line in cocktails, though,' the barman replied dully.

Duncan pointed to the optics hanging at the rear of the bar. 'I'll have a scotch.'

'We only serve doubles,' countered the barman.

'Yes, I thought you might say that,' nodded Duncan. 'Will it be a real double or one that's been strengthened with water?'

Before the barman could reply, a squeal of recognition came from one of the girls at the end of the bar. 'Oh, it's the soldier from the light company!'

Duncan looked up to see Wanda Williams swivelling on her stool and pointing at him. His first impression was of the transformation in her. When he had seen her earlier at her flat, he had thought her a rather sad figure but now she appeared a totally different being. Her fair hair was neatly bobbed and the low cut tapering dress showed her slim figure to its best advantage. 'Oh, I know you're not really in the light company,' she giggled, 'but it's how I remember you.'

'Are you buying the young lady a drink?' asked the barman pointedly.

'I didn't know the young lady wanted one,' said Duncan cynically, 'but I'd be bloody amazed if she didn't!'

'Now look 'ere,' began the barman aggressively, 'don't go thinking that Commando flash cuts any ice in 'ere, mate, 'cos it don't.' He glanced ominously around the room. 'We're dealing wiv your sort all the time. So if yer want ter stay, keep a civil tongue in yer 'ead, otherwise yer might git separated from it. Got it?'

'It's all right, George,' soothed Wanda, placing her tiny hand on the barman's massive forearm. 'He's not a client, but a friend of Rita's. She's upstairs with a regular at the moment but she's told me to keep an eye on him until she comes down. Perhaps you'd better give us both a decent scotch after all and not that cat's piss from the optic.' She smiled. 'Because I don't think Rita's in a particularly good mood tonight.'

'Well, that's a novelty, I must say,' replied George acidly as he reached under the bar for a bottle of Chivas Regal. 'Ain't she 'ad a client frail enough for 'er ter roll yet then?' He mutteringly poured two generous measures of best malt whisky in utter silence before moving down the bar to another two customers.

'He's a happy little soul,' said Duncan.

Wanda gave a nod of agreement. 'I think the only reason that Swinger keeps him on here is for the odd occasion when the wheel comes off. In the event of a rough-house, he can be an animal. You may find it difficult to believe but disturbances here can occasionally be the fault of the customer.'

'Perhaps it would be better to put the Chivas Regal in the optic,' suggested Duncan, 'instead of that cabbage water that currently lurks there.'

She smiled ruefully. 'As it happens, I think you're right. Swinger makes a great deal of money from this place, but I feel he could make more if folks did not wake up the following morning thinking they've been robbed blind.'

'Don't worry about it,' said Duncan dismissively. 'Soldiers have been parted from their cash ever since there have been soldiers. If Swinger and his team didn't do it, someone else would. In any case, few soldiers wake up in the mornings with any idea of where they spent the night before. It's one of the few advantages of being a soldier. It's far more important for you to tell me about yourself and why someone as sweet as you works in a tip like this.'

The compliment took her by surprise and she faltered before replying, 'Er – Rita would say you've got that the wrong way round. *We* are supposed to get *you* talking so you don't realise how much you're spending.'

Duncan leaned over and, besides looking down her neckline, also whispered in her ear, 'Don't tell anyone but so far I've not spent a penny. Though I think your barman has plans to alter that before the night is out.' She laughed and he was again surprised how much more sophisticated she was. 'That's the first time I've seen you laugh,' he said in genuine admiration. 'You should do it more often, it suits you.'

They talked in such a fashion for some time and it was only when a balcony door opened and he saw Rita coming down the steps that he realised how the club had filled in the last hour or so. If he had been surprised at Wanda, he was almost knocked out at Rita. Her jet black hair seemed a perfect accessory for her startling, dark red, off-the-shoulder dress. She was vivacious in every respect and everything about her seemed icily correct. Every instinct he had told him that this was a dangerous woman, but she was also a challenge that it was not in him to refuse.

In spite of her apparent hardness, he had known from the

outset she was an attractive woman, but tonight, for the first time since he had known her, she was devastating, and he suspected he might soon be disregarding life-long instincts. As much as he admired the sweet, almost innocent air of the younger girl, he knew that for pure animal magnetism it was no contest between the two women. Rita looked like every diamond-hard moll he had ever seen in a gangster film. The flattering soft approach that had worked well with Wanda would be water off a duck to the worldly Rita. Yet in spite of that, he correctly sensed she had an affinity for him. Why else would she pave his way so easily at the club?

Before she had descended the last step he decided where he was going to spend the night and the idea of paying for the privilege did not even enter his head. His first action was to invite Wanda on the floor to dance with him. Nothing like dancing with one woman, he thought, to interest another. Pretending not to see Rita he led the girl between the tables to the tiny floor. 'Why is it so small?' he asked as he took her in his arms to the appropriate tune of 'The Nearness of You'. 'I've seen bigger tablecloths.'

'It's a trade secret,' she whispered, 'so keep it to yourself. It's so the customers who intend to limit themselves to just drinks, can feel the girl so close to them that they become customers for . . . well, you know . . . the other thing.'

He glanced swiftly around the floor and instantly saw the validity of the girl's remark. Of the ten hostesses he could see, there was not one whose buttocks were not covered by her partner's widespread palms. This in turn pulled the girl even closer into her partner's groin. 'Looking around here,' he whispered, 'you realise that if I don't play with your bum a little, people might think I'm a pouf.' He gave a little shrug. 'Can't have that now, can we?'

She shrugged in return. 'It's not the hands on our bums that give us the clue, it's the push up our fronts that gives the game away. As a matter of interest, I can already vouch you're not a pouf.'

He lifted his gaze to see what sort of effect his flirting was having on Rita and was delighted to see it was considerable. In the few seconds he watched her she turned down the attention of a well-heeled potential client with what appeared to be an irritable response. Finally the music stopped and with his arm around the girl they eased their way back to the bar.

'I hate to interrupt,' said Rita curtly to Wanda, 'but aren't you supposed to be working?'

'Oh er—' stammered the girl, obviously in awe of her mentor, 'I'm s-sorry, Rita. I was just l-looking after him l-like you t-told me and—'

Her conversation was cut short by a loud whistle blast. The door of the club room suddenly burst open and the place began to fill with blue uniforms.

'I don't believe it! It's a bloody police raid!' snapped Rita. 'You'd think they'd have something better to do in a blitz besides raiding places like this, now wouldn't you?'

'So what happens now?' asked Duncan.

'They'll take everyone down to the nick and we'll spend half the night there while they check our names, addresses and service units. It's a real pain, I can tell you.'

'I've not got time for that, quick!' said Duncan to the two women. 'Get behind that curtain, no one's noticed us yet.' An extremely thick blackout curtain hung down over the recess of a full-length window. There was certainly a cover of sorts there but nothing that any searcher would miss. He sensed their lack of enthusiasm before adding, 'Well, it's better than nothing, c'mon, give it a try.'

They quickly shuffled behind the curtain and Rita immediately complained about the draught that cut through the blast-damaged frames. 'If we could undo this, we could get out into the alley at the back,' she said, tugging at a catch. 'It wouldn't be much colder than standing here anyway.'

Further conversation was stopped when the curtain was thrown back and all three were revealed to a searching policeman. 'You surely never expected to hide in here?' asked David Diamond, closing the curtains back into place behind him. 'I saw you dash in here but I thought you'd have a better plan than this.'

'Aw, c'mon, Dave,' pleaded Duncan. 'I've not got much of my leave left. I don't want to spend it in your nick. There must be a way out.'

'I was trying to tell you not to come here this afternoon when you called at the station but you were too bloody thick to notice. Quick, kick that frame hard.' In the event, the frame required little more than a severe push before it collapsed outward. A blast of cold air surged into the recess.

'I'm not going out there dressed like this,' protested Rita. 'It's bloody freezing! Can't you get our capes from the two stools at the end of the bar?'

'Anything else you'd like me to do?' asked David acidly. 'I'll get the black maria to run you home if you wish.'

'Go on, Dave, be a sport,' Duncan encouraged him. 'Once you've got their wraps we're out of your hair and you can go nicking people to your heart's content.'

The policeman gave a great sigh before rapidly slipping from behind the now windswept curtain and returning just as sharply with two ladies' wraps. 'Sod off quick,' was the sum total of his farewell speech.

As the trio climbed the basement steps into the street, the commotion at the front of the building almost drowned the noise of the customary air raid. The distance from the club to Wanda's flat was no more than a few minutes' walk but it was a shivering tortuous journey for the two women dressed as they were. Duncan had placed himself between them and they huddled tightly against him for warmth, a position he enjoyed greatly. They had just turned into Collinson Street when a great shower of shrapnel fell across the road, missing them narrowly but it was some indication of the girls' discomfort that they barely noticed it and certainly did not break step. They were hardly in the room before Wanda had climbed a chair to plug in the small, one-bar electric fire to the light socket.

'And I wouldn't even care if you were the chairman of the light company,' said Wanda, rubbing her body vigorously, 'because my bum's about to drop off.'

Further conversation was cut short as a massive explosion somewhere nearby caused the building to tremble, the power to fade and the little fire to extinguish.

'That settles it, Wanda,' said Rita as she lit the emergency candle. 'It's bed as soon as possible. It's the only place we can cuddle up to keep warm.' She turned to Duncan. 'As for you, my dear Sergeant, you can lie in between us so we'll not freeze, or you can doze in the chair. But if you think your luck's changed don't bet on it. We're so cold you'd scream the place down the instant we curled up to you.'

'Don't think I haven't thought of that,' said Duncan ruefully. 'If there's one thing that can destroy a man's ardour quicker than one icy bum, it's two of them. Call me ungallant if you will, but I'm heading for the Union Jack Club. Nothing personal, girls,' he added hastily, 'and I never thought I'd hear myself say it, but can I have a ticket to come back in the summer, though?'

'I thought you Commandos were supposed to be tough,' said Wanda disappointedly.

'Tough, yes,' agreed Duncan. 'Suicidal no.'

'What route are you taking back?' was the surprising question from Rita.

'Route?' he shrugged. 'Dunno, Borough Road, Waterloo Road, I suppose. Why?'

'Wouldn't mind going back by way of the Clinkside, would you? It's only a short detour.'

'Why, what else have you forgotten?'

'Judging by the direction and distance of that explosion, I'd say it must have been pretty close to the club. Perhaps you may be able to return your friend's favour for letting us escape.'

'Rita!' he exclaimed. 'You must be softening in your old age. It's not like you to be concerned, least of all for a copper.'

'He showed me a kindness . . . but as to anyone else in there—' she opened her palms and hunched her shoulders. 'Be they clients or staff, I don't give a toss. If it was the Clinkside that was hit, d'you think you could let us know in the morning? After all, there's no point in us girls dolling ourselves up tomorrow evening if we don't have to work, is there?'

He shook his head at her callousness but promised he would at least call to let them know the location of the explosion. He then let himself out into a world of smoke, dust and ringing fire-bells.

Within minutes of reaching the Clinkside he knew that Rita's fears had been more than realised. He could see by the ambulances that were still racing to the scene that casualties were obviously heavy. God, how lucky the three of them had been. If it had not been for the police raid they would have been in that lethal basement. He suddenly saw a blood-stained Canadian soldier staggering blindly through the dark. 'Was it the Clinkside?' Duncan demanded.

The man stared at him as if in a trance. 'Through the roof,' he muttered. 'It came through the roof . . . exploded on floor . . . blew everyone to bits . . . Everyone . . . every one.' The man then staggered off into the smoky dark. As Duncan turned the corner his worst fears were realised. The club was virtually flattened. It had been a direct hit, of that there was no doubt. Poor David, the only thing that could be said was it would have been doubtful if anyone in the main room of the club would have known what hit them. If it exploded when it hit the dance floor death would have been messy but instantaneous. He sought out a warden and asked if there was any way he could help.

'No,' the man replied wearily. 'There's not much rescuing to be done, mostly just gathering up. There are no more than a dozen injured.' He pointed to a group of people searching at one of the few pieces of the building still upright. 'You could give a hand there if you like.'

Duncan picked his way over the rubble but was soon assured by a pretty young ambulance girl that there was nothing to be done. He was about to turn away when a familiar voice came from one of the injured about to go into an ambulance.

'Is that your voice, Duncan?'

'*David!*' he responded. 'You're alive! Thank heaven for that. Where're you injured?'

'I – I don't know,' came the faltering reply. 'I c-can't see very well.' He gave a wry little laugh. 'Though I've you three crooks to thank for my escape.'

'Us?' asked the surprised Duncan. 'How?'

'After you three left, I decided to put the door-frame back in place in case someone should realise I had let you all escape. That curtain was thicker than any blanket and, though I was blown into the basement, it acted as a shield.' A gust of wind caught the flames of a nearby fire and gave a momentary surge of light. In that instant Duncan saw that the top of his friend's face was covered in a bloodstained bandage. He glanced quickly at the ambulance girl. She said nothing but pointed to her own eyes and shook her head.

'Can I go with him?' asked Duncan.

'It wouldn't help,' she said. 'Firstly the ambulances are already crowded, secondly, judging by what was left of his eyes, the hospital will transfer him as soon as possible to a specialist unit. His colleagues in the force already have the matter in hand, I suggest you leave it with them.'

Seeing the wisdom of the girl's remarks Duncan nodded an agreement and bent to comfort his friend before sliding him into the ambulance. As he turned away he realised the guns had ceased firing and the searchlights had faded. A strange silence seemed to have settled over the city as if some deciding point of a game had been scored and there was now nothing else to play for. By the light of the stars he could just make out the river and beyond that the outline of St Paul's Cathedral. Just for a moment he thought of the happy times he had spent on that river walk with Julia. Oh, where the hell was she? They had been in and out of each other's lives for as long as he could remember. Surely they were not destined to spend the rest of their days this way? He now realised just how much he wanted her, yet he had little more than two days to find her. His flippancy had now faded and he knew he must find this woman, but where was she? With the first tear of his entire adult life trickling from the corner of his eye, he picked his way wearily through the debris towards the Waterloo Road.

22

Julia stirred slightly and wondered if she should open her eyes. There is something really special about a goose-feather bed when it's really cold, she thought, as she burrowed deeper into it. She had burrowed so far into the feathered pillow that it was almost wrapped around her head, whilst the patchwork eiderdown was piled high enough on top of her to cut out half the early sun. Bed always felt good on cold Norfolk mornings. Julia could never understand why Eve should have been tempted with an apple. If she had had the sense to have held out for a feather bed, who knows, the whole course of history might have been different. If she were to open one eyelid and look to her left she would see the bedroom clock. But why would she want to do that? As soon as she saw the time then reality would start. She would know if she was either late or could afford another luxurious five minutes under the eiderdown. She moved a foot tentatively across the bottom of the bed but all she discovered was a chill spot where a warm leg should be. Oh dear, that meant Stuart was already up and about, that was particularly bad news. He was as fond of his bed as she was; if he had vacated it then time must indeed be running on.

The drone of aircraft at the distant Massingham airfield reminded her that full reality would begin the instant she assembled her thoughts. Playing for time she left them deliberately muzzy as she drew up her knees and hugged herself into a ball. He was such a lovely man that she wondered why she did not love him. Stuart himself was well aware of the fact and yet he accepted it. They lived together, slept together and on rare occasions actually made love together. She was probably as close to him as it was possible to be to almost any man but without that precious final commitment. She told herself it wasn't so wrong and she thought that one day they might even marry. People far less close to each other married: arranged marriages; royal marriages; shotgun marriages; marriages of convenience. One thing she was sure of, if they did marry, they would be as happy as any pair had a right to expect in such a situation. All right, so it would be a compromise, but it was one that she was beginning to think she could make. Interspersed with aircraft engines she thought she could hear a hammering noise. Not being fully awake, at first she took little notice. Then, as it became more distinct to her clearing brain, she knew exactly what it was. It was the blacksmith in his forge opposite! Good God, if the blacksmith was working then she must be really late. Their home was five miles from the aerodrome and without looking at the clock she guessed she should have been on duty at least an hour ago. Why hadn't Stuart called her? Leaping from the seductive warmth of the bed, she reached for her housecoat whilst shuffling her feet blindly around in search of her slippers. Still tying the cord she was halfway down the staircase when she smelt toast. He had been up long enough to cook toast but he still hadn't called her. Just what was going on?

She opened the kitchen door and saw Stuart sitting on a stool in front of the kitchen range, toasting fork in one hand and newspaper in the other. 'Shame,' he grinned, 'you caught me and spoiled the surprise.' He nodded to a small pile of toast already on a plate. 'Last slice, too.'

'Stuart,' she said firmly but not unkindly, 'why didn't you wake me?'

He rose to his feet and, crossing the fireside rug, lightly kissed the tip of her nose. 'I could say it was because you looked so beautiful as you slept that I hadn't the heart to disturb you.' He gave a mild shrug. 'On the other hand, I could tell you the truth and remind you that it's your birthday and we both have taken a couple of days' leave.'

She put her hands to her open mouth. 'Oh, of course!' she cried. 'Is this what happens when you get older? You not only forget your birthdays but you forget the time you have taken off to celebrate them.' She bent forward and returned his kiss. 'Oh, you are such a sweetie and here I am, spoiling your treat.'

'You couldn't spoil it, darling, because it's a shared treat. You surely don't think you're going to have an old-fashioned pre-war breakfast on your own, do you? I claim cook's rights to share a real peace-time breakfast with you, or else it's just watery porridge.'

Twenty minutes later she pushed away an empty plate. 'That was delicious, Stuart,' she complimented him. 'And all the better for being such a surprise. So what do you want to do today? I can hardly believe we have the sheer luxury of two days' leave. I feel like the war is over.'

'Then for two days, it is,' he said. 'Simple, really.'

There was such a change in his tone on the last two words that she looked up anxiously. 'Stuart,' she whispered, 'is something wrong?'

For a moment he made no reply, then said quietly, 'Your Duncan, what was his surname?'

'Surname – why . . . why . . . Forbes. Duncan Forbes.' A look of concern clouded her face. 'Why, what is it, Stuart? Tell me please,' she implored.

'Because we are up and about a couple of hours later than usual this morning, the paper had already been delivered. I thought it would be a luxury to read it before breakfast instead of after dinner when I usually manage it. There's something in it you ought to see.' He slid the paper across the table. 'I've marked it with a pen, there at the foot of the front page.'

Trembling, she picked up the broadsheet. There, from 'Our Special Correspondent', was a somewhat dramatised account of the daring Channel rescue of the aircrew of a Wellington bomber, plus 'Sergeant Duncan Forbes who had carried out a valiant attack on German fortifications on an undisclosed part of the enemy coastline.'

'Duncan!' she exclaimed. 'It's Duncan! He's alive!'

'It would appear so,' he agreed quietly. 'Seeing as I couldn't possibly be glad at anyone's demise, I'm happy for you. If you want to use the phone feel free. Happy birthday.'

She ran over to him and kneeled beside his chair. 'I've got to find out for myself, you know that, don't you?' she asked through flooded eyes.

He patted her arm. 'Of course,' he murmured. 'In fact he's done me a favour. I know how you feel about him but I also know how I feel about you. As long as there's the slightest chance he's alive you'll never rest. This way . . . well, it's like surgery, I suppose. If it doesn't work proper and we can't fix it, we take it out. Us surgeons do it all the time.' He gave an unconvincing smile. 'Now someone's doing it to me.' He held both her hands and stared into her wet eyes. 'You've got two full days' leave. It's amazing what can be achieved in that time by a dedicated woman, so I doubt I'll be kept waiting long.' He rose to his feet and, pointing to the telephone, walked quietly from the room.

He had barely closed the door before she was dialling Queenie's number. 'Where the hell have you been?' Queenie greeted her curtly. 'You've sent everyone to distraction with worry.'

'I know, Queenie, and you have every reason to be as angry with me as you wish, but could we postpone your recriminations for a while? I have just two days to try to find Duncan

332

and I've got to start somewhere, so I've started with you.'

'Right, first give me your telephone number and your address so we don't lose you again.'

'Well, it's Gayton 6097, but it's not our number so it's not in the book, we are renting a three-month lease. The address is The Old Chandlers, East Winch Road, Gayton, Norfolk. Look, I read the *Telegraph* this morning and it looks like he's not just alive but back in this country. Have you heard from him?'

'Not only heard from him,' said Queenie with just a hint of smugness, 'but I know he's searching for you and I also know where he's staying, at least for the next twenty-four hours. It's the Union Jack Club in Waterloo Road.'

'Do you have their number?'

'No, but if you haven't much time you'd be wasting most of it by telephoning. He's hardly ever there, he's out most of the time looking for you.'

'I'll be on the next train out of King's Lynn,' said Julia emphatically. 'If he rings you tell him as much . . . oh, and by the way, ring the Union Jack Club to leave a message to that effect for him. I can't stop now, Queenie . . . see you soon. Bye!'

As soon as the line cleared Queenie shook her head and asked the operator for the number of the Union Jack Club. Minutes later she was dialling the place.

'Yes, ma'am,' said the clerk cheerily, 'if you can bear with me whilst I find some paper I'll be with you.'

Paper, being one of the great wartime shortages, was at a premium and he finally had to settle for two small pieces. On one he scrawled the address and on the other the telephone number, although he took the precaution of putting Duncan's name on each. It would have worked fine if the skinny clerk who relieved him twenty minutes later had not seen the clear space on the rear of the paper sporting the telephone number. It was just the size to write a brief note to Private Partridge of the Pioneer Corps to tell him cousin Jessie was up from Wiltshire and would dearly love to see him.

Private Partridge had no sooner walked gloomily away from the inquiry desk, note in hand, than Duncan entered the foyer on his way out. An instinctive glance up at the notice board told him there was a message for him. Borrowing a map he soon discovered Gayton was seven miles from King's Lynn, which in turn was served by the main line out of Liverpool Street. 'How can I find the time of the next train to King's Lynn?' he demanded of the skinny clerk.

'Well, I've got a dozen timetables,' said the clerk, 'but not one that's now reliable. You'll probably find it better to go direct to Liverpool—' He looked up but found he was talking to himself. Duncan was already out of the door and running. It must have been roughly about the same time that Duncan boarded his train for King's Lynn that Julia boarded hers for Liverpool Street, and they blithely passed in opposite directions somewhere in the vicinity of Cambridge. If there was one blessing for them it was that the lines were reasonably clear and neither train was much more than an hour late. Which, for the north-eastern line in wartime, was the peak of punctuality.

Julia was the first to arrive. 'No,' said the skinny clerk. 'Sergeant Forbes isn't in, but I'll leave a message to inform him of your presence on his return.'

The next move was to telephone Queenie and Billie. There was no reply from Queenie and, other than providing hospitality, Billie was unable to help except to say Queenie had told her that Duncan was frequenting all their old haunts in his desperate search. Julia had no set plan so she simply set off to wander around the same locations in the hope of a casual meeting. She instinctively made for the river and was appalled to see the total carnage at the Clinkside, with a cluster of wrecked barges settled on the riverside mud. From there she went to the remains of Queen's Buildings, then on to the Winchester public house.

Pushing open the saloon door, she looked quickly over the heads of the last of the afternoon customers. A quick glance was all she needed to assure her there was no six-foot Commando amongst the clientele. She had barely left the doorway when she heard someone call her name. Putting her head back in the doorway, she saw two young women, rather the worse for drink, sitting at a small corner table behind the door.

'It's Julia, ennit?' said one. 'Yer remember me? We met that Sunday . . . by river . . . when your bloke fell in – ha! Have drink while you're here, gel, you look as if yer need it.'

'Oh yes, of course,' said Julia, after a moment or two's recollection. 'I remember you now.' She raised her hand in protest. 'No, no, thanks very much. I don't have time, I'm looking for him – Duncan, that is. Haven't seen him, I suppose?'

'S'down!' insisted Rita. 'Have a little drop of somethin' and we'll tell yer as much as we know.'

Julia did as she was bid and over a port and lemon heard about the trio's lucky escape from the Clinkside. 'You're soddin' lucky with that bloke,' slurred Rita enviously. 'All I've met in me life is pigs. Married the biggest of 'em.' She snorted. 'Thought I'd no more time for men . . . 's why I shacked up with 'er.' She gestured towards an aloof Wanda. 'But he's bit speshul, that Duncan . . . an' you're a dopy cow if you don't see it . . . yer really are.'

'So what are you two going to do if there's no Clinkside any more?' asked Julia, trying to change the subject.

Rita swayed lightly and put her fingers to her lips. 'Shush, secret.' She looked quickly around her. 'We're leavin' soon. Goin' away.' She nodded an agreement with herself. 'Far, far away. Leavin' this rotten 'ole for good, ain't we, Wanda?'

Wanda made no reply but shook an even wearier head than

Rita seemed to possess. 'Got certificates . . . ain't we, Wanda?' she persisted. 'Got certificates . . . ter say we ain't well enough ter keep bein' bombed by old 'Itler. Paid enough for 'em, mark you.'

Julia tilted her head and drained her glass. 'Look,' she said, 'I've come down from Norfolk for this search so I've very little time. Thanks for the drink and I wish you girls the best of luck, bye.'

'You just 'member wor I said about ole Duncan, though,' persisted Rita.

'I will, I will,' promised Julia. On leaving the Winchester, she decided to call in at Stones End police station, in case there was a chance of seeing David Diamond. Even if he was unable to help, she always suspected David had a soft spot for her and her spirits needed a boost at the moment.

'And who are you, love?' asked the old station sergeant.

'Close family friend, practically a relative. Why, something wrong?' she asked anxiously.

The old sergeant nodded. 'Could be,' he agreed as he began to recite the events at the Clinkside.

'I must see his wife Grace, please tell me where I can find her,' she pleaded. 'I'm a nurse on leave and I have very little time.'

'That case you'd better try the Royal Eye Hospital at St George's Circus. David's in there while they try to save his sight and she's hardly left his side since.'

Julia thanked him and hastened from the station. The hospital in question was mercifully less than ten minutes' walk and a staff nurse was soon showing her into a small room near the entrance to one of the wards. There, a figure that could have been David lay bandaged and motionless in a bed, whilst a woman who was unquestionably Grace sat uncomfortably at his side, but was sound asleep with her head on his bed.

'She's hardly left him,' whispered the staff nurse. 'I'd guess she's totally exhausted. If she wakes, try talking her into going home for a rest, otherwise he'll last longer than her.'

'What're his injuries?' asked Julia.

'Pretty formidable, I'm afraid. The surgeon said he's more concerned to be saving his life than his sight. He was not actually struck by anything except the blast. He does rally from time to time, though, but I don't think he knows where he is, or what has happened to him.'

'Curse this bloody war!' hissed Julia. 'It only seems the good people that suffer!'

'Oh, I don't know,' said the staff nurse with a sympathetic look. 'I've seen the odd first class bastard in here.' She reached out and put a hand on Julia's forearm. 'I think it evens itself out in the end, you know.'

'Julia? Julia, is that you?' A glance at the bed told her the voice came from beneath the bandages.

In an instant Grace was wide awake. 'He spoke, did you hear him?' she cried, seizing the free hand of the staff nurse. 'He spoke! Can't you ease the bandages from his mouth, please!'

'Grace, is that you? Are you there too, Grace? Where am I? Get this stuff off me and tell me what's happened!' he demanded. The staff nurse gently restrained his movements and told him that both Grace and Julia were present and he needed to relax so she could ease his dressings and send for the doctor. He calmed as soon as the two women each took a hand whilst Grace kept up a flowing whisper to his covered ear. Almost at once the staff nurse returned to be followed seconds later by a running doctor.

'I'm afraid you must both leave,' said the nurse as she hurtled the screens around the bed. 'Why don't you go home for a rest, Mrs Diamond? There's nothing more you can do here now. Come back in the morning after a good night's sleep.'

'She's right,' agreed Julia. 'I'll give Queenie a ring, I'm

sure she'll put us both up for the night. C'mon,' she coaxed, 'give them a night to work on him and I'll return with you to start all over again in the morning. What d'you say?'

The sheer effort of the past two days suddenly seemed to have drained Grace and she swayed for a moment but soon recovered and nodded an agreement.

On reaching the hospital exit they met two uniformed constables. 'Hello, Mrs Diamond,' said the older man cheerily. 'We've just popped in for a moment to see how Davy is.'

Grace left Julia to give the progress report and after she had completed it the constable asked their destination.

'Streatham Hill,' replied Julia. 'We're hoping to stay with David's parents.'

The policemen exchanged the swiftest of glances and reciprocal nods. 'Get in the back of the car, love,' said the older man. 'My driver'll have you there in no time.'

Because of the odd diversion and crater, it turned out to be a little longer than 'no time' but it was still only fifteen minutes door to door. It was during that fifteen minutes that Grace asked Julia about the reason for her sudden reappearance.

This conversation took place at almost the same moment that Duncan was having a similar heart-to-heart with Dr Stuart Rawlings over a cup of tea in the kitchen of the Old Chandlers in Norfolk.

'My gut feeling,' said the doctor quietly as he leaned back in his chair, 'is to shoot you and claim it was done by a German parachutist. If I thought I'd get away with it, I probably would. You know, Duncan, I'm not a particularly young man and I have been around a bit and what I haven't experienced, I have seen. But I tell you this, that girl of mine . . . yours . . . ours . . . is a twenty-two-carat cracker. Unfortunately for me, she seems to still be carrying a torch for you. God knows why! Even when you were supposed to be dead she wasn't free of you. Tell me, have you ever seriously thought about dying? I could help you, you know,' he said wryly.

Duncan smiled and put up two hands in token surrender. 'I know, I know,' he repeated. 'I think it finally came to me what a cretin I'd been when I was floating around in the Channel. I agree it took me long enough and I certainly feel guilty as far as you're concerned,' he conceded.

'How about as far as Julia is concerned?' asked the doctor dryly. 'Or doesn't that matter?'

'It matters to me now,' confessed Duncan. 'Put it down to selfishness if you like. In all honesty I doubt if I could offer any other excuse.'

'Do you know,' murmured Stuart ruefully, 'given another two months I think I might have beaten you. Anyway, I suppose I'm still in with a chance seeing as you're up here and she's down there. Do you two ever get anything right?'

'Not a lot,' grinned Duncan. 'I think our last ten years are pretty much cluttered with cock-ups.'

'Oh well, I can still have hopes,' said Stuart. 'But look, I don't want you to think I'm being mean-spirited just because you're about to take up again with the woman I love, but I thought you didn't have much leave left?'

'True,' agreed Duncan.

'Well, the train service between King's Lynn and Liverpool Street only ever runs punctually when the King goes to Sandringham, so I suggest you make a move soon or you'll still be up here when your leave runs out.'

Duncan's reply was interrupted by the telephone. Stuart answered and swiftly glanced across to Duncan. 'If it's Duncan you're concerned about he's here now ... Yes, Duncan! He arrived an hour or so ago ... I don't know, I'll put him on and you can ask him yourself ... What? Okay, then give me the details and I'll see what we can do from this end. D'you have any ideas where they could have gone? ... But they had no money surely? . . . Yes, don't worry, I've the address here somewhere. We'll leave now and I'll keep you posted . . . You sure you don't want a word with him? . . . Okay, but he'll never believe me, bye!' He replaced the handset and looked across the room at Duncan. 'We have another big problem, soldier. Julia's friend, David Diamond, was apparently severely injured, possibly blinded, in an air raid a couple of nights ago.'

'I know all about that,' replied Duncan. 'I was on the scene at the time.'

'Yes, but what you don't know is that David and his wife Grace were due to make their monthly visit to the children tomorrow. Grace wrote a quick note to tell Clara Maclure why they would not be coming. Unfortunately, Clara left it lying around and Freddie found it and showed it to Benji and Rosie. The result is they've gone.'

'I don't understand,' said Duncan anxiously. 'Who's gone?'

'The children, they've run away. They have no money, no food, just the clothes they stand up in. Clara is apparently in a terrible state and blames herself for not putting the letter away. She notified the local police but so far there's been no trace of them.'

'Poor Grace,' exclaimed Duncan. 'She must be almost out of her mind. But how did she find all this out? She's been at the hospital almost since Davy was injured.'

'Clara couldn't contact her direct but she had fortunately been given Queenie's telephone number for emergencies.' He glanced swiftly at the clock. 'Listen, Whicham Marsh is only a few miles across country from here. How do you feel about postponing your return to London for a few hours?'

'Of course! But how do we get to this place?'

'In my car. I'm only authorised to use petrol for my journey to and from the aerodrome but if we are stopped by the police I could just about stretch a point because it does lie in the same direction.'

'What're we waiting for?' asked Duncan, buttoning up his tunic.

Half an hour later the little Standard Eight car rolled to a halt outside Clara's cottage. A huge bicycle lay propped against her side gate whilst the front door of the cottage was wide open. Both men hastened from the car through the door but stopped in their tracks as they faced the scene in front of the tiny living room fire. There an elderly, ashen-faced lady lay motionless on the hearth rug and a massive policeman, still wearing his helmet, cape and cycle clips, knelt at her side gently rubbing her hands. In the chair a pretty, fair-haired, plump young woman sat quietly sobbing.

'Bloody hell,' Duncan whispered to the doctor, 'it's never-ending.'

23

Dr Stuart Rawlings spoke gently to the old lady. 'It's not *your* fault, Clara,' he assured her, 'don't worry, we'll find them. Look,' he pointed at Duncan, 'I've even got a good-looking Commando sergeant here to help. Now what more could you ask?'

Clara gave a weak smile. 'I should a'been more careful where I left the note, doctor. I knows that now.'

'Is she all right?' asked June Bumpstead through her tears. 'She's a real lady, is Mrs Maclure, she didn't deserve this.'

'She's going to be fine,' replied Stuart. 'She's just a bit distressed and blaming herself for everything. She's not to blame, no one is. It's something that even the best of children are liable to do.'

'D'you think she should go to Lynn hospital, doctor?' asked the village policeman.

Stuart looked down at her. 'What do you think, my dear, do you want to go?'

'Good heavens no!' she cried, struggling to sit upright. 'I've never bin in a hospital in me life and I've no intention o' goin' now.'

'I think that answers your question, Constable,' smiled Stuart. He turned to June Bumpstead. 'And now, ma'am,' he said quietly but firmly, 'I think it would be a good idea if you pulled yourself together and made these two people a nice strong cup of tea. Sergeant Forbes and I have some searching to do so we'll be off now.'

'I also need to be gettin' along,' said the policeman. 'I'll need to circulate their descriptions.'

'I'm sure you do,' agreed Stuart, 'but official wheels always take time to roll. I think the sergeant and I can contribute a lot before the trail gets too stale. Now, if you make sure you keep Mrs Maclure warm and not too excited, we'll be going. I promise you, Clara, if we find them you'll be amongst the first to know.'

'In that case,' said the constable, nodding his head in agreement, 'I'll not say no to a swift cup o' tea.'

'Please, one more question before we go, Mrs Maclure,' said Duncan. 'Have you missed any cash?'

'Bless you, boy!' she cried. 'Those children wouldn't take money from me!'

'But we need to be sure. I can't see how they expected to get to London without it. Can you check?'

She pointed to a vase that stood on a davenport desk in front of the window. 'If there be five pounds in silver in that there vase, then you owe all three children a big apology, Sergeant.'

Duncan tipped the contents of the vase into his hand to the instant accompaniment of jingling coins. 'You're right,' he smiled. 'I certainly do owe them an apology. Sorry, ma'am.'

'Come on then, Sergeant,' Stuart said, making for the door, 'let's try to make it a quick apology.'

The pair then made their farewells and slipped into the front of the car.

'Where d'you propose to start?' asked Duncan.

'Well, seeing as we are over a hundred miles from London,' replied Stuart, 'I'd say that we need to go to King's Lynn. Even without cash, there is no other transport over that distance for three kids in wartime, than jumping a train. We'll start at Lynn station. I'm sure they won't be too far from there,' he added confidently. He was about to negotiate a three-point turn when the spluttering of a Massey-Ferguson tractor towing a trailer laden high with potatoes could be heard coming around the bend behind them. Stuart paused to let it pass.

'Where does that road lead?' snapped Duncan.

'Nowhere in particular,' answered Stuart. 'It eventually fans out into a scattering of villages.'

'But it's dead straight.'

'So it's dead straight,' conceded Stuart. 'That still doesn't make it go anywhere.'

'Yes, but it leads south! If you were a kid without money and you had to travel a hundred miles, what would you sooner do? Go in the wrong direction to catch a train that you had no money to pay for, or make your way along a straight road that points in the direction of home and hope something else turns up?' He was almost out of the car as he was asking the question.

'But—' began Stuart.

'But nothing,' replied Duncan. 'You go to Lynn station and I'll follow this road. If I dash now I may just make the back of that trailer.'

'You'd better take this, then,' said Stuart, snatching a small map from the glove compartment and stuffing it down the soldier's battledress, 'because all signposts have been removed.' He then watched as the sergeant sprinted down the lane and finally swung aboard the back of the rattling trailer. With the luck they had experienced so far he half expected it to turn into the next field and stop. He waited for a few minutes until it receded into the distance before putting his car into gear and driving off in the opposite direction towards King's Lynn station.

Though Duncan's plan was little more than a gut feeling, he was closer to events than he could have realised. For certain months each wartime year, many Norfolk roads were continually criss-crossed by slow-moving, open-backed trucks and trailers taking high-piled loads of sugar-beet from the far-flung farms into the processing factory at King's Lynn. On a laden truck there would be scarcely room for a field-mouse but the unladen ones were a vastly different matter. Though they usually rattled along at a fair speed, many of the lanes had sharp bends, restricted views and cattle exits where the lorries would need to slow to a virtual standstill, or at least to a speed that would present no problem to three determined young travellers. However, selecting an empty truck was the easiest part of the task, the biggest difficulty was knowing where it was going.

The children too had had their problems. The first of these was when Freddie Foskett saw the River Nar. He remembered a lesson from Charles Dickens School in which his teacher, Miss Jones, explained that small rivers usually flowed into large rivers. As far as Freddie was concerned, this theory made the river he had spotted a direct pointer to home. It was a small river and the Thames was a great river, biggest in the world, he reckoned. Therefore all they had to do was walk the banks of the Nar to come out somewhere they could recognise, probably Battersea Park. The trouble was the River Nar was indeed a small river. In fact, in the usual run of rivers it was little more than a stream. Even worse, it flowed in entirely the wrong direction, a fact that it took Rosie all of four seconds to notice. Sadly it was four seconds *after* they had alighted from their best lift of the day.

'Well, look at it, you twerp!' she demanded. 'Don't even look like a bloody river . . . an' it goes the wrong way!'

'If yer followed it I reckon yer'd come ter Ireland,' observed Benjamin glumly. 'Or p'haps Scotland,' he added, as a helpful afterthought.

Freddy gave momentary thought as to whether Ireland or Scotland would be closer to London than King's Lynn but wisely decided not to risk an opinion.

'We've got ter keep goin' that way,' instructed Rosie, pointing due south.

'Yeh but I'm 'ungry,' complained Freddie. 'We've 'ad nuffin' since breakfast.'

'Yer right there,' agreed Rosie. 'I think we ought ter stop fer grub. Let's see what we've got.' The children may have been scrupulously honest in not taking Clara's cash but they had given her pantry a fair mauling. In their three satchels were bread, apples, carrots, turnips, a jar of blackberries and, in Freddie's satchel, a solitary Oxo cube. 'What's that for?' asked Rosie with mild curiosity.

'I like Oxos,' explained the lad.

'Yes, but we ain't got any 'ot water,' pointed out the practical Benjamin.

'I'll have it cold, then,' replied Freddie philosophically. 'There's plenty of water in the river.' So saying he emptied out the blackberries and tilted the jar below the surface. As the Oxo crumbled in the cold, blackberry-stained water, so did his confidence.

'Bloody 'ell, Benji,' cried Rosie, screwing up her face in disgust. ''E reckons 'e's goin' ter drink that. What *does* it look like?'

Benjamin, whose cooking experience was limited to toast and the odd hard-boiled egg, did not feel qualified to pass a full opinion so he thoughtfully settled for, 'Cow shit.'

If that was Benjamin's assumption of its appearance, it was probably an accurate description of its taste, because Freddie took no more than one mouthful before rendering further opinion academic by shrewdly dropping the jar onto a large riverside stone. His plaintive cry of, 'Oh dear, it's broke,' fooled no one.

Duncan, meanwhile, had found himself in just the sort of dilemma the children had a few hours earlier. His tractor had stood him in good stead before it turned into a farm entrance. On jumping off he saw a five-way road junction some quarter-mile ahead. A large signpost clearly dominated the hedgerow but a signpost without a sign is like a boat without a bottom. A scruffy, grey-bearded farm worker with a clay pipe was scything back an overgrown grass verge. 'Afternoon,' Duncan greeted him. 'Can you tell me where I am?'

The man did not look up but responded, 'Afternoon. Nope.'

'Nope?' Duncan echoed. 'Why not?' he added irritably.

''Ow do I know who y'ar? Fer all I knows yar might be one ô' them there Nazis.'

'Well, do I look like a Nazi?' pleaded Duncan. 'Oh, come on man, it's an emergency.'

'Yes, but I don't know that, do I?' explained the man slowly. 'So I can't tells yer where yer is. Wouldn't be proper.'

Duncan pulled out his map but it was a cheap one and, without a landmark, it was going to be difficult to locate a reference point. He pointed to the first junction on the left. 'Okay, so you won't tell me where I am. But will you tell me where that road leads?'

Without looking up the man replied, 'Carstle Acre.'

'Castle Acre, eh. And that one?' requested Duncan, pointing to the centre road.

'South Acre.'

'South Acre . . . I see . . . and that one?'

'West Acre.'

Duncan pored quickly over his map. 'Castle Acre, South Acre, West Acre. Hmm, and that one there, where's that lead?'

'Narborough,' replied the man, still without looking up.

'Narborough, eh?' He studied the map for a few moments more before adding acidly, 'Thanks, you've been a great help.'

''S all right. Ain't got any baccy, I suppose? I'm right out.'

'Sorry,' said Duncan, 'but there's a convoy of the Waffen SS Death Squad following me in a squadron of tanks. Ask them, they've got stacks of it.'

As he marched briskly down the road to Narborough he suddenly realised the difficulty he'd be in if he could not scrounge a lift. This fear was partially offset when an RAF mail-truck responded to his hitch-hiking thumb and dropped him three miles further on at the edge of Narborough, but he could not rely on such good fortune indefinitely. The answer came as the truck left him before it turned west towards the large air base at Marham.

In a nearby field a scattering of workers were busily engaged in the threshing of a wheat-stack. Those who were not fully occupied with the thresher were equally busy keeping the dust and chaff out of their eyes. There was a broad selection of six cycles lying against the hedgerow from which to select. He slipped the cycle chain from five of them and pedalled away frantically on the sixth, a drop-handlebar, highly-geared beast of a machine with an uncomfortable saddle and a picnic-box in the pannier.

Deciding that Narborough might not be the best place for such a distinctive machine he decided to pedal the extra six miles to the small market town of Swaffham. By this time the daylight was fading and he decided to put himself in the children's shoes. Providing he had been right so far in his guesswork, he thought they would not continue to travel after dark. Apart from their natural fears, the Swaffham Heath would have been particularly black in wartime so he guessed he was looking for some sort of shelter that would appeal to children, but what?

Two miles south of the town he stopped to sample the delights of the thresher's picnic-box. The jam tart was excellent but the bottle of cold, unsweetened, milkless tea, though refreshing, was an acquired taste and certainly took some swallowing. It was whilst he stood with his head tilted back that he saw the cluster of sheds beyond a stout wire fence. In itself this was no great surprise; with so many air bases scattered around East Anglia, half the countryside was fenced off in one shape or form. Yet this fence had a small interesting gap at ground level that was barely conspicuous from the road. Dusk was approaching fast and even he would be unable to make headway in the dark. If he could conceal the bicycle until morning there might be shelter to be obtained in one of the huts. Lifting some brambles he covered the cycle as best he could. Then, with a quick glance around, he crouched and began to wriggle his way through the gap in best Commando fashion. When halfway through, a strand of the wire slipped and hooked into the back of his uniform. He was in no great rush so he lay face down and ran his hands up his back in an effort to unhook his tunic. At this stage he thought he heard both a cough and a footstep, but before he could react a crack to his head ensured that his world was instantly illuminated by splintering lights before it plunged into total blackness.

Up until that evening, little Hilda Hegsworth had thought the war boring. She had been a member of the Women's Auxiliary Air Force for almost a year now and, other than being a general dogsbody around the camp, had done little but picket-duty. Then, an hour after catching three kids breaking in, she had arrived to secure the fence and discovered even more drama. She had first wondered how to approach him. He was in a uniform of sorts, but she could not make out the details in the fading light. He was also very big, whilst she was very small with the beginnings of a cough. Usually she patrolled with her friend Ira Richardson but Ira was now guarding the children whilst Hilda repaired the fence. Fortunately she also had her ash-wood pick-handle. Although she was never trusted with anything as lethal as a gun, standing camp regulations did permit pick-handles, though what exactly one was supposed to do with them was never fully explained. She did think of asking the man to surrender but supposing he refused, what then? She could have run for help but who was to know what sabotage he could commit in the meantime? The third option – cracking his head as he lay on the ground –

seemed a more sensible course to take. And so Duncan Forbes, a physically perfect, six-feet, thirteen-stone, highly trained sergeant in the British Commandos, was severely flattened by a wisp of a girl called Hilda, with a pick-handle and a nasty cough.

Duncan eventually came round, to the accompaniment of a splitting headache. As his vision improved he was aware he was sitting in a large wooden armchair in a dimly lit Nissen hut. Around him were two little WAAF girls with pick-handles on their laps, an RAF corporal, and a Norfolk Constabulary constable. 'Ah!' said the corporal. 'With us at last. How's your head?'

Duncan ran his hand down the back of his skull. 'Oh, so that's what it is,' he mumbled. 'A head? I thought it was a box of loose nuts and bolts. What hit me?'

Hilda Hegsworth gave a bronchial cough before replying, 'I did, I'm afraid . . . but I didn't realise you were on our side. I . . . er . . . I thought you might have been a German.'

'Oh, that's made me feel a whole lot better,' observed Duncan tartly.

His pockets had obviously been emptied and all his documents were strewn over the table. 'These yours?' asked the corporal. Duncan nodded, although the movement caused every bone and membrane in his head to savagely attack its neighbour.

'Tell me who you are, your unit, your name, your army number. Then tell me what you're doing in this part of the world creeping under our fence.'

Duncan recited his personal details whilst the corporal checked against his documents. 'That side of it seems okay,' conceded the corporal. 'Now, why were you breaking into this camp?'

Duncan did his best to explain what had happened since he had alighted from the train in King's Lynn those few hours ago.

'These children you're a'searching for,' said the policeman, 'whar be their names?'

'Oh – er,' began Duncan, delicately fingering his skull, 'Freddie, Benji and – let me see now – oh yes, Annie.'

'Annie?' queried the constable.

'Me name ain't bleedin' Annie,' protested a childish voice from his rear. 'Dopy sod always calls me Annie. Me name's Rosie!'

He spun around, which was a great mistake because his head appeared to follow three seconds after his body. 'Yeh, that's right . . . Rosie,' he muttered.

The corporal and the constable exchanged meaningful nods. 'You're a lucky man, Sergeant,' said the corporal, 'and you've got the diligence of these two young WAAFs to thank for it.'

'D'you reckon?' answered Duncan without conviction.

'I do reckon. If they hadn't spotted this trio breaking into the base they would not have spotted you. Then where would you have been?'

'I have no wish to compound the trouble I'm already in by telling you that, Corporal. Perhaps I'll enlighten you after the war.'

The corporal laughed. 'Come on down the messroom and have something to eat. I think we can just about nip this thing in the bud before it gets out of hand.'

'Thanks,' said Duncan gratefully, 'but first can we just make a couple of phone calls to put folk's minds at rest?'

'We'll do it from the picket office on the way down. Are you thinking clearly enough to walk?'

'Well, I think I remember we're still losing the war. That any guide?'

'Spot on!' replied the corporal. 'Your recovery's practically complete.'

Within an hour they had eaten, telephoned Queenie and telephoned the police office in Whicham Marsh to put Clara's mind at rest. They had hardly finished eating when Stuart Rawlings entered the messroom. 'The police at Lynn station told me the children had been found here,' he said. 'What do you propose to do now?'

Duncan sighed uncertainly. 'Well, they need to go home, to London I mean. At least for the time being. It'll give everything a chance to settle. What their parents decide after that—' he shrugged. 'But the first problem is their fare. I haven't enough money for all their train tickets.'

'I think you're right but don't worry about the fare. I'll run us back to Clara's, then, before we go to the station, I'll take you to my place to pick up some ticket money. How's that suit?'

'Fine, and that's very kind of you, but Clara's going to be terribly upset at losing the kids,' pointed out Duncan.

'Upset?' exclaimed Stuart with uncharacteristic sharpness. 'She's going to be bloody devastated! But these things happen to relationships in wartime, as I've recently discovered.'

'Er – just one final thing,' said the corporal, as the group climbed in the car. 'As far as the RAF is concerned, this matter never happened. We've fixed the fence, you've recovered the children and there was no damage to government property.'

'If there was no damage to government property,' queried Duncan, gingerly fingering his head, 'why doesn't my hat fit?'

'Well, of course,' said the corporal pointedly, 'if you'd care to stay and make a report and have the whole matter investigated . . . ?'

'No, no,' Duncan responded quickly, 'but if you can get someone to drop that little WAAF somewhere behind German lines, I'm sure she'd shorten the war.'

Stuart, who had been sitting, hands on the wheel and engine running, asked impatiently, 'Can we go now?'

'Yes,' side-mouthed Duncan, 'and quick, before some bugger finds that bloody bike.'

* * *

The forecast that Clara would be devastated was not far short of the mark. Even the children realised the emotion the old lady felt and the warmth of their embraces to both Clara and June showed this. To a chorus of 'Write soon' they waved frantically as Stuart drove them away from the cottage. Eventually they arrived outside his house at the Old Chandlers. His plan had been to run quickly indoors to pick up the necessary cash for the fares. However, the numerous drinks the children had absorbed ensured a triple demand for his lavatory.

It was whilst they waited for Rosie to finish that his telephone rang. Stuart made no more than a few terse replies before handing the receiver to Duncan. 'It's for you,' he said quietly. 'I'll wait outside.'

'Me?' said the surprised Duncan. 'Who knew I was here?'

'No one actually *knew*,' replied Stuart tersely from the doorway. 'It's just the way my luck's been running lately.'

At the very sound of Julia's voice Duncan felt he wanted to hug himself with pleasure, even if she did blast him for his thoughtlessness, selfishness, and for leaving London for Norfolk as she left Norfolk for London. She was well into a garbled account of the chase she had made around the capital before he interrupted with the demand, 'Stop and bloody listen for a minute, woman!' Her silence was caused as much by surprise as acquiescence.

'Right, listen carefully because I haven't much time,' he continued. 'We should all arrive at Liverpool Street sometime this evening. My pass expires shortly so instead of having a go at me, why don't you use the time constructively by arranging our marriage by special licence as soon as possible? If there's a problem, tell them you're pregnant and you need the allowance, or something similar.'

'Oh very romantic, I must say!' she replied angrily. 'And if I say no, what then?'

'You can't possibly say no,' he complained. 'Not after I've swum the Channel, landed in Portsmouth in a flying bedstead, nicked a bike, chased three kids halfway across Norfolk and been virtually beaten to death by some nutty bird named Hilda Hegsworth with a pick-handle and a hacking cough! It wouldn't be fair!'

'Duncan Forbes, I have no idea what you are talking about but if you don't marry me this time there'll be two nutty birds you'll need to contend with and this one won't stop at *practically* killing you. Do I make myself clear?'

'Oh, very romantic, I must say,' he mimicked. 'But just get that licence before the shop closes. Oh by the way – I love you, you belligerent cow.'

It was a very subdued Stuart that drove the quartet the few miles into King's Lynn railway station, but his farewell was sincere and generous.

'I will never be able to thank you enough for everything – and I mean everything – you have done,' said Duncan almost sadly. 'For what it's worth, I feel . . .' his voice trailed away as he gripped the doctor's hand in a powerful squeeze.

'Forget it,' said Stuart dismissively. 'Though you could tell Julia that I've used up my petrol ration for the next few weeks and I'm going to have to cycle to the aerodrome every day. That'll keep her in London, if anything will.'

The whistle blew and the doctor raised a hand in farewell to Duncan and the children. As the train eased its way out of the station Duncan also raised a hand. 'See you!' he called cheerily, but both men knew they would never meet again. For each of them the other represented a chapter that had closed for the rest of their lives.

Throughout the journey to London, Duncan had been thinking how best to make the journey to Queenie's house in Streatham. It was a needless worry as, to the delight of the children, Grace and Julia met them at the station. Even Duncan was surprised at his own excitement at seeing Julia again. He asked about David's condition and was told that though his sight was now expected to be saved he would never work as a police officer again. The news placed a dampener on the homecoming but as Grace said with rather unconvincing bravery, 'Life goes on.'

'Speaking of which,' said Julia to Duncan, 'how do you feel about being married at Brixton register office at ten-thirty the day after tomorrow?'

'Do you mean it?' he exclaimed. 'You've actually arranged it? It's not a leg-pull?'

'It better not be,' she said tartly. 'I had the devil's own job to get an extra two days' leave.'

'That's a point,' said Duncan. 'What're you doing about your job at the aerodrome?'

'I'll arrange another transfer, I suppose.' She shrugged. 'Everyone is short of nurses these days but in case I have to serve overseas, I'd like to be married first.'

Queenie made them all extremely welcome and Duncan was particularly pleased when they were joined by Jackie Blackwell, who hardly ever stopped hugging his daughter.

The following day was a chaotic round of hospital visits, reception arrangements and dress fittings for Rosie and Julia. In fact Julia was relatively easy but it was only when the sixth dress for Rosie had been turned down that the reason became apparent; no one had seen her in a dress for months and by her incessant complaining it was going to be a fair time before anyone saw her in one again. It was only when they sat down to a late tea that day that the arrangements had all been completed. Billie Bardell, Grace, Rosie and Julia were to sleep in one spare room, whilst the two boys, Jackie Blackwell and Duncan were to sleep on the floor in the other. As a good omen, a heavy fog ensured a raid-free night and a reasonable sleep. There would doubtless be a scramble for the only bathroom in the morning but there was little to be done about that. It was then off to Brixton register office to be followed by a hospital visit to David, before lunch at the Anchor pub by the riverside at Southwark Bridge, where they would be joined by several old friends and neighbours. The old superstition of the bride and groom not seeing each other on their wedding day had to go by the board, but then so had many other rituals in a wartime wedding.

As the group sat round the fire that wedding eve, Jim thought Queenie looked particularly pensive. Pouring her a drink he asked, 'Why so glum? I thought only the groom had second thoughts before the wedding?'

'I can't help it,' she admitted. 'Everything has been so frantic this last day or so. I'm sure we've forgotten something. Before the war we would have spent weeks just planning and working everything out, now it seems to be done in minutes.'

'I know, old girl,' he said quietly, 'but those days were light years ago. Time now seems as short as every other commodity. At this rate the government'll soon ration it. We'll probably only be allowed sixteen hours in a day.'

Julia laughed. 'I don't know why you two old fogies are worrying so,' she said. 'I've waited years for this day and no one and nothing is going to spoil it, I assure you of that. I simply won't let them,' she added confidently.

Her prediction appeared to be right. The fog had cleared, it was a lovely morning and the rota for the bathroom had worked a treat. Everyone seemed in the greatest of spirits and even Rosie seemed resigned to her frock. Benjamin and Freddie were passably smart, Billie and Queenie seemed years younger, Grace looked beautiful, Jim oozed dignity and Duncan was, well, just Duncan. The greatest surprise, however, was Jackie Blackwell. After seemingly ages of wearing his warden's overalls and helmet, the curly-brimmed bowler that topped off a bow tie and three-piece, pin-striped suit stunned everyone, his daughter most of all. No praise gave him greater pleasure than her stunned observation, 'Dad! Yer a toff!'

In fact as they arrived in two taxis at the register office everything was almost perfect, almost, that is, except for just two things. These were in the shape of a pair of giant military police sergeants, who jumped from a truck and greeted Duncan with the evocative words, 'Duncan, you're nicked!'

24

'Bill Voisey!' exclaimed Duncan. 'What're you doing here?'

'I'm afraid me and my oppo – Sergeant Len Frampton – are nicking you, sunshine,' said Bill. 'Sorry, an' all that, but you're a naughty boy and the army's got the right hump with you.'

'Me! Why?'

'Well, first of all, you're absent without leave. No, no,' he said, raising his hands to stifle Duncan's protest, 'your pass expired yesterday. Secondly, your unit has been trying to contact you at the address you gave – the Union Jack Club – for two days but they say your bed hasn't been slept in for at least two nights. So, one – you're AWOL; two – you're overdue; three – you've not resided at the address on your leave form; four – you've not responded to a recall to duty. That's just for starters! If I remember anything at all about you and your misdemeanours from India, I'll lay odds once we go into it, we'll be dusting off King's Regulations for half-a-dozen more.'

'But how did you find me?' asked the bewildered Duncan.

'Ah ha! Brilliant detective work,' said Voisey smugly. 'A Pioneer Corps squaddie returned a note to the desk that had your name and a telephone number on the back. The clever lad thought it might be important. Len here rang the number and a doctor someone-or-other gave him a Streatham address. We got there in time to see you doing a runner, so we followed. Clever, weren't we?'

'But I wasn't doing a runner, you berk, I'm getting married!'

'Married?' queried the now hesitant Voisey. 'When . . . where?'

'Now! Here! Ten-thirty, to be precise. This is a register office.'

The sergeant looked quickly around, not really sure what King's Regulations had to say about arresting someone in such an establishment. He wondered if it was like feeling someone's collar in a cathedral. He gave the situation a swift thought before deciding to bluff it out. 'Sorry, Duncan old mate, but you can't marry, we've just nicked you. Your CO's been screaming for you for two days so he can brief you for some bloody Commando raid. He's not going to wait till your honeymoon's over, that's for sure.'

'Listen, you!' snapped the furious Julia. 'I've spent the best part of ten years getting this oaf to our wedding. If you think you and your thick mate here' – she pointed at the sergeant's less verbose colleague – 'are going to put a block on it now, you've another think coming. At ten-thirty we're getting married, at eleven-thirty you're at liberty to shoot him if you wish. In fact, at this precise moment the idea of being his widow does have a certain appeal to me, but until then he's not yours . . . *he's mine!*'

'Look,' said Jim soothingly, 'there must be a better way of dealing with it than just dragging the groom off ten minutes before his wedding, surely? The army can't be that desperate for him. They've waited two days, another hour or so is not going to lose the war. What d'you say, eh?'

'Who are these two bloody idiots anyway?' cut in Billie Bardell aggressively.

Duncan wearily pointed at Voisey and said, 'The sergeant here is Bill Voisey. I knew him in India before the war. He's now a military policeman. The other bloke is his side-kick, but we've not had the pleasure of meeting before.'

'So you actually know this geezer?' queried Billie, gesturing to Voisey.

'Well, not for some years now but yes, I do know him,' agreed Duncan.

She then turned her attention to Voisey. 'And where do you intend taking him, Sergeant?'

'Eventually to his unit at Shoreham, ma'am,' he replied, 'but at the moment we're only taking him to their holding company . . . that's in the Tower of London.'

'The Tower of London,' cried Julia. 'They *are* going to shoot him, then! Good! If I pay you, can I give the order to fire?'

Both Jim and Queenie felt the hostile reception the sergeants were receiving was really no help to their cause. After a quick exchange of whispers they began to pursue the possibility of a postponement in the arrest. 'I've just spoken to Grace,' whispered Jim. 'She's going to have a word with them. She'll soften them if anyone can.'

It was no mean observation. When she put her mind to it, Grace could cultivate an overwhelming air of sexuality and charm. Of course, being stunningly attractive helped. At such times she was certainly more than aptly named. Their first object, though, was to remove Julia and Billie from the firing line. Their current aggression could well cause the escorts to handcuff Duncan and dash off to the Tower in fright.

'Look,' said Grace softly to the two sergeants, 'would you two gentlemen mind just sitting quietly with me in the foyer and having a confidential chat about the best way to handle this impasse . . . please?'

Duncan would have cheerfully bet his last penny that Voisey did not have the faintest idea what an 'impasse' meant; on the other hand a 'confidential chat' with such a good-looking woman was an offer he knew the old sergeant would be unable to refuse.

At that moment, Voisey himself had not the slightest

intention of releasing his prisoner, yet the idea of sharing an intimacy with such a woman predictably appealed. She took both men to the furthest part of the foyer and deliberately sat between them. Time and again she spoke softly to one, then to the other, neatly interspersed with much touching of arms. Throughout this conversation neither man spoke, though they nodded frequently and their eyes never once left her body. After some few minutes Jim looked anxiously up at the clock. Not only was time slipping by but Julia's nostrils were starting to flare again. As if to remind them the clock was racing the first guests of a later wedding were starting to drift into the foyer. Very soon Duncan's entire party would need to be gathering in the inner office. The two military policemen suddenly nodded in unison, but still no move was made.

'This is going to be a bloody close-run thing,' muttered Duncan. 'Voisey always was a stubborn old sod.'

Suddenly Voisey rose to his feet and hastened to a public telephone box in the corner of the foyer where he was soon deep in conversation. During this time Grace appeared totally relaxed but her eyes never once left him. Every few seconds he glanced towards her and she returned his glance with a dutiful smile of encouragement. After what seemed an eternity but was probably little more than a few minutes, he replaced the receiver and, returning to her side, gave her a nod of assent. Grace gave a yelp of delight and reached out and squeezed both men's hands and planted a fleeting kiss to each of their cheeks. Voisey then spoke earnestly to her for a few moments and she nodded throughout his conversation. The onlookers heard her say demurely, 'I'm sure he'll agree to that, Sergeant,' as she rose to her feet with a beaming smile, and walked back to them.

'Now listen, Duncan,' she began, 'these two gentlemen have been extremely kind. Sergeant Voisey has agreed to the wedding taking place as arranged and has agreed to accompany us to see poor David in hospital immediately after the ceremony. Isn't that kind?'

'Kind?' murmured the astounded Duncan. 'It's a bloody miracle.'

'No it's not,' whispered Jim. 'It's pure sex.'

Grace had her back to Duncan at that moment so he could only see her rear. 'Yeh,' he said thoughtfully, 'you could be right. If there's one thing in the world better than that woman's rear, it's that woman's front. Ten more minutes with her and they'd have agreed to drive us on a honeymoon to Skye.'

'And the reception at the Anchor?' asked Julia. 'Is he okay for that as well?'

Grace shook her head sadly and turned to Voisey. 'You'd better tell them about that, Sergeant.'

'I've just spoke on the blower to a Colonel Baker at the Tower,' said Voisey. 'He said he wants nothing more than Duncan back in time for a briefing for something special that's taking place soon. He's allowed the marriage and the hospital visit but he wants him back in the Tower before one o'clock today because the whole unit is moving off for Shorncliffe. The wedding reception – at least for the groom – is out. Sorry, folks.'

'So there's to be no discipline charges?' asked Duncan.

'If you're back before one o'clock, no.'

'Thanks a lot, Bill,' said Duncan gratefully. 'You couldn't have done more. There's no reason why the reception should be cancelled, though. It's been paid for and many of our friends will already be on their way. It just means the groom won't be there, that's all.'

'Neither will the bride,' cut in Julia obstinately.

'Listen,' whispered Duncan to her, 'we've had a result here, we really have! Let's not spoil it, not for the sake of a lunch.'

'I don't intend to,' she said, before turning her attention to the two military policemen. 'When we leave the hospital, will you be escorting my husband to the Tower in your truck?'

'Yes, ma'am,' agreed Voisey.

'Then take me too. You don't have to worry, you can drop me at the gate, I'll consider it part of my nuptials. There can't be many brides whose going away journey is to the Tower! It'll be something to tell my grandchildren, that's for sure.'

'Are you positive that's what you want?' asked Duncan.

'Of course,' she replied. 'A few minutes ago I didn't think I was getting married but now I am, so what's the big problem? You're right, we'll do without lunch. Oh, and by the way,' she said, turning to the two sergeants and adopting her most demure pose. 'I do apologise, boys, but you can understand my disappointment when I thought you were taking my future husband away. Whatever must you be thinking of me?'

'Well, I was a little surprised when you said you wanted to shoot him, ma'am,' said Voisey, with just a hint of sarcasm in his tone. ''Cos he ain't that bad a bloke. But I guess you'll keep him now, eh?'

'How understanding of you, Sergeant,' she smiled. 'When I now think of some of the types the army could have sent to capture my Duncan . . . well, I go cold, I really do. Bless you both.'

'Don't overkill,' hissed Duncan, 'we're winning.'

As they all filed rapidly into the register room, Julia looked anxiously around, wondering what else could misfire. She even pricked her ears in case she could hear a distant siren announcing an imminent air raid, or running footsteps to say the building was on fire, but there was only the voice of the registrar and the participants' responses. Then, virtually before she knew it, she found herself a married woman. There was almost a feeling of anti-climax – almost, but not quite. She turned and looked up at Duncan and whispered, 'I withdraw my bid to take part in your execution. I think I'll just love you instead.'

He gave a slow intake of breath and shook his head. 'Not sure I approve of that,' he whispered back. 'Could be even more dangerous.' He gave a thoughtful 'tch' before adding, 'No thanks; given a choice, I'll settle for being shot.'

Her response of a sharp dig in his ribs caused the registrar to sigh and silently yearn for a swift return to the dignity of peace-time weddings.

Ceremony over, the group emerged out onto the sunlit Brixton Road with the nervous small talk and the slightly lost air that wedding groups have at such times.

Queenie was the first to begin to instil some form of order. 'If we're going to see David, what are we going to do about the children?' she asked. 'The hospital won't allow anyone under fourteen years of age in the ward. They are only taking the rest of us under sufferance because visiting time is usually between two and three this afternoon.'

'Well, I can visit David any time,' pointed out Billie. 'As it's a nice day why don't I take the kids to the Anchor? We can have a drink on the forecourt and keep the rest of the guests entertained until you all arrive, though I'll keep it a secret that the groom's been nicked.'

'Bit hard on the kids, though, isn't it,' said Duncan, 'considering they scarpered from Norfolk because Benji wanted to see his dad?'

'I've been thinking about that,' murmured Grace. 'I think it would be best if I smuggled him in the ward later during evening visiting. With us lot clustered round the bed this morning the matron is bound to be a bit edgy. Not only that, if there is only Benji and me, it'll give David more time with the boy.'

'Good, that's settled, is it?' asked Billie, looking around in case any other suggestion was forthcoming. 'Okay? Very well, kids, we'll be making our way to the Anchor now and see the rest of you later. Cheerio.'

After a brief wave, Jackie, Queenie and Jim climbed in a taxi destined for the hospital, whilst the bride and groom followed in the military truck accompanied by their escorts. 'Not quite the start I was seeking,' admitted Duncan. 'Still,' he said as he turned to kiss his bride, 'no one can say we were conventional.'

Two miles away, another unconventional couple were about to change their way of life. Rita Roberts and Wanda Williams had finally decided it was time to move on. 'We've done particularly well,' admitted Rita. 'If we're careful we have enough goodies for us never to work again. It was a bit of a scare when the Clinkside copped it,' she admitted, 'but really it was the best thing that could have happened. Now there's no one to come looking for us and all we've got to do is to change some of our more bulky stuff into smaller negotiables. Then it's no more scrimping and saving, no more being mauled by those stinking apes at the club, no more posing for those sick films and no more bug-infested tenements.'

'I don't know what I would have done without you,' said Wanda gratefully. 'Honest, I don't. I feel so excited about our new life, but it won't change nothing between us though, will it?' she asked worriedly.

'What d'you mean?' asked Rita curtly.

'Oh well . . .' Wanda became flustered. 'You know . . . take that soldier Duncan . . . I mean, he really fancied you. It made me feel . . . well . . . sort of jealous, I suppose,' she said bashfully.

'Jealous! Of me?'

'No, no, not you,' replied Wanda hastily. 'I was jealous of him. You know I love you, Rita, I could never love anyone else . . .' She faltered for words. 'I, I don't know what I would do without you now. You always seem to know what to do and what to say. I know now you're the best thing for me. I'll do whatever you want, Rita, just you and me, right to the end, yes?'

Rita suddenly stared at her with a gaze as hard as Wanda had ever seen. 'Why are you looking at me like that?' she asked fearfully.

Rita's expression changed instantly and she put a comforting arm around the younger woman and kissed her firmly on the mouth. 'Your imagination's running away with you. Once we get settled in our new place things will be different, you'll see. Tell you what, before we go let's finish up the rest of the gin in that bottle, there's only a little left, c'mon.' So saying she poured out two hefty measures. 'Here's to the German pilot who flattened the Clinkside. May he have a long and fruitful life for doing us such a favour.'

'I suppose there's a lot about you I don't really understand, Rita,' confessed Wanda, now a little uncomfortable, 'and sometimes you can seem a bit . . . well, perhaps a bit hard . . . Oh, I know you don't mean it,' she added hastily.

'How do you know what I mean and what I don't?' asked Rita sharply. 'Just now you were uneasy because I toasted the German who bombed the club. I'll tell you why you were uneasy, shall I? You were uneasy because you read the papers and take in all that shit on the wireless about the *wicked* Germans and the *good* British and you think therefore we must win the war . . . that's what you think, don't you?'

'I don't really know,' mumbled Wanda. 'But yes, in a way I suppose I do.'

'Of course you do, but listen to me. If the Germans win the war my actions won't matter a damn. If the Allies win I will have made my pile and left, so why should I care?'

'But you're British,' protested Wanda. 'You must want us to win?'

'The only person I want to win is me – sorry, I mean us. I bet you think I'm a traitor for toasting that German pilot, don't

367

you? Well, perhaps I am. But I'd sooner be a traitor than a hero. Traitors are usually thinking people, heroes are usually thick and get killed or maimed. When wars are over everyone forgets the cripples. Therefore you may as well be a traitor, because if the enemy wins you've backed the winner and if your side wins, well, no one gives a damn after a few months anyway. This war is the best thing that has ever happened to me because I can now see the world for what it is. You can lose your kids, lover, friends, even pets, but no matter how great the sacrifice you've made, after a while your enemy, who you hated, becomes just another country like every other country and you ask yourself, What it's all been for? Even now, if you walk around you'll see disabled people, hurt people, people like that David, maybe blind for the rest of his life – and for what? In a few years' time the two nations will be friends again, but that won't give him his sight back, will it? That won't grow new limbs that have been torn off. That won't fetch back all the people who died in Queen's Buildings, will it? Of course it won't, we'll just fall out with some other bloody country and do the whole thing again. Well, they won't be doing it with me, not this time, not next time, nor any other bloody time. Count us two out, eh Wanda?'

Wanda, who by now was totally out of her depth, murmured, 'Er – yes,' and swallowed the last of her drink. 'Come on, girl,' said Rita. 'We can leave most of this stuff here, it's rubbish anyway. There's a train from Paddington about six o'clock and I'd like to check our final inventory on the barge and pick up Tibs before we catch it.'

Wanda slipped into her coat and almost skipped down the few stairs to the street. She could not remember being so happy since she was a child.

Fifteen minutes later, they had taken a small coracle from the burnt-out remains of the Clinkside's pier and paddled it round to the far side of a trio of derelict barges, well out of

368

sight from the river wall. After climbing the fixed iron ladder they slithered down into the converted hold where Rita called, '*Tibs!*' As the cat appeared from nowhere, Rita tipped out an unappetising mish-mash of cat food onto a grimy dish. Meanwhile, Wanda Williams was already trying for size a bracelet that sparkled even in that subdued light.

As she continued to finger the many small treasures, Rita spent her time calculating their worth. Sadly for Wanda, and contrary to expectations, Rita's sums did not quite equate to the financial security for two people she had prophesied. On the other hand they promised excellent security for one. She stared for a moment at the rear of Wanda's exquisitely smooth white neck. 'Pity,' she thought, as she planted a warm kiss firmly in its centre.

Wanda gave a shudder of pleasure. 'Mmm, nice,' she murmured. 'Do it again.' This time the girl closed her eyes in loving expectation.

Rita slid her hands seductively over Wanda's slim shoulders and gently around to her throat. Although the struggle was violent it was brief and there was only one sound. That was a solitary, ear-piercing scream that caused the cat to leap from its dinner and race across the tops of some boxes to seek the sanctuary of the barge deck. Meanwhile, below, Wanda slipped wide-eyed, open-mouthed and dead to the floor just as quietly and smoothly as any river eel.

Relinquishing her hold, Rita hastily filled a sturdy bag with the more expensive jewellery and watches, plus a box of golden guineas. The rest of the stuff would have to wait, if indeed she ever returned for it. All that remained was to tuck Wanda away in one of the many convenient recesses and make that difficult climb up to the deck.

Fifteen minutes earlier, and three hundred yards away, a taxi had stopped at the Anchor public house. At the first sight of the river the three children were ecstatic. They had quite liked Norfolk and they loved Clara dearly, yet at heart, all were born street-rakers. Here at last, by the river, they were in their element. 'Don't go away!' had been Billie's parting words as she gave each a lemonade before searching the beer garden for early guests.

'Can we just go to the bridge?' Freddie had asked. 'We might see a submarine,' he had added hopefully.

'To the bridge but no further then,' Billie had conceded. 'I don't want to search half of London for you when the rest arrive.'

Each of the children had known that the permission to go as far as the bridge was not quite enough. Just *past* the bridge, opposite St Paul's, was their real destination. It was there, early in the war, they had first seen German pirates. Though they had not been able to interest one single adult at the time, perhaps now would be an ideal opportunity to see if the same pirates were still functioning. They downed their drinks and hastened to the south-east corner of the bridge. Glancing back, they saw Billie was already in conversation with the first of the guests. Running eagerly through the archway beneath the bridge's southern approach, they were delighted to see – a hundred yards or so upstream – the same three barges! Well, at least they looked like the same three barges. On the other hand they also looked like every other barge on the river. Still, there were three of them and they were in the same place and that was close enough.

'Look,' said Freddie sadly, 'they've bin bombed! I bet there was a battle when we were in Norfolk an' we missed it. I knew we shoulda come 'ome earlier!'

Running excitedly along Bankside, they made for the river steps. 'Look there!' cried Freddie 'It's a cat on a barge!'

''Ow's it get there?' asked Benjamin.

'Swum,' answered his friend.

'Cats can't swim,' pronounced Rosie.

'Well, 'e must be able to,' retorted Freddie. ''Ow did 'e get there otherwise?'

It was a question neither felt qualified to answer. 'I reckon we orter rescue it,' said Freddie gallantly. Spies had suddenly faded from their thoughts; here was something really worthwhile. If they were really lucky they could save a cat from drowning! Wouldn't that be something to tell everyone!

''Ow we goin' ter get on it?' asked Benjamin doubtfully. 'The first two barges are so rotten they're fallin' apart!'

'Same as before,' suggested Rosie. 'We can swing on the rope.' She looked hastily up and down stream. 'There's no coppers about, c'mon.'

Now totally fired with thoughts of feline salvation they quickly made their way across the rope to the first barge. Below them the tide was receding and the first two barges were resting on the river bed in shallow water, although the furthest barge clearly floated. Meanwhile, the cat, fearful of the noisy new-comers, had dropped down into the coracle and out of their sight.

'Cat's gone,' announced a worried Rosie. 'D'yer reckon 'e's fell in?'

'Nah,' replied Freddie, 'I should think 'e's just frightened an' popped back in the barge. Poor little thing.'

'That's all very well,' said Benjamin, 'but 'ow are we goin' ter get 'im out? We cut the rope last time an' all the barges nearly floated away. We can't do that again, my dad nearly got the sack.'

'I've got an idea,' exclaimed Rosie. 'We needn't go out there on the barge at all. All we've gotter do is pull that barge back tight next ter this'n.'

'Well, 'ow do we do that?' asked the dubious Benjamin. 'Barges weigh tons!'

371

'Not when they're floatin,' they don't. Yer just pulls 'em an' they comes, 's easy.'

Fired with Rosie's scientific knowledge, they found themselves footholds and unhooked looped rope from the bollard. Holding the rope firmly, they took the strain of the barge. The pull of the current was greater than anticipated and, although they were just about holding their own, indeed even gaining the occasional inch, they were tiring fast.

Already Rosie was regretting wearing her new frock. If she had worn her old frock she would have worn her old knickers. Unfortunately Queenie had decided that a new frock merited new knickers. Now, if there was one thing that Rosie liked, it was a bit of give in her knicker-elastic, but wartime elastic being what it was, it had one overriding fault – it rarely stretched. As the elastic finally parted, she snatched at her knickers to avoid them falling to her ankles. In this she was successful, which is more than she was when she attempted to regain her hold on the rope. If three kids could just about hold on to a barge, two kids can just about lose one. The rope slid through their hands, giving them friction burns, before dropping into the swirling Thames.

The barge then swung out into the five-knot current and spun around a couple of times, as if seeking a suitable place of impact. Finally choosing its spot, it broadsided into the concrete base of the second arch of Southwark Bridge. The craft seemed to hold this position for some seconds, time enough to give momentary hope to its sole live occupant, but it was to be a false dawn. As the barge split, the first rush of water lifted the corpse of Wanda Williams and carried it round in a speeding circle before hurtling it – still wide-eyed and open-mouthed – straight into the chest of the struggling Rita Roberts. For the first time in her whole life Rita screamed, which, discounting a gurgle, was also the last sound she made on this globe. Within seconds the entire barge had disintegrated. The patched panels came off like wallpaper and the few contents that could float spiralled their way up to the surface and out towards the sea. Those that could not float tumbled out into the angry Thames and sunk deeply into its muddy bed. As the bulkhead had splintered, so the little coracle drifted downstream, with a rope trailing from its stern and a cat staring from its bow.

'Blimey, Rose!' exclaimed a wide-eyed Freddie. 'You've bin an' gone an' done it nah!'

Rosie gave a quick glance up and down the river where, apart from the cat, there was now little to be seen. 'Weren't my fault,' she protested. 'It slipped.'

Up on Southwark bridge and unaware of the action below, Sergeant Frampton had just eased the truck into the kerbside. Julia leaned forward and planted a kiss on the side of his cheek. 'Thank you, Sergeant, it was kind of you to come this way. This spot has so many memories for both of us.'

'Er – n-no problem, ma'am,' he replied in a tone that indicated that he was rarely awash with compliments. 'It's only a few minutes' detour.'

Bill Voisey glanced at his watch. 'I'm afraid you haven't got time to leave the truck. We've only got ten minutes to get to the Tower.'

'I know, I know,' agreed Julia, clutching Duncan's hand tightly. 'But as I can't have my husband at our wedding reception, I thought I'd like to see this spot with him on my wedding day. I don't know what it is about Southwark Bridge, but in comparison to any other bridge in London, it always seems so tranquil and romantic. Even on a working day.'

'If it's tranquil and romantic,' asked Duncan wryly, 'why am I being taken to the Tower?'

'Oh c'mon, Duncan,' she chided, 'you can't fool me. You're loving every minute of this and you know it.'

'And you?' he asked. 'What're your feelings about the way things have turned out?'

'I'm also guilty of loving every minute of it,' she smiled. 'I always told myself we would marry. Mind you, I didn't always believe it because it was a totally illogical thing to do,' she added, 'but then I suppose our whole relationship has been illogical.' She kissed him and tapped Sergeant Frampton's shoulder. 'To the Tower, my man, and don't spare the horses.'

The sergeant thrust the truck into gear and roared away across the bridge. Two minutes later, with the Tower in sight, it was racing past the lorry bays of the old Billingsgate Fish Market. Parallel with the truck and floating along on the other side of the fisheries, a lone cat in a coracle sniffed the heavy aroma of smoked herrings and assumed he was in heaven.

A selection of bestsellers from Headline

LIVERPOOL LAMPLIGHT	Lyn Andrews	£5.99 ☐
A MERSEY DUET	Anne Baker	£5.99 ☐
THE SATURDAY GIRL	Tessa Barclay	£5.99 ☐
DOWN MILLDYKE WAY	Harry Bowling	£5.99 ☐
PORTHELLIS	Gloria Cook	£5.99 ☐
A TIME FOR US	Josephine Cox	£5.99 ☐
YESTERDAY'S FRIENDS	Pamela Evans	£5.99 ☐
RETURN TO MOONDANCE	Anne Goring	£5.99 ☐
SWEET ROSIE O'GRADY	Joan Jonker	£5.99 ☐
THE SILENT WAR	Victor Pemberton	£5.99 ☐
KITTY RAINBOW	Wendy Robertson	£5.99 ☐
ELLIE OF ELMLEIGH SQUARE	Dee Williams	£5.99 ☐

All (*Group Division*) books are available at your local bookshop, or can be ordered direct from the publisher. Just tick the titles you would like and complete the details below. Prices and availability are subject to change without prior notice.

Please enclose a cheque or postal order made payable to *Bookpoint Ltd*, and send to: (*Group Division*) 39 Milton Park, Abingdon, OXON, OX14 4TD, UK. Email Address: orders@bookpoint.co.uk

If you would prefer to pay by credit card, our call centre team would be delighted to take your order by telephone. Our direct line *01235 400414* (lines open 9.00 am–6.00 pm Monday to Saturday, 24 hour message answering service). Alternatively you can send a fax on *01235 400454*.

TITLE		FIRST NAME		SURNAME	

ADDRESS	
DAYTIME TEL:		POST CODE	

If you would prefer to pay by credit card, please complete:
Please debit my Visa/Access/Diner's Card/American Express (delete as applicable) card number:

Signature .... Expiry Date ....

If you would *NOT* like to receive further information on our products please tick the box. ☐